The Romance of the Western Bower
by Wang Shifu
Adaptation by Zhang Xuejing

Zhao the Orphan
by Ji Junxiang
Adaptation by Wang Jianping and Ren Yutang

Snow in Summer
by Guan Hanqing
Adaptation by Chang Xiaochang

Revision by Liu Yousheng

Better Link Press

Copyright © 2008 Shanghai Press and Publishing Development Company

All rights reserved. Unauthorized reproduction, in any manner, is prohibited.

This book is edited and designed by the Editorial Committee of *Cultural China* series

Managing Directors: Wang Youbu, Xu Naiqing
Editorial Director: Wu Ying
Editors: Yang Xinci, Mina Tenison

Adaptation by Zhang Xuejing, Wang Jianping and Ren Yutang, Chang Xiaochang
Translation by Kuang Peihua and Liu Jun, Paul White, Paul White

Interior and Cover Design: Yuan Yinchang, Xia Wei

ISBN: 978-1-60220-212-2

Address any comments about *Love Stories and Tragedies from Chinese Classic Operas (IV)* to:

Better Link Press
99 Park Ave
New York, NY 10016
USA
or
Shanghai Press and Publishing Development Company
F 7 Donghu Road, Shanghai, China (200031)
Email: comments_betterlinkpress@hotmail.com

Computer typeset by Yuan Yinchang Design Studio, Shanghai
Printed in China by Shanghai Donnelley Printing Co. Ltd.

1 2 3 4 5 6 7 8 9 10

The Romance of
the Western Bower
5~118

Zhao the Orphan
121~279

Snow in Summer
281~418

The Romance of the Western Bower

	About the Original Work	6
Chapter 1	Enchantment at the Hall of Buddha	9
Chapter 2	An Exchange of Verses	30
Chapter 3	Uproar at the Funeral Service	36
Chapter 4	Delivery from the Bandits	41
Chapter 5	The Promise Broken at a Family Feast	55
Chapter 6	The Love Message of the Lute	63
Chapter 7	Repudiation	75
Chapter 8	The Tryst	86
Chapter 9	A Handmaid in the Dock	89
Chapter 10	A Tearful Farewell Feast	97
Chapter 11	The Wedding	104

About the Original Work

THE LOVE STORY of Oriole and Zhang Junrui has been loved both by scholars and ordinary people for hundreds of years. *The Story of Oriole*, written by Yuan Zhen of the Tang Dynasty (618-907), defined the story's basic framework, but had a tragic ending with Master Zhang finally abandoning Oriole. In the Song Dynasty (960-1179), a version appeared in the colloquial language (as opposed to the classical language of the earlier versions), followed by two separate versions, *The Story of Oriole* by Qin Guan and Mao Pang, which was composed in the *Daqu* style, (a style in which the narrative parts are written in prose and the lyrical parts are written in verse) and *Shangdiao Dielianhua*, with the same theme, by Zhao Delin. In the Jin Dynasty (1115-1234), two *zaju* dramas titled *The Rose* and *The Chastisement of Rose* were created respectively. In the same period, *The West Bower Zhugongdiao* written by Dong Jieyuan (later known as *Dong's West Bower*) became the most influential version of the story. In the Yuan Dynasty (1279-1368), Wang Shifu wrote a *zaju* drama titled *The Romance of the Western Bower*, including 21 scenes that fall into five acts. This work is considered the most important lyrical drama in the history of Chinese classical theater. The work is noted for its brilliant anti-traditionalist theme, excellent artistic techniques, and a classical style. The drama is much admired for its beautiful and resourceful language. Like an eye-catching flower, the story has attracted readers and tugged at their heart-strings for years.

However, the version by Wang Shifu is a story that can only be read by well-educated readers, and is not very suitable for performance. There are no records of the play being performed during the Yuanzhen and Dade reign periods (1295-1307) of the Yuan Dynasty, when *zaju* dramas were thriving, and it was not until the Ming Dynasty (1368-1644) that the version by Wang Shifu was spoken highly of by the literati, and became fashionable. Since the Ming Dynasty, there have been more than 30 versions of this love story, proving how great the artistic charm of the story is.

To make this excellent classical opera better known, especially among younger readers, we have adapted it into a novel in the vernacular, while striving to be faithful to the original. As novels and operas are different kinds of artistic forms in terms of performance and literary technique, we have edited the original and added chapter headings accordingly.

Liu Yousheng

CHAPTER ONE

Enchantment at the Hall of Buddha

DURING THE REIGN of Emperor Dezong of the Tang Dynasty (618-907), a scholar named Zhang Gong, styled Junrui, lived in Luoyang. Zhang Junrui was born into a family that had produced officials for generations. His father was the president of the Ministry of Rites. As the only son of the family, Junrui was adored by his father. His father personally instructed the boy whenever he had time to spare from his duties, and engaged famous teachers to reside in his mansion and give Zhang Junrui lessons. It was his cherished wish that his son would become well enough versed in both polite letters and martial arts to be fit to attend the emperor himself, and bring honor to the Zhang family. Junrui was a bright boy. At the age of seven he began his studies, and proved so intelligent and adept that he could recite a passage of his books by heart having read it no more than once. As time went by, he acquired a good command of *The Four Books* [namely, *The Great Learning*, *The Doctrine of the Mean*, *The Analects of Confucius* and *The Mencius*] and the *Five Classics* [namely, *The Book* of Songs, Collection of Ancient Texts, The Book of Changes, The Book of Rites and The Spring and Autumn Annals], as well as of the four accomplishments of Chinese poetry, music, chess, and calligraphy and painting. In addition, he was as handsome as Song Yu and Pan An (two ancient Chinese heroes), and had an outstanding poise and manner. However, when he was 17, his father, distressed by the corruption at court, died of apoplexy. One year later, his grieving mother passed away too. From then on, Zhang Junrui had only a small legacy to live on. He dismissed all his family servants, keeping only one young boy as his page, with whom he left home to travel, visit friends and seek out teachers. To broaden his knowledge and widen his horizons, Junrui was determined to "travel 10,000 miles" and "read 10,000 books."

In the spring of the 17th year of the Zhenyuan reign period, Emperor Dezong issued a decree, announcing that the civil service examinations would be held in the following year at the capital to recruit people of talent for official positions. At the news, scholars all over the country lost no time making preparations for the journey to the capital, where they could study for the examination and present their essays to influential persons, hoping to be recommended for the emperor's attention.

Confident that he would easily pass the examination and make his name resound throughout the country, Zhang Junrui packed his belongings and set off with his page boy for the capital.

On the way, the sun shone and spring breezes blew. Letting his horse plod along at its own pace and his thoughts flow wherever they would, Zhang felt as if he were soaring like a swallow. One day, he saw before him by a fork in the road a boundary marker with the words Pujin Pass written on it. Startled, he suddenly thought of his old classmate Du Que.

His former classmate and good friend, Du Que had similar tastes and interests with him. They had been inseparable, and finally became sworn brothers. Du Que was fascinated by The Art of War, written by the master strategist Sun Zi of the Warring States Period (475-221 BC), and later gave up the pen for the sword. Coming first on the list in the imperial military examinations, Du was appointed General of the Western Front, commanding an army of 100,000 men stationed at the Pujin Pass. Zhang, who had not met Du Que for quite a few years, thought to himself that this was a good opportunity to renew their acquaintance and at the same time enjoy the scenery of the pass.

Soon Zhang found himself in Pujin. The Pujin Ferry faced Xiayangjin, across the Yellow River. Standing on the bank of the roaring river, he felt a poem well up inside him:

> *Of the tortuous, turbulent Yellow River,*
> *Where is the most perilous part?*
> *Surely it's there.*
> *The River girds two Eastern States*
> *And keeps two Western States apart*
> *And bars the Northern Gates.*
> *White-crested waves surge up high*
> *Like autumn clouds in the boundless sky.*
> *The floating bridge, boats joined by ropes of bamboo.*
> *Looks like a crouching dragon blue.*
> *From west to east its waves through nine states go;*
> *From north to south a hundred streams into it flow.*
> *The river, like the Milky Way, falls from the sky;*
> *Beyond the clouds its source hangs high.*
> *It runs its course unchanged to the Eastern Sea.*
> *It makes a thousand Luoyang flowers dance with glee.*
> *And waters ten thousand acres in the Eastern land.*
> *Skyward I'd sail till sun and moon are near at hand.*

Zhang then fell to musing: "In spite of having studied for years and acquiring a deep knowledge of literature, I'm still a wanderer and do not know when I can achieve my goals. Lofty talent cannot be confined to lowly posts, and a noble character cannot fulfill his ambition in troubled times. O Yellow River, you run directly to the Eastern Sea. Do you know what the future holds for me?" So thinking, he could not help shedding tears.

> *My precious sword lies hidden by the autumn streams;*
> *My sorrow-laden saddle's bursting at the seams.*

Suddenly Zhang heard the din of horses and carriages. Looking around, he saw a throng of people all jostling each other. Unbeknownst to himself, he had already reached Puzhou City. The city lay on the bank of the Yellow River, facing Shaanxi Province and separated from Henan Province in the south by Mount Zhongtiao. Legend has it that Puzhou was the capital of a kingdom in remote antiquity. During the Warring States Period it was under the jurisdiction of the State of Wei, and was called Puban. In the Tang Dynasty it was the capital of Hezhong Prefecture. The ancient stone streets were lined with shops, tea houses, taverns, restaurants and inns. Though the city was not as prosperous as the other major cities, it was the hub of traffic bound for the eastern and western states, and on a post road leading to the capital. The city was bustling with people.

Zhang's first thought was to find an inn where he could stay for the night. Suddenly he caught sight of a signboard inscribed with three Chinese characters: "No.1 Scholar Inn". The innkeeper, who was standing in front of the door, saw the handsome young man with a dignified bearing mounted on a horse followed by a page. Immediately, he suspected that the young man must be from an aristocratic family. And so he hurried over to catch hold of the horse's reins. "Please come in, Master!" he cried. "If you are going to the capital to take the examinations, you should put up at our No.1 Scholar Inn. It is an auspicious place. I guarantee you'll be a successful candidate if you stay with us. You can have the best room in the house — with immaculate and comfortable bedding, and a superb view."

Zhang was pleased to hear this, and thought that indeed the No.1 Scholar Inn was an auspicious name for an inn. So he decided to put up at the inn. "We'll stay here," he told the page. Dismounting, he said to the innkeeper: "Very well, give me your best room, and unsaddle my horse and feed it with fine forage."

"Don't worry, Master," said the innkeeper, "we have a special man to take care of your horse." He then called out, "We have an honored guest. Take the horse to the stables, and prepare some tea."

An attendant appeared, took the horse's reins from the page and led the horse to the yard at the back of the inn.

Following the innkeeper, Zhang was shown to the best room in the inn. It had white walls, bright windows and clean furniture. There were some tasteful paintings and works of calligraphy hung on the walls. Zhang was satisfied with the room, and ordered his page to unpack their things.

Soon afterwards, the innkeeper brought in a basin of clean water for Master Zhang to wash with, and prepared tea personally for the guest. Sipping the delicious and refreshing tea, Master Zhang immediately felt relaxed. He then began to question the innkeeper about the local attractions. "Are there any famous mountains, scenic spots, historical sites or ancient temples here?" he inquired.

"The most famous attraction around here is the Salvation Monastery to the east of the city," the innkeeper answered. "You really should pay a visit to it, sir. It was erected by the imperial order of Her Majesty Empress Wu Zetian. It has magnificent buildings. Visitors come from all over to see it. It is really the only thing worth seeing in the city. In addition, the abbot of the monastery is a learned man. You may discuss sutras and the classics with him."

This piqued Zhang's fancy, and, giving his page orders to prepare lunch, he said that he was going to see the monastery and would be back before long.

Leaving the bustling streets of the city behind, he came to the main road leading out of the eastern gate. In the full bloom of spring, the road was lined with green grass, tall trees, red peach blossoms and white plum flowers. In the distance, tree-covered mountains could be seen, with tumbling streams, swallows feeding their young, and other birds chirping merrily. Viewing the scenery along the road was just like appreciating a beautiful landscape painting. Zhang felt relaxed and happy. Before long, he saw a grand monastery with lofty buildings shrouded in trees on the slope of the mountain ahead of him. "That must be the Salvation Monastery," he thought to himself. Walking closer, Zhang found that the monastery, shaded by thick stands of tall pine and cypress trees, had red walls and was roofed with green tiles; its main buildings and pavilions were scattered here and there in picturesque disorder. In front of the monastery, there was a flat, open space big enough to hold 10,000 people. The whole setting seemed to him to be ideal for a place of worship and meditation.

Looking up at the cluster of buildings from the foot of the mountain, Zhang saw a flight of 108 steps leading to the gate of the monastery. In the middle of the gate there was a horizontal board inscribed with six elegant characters, announcing "The Salvation Monastery, constructed by imperial decree", and above them there was a line of smaller characters, reading "Built in the second year of the Chuigong reign of the Tang Dynasty". Zhang plodded up along the steps. At the gate he saw an acolyte of about 16 years old coming out of the monastery. Seeing Zhang, the monk pressed his palms together and chanted, "Amida Buddha! May I ask where you are from, sir?"

Zhang was pleased at this gentle greeting. He replied, "I come from Luoyang. Having heard that your renowned monastery has a quiet and elegant environment and beautiful scenery, and that the abbot is a learned man, I have come to worship Buddha and pay my respects to the abbot. May I ask if the reverend gentleman is in?"

"I am afraid that my master left the monastery this morning to conduct a religious ceremony. I am Fa Cong, a disciple of Abbot Fa Ben. Since my master is absent, perhaps I may keep you company. May I invite you to have tea in the hall?"

"Since the abbot is out, I will not trouble you to offer me tea," Zhang replied. "But may I prevail upon you to show me around the monastery?"

"With pleasure, sir." So saying, Fa Cong led Zhang into the monastery grounds. While Zhang was being shown around the Hall of Buddha, the Bell Tower, the Pagoda Courtyard, the Arhats Hall, the kitchen, the monks' living quarters, etc., let us recount the details of the connection of the monastery with the late Prime Minister Cui Jue.

The Salvation Monastery was a temple dedicated to the merit and virtue of Empress Wu Zetian. The abbot, Fa Ben, had been sponsored for his post by Prime Minister Cui. When the latter was in charge of the monastery's renovation, he contributed funds to have a courtyard built adjacent to the west wing for himself to live in after his retirement. Wearing straw shoes and leaning on a bamboo cane, he would worship Buddha every day and took good care of himself, so as to fulfill his allotted life span. But he had unexpectedly died of illness three years previously in the capital; now that the three-year period of mourning was about to end, his wife, Madam Cui, his daughter, Oriole, his adopted son, Merry Boy, and their maids and servants, a total of a dozen people, were on their way to take his coffin to his family graveyard at Boling, his hometown. However, as the prefect of Mid-River Prefecture had just passed away, Puzhou City was in great disorder. Thus, it was not safe for Madam Cui and her party to continue. Madam Cui decided to put her husband's coffin temporarily at the Salvation Monastery. Then she wrote a letter to her nephew Zheng Heng, to whom Oriole had been betrothed, to ask him to come right away and take charge of matters. Madam Cui was a capable lady, especially good at handling family affairs. She had been very strict with her daughter, seeing to her education and keeping her as much as possible in seclusion. Thanks to her mother's efforts, Oriole was able to sew and embroider, write poetry, and do calligraphy and mathematics.

That very afternoon of Zhang's visit to the monastery, Madam Cui had just woken up to the sound of her daughter singing sadly, accompanying herself on the *qin* [a seven-stringed zither]:

Here we are, east of Puzhou City, when spring is late,
Shut up in a lonely temple with a barred door and gate.
The flowing stream is red with fallen blooms,
Laden with gloom,
I bear a silent grudge against the eastern breeze,
Blowing down flowers from the trees.

Upon hearing this, Madam Cui felt a pang in her heart. She raised her head, looked out of the window, and saw that the spring scenery was very attractive. Believing that her daughter must be very lonely all by herself in her room, she called to Rose, Oriole's maid: "Rose, it is such a warm and sunny day, and the spring scenery is charming. There is no one in the front courtyard or in the Hall of Buddha now. Why don't you take your young mistress to divert yourselves there for a while. I'm afraid she will be bored staying in the room all day long."

Rose was a girl of about 15. She had been attending Oriole since they had both been children, and the two girls were as close as sisters. In the previous few days, as Madam Cui had prevented them from going out, neither of them had dared set foot outside their quarters. So, upon hearing Madam Cui's suggestion, Rose responded with delight. She ran to Oriole's room right away. There she chattered to her young mistress: "Miss! Get ready to go out right now! Your mother has given permission. We can go to the Hall of Buddha."

Oriole feigned indifference. "Oh, is that all?" she said. "I thought it must be something important. But if you are so keen to go, let's go." Oriole tidied herself up, and the pair headed for the Hall of Buddha.

Now let us return to Zhang. In the company of Fa Cong, he had visited the Hall of Buddha, the quarters of the monks, the bell tower and the monks' cells. He had climbed the pagoda, traversed all the passages, counted the Arhats, worshipped Buddha and bowed to saints and sages. In high spirits, he walked out of the courtyard where the pagoda was located, and came to another spacious courtyard at the end of the western wing of the monastery. There he espied a horizontal board bearing the words "Pear Blossom Yard". The two-leaf door in the shape of a crescent moon was slightly open. Zhang pushed open the door and tried to step in. But he was pulled back by Fa Cong. Turning round, he asked in surprise: "Why do you stop me?"

Fa Cong lowered his voice, and said, "I'm sorry, sir, but you shouldn't go in there…"

"Why not?" Zhang asked sharply.

"Sir, it is the residence of the family of His Excellency the late Prime Minister Cui."

"Why do they live in a monastery?"

Fa Cong looked around, and seeing that no one was near, said,

"When our monastery became dilapidated, Prime Minister Cui had it rebuilt, and constructed this courtyard residence adjacent to the western wing for himself. He had planned to live here after his retirement to worship Buddha, study the scriptures and spend his remaining years in tranquility. But unfortunately, His Excellency died before he was able to enjoy the use of the residence. Now his widow, together with her daughter and adopted son, is taking the late prime minister's coffin to his hometown, Boling, to have it buried there. It so happens that the officials have lost control of this region, and Sun the Flying Tiger, a bandit chief, is rampaging everywhere with his 5,000 men. Madam Cui is afraid that they will run into the bandits if they travel, so they are temporarily staying at the monastery to await the end of the emergency."

The young man nodded his understanding, and said, "Oh, I see." On his way back past the Hall of Buddha, Master Zhang suddenly got a whiff of an exquisite perfume. He turned his head to see where the delightful scent was coming from, and was immediately rooted to the spot: An incredibly beautiful girl was coming out of the hall. Her eyebrows were arched like crescent moons, slanting upward towards her cloud-like hair. Her lips were cherry-red, and her teeth as white as jade. Dressed in a flimsy silk robe, she held a rose in her hand. She looked like an angel from Heaven to Master Zhang, who thought to himself: "I have seen thousands of beauties as I traveled here and there, but I have never seen such a charming face. This is surely no monastery inhabited by dreary monks, but a paradise where lovers engage in dalliance. Who would have thought that I would meet an angel here? This beauty must have seen me. But instead of hastening away, she lingers and caresses that flower. Perhaps she is not unimpressed by my appearance." Zhang's eyes were dazzled, and his soul seemed to soar up into the sky.

The girl called her maid hesitantly, like an oriole warbling in a flower garden: "Rose, Rose!"

"I'm coming, young mistress! It's really a fine building!" So saying, Rose ran out from the hall.

Oriole knitted her brows and sighed. She then recited two lines of verse:

The monks are gone; empty their rooms,
The steps are covered with red fallen blooms.

Master Zhang was impressed by the girl's ready turn of phrase. Just then, Rose noticed the young man standing there staring at her mistress as if transfixed to the spot. She said to Oriole: "Miss, there is a stranger over there. Let's go back." So saying, she pulled Oriole by the sleeve, urging her to leave.

Oriole blushed. She lowered her head and walked slowly back towards her quarters. When she arrived at the threshold, she turned and cast a shy glance at the young scholar before vanishing inside, which sent Zhang into transports of delight. He rubbed his eyes, and asked Fa Cong: "Was that the Goddess of Mercy that appeared just now?"

Fa Cong smiled and said, "Sir, the very idea! She is the daughter of the late Prime Minister Cui. The Goddess of Mercy indeed!"

Zhang sighed, "I never thought there could be such a beauty on this earth. She is the most charming girl I have ever seen. And she has such exquisitely tiny bound feet!"

Fa Cong could not hold back a guffaw: "She was standing over there, and she was wearing a full-length gown; how could you see her feet?"

Zhang took Fa Cong by the hand, and led him to where the girl had been standing. Pointing to her footprints on the petal-strewn path, he said, "Look, there you can see how delicate her feet must be. Her glance showed the feelings in her heart, and the tiny footprints also convey her love."

Fa Cong opened his eyes wide, and examined the path carefully. But he had to confess that he saw nothing.

"Ah, well, if you could see such things, you would not be a monk," Master Zhang teased him.

Remembering how Oriole and Rose had walked into the Pear Blossom Yard with their ornaments tinkling—like two fairy maidens returning to paradise—he ran towards the yard, hoping to catch another sight of them. But he found that the red doors were already closed. Looking about him, Zhang felt that the poplars and willows seemed to be weeping and the birds mourning. The gate was shut at the yard where pear trees bloomed and the whitewashed walls seemed as high as the azure sky. Zhang bemoaned his lot: "Why does Heaven not help me? How can I endure my tedious life? Young mistress, the musk and lily fragrance you spread still lingers. I am undone by your bewitching glance, and I am at a loss what to do this long day. The willow branches wave in the east breeze, and gossamer threads retain the petals of the peach trees. Your lotus face has disappeared behind the beaded screen. Is this the residence of the former Prime Minister Cui or the Temple of the Goddess of the Southern Sea?"

Seeing that Zhang stood in a trance in front of the Pear Blossom Yard, Fa Cong tried to take him away: "Sir, please don't make trouble. This way please."

Zhang had lost all interest in sightseeing. He muttered, "I will give up everything for this charming girl. I'm not going to the capital to take the civil service examinations."

"Are you mad?" Fa Cong exclaimed. "How can you give up your official career?"

Zhang thought to himself: "Love has penetrated to the marrow of my bones. How could I forget her bewitching glance? Even if I were made of iron or stone, I could never forget her in my heart. Rank and wealth and fame mean nothing to me now. Suddenly, this monastery has been converted into a fairyland." After a long pause, he hit upon an idea. He made a deep bow to Fa Cong, and said, "I want you to do me a favor."

"Just tell me what I can do for you," Fa Cong said.

"As you know, I'm going to the capital to take the civil service examinations. So I should make good use of my time to review the classics. However, the inn where I am staying is so crowded and noisy that I cannot concentrate on my studies. Your monastery is a quiet place, with plenty of empty rooms. Could you please ask your master if I can rent a room here so that I can spend my time reviewing my lessons? Please say a few good words for me. I'll come back tomorrow to receive your reply."

Fa Cong showed signs of reluctance. "This is no easy matter. You see, our monastery has never rented out rooms before."

But, seeing that Zhang was determined to move into the monastery, Fa Cong finally agreed to see what he could do.

Thereupon, Zhang returned to the inn.

In the meantime, Abbot Fa Ben had been overseeing a religious ceremony in a nearby village, and did not return to the monastery until nightfall. As soon as he had crossed the threshold, Fa Cong reported to him Zhang's visit to the monastery, and told him that the young scholar wanted to rent a room at the temple. He described Zhang in glowing terms, hinting that a little favor done now for a person from an excellent family with an illustrious official career ahead of him would be a wise investment for the future.

Fa Ben nodded in agreement, and said: "Oh yes, I have heard of Zhang Junrui. He is a gifted scholar. It's a pity I failed to meet him today. Fa Cong, keep watch at the gate tomorrow, and let me know the minute he arrives."

"Certainly, sir," the acolyte replied. Walking out of the room, Fa Cong thought to himself: "The silly young fellow will surely come tomorrow. The 'Goddess of Mercy' who lives here has captured his soul even before he dies."

There was little sleep night at the No.1 Scholar Inn that night for Zhang. Regardless of whether his eyes were open or closed, the divine beauty of Oriole loomed in front of them. The glance that she had given him showed the feelings in her heart, he was convinced. He then decided that fate had stepped in and brought them together. Finally, day dawned, and brought an end to his tossing and turning. He washed and dressed as hastily as if the inn were on fire, and set out alone for the Salvation Monastery. Long before he got there, he saw Fa Cong standing in front of the temple gate, craning his neck and looking down the path. Zhang quickened his pace, reached the gate, and bowed to Fa Cong: "Good morning!" he said.

Fa Cong bowed in return. "Good morning, sir," he said. "My master is waiting for you. Please wait while I go and inform him. The abbot will come to welcome you in person."

Zhang protested, "But I cannot trouble the abbot to lower himself to come out to greet such a worthless person as myself."

Nevertheless, Fa Cong insisted that it was the wish of the abbot himself, and without more ado he fetched his master.

At the sight of Master Zhang, Fa Ben pressed his palms

together before his chest, and said, "Amida Buddha! Please come in and take a seat, sir. Yesterday I was not at home, and failed to welcome you. I hope you will forgive me."

Zhang found Fa Ben to be an elderly monk with snow-white hair. Yet his face still maintained the vibrancy of youth. He had an air of profound sanctity about him, and his voice was strong and clear. In fact, he looked as serene as Buddha himself. Zhang was filled with a deep sense of awe. He bowed to the abbot, saying "I have long heard your renowned name, and wished to come and hear you preach. I am sorry to have missed you yesterday. But now that I have met you at last, I am truly happy."

Following this exchange of greetings, they entered the abbot's room, and took seats. Fa Cong presented each of them with a cup of tea, and then stood behind the abbot.

The abbot started the conversation by saying, "Sir, you are a famous scholar from the City of Luoyang. What brings you here to Mid-River Prefecture?"

Zhang replied, "Since my parents died, I have been living the life of a wanderer. In the course of my travels, I heard of the magnificence of the Salvation Monastery and of the lofty scholarship of its abbot. As I was passing through here on my way to the capital to take the civil service examinations, I thought I would take this opportunity to pay you a visit."

Fa Ben said, "You have a dignified and imposing appearance. I suppose your late father bequeathed a great deal of property to you?"

Zhang shook his head. "My late father enjoyed great renown as the president of the Ministry of Rites. During his life he was just and upright, but, alas, after his death he left no legacy. I have come here hoping to hear you preach, but I am afraid that, as a homeless vagabond, I have not the means to show my proper respects to you. A poor scholar's gift is as light as a scrap of paper." So saying, he took an ounce of silver out of his sleeve, and said, "I can only offer this ounce of silver for the upkeep of the monastery. Would you kindly accept it?"

"You are my guest, sir; such a thing would be unthinkable," Fa Ben protested. This superficial banter went on backwards and forwards for some time. Knowing that if his gift was not accepted, he could proceed with the next stage of his plan, Zhang shot an appealing glance at Fa Cong.

The acolyte understood well what was on Zhang's mind, and he thought: "Why are you so anxious, Zhang? Silver does not entice us monks. We don't care about your money." Fa Cong avoided Zhang's eyes.

Fa Ben too knew exactly what was behind the young man's generosity, as Fa Cong had told him what he wanted. Confronted with the abbot's intransigence, Zhang blushed, and finally blurted out, "To tell you the truth, reverend sir, I want to request a favor from you."

The abbot burst out laughing, and said, "A favor? Well, don't be shy; let me know what it is."

"I am a stranger here, without any relatives or friends," Zhang said. "At the moment I am living in a crowded inn. It is noisy from morning to night, and I am unable to study there. I wish to rent a room here, so that I can concentrate on studying and also benefit from your teaching. As for the rent, I will pay whatever you wish."

The abbot said, "It is true that there are plenty of spare rooms in our monastery, but most of them are old and bare. I am afraid that they are not suitable for you, sir. If you like, you may share my room."

Zhang groaned inwardly. To get out of this situation, he said, "Thank you very much for your kindness, reverend sir. I would be happy to share a room with you and learn from your esteemed teaching. But it is my habit to recite the classics at night; I am afraid I would disturb you. It would be far better, I think, if I lived by myself."

Fa Ben was impressed by this line of reasoning, and finally consented, "You may choose whichever room you wish."

Inwardly rejoicing, Zhang explained that a room on the sequestered side of the monastery would be most suitable for his study purposes; in fact the nearer the western bower the better, he added, as if an after-thought had just struck him. Nodding, Fa Ben said, "It is quiet there, an ideal place for you to read books. I'll have the room cleaned, and then you may move in. May I ask how much luggage you have?"

"One load. I also have a page boy."

"When do you wish to move in?"

Zhang, who couldn't wait to move in, jumped up and said, "Today." As he was about to take a hasty leave of the abbot and the acolyte, a girl appeared in the doorway. Zhang was surprised to find that it was the maid he had seen the previous day. Thereupon, he sat down again.

Clad in a mourning dress of pure white, Rose wore her hair in two coils, in one of which was stuck a purple silk flower. She had thin eyebrows and clever eyes. She stole a look at Zhang, but her eyes revealed not a hint of her thoughts.

Zhang heaved an inward sigh, and thought to himself: "What a nimble girl! If I could put my head on your young mistress' pillow, I would not trouble you to make the bed for us. I would ask your mistress and her mother to set you free. I would even write a guarantee for you myself. Though you are young, your manner shows not the slightest trace of coquetry. You have the graces of a girl who has grown up in a rich and influential family."

Rose approached the abbot slowly, and made a deep bow. She said, "Ten thousand blessings, Reverend Abbot! My mistress has ordered me to inquire when it will suit you to perform the funeral service for my late master."

The abbot put his palms together before his chest and said, "Amida Buddha! The offerings and other preparations are all ready for the service in the Hall of Merits and Virtues. The 15th is the day Buddha will receive the offerings and I shall perform the funeral service for your late master."

"May I go with you to the hall to view the preparations before I report to Madam Cui?"

"Certainly you may." The abbot then turned to Zhang and said, "Would you mind waiting here for a little while? I will soon be back." So saying, the abbot stood up.

Zhang realized that he must become well acquainted with Rose and make a good impression on her if he was to gain access to her young mistress. So he decided to waste no time, and said to Fa Ben, "Abbot, why do you leave me alone here? Please let me go with you."

The abbot replied, "There is no need to trouble yourself about monastery matters, young sir. I assure you, you will find this business of no interest to you at all."

This dismayed Zhang, but suddenly an idea came to him. "What I mean, Reverend Sir, is that you must be more discreet."

Fa Ben stopped and looked back. "What do you mean, Master Zhang?" he asked.

The young man feigned surprise. "How can such a large family have no male servant, and have to send a maid as a messenger?"

"Madam Cui insists on having no male servants in her household," the abbot replied. "Then do you think Madam Cui or the young mistress should have come to inquire about the date of the ceremony in person?"

Zhang pursued, "An old saying goes: 'Don't pull on your shoe in a melon patch, and don't adjust your cap under a plum tree.' Aren't you afraid that you might arouse suspicion by going into an empty hall with a pretty young girl?"

Abbot Fa Ben was stung by this remark. "How dare you say such a thing?" he cried. "As a monk, I have long been free from all human desires and passions. I do not need to avoid suspicion."

"Please don't be angry, Abbot," Zhang said. "You misunderstand me. But I cannot help reminding you that gossip is a fearful thing."

"That is preposterous!" the abbot snorted. "However, if you want to put your mind at rest, you had better come with us."

"It would be my pleasure to go with you," Zhang said, with a solemn countenance but gleeful inside.

Zhang hurried to follow the abbot. "It would be more seemly, I think, to allow the maid to precede us by a few paces," he suggested.

Fa Ben nodded his agreement, saying, "Spoken like a true gentleman! You are a worthy disciple of Confucius."

Both Fa Ben and Zhang followed Rose to the Hall of Merits and Virtues. Located at the northeastern corner of the monastery, behind the Hall of Buddha, the Hall of Merits and Virtues was also known as the Beamless Hall, because it had been constructed without the use of beams. Above the door of the hall there was a horizontal signboard painted blue and inscribed with the three golden characters: Hall of Merits and Virtues. An antithetical couplet hung on both sides of the door, reading, "This hall abounds in merits and virtues, and the Salvation Monastery saves all monks who come to it." It had been written by Ouyang Xun, a famous calligrapher of the Tang Dynasty. The three of them inspected the hall, finding everything in readiness for the funeral service, including yellow curtains, cloth flags, bells, wooden fishes (percussion instruments made out of hollow wooden blocks and used by Buddhist priests to beat the rhythm when chanting scriptures), mourning articles, paper horses and money, incense burners and candles. Fa Ben said to Rose: "The offerings are ready, and all the other preparations have been made for the service. I request that Madam Cui and your young mistress come on the 15th day of this month to offer incense."

At this, Zhang interrupted: "May I ask why you need to offer incense?"

Fa Ben replied, "It is to express the filial piety of the young mistress towards her late father, ahead of the funeral service, as the mourning period is about to come to an end."

Zhang was intrigued at this news. "So the young mistress will come here on that day!" he mused to himself. "That will be a good opportunity for me to meet her. I must not let this opportunity slip from my grasp." So thinking, he suddenly hit upon an idea. He burst into tears, and sobbed, "I'm so ashamed!" "What's the matter, young sir?" cried Fa Ben, in consternation.

His voice choking with tears, Zhang said, "You have reminded me of what an undutiful son I am. I have neglected to burn incense in honor of my deceased parents ever since I started my wanderings. How I wish to repay them for their boundless kindness, just like the young lady!"

Upon hearing this, Fa Ben was filled with a feeling of deep veneration, impressed with how well educated, dutiful and filled with a sense of propriety he was. "Zhang," he urged gently, "I beg of you to restrain your grief. Please do not be too sad."

Zhang wiped his eyes and said, "Will you be kind enough to allow me to subscribe something so that I may be included in the service, for the salvation of the souls of my deceased parents?"

The abbot replied, "Since your purpose is to fulfill your filial duty, I must of course consent."

Zhang, delighted to hear this, said, "I only have five thousand cash on me. I don't know if it is enough."

"It is enough, if your desire is sincere," the abbot said. Then he called to Fa Cong: "Arrange to include Master Zhang in the service."

"Yes, Master," Fa Cong answered.

Zhang bowed to the abbot, and said, "Thank you very much for everything you've done for me. But I'm not sure if Madam Cui and the young mistress will agree to my request. If they do not, it will be difficult for me to fulfill my filial duty."

"Do not worry about that, Master Zhang," Fa Ben said. "I will persuade Madam Cui of the rectitude of your intentions. But both Madam Cui and her daughter are reasonable people; I don't believe that they will object."

Zhang saluted the abbot again: "I'll never forget your kindness," he said, glancing at Rose, who betrayed not a hint of what she was thinking.

"Well now," said Fa Ben. "Everything is arranged. Would you like to come to my room for a cup of tea?"

They left the Hall of Merits and Virtues, Rose walking in front, followed by the abbot. Zhang fell behind so that he could have a word with Fa Cong. "Will the young lady be present at the service?" he whispered to the acolyte.

"How could she be absent from a service being held specially for her father?" Fa Cong answered.

Zhang felt as though a load had been taken off his mind. "Then that was five thousand cash well spent," he thought to himself with satisfaction.

The next step in his plan, he decided, was to worm himself into the confidence of Rose. He made an excuse not to go to the abbot's room to drink tea, but lingered outside until Rose should come out.

Saying good-bye to the abbot, Rose set off back to the Cui family quarters. As she was walking along, with her head bent modestly, who should suddenly appear in front of her but the young scholar who had cried so sadly in the Hall of Merits and Virtues! Although she was somewhat displeased to be so accosted, Rose had no choice but to return the young man's greeting: "Ten thousand blessings on you, sir."

Rose's reserved manner was not lost on Zhang. Although he knew the answer, he asked, "Are you the personal maid of Miss Oriole?"

Rose replied in an icy manner: "I am, sir. Why do you ask?"

Zhang was at a loss what to say. But, afraid that he would miss his chance if Rose left right away, he forced himself to ask, "May... May I tell you something?"

Rose scoffed at him: "What a strange person you are! An old saying goes, 'Like arrows, words must not be freely spread. Once they are heard, they cannot be unsaid.' So, if you have anything to say, please say it with decorum."

Zhang felt ill at ease in the presence of this self-assured girl. After hesitating a short while, he spoke evasively: "I am Zhang Gong, styled Junrui, a native of Luoyang. I was born on the 17th day of the first moon. I am 23 years old, not yet married..."

Rose found the young scholar both annoying and amusing. She gave him a supercilious look, and said, "Why do you entrust me, a stranger, with such deep secrets?"

Regardless of the consequences, Zhang plunged ahead: "I have another question to ask you. Does your young mistress sometimes go out of doors?"

Rose was taken aback at this. She thought to herself: "This young gentleman must be up to no good, asking about my mistress." she replied in a haughty manner: "You are an educated gentleman. So you should know that the revered sage Mencius said, 'Is it not the rule that males and females shall not allow their hands to touch in giving or receiving anything?' The ancients said, 'Speak not a word and make not a movement contrary to propriety.' Cold as ice and frost, my mistress rules her family strictly. Even a servant boy dare not enter the western bower unbidden, and my young mistress is seldom allowed to leave her room in case she is seen even by the monks. Now you, who are no way connected with the family, come asking impertinent questions. You really must recover your sense of propriety." With that, Rose stalked away, leaving the young man very discomfited.

Zhang stood there, his knitted eyebrows showing his grief and gloom. He mused, "Rose said that her mistress is as cold as ice and frost, and no one, unless summoned, dare enter her room. Oriole, if you stand in awe of your stern mother, perhaps you will never give me so much as another glance before you depart. Even if I never see you again, I will never be able to stop yearning for you. Your image is so deeply engraved on my heart. If we could be joined like twin lilies in this life I would hold you for ever in my warm embrace and set you in my heart! The Amorous Hill is far away in the celestial sphere, but the place of our meeting seems even farther away. What Rose said makes me feel you're too high to reach. Would you dare to defy your stern mother, and confess the feelings in your heart to me, your forlorn lover? Are you not aflame with love when you see the butterflies flying in pairs? Could I but hold you in my embrace, I would steal your fragrance like a bee steals the pollen from the flowers. I cannot banish from my mind your lightly penciled brows and thinly powdered face, your jade-white neck and lily-like feet, your crimson sleeves and exquisitely tapered fingers..."

Waking from his reverie, Zhang recollected where he was, and decided to go and say goodbye to the abbot. He found Fa Ben waiting for him. Asked about the arrangements for Zhang's lodgings in the monastery, the abbot explained, "There is a room adjoining the western bower. It is delightful and quite suitable for you. It has already been cleaned. You may move in at your earliest convenience, sir."

"You have been very kind, abbot. I will return to the inn and bring my luggage here."

"There will be a meal ready for you when you return," the abbot said.

Zhang took his leave. On his way back to the inn, he pondered, "After I move to this quiet monastery, I will have only vegetables to eat, and no wine will be available. How will I be able to while away the lonely hours? Even if I attain my goal, there will still be many lonely nights to be endured before that happens. I'll be alone in a room deep in the heart of a courtyard, with only a flimsy mat and a single oil lamp throwing fitful shadows on old books for company. Sleepless at night, I'll toss from left to right. How many times will I sigh and groan, and beat the pillow all alone, pining for Oriole?"

CHAPTER TWO

An Exchange of Verses

EVER SINCE SHE had seen Zhang at the Buddha Hall the day before, Oriole had been in a trance, as if her soul had left her body. The handsome and graceful young scholar was ever-present in her mind. Whenever she remembered that her father had betrothed her to Zheng Heng, her ugly, ignorant and incompetent cousin, she would think, "How wonderful it would be if my cousin were like that handsome young scholar!"

Suddenly she thought of Rose, and wondered what was keeping her so long on the simple errand she had been sent to perform. She made up her mind to scold the little truant as soon as she got back.

At this moment, Rose entered the room, beaming. Oriole put on a grave expression and asked, "Rose, what about the funeral service? Why did it take you such a long time to find out?"

"I have just told my mistress about it, and now I want to tell you. The 15th day of this month is the date on which the service will be held, and the abbot requests that you and your mother burn incense on that date." So saying, Rose laughed again.

Oriole gave Rose a stern look and said, "What are you laughing at?"

Rose burst into louder laughter.

Oriole, puzzled and somewhat annoyed, said, "Rose, have you taken leave of your senses? You're behaving most improperly!"

Rose became serious. "Miss, I have something amusing to tell you. The young scholar we saw the other day was today sitting in the abbot's room."

On hearing this, Oriole blushed, and with feigned indifference asked, "Why do you think that that is so amusing?"

"But let me tell you more, Miss," Rose said, with a smile. "When the abbot took me to the Hall of Merits and Virtues, the young scholar followed us. After we went back to the abbot's room, the young man waited for me outside. When I left the abbot's room he stopped me, and said, 'I am Zhang Gong, styled Junrui, a native of Luoyang. Born on the 17th day of the first moon, I am 23 years old and not yet married.' I said nothing. Then he asked me: 'Are you the personal maid of Miss Oriole? Does your young mistress often go out of doors?' I, of course, berated him for his impertinence. Young mistress, I don't know what on earth he was thinking about. I never imagined there could be such a foolish young fellow!"

Oriole joined in Rose's merriment, but in spite of her mocking tone, she was secretly impressed by Zhang's forwardness. She abruptly checked herself, and put on a serious expression. "There's no need to mention this to my mother, Rose. I hope you understand," she said.

Rose assured her that she did.

Afraid that Rose would start to guess what was on her mind, Oriole looked out of the window and suggested, "It's a fine day today, and that means a bright moon tonight. Arrange the incense table, and we shall go to the garden to offer incense to Heaven later."

Meanwhile, Zhang finished his preparations for moving into the monastery together with his page. A small room near the western bower had been made ready for him by Fa Cong. Though somewhat small, it had been charmingly furnished. Under the green screen window stood a purple sandalwood desk, on which there were the four treasures of the study (writing brush, ink stick, ink slab and paper). Beside the desk, there was a tea table, on which sat a potted landscape, with a miniature pine tree growing from a curious white stone. In a small niche in one wall was a white jade statue of the Buddha Avalokitesvara. Flanking the niche, there was an antithetical couplet, which read, "Avalokitesvara is free from trammels in the purple bamboo grove; and Tathagata sits on the White Lotus Altar." In front of the statue there was a gilded incense burner, with wisps of smoke and the fragrance of joss sticks coming from it. A traditional Chinese painting titled *Crossing the River on a Reed*, painted by the famous painter Wu Daozi hung on one of the white walls, together with an antithetical couplet written by Yan Zhenqing: "An elegant room need not be large; and fragrant flowers need not be many." Zhang pushed open the green screen window, and found himself gazing out onto a small courtyard with green grass, two weeping willows and a clump of peach trees. In one corner of the wall, there was a rockery made of stones brought all the way from Lake Taihu. The young man was charmed by the scenes both indoors and outdoors. He expressed his gratitude to Fa Cong, and complimented him on his fine taste. The acolyte demurred, but was delighted with the compliment all the same. He knew full well, of course, why Zhang had moved into the temple, but he assuaged his conscience by reminding himself that his duty to Buddha was to help others. He said to Zhang: "Sir, let me tell you something. Miss Oriole goes into her garden to offer incense to Heaven and pray to the moon almost every night."

The young scholar was excited when he heard this, and asked, "Where is the garden?"

"On the other side of your own garden wall, sir." So saying, Fa Cong took his leave.

Zhang ate his supper absent-mindedly. Then he sent his page to bed. He sat up until the moonlight shone on the eastern wall and he judged that all the monks must have gone to sleep. Zhang walked on tiptoe out of his room, and furtively climbed up the rockery in the corner of the wall. Peeping over the top of the wall into the other garden, he saw that it was full of spring flowers.

Meanwhile, there was not a speck of cloud in the jade-like sky, in which the Milky Way sparkled like diamonds. The silver moon sailed on high, shedding its light on the enchanting scene.

Just as he was wondering if and how he should approach Oriole on this night, Zhang heard the creaking of the garden gate, and caught a whiff of fragrance borne on the wind. Still on tiptoe, he fixed his eyes intently on the gate. Rose entered the garden, holding a green lantern and followed by Oriole. "Ah, she is more charming and graceful than ever tonight," thought Zhang. "She is like a fairy who has fled from the Heavenly Palace." With her hair tied up in a bun, Oriole wore a light green jacket buttoned down the front and a white silk scarf. Below the jacket, she wore a silk skirt. She looked like the Fairy Queen standing in front of the crimson door of the imperial temple or Lady Chang'e in the moon, worthy of the praise of a great poet. Zhang's soul was ensnared at that instant.

Oriole told Rose to place the incense table near the fantastic Taihu Rock.

Rose did as she was bidden. "Young mistress, everything is ready for you to light the incense," she said.

Oriole placed three sticks of incense in the incense burner, one by one, and, with a bow, started to pray to the moon: "As I burn the first stick of incense, I pray that my deceased father may soon ascend to Heaven. As I burn the second, I pray for longevity for my dear mother. As I burn the third...."

Noticing her young mistress hesitate, Rose said, "You're always silent when it comes to the third one. Let me pray for you. I pray that my young mistress may marry a man whose literary talents are second to none, and who is talented and good-looking, gallant and gentle, and who will also be kind to me, Rose."

Oriole was overcome with shyness. "Don't talk nonsense, Rose," she said. Then she raised her head, bowed to the moon again, and stood up slowly. Leaning on the balustrade, Oriole heaved a deep sigh as she pondered what was in her heart.

Zhang, having observed all this, thought to himself: "She burned the third stick of incense praying that she could meet her ideal husband. This scene has inspired me to compose a poem. And he recited:

The moonlight dissolves the night,
Spring's lonely in flowers' shade.
I bask in the moonbeams bright
Wondering, where is the lunar maid?

Oriole and Rose were startled to hear these murmured lines. "Someone is chanting a poem over by the corner of the wall!" Oriole exclaimed.

Rose said, "It sounds like the voice of that foolish young scholar, who is 23 years old and still unmarried."

Oriole felt a surge of excitement running through her. She thought, "I have been thinking of him, and now he has been brought near, to recite an affectionate poem for me!" She could not help saying: "What a pure and fresh poem! I will compose one to match it."

And, without further hesitation, she recited as follows:

In a lonely room at night,
Spring and youth wither and fade,
You who croon with such delight,
Pity the sighing maid!

Zhang was surprised and overjoyed. He thought, "Not only has she captivated me with her beauty; now I discover that she is intelligent and accomplished too! She matched my verse perfectly and effortlessly. Each word revealed what her heart is feeling. Her words and rhymes were soft, clear and apt."

Thereupon, completely under the spell of the moonlight and infatuation with the beautiful and talented Oriole, Zhang stood up, ready to climb over the wall into the garden. As he did so, he looked straight into the face of Oriole, who was gazing at that part of the wall.

Oriole startled when she saw him.

Rose saw him, too. "Miss, there's someone looking over the wall," she whispered urgently. "We ought to go back indoors, or else the mistress will be displeased."

Oriole reluctantly followed Rose out of the garden. But as she did so, she could not help glancing back, giving Zhang a look that was full of tender feelings. The young man stood where he was, mute and stupefied at this turn of events, and it was only when the garden gate clicked shut that he came to his senses. Uttering a sigh, Zhang heaved a deep sigh, as if awakening from a dream, and gazed around him. It was the dead of night. Cold dew glistened on the green moss, the bright moonlight filtered through the shadows cast by the flowers and a soft breeze blew, making the dark trees shiver. The Dipper hung crookedly in the heavens.

Zhang came down from the rockery, and shuffled back to his room in low spirits. With only a flickering oil lamp for company, Zhang lay sleepless. Gusts of chilly wind filtered through the shutters, tearing the paper that covered the windows.

As he tossed and turned, he longed for the day when, amid flowers and beneath a willow tree, behind a mist-like curtain or surrounded by a cloud-like screen, he and Oriole would swear an oath as everlasting as the mountains and seas. Then at the dead of night they would enjoy their fill of love. And the future would unfurl, shining before them.

These thoughts cheered him up, and he blessed his good fortune.

Truly, his situation was like this:

Feigning leisure, I seek lore
From the abbot's learned store.
But my verses are addressed
To the bower in the west.

CHAPTER THREE

Uproar at the Funeral Service

ON THE 15TH day of the second moon, the Hall of Merits and Virtues was all set for the funeral service for the late Prime Minister Cui to begin. Banners waved to and fro, and clouds of incense smoke formed a dense canopy overhead. The sacred drums and bronze cymbals sounded like thunder, bells pealed, and the steady chanting of the monks reverberated through the air.

Abbot Fa Ben, who had been moved by Master Zhang's filial plea a few days before, and agreed that he be allowed to offer incense to intercede for his deceased parents during the service, had had second thoughts. Afraid that Madam Cui would be unhappy about the arrangement, he planned to let Zhang burn incense first to avoid him meeting Madam Cui and her daughter. So he sent Fa Cong first thing in the morning to summon the young man to the hall. The latter, who had long been ready, lost no time following the acolyte. On the way, he was looking forward to feasting his eyes on the object of his infatuation.

Fa Ben greeted him at the door of the Hall of Merits and Virtues. "Amitabha! Good morning, sir!"

"Good morning, abbot!" Zhang replied, bowing low.

Fa Ben led Zhang to a table set up for him to sacrifice to his deceased parents, and invited him to burn incense.

Zhang picked three sticks of incense from the table, lit them with a burning candle, dropped to his knees, and prayed silently: "In burning the first stick of incense, I pray that those who are alive enjoy long life and happiness. In burning the second stick of incense, I pray that those who have passed away be happy in Paradise. In burning the third stick of incense, I pray that Rose will hasten my suit and Madam Cui may be kept long in the dark about my coming trysts with her daughter. Oh Buddha, show me your favor." Then he made three kowtows in great earnest before getting up.

Seeing that Zhang had finished his offering, Fa Ben came up to him, and said, "If Madam Cui asks you, please tell her that you are a relation of mine."

Zhang knew by this that Fa Ben was somewhat afraid of the imperious Madam Cui. But he was grateful to the abbot, and promised him to do as he asked.

At this moment, there was heard the clatter of jade pendants and a medley of footsteps. An elegant and dignified old lady entered the hall, surrounded by a group of female servants. It was Madam Cui. Then came a middle-aged female servant with a boy of about seven or eight years old, who were followed by Oriole and Rose.

Fa Ben hurried to greet Madam Cui: "It was remiss of me not to come out to greet you, Madam Cui. I hope you'll pardon me," he gushed obsequiously.

Madam Cui gave him a curt nod of recognition, and said, "You don't have to stand on ceremony, Abbot." She raised her head, and caught sight of her husband's tablet on the table. Immediately, tears welled up in her eyes, and she tottered over to the table, lit the candle, went down on her knees, and made a deep kowtow. As she did so she reminisced to herself, "When my husband was alive, we had hundreds of attendants and many a sumptuous banquets, the courtyard was as crowded as a market place every day. But now my husband has ended his life in the capital, and has left his children fatherless and me a widow. Now I have for company only a few faithful servants, visitors are few and far between, and my children and I have no one to rely on. My late husband's coffin has a long way to go before it reaches its final resting place. Though I have written a letter to my nephew Zheng Heng, to whom my daughter is betrothed, not a single word has been heard from him. I planned to depend on Zheng Heng in my remaining years. But no one knows where he is."

These gloomy thoughts made her burst into tears. Finally, after being comforted by some of her servant girls, she recovered sufficiently to order her young son to burn incense for his deceased father. The child, known as Merry Boy, did so, with the help of his nursemaid.

Then came Oriole's turn. Before she reached the table, tears were cascading down her cheeks. She lit three sticks of incense and planted them in the incense burner. Then she fell to her knees, and made several kowtows, sobbing.

Zhang, standing at the back of the hall, had his eyes fixed on Oriole all the time. He whispered to Fa Cong: "Young monk, your piety has brought an angel down to earth."

"It is your own merit that has done that," replied Fa Cong.

Zhang ignored him, and returned to gazing at Oriole. He noticed that her lips were cherry-red, her nose jade-white, her face like the flower of the pear-tree, and her figure as slender as a willow branch. Having time to ponder her charms, Zhang found himself falling deeper and deeper in love.

Abbot Fa Ben, conducting the ceremony from the pulpit throne, also could not tear his eyes away from Oriole. Fa Zhi, the head monk, who took the lead in chanting scriptures, was so fascinated with the girl's beauty that he absent-mindedly struck Fa Cong's head instead of the bell. The acolyte forgot which candles to light, and the monk in charge of the incense had to be constantly reminded to keep his mind on his duty.

Zhang, deaf to every other sound, heard Oriole weep like a stricken bird in a deep and gloomy forest, and saw her tears running down like pearly dewdrops on flowers. He longed to call out, "Miss Oriole, please don't be too sad!" Seeing Oriole shedding tears made Zhang's heart ache unbearably. But he dared not go to comfort her. Instead, he went back to the sacrificial table set up for his parents, dropped to his knees and began to sob. What was going through his mind was: "I am alone in the world, and drifting here and there. I have neither married, nor started my career. Though I've found my true love, it seems unlikely that I will ever be able to marry her..."

The more he thought about his apparently hopeless situation, the more upset he felt, until eventually he could not help wailing out loud. Everyone in the hall heard him cry out. Rose recognized the voice at once. "Oh, it's that foolish scholar!" she thought to herself. "What's he doing here? Oh, I remember: They said that he had paid 5,000 cash to be included in the service. But it's too bad that he should be making such a show of himself."

Oriole too was startled by the disturbance. She stopped weeping, and turned her head to see what the matter was. Perceiving Zhang crying bitterly in front of a sacrificial table, she remembered that Rose had told her that the young scholar was to be included in the service. Seeing him in this state, she was impressed by what a dutiful son he was. Rose went over to help Oriole rise and return to her place.

Madam Cui, meanwhile, was most annoyed at the disturbance. "Where on earth did this man come from, causing this most unseemly row," she thought, with indignation. "How dare he take such liberties?" It was then that she noticed the other sacrificial table. "Good Heavens, another family is taking advantage of our funeral service to perform a sacrifice for themselves! This is most outrageous! The things some people will do to save money!" Madam Cui then demanded of the abbot what the meaning of this outrageous behavior was.

Fa Ben, startled at Zhang's outburst, hurried over to Madam Cui with a hurried explanation: "I hope Madam will forgive me. A relation of mine, who is a scholar on his way to the capital, asked me to include him in the service to show his gratitude to his deceased parents when learning that Miss Oriole would make an offering for the soul of the late Prime Minister Cui. Moved by his filial piety, I promised him I would. But I did not find time to report it to you. I am afraid I have incurred your displeasure."

Madam Cui, somewhat mollified, said, "How could I be

displeased to see anyone show his gratitude to his deceased parents? Why don't you introduce him to me, since he is your relative?"

"I certainly will, Madam," said Fa Ben, breathing an inward sigh of relief. He went to Zhang, thinking that since the young man had a pleasing appearance and polished manners, there would be no harm in his meeting Madam Cui. "Sir, please restrain your grief," he urged. "Madam Cui wishes to meet you."

Zhang was delighted to hear this. He wiped away his tears, and followed the abbot to the center of the hall, where he was duly presented to the widow of the late prime minister.

The funeral service proceeded. All through the night and until dawn the next day, candles flickered, incense burned, gongs boomed and chants resounded. Zhang kept himself busy attending to Oriole as she went through the prescribed rituals.

Finally, Fa Ben recited some prayers, and burned paper money as a symbolic gift of wealth for the deceased in the afterlife. Then he said to the mourners: "It is dawn now. The service is done. Please return to your quarters, Madam and young mistress."

Madam Cui got up: "Thank you, abbot, and your monks too. You've worked hard. I'll take my leave now." So saying, she led her entourage back to their quarters in the western bower.

Alone in the Hall of Merits and Virtues in the gray light of dawn, all the candles and incense sticks snuffed out, Zhang pondered in anguish: "Oh, Abbot, what am I to do now? Did you see Miss Oriole cast glances towards me time after time, her eyes full of love? She must know that I am dying for her love."

CHAPTER FOUR

Delivery from the Bandits

AFTER THE FUNERAL service, Oriole found herself so restless that she could scarcely do needlework, read books, or even eat or drink. What was more, she was distressed to see that the spring was departing — blossoms were falling in showers and ten thousand petals were whirling in the wind. White butterflies and willow down mingled, so that the air was filled with snow-like flakes, and swallows packed their nests with fallen blooms. Seeing the pond full of green weeds, but with only a few flowers, Oriole felt sadder still. When Rose saw her young mistress shed tears at the fast disappearance of the flowers, she determined to try to cheer her up by encouraging her to go out for walks. But Oriole felt so sluggish and disconsolate that she only wanted to lie in bed. So Rose made her coverlet fragrant and her pillow soft, so that she might sleep well. However, Oriole did not appreciate her attendance, and petulantly upbraided her: "I do wish you would not hover around me like a shadow all the time!"

Rose protested that it was Madam Cui who insisted on her never letting her young mistress out of her sight. At this, Oriole felt resentment well up inside her. "My mother is far too much of a tyrant," she thought to herself. "Especially in the past two years, she has been making sure that Rose keeps a particularly close eye on me. It seems that she is afraid that I will bring disgrace to the family. The very idea!"

Meanwhile, Rose was wondering what had come over her young mistress. She was bright enough, however, to realize that this melancholy and listlessness had started soon after she had first met that foolish young scholar. "Has she fallen in love?" she wondered.

One fine day, Oriole was gazing out of the window, lost in thought. Noticing that butterflies and swallows were fluttering about in pairs, she began to shed tears. She thought, "I'm already 19 years old, and unmarried. I am not satisfied with the fiancée chosen by my late father. Though my cousin Zheng Heng is from an official family and a son of a minister, he is ignorant and clumsy. He is not an ideal lifetime companion. He by no means compares with that scholar who recited a verse on the other side of the wall on that moonlit night. I fell in love with him at first sight. It was a masterful verse that he composed, using fine words and natural sentiments. Besides his handsome face and fine figure, he has such a gallant air about him! I think of him alone these days. He lives so near to me — we are only separated by a wall — but how can I let him know how I feel about him?" All of a sudden, there came a knock at the door. When Rose opened it, she found Madam Cui and the abbot standing there. "Miss, my mistress and the abbot have come," she informed Oriole.

The latter stood up, tidied her clothing and came forward to greet her mother. "Ten thousand blessings, mother. Ten thousand blessings, abbot," she said.

Both Madam Cui and the abbot looked grave and flustered. As she took a seat, and before Rose could offer the visitors tea, Madam Cui started to speak hurriedly. "There is terrible news, my child," she wailed. "The bandit known as Sun the Flying Tiger has besieged the monastery with 5,000 men. He has heard that your beauty is such that it outshines that of the fabled courtesans of old. He is determined to take you by force." Then Madam Cui broke into uncontrollable sobbing.

The bandits were entrenched in Mount Leishou, in Mid-River

delivery from the bandits

Prefecture. Sun the Flying Tiger had been an officer under Ding Wenya, military commissioner of the prefecture, but when Ding Wenya proved incompetent, he soon lost control of the troops under his command. Finally, the troops, not having received their pay for many months, rebelled, and Sun led a ragtag army of 5,000 men in a life of wandering banditry. They burned, killed and looted in the Mid-River Prefecture wherever they went. It was he who had prevented Madam Cui and her family taking the coffin of the late Prime Minister Cui to his hometown, as he had learned that in the entourage was the prime minister's beautiful daughter. He was determined to have Oriole as his wife. He thought to himself, "An old saying goes, 'A hero and a beauty is an ideal combination.' Just as Xiang Yu, the king of Western Chu, had Yu Ji to keep him company, so should I, Sun the Flying Tiger, have Oriole as my wife."

One day, he donned his armor, gathered his men and said in a loud voice: "Officers and men, hear my command! We are about to launch a silent night march to surround the Salvation Monastery. If I can have Oriole as my wife, then the desire of my life will be fulfilled, and I will reward you all handsomely."

All his men cheered in unison. Eager for booty, they lost no time marching to the monastery. They appeared before it at dawn the next day, and began to beat drums and gongs, wave flags and shout battle cries. The monks flew into a panic.

Sun's lieutenant stepped forward, and called out to the frightened monks: "Hear this! Sun the Flying Tiger demands that you hand over the young lady Oriole within three days to be his wife. If you refuse to comply with this order, we shall kill everyone in the monastery, and burn it to the ground!"

Abbot Fa Ben was horrified at this turn of events, and hurried to inform Madam Cui. The two decided that Oriole must be told of the situation at once.

Oriole fainted on the spot when she heard the grim news. Rose and Madam Cui managed to revive her, but Oriole could not be comforted. "An old saying goes," she thought, "that beauties are often ill-fated. This is certainly true in my case. Now I can neither stay nor depart. Where can we find a friend on whom we can rely?

43

Without my blessed father, we are completely helpless!"

At this moment, the drums started beating outside until they reached a crescendo, and the dust from the bandits' stamping feet raised a cloud of dust that floated to the heavens. Oriole stood up, and wiped away her tears, and thought, "What's the use of weeping in front of those bandits, who kill people without even batting an eyelid? I must think of a way to divert this calamity from my family members and the 300 innocent monks of the Salvation Monastery."

Madam Cui was surprised to see her daughter suddenly become so calm. Thinking Oriole was scared out of her wits, Madam Cui cried, "I am nearly 60 years old. For me, death would not be premature. But you, my dear child, are still young and not yet married. How can I bear to see you fall victim to this beast of a bandit?"

"Mother, I have an idea," said Oriole, with determination.

Upon hearing this, the others felt relieved, thinking, "Oriole is a worthy daughter of the late prime minister. She betrays no fear in an hour of danger."

"I think that all that can be done is to hand me over to the bandit, so that the lives of our family and the monks can be saved, and the monastery protected," said Oriole.

A cry of dismay arose, and Madam Cui was heartbroken. "My dear daughter," she cried piteously, "in our family no man has ever broken the law and no woman has ever been sullied. How can I bear to hand you over to that bandit and disgrace our family?"

Oriole was convinced that what her mother said was right. She reflected, "I am a daughter of the exalted Prime Minister Cui. How could I become the wife of a bandit? It is better that I die to maintain my chastity. That way, the bandit will have no further reason to harass the monastery, and my family members and the monks will be saved!"

She turned to her mother and said, "Mother, you'd better hand me over to the bandit."

"My dear, that is out of the question! How can you suggest such a thing?" cried Madam Cui in despair.

"My dear mother, in my opinion there are five advantages to handing me over. Firstly, your safety will be ensured; secondly, the temple will escape being razed to the ground; thirdly, the priests will be able to continue to pray for me and our ancestors; fourthly, my father's coffin will be allowed to reach its final resting place; and fifthly, Merry Boy will survive to be the scion of our family..."

Merry Boy, who was clinging to Madam Cui, interrupted at this point: "Elder sister, don't worry about me. I am not afraid," he assured her.

Oriole stroked the boy's head gently, and said, "You are the only one who can continue our family line. Should I disobey the bandit and fail to make this sacrifice, the temple and our father's coffin will be turned into ashes, and the monks who offer prayers for us will be slaughtered. How can I be so selfish?"

Upon hearing this, Madam Cui was deeply grieved. "I will never hand you over to the bandit," she said crying bitterly.

With tears in her eyes, Oriole said, "Mother, you must sacrifice me. I will take my own life with a white silk scarf. You may have my dead body presented to the head of the brigands. The bandit who wants me to be his wife will surely not accept my dead body. When I die, the bandits will withdraw, and you will all be saved..."

The others were all moved by her words. But Madam Cui shook her head, saying, "No, it won't do."

"Mother, you must bear to be separated from me. You should convince yourself that you never had a daughter. I will have to repay all your kindness of bringing me up in the next life," the weeping Oriole begged.

Seeing both mother and daughter so heart-broken, Abbot Fa Ben said, "Madam and young mistress, don't be upset. Let us go to the Hall of the Dharma and inquire of the monks and laymen there if they have any suggestions to offer, so that we can devise a plan. An old saying goes: 'For every 10 steps there must be grass, and for every 10 houses there must be someone of talent.' In addition, Madam may offer a generous reward to anyone who is able to induce the bandits to withdraw. For another old saying goes: 'When a high reward is offered, brave fellows are bound to come forward.' What do you say, Madam?"

"That sounds reasonable, abbot. Let's go at once," Madam Cui agreed.

Both inside and outside the Hall of Dharma there were throngs of people, alarmed and bewildered. Abbot Fa Ben escorted Madam Cui and Oriole into the hall, and he stayed outside to confer with the monks. However, no one could offer an acceptable proposal.

After a long while, the abbot stepped into the hall to report to Madam Cui: "Madam, no one is able to present a completely safe plan. What can we do then?"

Oriole cut in calmly: "Mother, at this very moment you must make up your mind to sacrifice your daughter. I have an idea. You should proclaim that if anyone in the monastery is able to induce the bandits to withdraw, you will present me to him as his wife, and give him a handsome dowry."

Madam Cui at first refused to hear of such a thing, but after having thought about it for a while, she came to believe that it was a good proposal after all. Though an uneven alliance, such a match would be better than Oriole's falling into the hands of the brigand Sun. At this critical moment, it was the only thing they could do. So she said, "Abbot, please proclaim to all the priests and laymen in the monastery that if anyone is able to induce the bandits to withdraw, I will give him my daughter's hand in marriage, together with a handsome dowry."

Fa Ben went out to proclaim this offer, which aroused great interest among both monks and laymen. They all admired the beautiful Oriole, but it seemed that no one had any idea how to drive away the bandits. Eventually Zhang stepped forward. "I have a plan for getting rid of the bandits," he declared in a ringing voice. When the abbot asked him what it was, the young man said, "Could you please inform Madam Cui that I want to see her?"

Fa Ben lost no time returning to the anxious Madam Cui in the Hall of the Dharma. "Heaven has extended a helping hand to you, Madam," he cried. "Someone has offered to drive away the bandits!"

"Buddha is merciful, Abbot! Who is this bountiful person?"

"I beg to inform you, Madam, that he is my relative who joined in the funeral ceremony. He is a young scholar by the name of Zhang Gong, and styled Junrui."

Madam Cui nodded her approval, and Oriole was delighted to hear it. She prayed in her heart: "May the brave young scholar drive away the bandits and keep us all safe."

"The young man is waiting outside. He wants to meet you, Madam," the abbot said.

"Please bring him in," Madam Cui urged.

The abbot thereupon hurried out to summon Zhang. In no more than a moment, the young man entered the hall, calmly and gracefully. He readjusted his hat, stepped forward and made a deep bow to Madam Cui.

The latter was impressed by the young man's dignified demeanor, and signaled to Rose to bring a chair for him. She lost no time explaining her dilemma: "Sir, a disaster has fallen on my family. Sun the Flying Tiger has surrounded the monastery with his troops. He demands my daughter Oriole for his wife. We, a widow and orphans, have no one to rely on. An old saying goes: 'Everyone has a sense of pity.' I hope you will rescue us from the danger. All the members of our family will be deeply grateful to you, and will never forget your kindness."

Upon hearing this, Zhang thought to himself: "What about her reported promise to give Oriole as wife to anyone who can drive the bandits away?" And he decided to keep silent until she made the offer in person.

Seeing that Zhang did not give an answer straightaway, Madam Cui immediately guessed the reason. She said, "Sir, just now I asked the abbot to convey my intention to give my daughter Oriole to anyone who can drive the bandits away."

Zhang was overjoyed to hear that it was true after all. "Do you really mean that?" he cried.

"What has been said cannot be unsaid," replied Madam Cui solemnly. "If you can get rid of the bandits, you may marry my daughter right away. The abbot will be the witness."

Zhang stole a glance at the beautiful Oriole, then said, "If that is the case, please let my future bride go back to her chamber. I have a plan for driving the bandits away."

Upon hearing this roaming scholar call Oriole his 'future bride', Madam Cui was somewhat displeased. But in this critical situation, she had no choice. So she said to Rose: "Escort your young mistress back to her chamber."

Oriole too, hearing Zhang call her his 'future wife', was disconcerted, but by no means displeased. Blushing, she allowed Rose to guide her back to her chamber.

"Now, sir," said Madam Cui, turning to Zhang, "what is your plan?"

"My plan, Madam, first of all requires the assistance of the abbot."

"An old priest is no fighter. I must ask you, sir, to find someone else to replace me," said Fa Ben, shaking his head.

Zhang smiled and said, "Do not be afraid. I do not want you to fight. Just go and tell the rebel chief that it is the decision of Madam Cui that her daughter in mourning cannot marry a general in arms. Moreover, the young mistress has been pampered since childhood. It would be a great pity if she was frightened to death by the sound of drums and gongs. If he wishes to marry her, he must take off his armor, lay down his arms and withdraw as far as an arrow can fly. Then he must wait for three days, until the funeral service is finished. After she bids farewell to her father's coffin and changes into her bridal robes, she will be escorted to him. If she should be escorted at once, it would be unlucky for his army because she is still in mourning. Hurry and tell him that."

"But what is to be done after the three days?" asked the abbot.

"Don't worry, Abbot. I am prepared for that contingency."

Sun the Flying Tiger was pacing up and down, consumed with impatience. Normally he would have simply stormed the monastery and seized his prey. But as Oriole was the daughter of the late prime minister, he felt that he had to employ some finesse in the matter. Unexpectedly, one of his men came in to report: "The abbot is requesting a parley with the general." Sun the Flying Tiger strode to the front gate of the monastery. Not being a man to beat about the bush, he roared, "Listen to me, you bald-headed old ass. Send Oriole out here at once, or I'll burn your monastery to the ground!"

The abbot adopted a conciliatory tone, saying, "Please do not be hasty, General. I am ordered by Madam Cui to inform you that..." He repeated what Zhang had said.

It sounded reasonable to Sun, who said, "All right. But if Oriole is not sent to me when three days have passed, I will have you all put to death. In the meantime, go and tell Madam Cui what an excellent son-in-law I will make."

Then he turned to his men, and shouted, "Withdraw as far as an arrow can fly!" Thereupon, all the bandits retreated out of sight.

Returning to the hall, the abbot reported to Zhang: "Sir, all the bandits have withdrawn. But if Oriole is not sent to him after three days, Sun says, he will kill all of us."

"Sir, what's your plan? Please tell me," the anxious Madam Cui urged Zhang.

The young man said calmly: "I have a friend whose name is Du Que and whose title is White Horse General. He is now in command of an army of 100,000 men, guarding the Pu Pass. He and I are sworn brothers. If I write a letter to him, he is sure to come to our rescue. But the pass is about 40 miles away. Who can deliver a letter there for me?"

"If the White Horse General comes, we need not be afraid of even a hundred so-called Flying Tigers," Fa Ben said, with great enthusiasm. "Sir, I have a disciple called Hui Ming," he went on. "He is most trustworthy. He can deliver the letter for certain."

"Excellent," exclaimed Zhang. "Please have a writing brush and some paper brought to me."

Upon being presented with the four treasures of the study, Zhang took up the brush and began to write. In only a few minutes, the letter was ready to be dispatched.

However, the abbot said, "There is one thing, young sir, which I forgot to mention. This man Hui Ming is a person of peculiar temperament. Remiss at reciting the scriptures and praying, his predilections are fighting and drinking. If you ask him to send the letter, he is sure to refuse, but if you can challenge his perverse spirit, nothing will deter him from going."

Zhang thought to himself: "He sounds like a real stubborn donkey. He will refuse to go when asked, but will volunteer to go if he is beaten. Well then, I will lead him a merry dance today!" Then he folded the letter, put it in an envelope, walked out of the hall and proclaimed to the assembled monks and laymen: "Sun the Flying Tiger has the monastery surrounded. How can we just sit here waiting for death? I have a friend known as the White

Horse General, who is guarding the Pu Pass. I have written a letter begging him to come and save us from the brigands. Who dares to take it to him?"

All the monks and laymen looked at each other, none of them daring to volunteer. "Isn't there a single brave man in such a large monastery?"

"I will go!" All of a sudden, a tall, strong monk came forward, with an iron club in his hand and a sword in his belt. "Sir, give me the letter. I'll take it to the White Horse General."

Zhang was inwardly delighted, but pretended to be quite unimpressed with the offer. He spoke deliberately: "This is no trifling matter. If this letter should fall into the hands of the bandits, we will all be put to death and the monastery razed. Are you sure you have the courage and skill required to deliver such an important letter?"

Hui Ming patted his chest proudly and said, "The quiet life in this monastery irks me, and a meatless diet is not to my taste. I am eager to pit my wits and strength against these 5,000 churls who have dared to be so insolent."

"Are you sure that you really have the courage to go?" the abbot asked.

Hui Ming retorted with a flurry of oaths that nothing would stop him delivering the letter, least of all a handful of ragged robbers. And so, Hui Ming departed on his mission. He left the monastery by the back door, where only a handful of bandits had been left on guard. They shot arrows at the monk as soon as they saw him, but he simply knocked the arrows aside with his iron club. When this incident was reported to Sun the Flying Tiger, he thought that one of the monks must have panicked and fled. So he gave it no more heed.

Hui Ming reached the Pu Pass before daybreak. He found General Du reviewing his troops. Granted an audience with the general, Hui Ming reported as follows: "The Salvation Monastery is surrounded by Sun the Flying Tiger and his 5,000 men. He demands that the daughter of the late Prime Minister Cui be handed over to him. I have brought a letter from Zhang Junrui, who requests Your Excellency to come to their rescue as soon as possible."

"Hand his letter to me," ordered General Du, frowning.

Hui Ming took it out, and handed it to the general.

General Du opened the letter and read: "Zhang Gong, your former fellow student and sworn brother, kowtows to you over and over again and presents this letter to Your Excellency General Du. Two years have passed since we met last, and I can never forget the windy and rainy nights when we shared lodgings together. On my way from my home to the capital, I came to Mid-River Prefecture and intended to pay you a visit. But the journey had so exhausted me that I fell ill. Now I am better, and there is no cause for worry. I have taken up quarters in a quiet monastery that has unexpectedly became a place of calamity. The widow of the late Prime Minister Cui brought her husband's coffin to the monastery on her way to its last resting place. But a bandit nicknamed Sun the Flying Tiger has besieged the temple with 5,000 men, determined to seize the late prime minister's beautiful daughter. Anyone who could see their pitiful and helpless state would feel indignant and do all he can to drive the bandits away. But, to my regret, as I am a mere scholar unable even to truss a chicken, I can do nothing to help them, even if I sacrifice my life. Then I thought of you, who have command of a huge army of gallant troops. You who follow the tradition of the heroes of old are in no way unworthy of them. I am now in grave danger, along with the kin of the late prime minister and the monks of this monastery. I beseech you to come to our aid as soon as possible. We would be as grateful to you as a fish stranded on dry land to the person who brings it water from the far-off West River. The late Prime Minister Cui, though in the eternal shades below, would also be grateful to you for your timely assistance. Anxiously awaiting your timely arrival, Zhang Gong salutes you again."

After having read the letter, General Du flew into a rage. "I heard that Ding Wenya lost control of the prefecture and that Sun the Flying Tiger has been running amok, causing all kinds of havoc," he thought to himself. "But this is outrageous! There is nothing else for it but to punish that scoundrel of a bandit once and for all." He said to Hui Ming: "I understand that the matter is urgent. Go back to the monastery and tell them to be of good cheer, for I will set off this very night to relieve the siege."

"The monastery is in a perilous situation," said Hui Ming. "I beg Your Excellency to make haste."

"Don't worry. Though I have not received an imperial order, it is my duty to save the people from disasters. Adjutant, select 5,000 of my crack troops, and tell them to get ready to march to the Salvation Monastery in Mid-River Prefecture. Their mission is to crush Sun the Flying Tiger."

Before long, General Du, resplendent in full armor and mounted on his white charger, set out at the head of 5,000 picked troops for the monastery. Sun the Flying Tiger was taken by surprise and, after a brief skirmish, captured. The other bandits either fled or surrendered.

It had been a time of great tension and worry for the people in the monastery. After Hui Ming had left to seek help from General Du, Zhang tried to instill hope into everyone by assuring them that his sworn brother would come galloping to their rescue in no time at all, and give that villain Sun the Flying Tiger his just deserts. Nevertheless, he was consumed with worry: If anything should go wrong, all the people in the temple would die and he himself would lose a beautiful wife.

Two days of the three-day respite that Sun the Flying Tiger had given them had dragged by, when Madam Cui and the abbot came to see Zhang. As soon as she entered the room, Madam Cui said, "The letter was sent two days ago, but no reply has come yet. There is only one day left before that monstrous brigand comes to claim my poor Oriole. What are we to do?"

At that moment, a deafening commotion was heard outside the gate of the monastery. Zhang was beside himself with joy. "My sworn brother must have arrived," he cried out in exultation. "Abbot, let's go to the Bell Tower and take a look." So saying, he clambered to the top of the Bell Tower, followed by the abbot. From there, they saw that the area in front of the gate was a bedlam of dust and smoke, and hundreds of battle flags waved. Among them there was a large flag on which the surname of the general, Du, was embroidered. The enemy were in great disorder, and before long they laid down their arms, fell to their knees and surrendered. Sun the Flying Tiger was captured alive. General Du had won a great victory.

Zhang and the abbot hurriedly descended the tower, and opened the gate of the monastery to welcome General Du. Zhang made a deep bow to Du: "It is so long since we parted that our meeting seems like a dream," he gasped.

General Du saluted him in return. "I am so pleased to see you," he said. "May I ask why you did not come to pay me a visit?"

"I happened to be indisposed, and besides I was busy trying to protect Madam Cui and her entourage. I hope you will forgive me."

Upon learning that the bandits had been eliminated, Madam Cui was so relieved that tears ran down her cheeks. She immediately ordered a banquet prepared to celebrate the victory of the White Horse General.

General Du bowed to Madam Cui, and said, "I had not taken proper precautions against these bandits, and as a consequence you have been needlessly troubled, for which I should bear the blame."

"I will not hear of it, General Du," said Madam Cui. "We were in such a hopeless situation that we deemed death inevitable. It is due to you that we are able to continue our lives. I do not know how to repay your kindness."

"It is merely my duty," said General Du.

Zhang explained: "I wrote you the letter to ask you to rescue us from the siege, because Madam Cui had declared that if anyone were able to induce the bandits to withdraw, she would present him with her daughter as his wife."

Du Que said, "My heartiest congratulations and best wishes to you." Then he said to Madam Cui: "Zhang proposed a plan for defeating the bandits, and you, Madam, made a promise. If you keep your promise, your beautiful daughter and this talented young man will make an ideal couple, I think."

Madam Cui smiled, saying: "I am afraid my daughter is not worthy to be his wife. Anyway, I have still other arrangements in mind. Let dinner be served."

Du Que declined, "It is unnecessary to go to such trouble for what was merely a matter of duty. Besides, as the bandits have just surrendered, I must go and deal with the matter. Moreover, I am in charge of guarding the Pu Pass, so I must not be away from my regular post for too long. But I will certainly come on the wedding day of my sworn brother. I hereby take my leave. I hope you, Madam Cui, and Zhang will forgive me."

"I dare not detain you, lest it should interfere with your duties," said Zhang.

They saw the White Horse General off at the gate of the monastery, and together with all his officers and men returned to the Pu Pass in triumph.

The horsemen leave the temple 'mid the cymbals' sound;
The soldiers sing victorious songs, for the Pu Pass bound.

After they had gone, Madam Cui said to Zhang: "We are deeply grateful for your invaluable help. From now on, you should no longer dwell in your present quarters, but move to our library, which has been cleaned and made ready. You may move in at any time. A special dinner will be prepared tomorrow, and Rose will come to invite you. I insist on your presence." So saying, she and her maids left.

Zhang was overjoyed at this turn of events. He said to Fa Ben: "I thank you for everything you've done for me. But I am not sure about my marriage."

"It is all settled," said Fa Ben. "Oriole is destined to be your wife. You're very lucky. The disaster posed by the bandits has turned out to be a blessing after all! Get ready to be a bridegroom."

In high spirits, Zhang packed his things, and moved to the library of Madam Cui's quarters.

CHAPTER FIVE

The Promise Broken at a Family Feast

NOW THAT THE danger had passed, Madam Cui started to have second thoughts about her rash promise. First, Oriole had been betrothed to her nephew Zheng Heng at the express wish of her late husband, and she feared to face the wrath of her elder brother if she broke off the engagement. Second, and just as important in her eyes, was the fact that Zhang came from a family that had gone down in the world, and currently he had no official title. All that day, Madam Cui was so perturbed that she could neither eat nor rest. She was forlorn and tearful as she thought, "When my husband was alive, he took care of everything. Now I have to make all the decisions. As a widow and an orphan, I and my daughter are prey to bullying by all sorts of rascals."

Nevertheless, to thank Zhang for his help, Madam Cui had a feast prepared in the guest hall of the monastery, and sent Rose to the library to insist on Zhang's attendance.

Rose thought to herself: "Madam does not need to worry about that; the foolish young man is only too eager be anywhere where

Oriole is likely to be present." So off she went to find Zhang.

After the White Horse General had crushed the bandits headed by Sun the Flying Tiger, Zhang moved to live in the Western Bower at the invitation of Madam Cui, fully expecting her to keep her promise and allow him to marry Oriole. He had already been informed of the upcoming banquet, and was unable to sleep that night for excitement. Long before dawn, he woke his page, and started to wash and dress. With the help of the page, he scrubbed himself till his skin shone, using up two pieces of soap and two buckets of water. He then put on a black silk hat and a scholar's robe of pure white with a gilt-buckled belt. No sooner was he ready than he heard a knock at the door.

"Who is it?" he asked eagerly.

"It's me," said Rose.

Zhang invited her in, and lost no time asking, "Rose, why is Madam Cui holding this banquet?"

Rose smiled mischievously: "In the first place," she said, "it's being held to celebrate our escape from danger. And in the second place, it's being held to thank you for your kindness." Then, after a moment of hesitation, she said, "Oh, I almost forgot! It's also being held in honor of your marriage to Oriole."

Zhang was overjoyed. "How do I look, Rose?" he cried. "There is no mirror in the room, so do tell me!"

Rose burst into peals of laughter: "You are so polished and dazzling that no one will be able to look at you for the glare!"

Zhang's face turned bright red, and he pleaded, "Don't tease me, Rose. Tell me, is it really decreed by fate that I am to marry Miss Oriole today?"

"Indeed it is," Rose said. "A truly happy union cannot be decreed by mortals, but by fate alone. Just as plants and trees grow together naturally in the spring breeze, you and Miss Oriole are meant for each other."

Zhang was even more pleased than ever. "Rose, will your young mistress be faithful and true?" he asked.

"You two will have to decide for yourselves who is faithful and who is not. But I want to warn you, Master Zhang, that you must be gentle to my young mistress tonight. She is very delicate."

Scarlet-faced, Zhang replied, "Don't worry, Rose; I have a tender heart. Now, tell me what arrangements have been made and how the chamber is decorated."

"The bed curtains are embroidered with a full moon and pairs of love birds, and there are two screens of the finest jade adorned with images of peacocks. There is also an orchestra, which will play "The Song of Happy Union". You must prove yourself worthy of these lavish preparations tonight."

Though Zhang knew that Rose was making fun of him, he was pleased to hear this. But then it occurred to him that he had nothing to offer as a gift for the bride and her family. He mentioned this worry to Rose, who assured him that in the circumstances, with no other guests at the banquet — not even the abbot — the normal etiquette would not apply. So it was with a feeling of relief that he allowed Rose to depart.

No sooner had the door closed behind her than Zhang fell into a pleasant reverie. He imagined his reception by Madam Cui. "She will say, 'Here you are, Master Zhang. You and my Oriole will make a happy couple, so drink a cup of wine each before you retire to the bridal chamber.' Then we two will go to the bridal chamber. After Oriole removes her clothes, we shall be as close as fish and water. In the dim lamplight, I will gaze on her black hair cascading over her shoulders, and her star-like bright eyes will gaze into mine. I can see them now — the jadeite-colored quilts and the socks embroidered with mandarin ducks!"

Meanwhile, Madam Cui was wracked by impatience, waiting for Rose and Zhang. When Rose finally returned and reported that the young man was on his way, she sent her to fetch Oriole. Zhang appeared soon afterwards. He straightaway saluted Madam Cui: "Madam, I have come to pay my respects to you."

"Please don't stand on ceremony, Master Zhang," Madam Cui said. "If it had not been for your timely assistance, we would not have lived to see this happy day. As you know, I have had a banquet prepared for you. Although it can in no way requite you for your splendid service, I hope you will not scorn this little token of my appreciation."

Zhang waved his hand dismissively, and said, "You are too kind,

Madam. It is said that on the good fortune of one person often depends that of multitudes. The defeat of the bandits was due to your good fortune, Madam. Nothing else is worthy of mention."

"Your modesty becomes you as a scholar," his hostess rejoined, and urged him to be seated at his ease.

But Zhang continued to play the role of the self-effacing scholar in front of his prospective mother-in-law: "I should remain standing, Madam, as prescribed in the ancient rites. How could I presume to sit down in your presence?"

"Do you not know the old saying that politeness is not as good as compliance? Please sit down, sir," Madam Cui urged him.

"You are right, of course. I will take my seat." Zhang said, eager to ingratiate, and proceeded to do as he was bidden.

Madam Cui ordered wine to be brought, personally filled a cup, and offered it to the young man with both hands, a singular honor.

Zhang, feeling extremely flattered, stood up to receive it, and said, "This is very kind of you, and though I'm not used to drinking wine, I remember that it says in *The Book of Rites* that younger people should unhesitatingly obey the orders of their elders." He thereupon drained the wine cup.

He then poured wine for Madam Cui. These formalities completed and all the polite protocols exhausted, an oppressive silence reigned in the banquet hall. Zhang sat fidgeting, and wondering when Oriole and Rose were going to put in an appearance.

All this time Oriole was doing embroidery in her room, unaware of the banquet that had been arranged. She was startled when Rose burst into the room, crying, "Miss, miss!"

Oriole paused in her work, and asked the girl: "What is it, Rose? What are you so excited and flustered about?"

"Madam is entertaining a guest in the main hall of the monastery. She asks you to join them."

"Go and tell my mother that I'm not feeling well today, so I beg to be excused."

Rose pouted. "You'll be sorry you refused to go when you find out who the guest is," she murmured.

"I don't care who he is; I won't go."

"That's what you say now, but wait till you hear who the guest is!" Rose said, archly.

"All right, tell me who it is."

"None other than that young scholar!" cried Rose triumphantly. "The unmarried one, remember?"

Oriole was delighted to hear this, but she was careful not to make this obvious to Rose. She thought to herself: "Master Zhang was the one who saved us from those savage bandits. The least we can do to show our appreciation is to hold a feast for him." She thereupon told Rose that, on second thoughts, she had decided that it was only right and proper that she should attend the banquet after all.

Upon hearing this, Rose teased her, saying, "Whenever the young scholar is mentioned, you become agitated. Aren't you ashamed?"

Oriole blushed and muttered, "Stop talking nonsense, Rose," aiming a playful slap at her.

Rose then helped her mistress to wash and dress herself, taking extra pains so that she would look her best when she met Zhang. She combed her hair into an elegant pile on the top of her head, and in it inserted a green peony that had just been picked from the garden, holding it in place with a gold hairpin. Oriole then painted her eyebrows, powdered her face and put on some lipstick. Then she changed into a pink jacket decorated with small flowers, a silk skirt, and a pair of pink shoes with a phoenix pattern. When her toilet was complete, she looked a veritable vision of loveliness.

"Your face looks so delicate that it seems even a puff of wind would hurt it, Miss!" said Rose. "What a lucky man Zhang is! My Young Mistress, you were indeed born to be the wife of a grand official!"

Though inwardly pleased, Oriole frowned and said, "How you talk, Rose! I have nothing but a friendly interest in that kind young man. Wife of a grand official, indeed!"

But Rose kept on teasing her: "Both of you are lovesick for each other. And now, finally, your long days of suffering have come to an end."

Oriole lowered her head, and thought to herself that Rose was absolutely right.

Suddenly, Rose thought of something, and said, "Miss, isn't it strange that your mother did not decide to throw a big banquet and invite relatives and friends, if you and Zhang are to be married today? It isn't like a wedding banquet held by a prime minister's family at all!"

"Rose, you don't understand the situation," Oriole said. "My marriage to the impoverished young scholar will bring a financial burden upon our family. My mother's only concern right now is to save money."

"Yes, I suppose you're right," Rose agreed. "Well, now that you are ready, let's go to the main hall."

As soon as Oriole entered the hall, her eyes met Zhang's arduous gaze. She hurriedly looked at the ground, walked up to her mother, and paid her respects to her.

The sight of Oriole in her holiday best, and groomed and made up like a bride brought a frown to her mother's brow. "My dear," she said coldly, "Now pay your respects to your elder brother."

All the people in the hall were aghast at hearing Madam Cui refer to Zhang as Oriole's "elder brother". The two words, indeed, hit the young man like a thunderbolt. Oriole was only prevented from falling down in a swoon by Rose, and Rose herself was flabbergasted. "The old woman must have decided to call off the marriage," the girl thought. "Everyone knows that a sister and brother may not marry."

With a vacant smile, Madam Cui said, "Rose, bring heated wine for your young mistress to fill the cup of her elder brother."

This was duly done. Sad and indignant, Oriole lifted the wine cup slowly, but did not fill it. Her mother urged her: "My dear daughter, you must present a cup of wine to your elder brother."

At this moment, Zhang stood up, and declined the wine. "I beg to be excused," he said. "But I cannot drink any more wine."

Oriole understood his reticence very well. With tears in her eyes, she ordered Rose to remove the wine. She wanted so much to pour out her feelings to Zhang, but with her mother at her side it was impossible. Although her lover was but a foot from her, he seemed as far off as the Milky Way. How could they have expected that the delight enjoyed beneath moonbeams would turn into empty dreams?

Madam Cui flew into a rage at this turn of events, yelling, "Rose, fill a cup of wine, and let your young mistress to present it to her elder brother."

Rose cursed Madam Cui in her heart: "You're an unfeeling old woman who is only interested in riches and decorum. You care nothing for the tender feelings of young people in love!"

"Rose!" Madam Cui shouted, seeing the girl hesitate.

"Yes, Madam," Rose answered. She filled a cup and gave it to Oriole, who immediately pushed it aside, spilling the wine. Angry that Oriole refused to bend to her will, Madam Cui ordered, "Rose, conduct your young mistress to her bed chamber."

Rose did as she was bidden.

Seeing Oriole leave in sadness and anger, Zhang felt as if a knife were piercing his heart. He went up to Madam Cui, and made a bow, saying, "Madam, I wish to consult you on a matter which I am not sure if it is proper to ask you about."

"If you have anything to say, please speak out," Madam Cui replied with a self-satisfied smile.

"Do you still remember the promise you made when the bandits were surrounding the monastery?"

"Yes..."

"At that time, you promised to give the hand of Miss Oriole to anyone who could make the bandits withdraw. Is that not what you said? Hence I wrote that letter in haste, requesting General Du to come and save the lives of your whole family. When Rose came this morning to summon me, I thought you were going to fulfill your promise, and I was to marry your beautiful daughter. I cannot for the life of me imagine what has made you suddenly change your mind and call me her 'elder brother'. But, if you think I am unworthy of being your son-in-law, I request that you allow me to leave your presence for ever, here and now."

Madam Cui heaved a deep sigh, and said, "It is you to whom we owe our lives. However, my daughter was betrothed to my nephew Zheng Heng when my late husband was still alive, and I have written to summon him here. So you see, it is out of the question for you to aspire to my daughter's hand. Now I think the best thing I can do is to reward you with a large sum of money, so that you may select another lady of noble birth and that both of us may carry out our matrimonial arrangements to our own satisfaction."

Zhang said: "What use have I for your money if Oriole is denied me? An old saying goes, 'There are gilded palaces in books, and there are beautiful ladies in books.' I will now bid you farewell." So saying, he turned to leave.

"Pray do not be so hasty, sir. I fear the fumes of the wine you drank have gone to your head," said Madam Cui. "Rose, see the young gentleman to the library. Tomorrow we will discuss the necessary arrangements."

Leaning on Rose, Zhang stumbled from the hall, his head reeling from the wine, but more so from the shock he had just received. "Alas, Miss Rose, I am afraid that I was born unlucky. I am doomed to pass lonely nights. And to think that I expected to pass this night in the bridal chamber!"

Rose uttered some words of comfort, but Zhang fell to his knees before her: "Miss Rose," he cried, "you must know that since I first set eyes on your young mistress, I have neither eaten nor slept properly. My sufferings have been unbearable. I thought I would marry Miss Oriole today. But to my utter consternation, Madam changed her mind! I am devastated with grief."

"Please do not despair, sir," Rose interrupted him. "I will do my best to help you."

This caused a ray of hope to gleam in Zhang's heart. "But what can you possibly do to save a lovelorn wretch like me?" he pleaded. "But if there is anything you can do, I will be grateful to you to the end of my days."

Rose said, "I have noticed that you possess a lute, so I suppose you are adept at playing that instrument. Now, my young mistress also loves the music of the lute. She will go with me to the garden to burn incense tonight. When you hear me give a cough you should start playing your lute. I will observe her reaction closely, and at the right moment I will tell her your sentiments. I will let you know early tomorrow morning what she says."

Zhang shed grateful tears and thanked the girl over and over again. But Rose cut him short, and departed to attend to her young mistress.

CHAPTER SIX

The Love Message of the Lute

ZHANG WAS DELIGHTED with Rose's suggestion, and could not wait for nightfall. He passed the time tuning his lute and preparing himself for a new expression of his love for Oriole. As the drumbeat announced the onset of the night hours, he sat before the instrument and addressed it thus: "Oh, lute, you have accompanied me through thick and thin for many years. I depend on you for the success of tonight's venture." Then he turned his eyes Heavenward, and prayed, "Oh, Heaven, graciously lend me a fair breeze to waft the music of my lute to Oriole's ears."

Meanwhile, Oriole was sitting dejected in her bed chamber, devastated by her mother's harsh treatment of Zhang and despairing of ever finding happiness. Unexpectedly Rose suggested, "Miss, how bright the moon is tonight! Let's go and burn incense in the garden. There we can pray for better fortune."

Oriole sighed, and wailed, "My mother's mind is made up. What's the use of burning incense now?"

"The Moon Goddess is always ready to lend an ear to the petitions of young lovers, Miss," said Rose, coaxingly.

Oriole was reluctant to go, feeling that everything was hopeless, but eventually she allowed herself to be led out into the garden by Rose.

Just as the girl had said, it was a brilliant moonlit night. The moon itself dazzled the eye, and fragrant flowers, wafted by the breeze, filled the air like a snow shower.

Rose lost no time setting up the incense table. Oriole picked up three incense sticks, and said in her heart: "Oh, Moon, what can I do now? *The Book of Songs* says, 'Good in the beginning, but usually bad in the end.' Mother, you are the widow of the late prime minister. How could you go back on your word? Why should something well begun be in the end undone? Zhang will now be only a dream lover to me. And I shall be a merely beloved image to him. I can only long for him in vain. We cannot meet, except in sweet dreams. Oh, my heart breaks when I think how I was attired in my bridal array! So close to happiness!"

Seeing Oriole wipe away tears, Rose said, "Look, there is a halo around the moon! It will probably be windy tomorrow."

"It will probably rain tomorrow also," Oriole sighed. "There is the moon and the wind in Heaven, but there is not a happy thing on Earth."

"What do you mean, Young Mistress?" asked Rose, puzzled.

"There is also the halo of the moon on earth too," replied Oriole. "A lovely jade-like face is locked up within embroidered curtains of lace. It fears to be profaned by the touch of a mortal hand. Just like the Goddess of the Moon traversing the sky from west to east, all alone. Her lover cannot visit her palace again, which is surrounded by screen on screen, lest she be seen and her heart above be moved to love."

Hearing this, Rose thought to herself: "Oh, Miss, you are seriously lovesick! Zhang must be waiting in great anxiety on the other side of the wall. I'd better give him a signal." Then she coughed lightly.

Zhang on the other side of the wall heard the cough, and a surge of excitement ran through him. He straightaway began to play his lute.

The melody flowed in an exhilarating medley of sounds: harsh like the clash of cavalry sabers; then soft like flowers dropping into smoothly flowing streams; then high like the cry of a crane in a breezy moonlit sky; and then soft like lovers' whispers. Oriole, who had been in no mood to appreciate the moon, was fascinated by the beautiful music.

Rose was happy to see her young mistress listening to the strains of the lute with great attention. She said, with a smile: "Please stay here and listen to the music, Miss. I am going to see if your mother needs me."

Oriole gave an absent-minded nod.

Rose's voice was heard by Zhang, who immediately thought to himself that he must seize this chance when Oriole had been left alone to express his love for her. He remembered that an ancient scholar had wooed a beautiful lady by playing a tune called "The Phoenix Seeks His Mate". So he began to play this old romantic tune, at the same time singing:

> There is a lady I cannot forget, I swear.
> Not a single day but she puts me in despair.
> Hither and thither see the phoenix fly,
> Seeking his mate low and high.
> Alas! Where is the lady fair?
> I cannot find her anywhere.
> I sit forlorn and strum my lute
> To help relieve my pain acute.
> When will you give your word
> To the wandering phoenix bird?
> When will we two soar,
> Wing to wing, evermore?

Oriole's heart was touched by the exquisite sadness of the tune and the bitter longing expressed by the words.

Suddenly, the music stopped, and she heard the player lament from the other side of the wall: "Alas, I, Zhang Junrui, am unlucky in love. Your mother may be ungrateful and unjust, but you, my dear Miss Oriole, how can you deceive one who believes in the sincerity of your feelings?"

But Oriole could not answer him. Now the moonlight seemed

to shed wan beams of desolation all around, and what had been a delightful vista was now a heart-breaking lonely scene. But she was not allowed to wallow in her reveries for long before she heard Rose saying, "Young Mistress, your mother is looking for you. Let's go back. Otherwise we will both be in trouble."

So the two left the garden of the Western Bower. From then on, Oriole languished in her bed chamber, unable to apply herself any more to her needlework. At the same time, Zhang found himself unable to concentrate on his studies. Both of them pined for each other, not knowing what to do to end their heartache.

One day when Oriole went to pay respects to her mother, Abbot Fa Cong came to tell them that Zhang was sick. Hearing this, Oriole was so distressed that she had difficulty restraining her tears. Upon returning to her room, she prevailed upon Rose to go and see how Master Zhang was faring, enjoining her to be as discreet as possible.

Rose tiptoed up to the outside of the young man's quarters, and peeped through a tear in the paper that covered the window. She saw the young scholar lying fully dressed on his bed. He looked pale and sickly. His breath came in labored gasps. Rose knocked lightly on the window frame.

"Who is there?" Zhang asked, in a creaking, strangled voice.

"The spirit of lovesickness," answered the mischievous Rose.

Pleased to hear Rose's voice once more, Zhang struggled to his feet and opened the door.

"Have you brought a message, Rose?" said the young man eagerly. "Did your young mistress say anything to you last night after having listened to me playing the lute?"

Rose pretended to be angry: "My young mistress has been feeling uneasy since she heard your lute playing last night," she said. "She does not attend to needle and thread, nor take any care of her appearance. She sheds tears as she gazes upon the flowers, and is sad and weary as she looks up at the moon. Her appetite has vanished, and all day she thinks only of you, Master Zhang. You are ill, and my young mistress is sick too. Your mutual malady is nothing but lovesickness. "

"Since Oriole loves me, it is worth suffering from lovesickness," thought Zhang. Then he said out loud: "Miss Rose, I have a letter to send to your young mistress; may I trouble you to deliver it for me?"

"Oh, no," Rose protested. "A letter is too dangerous! What if somebody should find it later? However, I can pass on a message by word of mouth."

But Zhang balked at this suggestion. "My message is only for your young mistress's ears," he explained.

"Even so, I am not sure how my young mistress will react upon receiving an intimate letter," Rose said. "Maybe she will pull a long face and say, 'Rose, from whom is this message you dare to bring to me? You little minx! How dare you be so impudent?' Then she will tear the letter to pieces without even reading it. What could I do then?"

"I'm sure you will think of a way to get your young mistress to read the letter."

"You're good at manipulating others."

"I will give you a handsome reward for your trouble," Zhang offered.

But this had the opposite effect to what he had intended. "What a disgraceful thing to say!" snapped the girl, flaring up. "Don't think that just because I'm a maid I can be bought to further your sordid little affairs!" And she turned to leave.

"Don't be angry, Miss Rose," the young man pleaded. "It was silly of me to say such a thing. Please forgive me."

"If you say, 'Have pity on poor, lonely me, I pray,' I may try to find a way for you. But if you presume on your wealth, I'll be treacherous and ruthless," Rose said.

"As you say, Miss Rose, have pity on poor, lonely me, I pray. Will that do?" Zhang said.

"Yes, that's better. Now write your letter, and I will deliver it for you," Rose said, smiling.

On hearing this, Zhang felt an enormous sense of relief. He lost no time preparing paper, a brush and ink. Even though she could not read, Rose was impressed by Zhang's penmanship. She could not help saying, "How nice your handwriting looks! Read it to me, please."

Zhang was most reluctant to read out his love letter to Rose, but as he was eager to stay in her favor he had little choice. So, after a great deal of throat clearing, he began:

"With a hundred salutes, Zhang Gong humbly presents this letter to Miss Oriole. The other day your mother rewarded my service, slight as it was, with undeserved unkindness. When the feast was over, I could not fall asleep. So I played my lute to express my helpless feelings and so that you might know that both the lute and its player would soon be gone forever. I am taking advantage of Rose's visit to send you a few lines in the faint hope that you, who are so near and yet so far away, may have pity on me and come to my rescue. While awaiting your decision, I add a poem that I hope you will condescend to read:

> Gnawed by lovesickness,
> I play my lute.
> Spring is happiness.
> Can your heart be mute?
> Love can't be disobeyed.
> Of vain fame make light.
> Pity the flower's shade;
> Don't miss the moon bright.

Though Rose could not understand the elegant language this missive was couched in, she thought that its contents were charming.

"Miss Rose," Zhang enjoined her, "You must be very careful not to let this letter fall into the wrong hands," he said as he handed it to her.

"I will take this letter for you, sir," Rose said. "But you must not forget your ambition to become a top scholar and a high official. You should concentrate now on your studies, and be prepared to postpone your happiness until you have succeeded in passing the civil service examination."

These words made Zhang think, "Though Miss Rose is young, she has lofty thoughts. She is really a girl of exceptional ability. But what is the use of an official career if I cannot have Oriole as my wife?" As he dared not offend Rose, he simply nodded his head.

"You must take good care of yourself, sir. Don't let worries take a toll on your health," said Rose.

"I will bear in mind your kind words. But as to the letter, dear Miss Rose, you must be careful."

"You can rest assured, sir," said Rose. "I will be very careful to convey it straight to my young mistress. I'll also use my own eloquence to convey your true feelings and get my young mistress to pay a visit to you."

Rose thereupon tucked the letter in her sleeve and left.

All this time, Oriole was waiting impatiently for Rose to return with news of Zhang. Night fell, and there was still no sign of the girl. Oriole went to bed, but tossed and turned all night long, and only fell asleep at daybreak.

It was not until after Madam Cui had finished her breakfast that Rose found time to go to see Oriole. She opened her young mistress' bedroom door, and saw that the room was lit by a single candle that had burned low. She gently drew aside the bed curtain, and gazed on Oriole's tousled hair, with its hairpin askew.

Rose took out Zhang's letter. Her first impulse was to wake Oriole up to give it to her. But then she thought, "What can I do if she refuses to accept it. It would be better to put it in her make-up case, and let her find it herself." So she put the letter in the case, leaving a corner of it sticking out, so that it would be quickly noticed. She went to stand behind the screen, and coughed.

Oriole woke up. She rose, stretched and sighed deeply. "Who's there?" she called out. But there was no answer. She got out of bed and sat at her dressing table. The first thing that caught her eyes was the corner of the letter sticking out of her make-up case. She took it out, opened it and read it. As she did so, her heart beat faster and her cheeks turned red. She read it over and over again. Then it suddenly occurred to her that Rose must have put it where she had found it. "I'll bet she is peeping me and giggling inwardly right now," she thought. "Rose!" she cried. "Come out from wherever it is you are hiding!"

"What can I do for you, Miss Oriole?" Rose said, emerging from behind the screen.

"You little minx!" barked Oriole. "Why were you skulking behind that screen? Where has this come from, Rose? I am the daughter of the late prime minister; how dare you make fun of me with such a letter? I've a good mind to report this misbehavior to my mother, and get her to give you a good thrashing."

"You were the one who sent me to the young gentleman," she retorted tartly. "And he gave me the letter. You know quite well that I cannot read. So how could I know what he has written? Anyway, it's nothing to do with me. In fact it would probably be better for me than for you to take this letter to your mother and tell her all about it." So saying she snatched the letter from Oriole's hand, turned and walked towards the door.

Mortified, Oriole chased after her, and grabbed hold of her gown. "Rose, Rose, Rose, Rose, Rose! I was only joking. Don't take it seriously. Now give me back that letter, there's a good girl."

"Let go of me Miss, if you please," said Rose coldly.

Oriole dared not let her go. "Dear Rose, could you please tell me how Zhang's health is?"

Rose cast a glance at Oriole, and then tossed her head, saying, "I don't know. His health has nothing to do with me."

"Oh, Rose, do tell me! You don't know how I feel..."

"I don't care how you feel. You're much better off than that foolish young scholar anyway. He has no desire to drink or eat. Facing the eastern wall, he sheds tears day and night. He has become so pale and wan that I fear he is in a state of terminal decline."

Rose's words made Oriole's heart ache. "We should call a doctor!" she burst out.

"No medicine can cure him; only his lover," said Rose.

Oriole, whose face had turned bright red, pretended not to hear. She took the letter from Rose and said, "Although my family is under an obligation to him, the relations between us are merely those of brother and sister, and nothing more. You are always discreet, Rose. If others get to know of this letter, what will become of the honor of our family?"

"Miss, you are the person who has made Zhang suffer so much.

What do you really want? You encouraged him to climb up the tree, and then you removed the ladder and gazed upon him with indifference. How can you and your mother be so heartless?"

Oriole's face turned now red, and now white. She lowered her head and picked up a writing brush. "Dear Rose, stop talking. Let me write a letter to him to tell him not to be so foolish."

After having written and sealed the letter, Oriole said to Rose: "Give him this letter and say, 'When my young mistress sent me to see you, sir, it was simply a matter of courtesy between sister and brother; it meant nothing else. If you persist in your nonsense, my young mistress will be obliged to tell her mother.' And Rose, you will have to answer for this!" So saying, Oriole threw the letter on the ground, and went to lie down on her bed, ignoring Rose.

Rose thought to herself: "You don't know how to restrain your tongue, you vixen, abusing others and making them feel sad by giving vent to your own bad temper. When you heard the lute beneath the bright moon, you didn't fear the cold on a dewy spring night. Was it because you were devoured by your flame for the scholar so that you felt no shame? You weren't afraid of freezing into stone for that crazy, gallant man. You are a flower thirsting for rain."

Rose picked up the letter from the floor, but hesitated. She was afraid of what her young mistress would say and do if she disobeyed her and refused to deliver the letter. But she was afraid that the letter would hurt Zhang. She thought about it over and over again. Finally she tucked the letter into her sleeve, and left for the library.

Zhang was waiting impatiently for Rose to bring him an answer to his own letter.

Accompanied by a clatter of jade pendants, Rose entered the library. Zhang was glad to see her: "So you have come, Miss Rose. What about the letter?"

Extremely worried, Rose heaved a deep sigh: "It failed to touch my young mistress' heart, I'm afraid, sir. I must advise you to put an end to your foolishness."

"My letter was a talisman to make lovers meet. How can it have failed? It must have been your fault, Miss Rose; you were not zealous enough," Zhang said.

Rose was stung by this remark. "To tell you the truth, sir, your letter was impertinent. It could have got me into trouble, too. From now on, meetings will be rare, and there will be no more moon viewing in the Western Bower."

As she turned to go, Zhang fell on his knees before her. "Miss Rose," he cried, "If you abandon me, who will there be to plead my cause? You must help me to win back my lover, and save my life."

"You are a learned scholar, sir. Can you not perceive how the matter stands? My young mistress is fickle. I can hardly understand her moods. I could easily be beaten for my involvement in your love affair."

Zhang wept. "If you won't help me, Miss Rose," he cried, "there can be no hope for my life."

Rose was in a quandary, hearing this. So she took her young mistress's letter from her sleeve, and handed it to him. "I can say no more," she said, with a sigh of resignation. "Here is her answer to your letter. You can read it for yourself."

Zhang took the letter, wiped away his tears, and began to read it. Suddenly he leapt up from the ground, exclaiming, "Today is indeed a happy day!"

Then he placed the letter on the table, and bowed to it time and again: "I should burn incense and make three bows to this letter. If I had known your young mistress's letter was to arrive, I should have prepared an honored reception. Now it is too late, so I hope I may be excused."

Rose thought the young man must have taken leave of his senses. "Perhaps the strain of disappointed love has been too much for him," she thought. "Sir, please pull yourself together," she urged him.

Zhang emitted a cackle of laughter. "Miss Rose, you will rejoice too before long," he assured her.

"I am afraid you must have lost your mind, sir, as a result of your lovesick grief. What does she say in the letter?"

"The meaning of her letter is the very opposite of what it says, you see," answered Zhang, with a crafty smile. "What she really means is that we should meet in the garden again tonight."

"I don't believe it," snorted Rose. "Be so kind as to read me the letter."

Zhang cleared his throat, and began to read:

Wait for moonrise in the Western Bower,
Where the breeze blows ajar the door.
The wall is shaded by dancing flowers;
Then comes the one whom you adore.

"What does it mean? Please explain it to me," Rose said.

Zhang explained, "'Wait for moonrise in the Western Bower' tells me what time to go to the garden. 'Where the breeze blows ajar the door' means she will open the door and wait for me. 'The wall is shaded by dancing flowers' tells me to climb over the wall screened by the shadows of the flowers lest I should be seen. And 'Then comes the one whom you adore' of course needs no explanation."

Rose began to laugh: "Are you sure she wants you to climb over the wall?"

"What else can she mean if not that, Miss Rose? I am a master at solving romantic riddles. I have made no mistake," Zhang said with great confidence.

"Then my young mistress has made a fool of me," said Rose angrily. "Who has ever seen a messenger fooled by the sender? Five words hint at the time; and four lines appeal to the lover missed. Oh, Young Mistress, you have treated me like a puppet on a string, playing your crafty games!"

"I'm sorry to have made you go through all this. I offer my deepest apologies to you on behalf of your young mistress," Zhang said, bowing to Rose.

Rose said: "My young mistress has shown affection to you, but she makes light of me. Her honeyed words will warm you in the depth of winter; but her frown makes me shiver even in midsummer."

"Don't be angry, Miss Rose. I still need your help. I have visited the garden twice, without any result. I am not sure how she will treat me," said Zhang, with a worried frown.

Rose offered words of encouragement: "This letter is proof of her sincerity, I'm sure."

Zhang was overjoyed to hear this. As he watched Rose depart, he thought, "All things are fated. Who could have anticipated the happiness Miss Oriole would send me in her letter? I'll hold my young lady in my arms soon." He read the poem time and again, regarding it as a treasure. Looking forward to their happy meeting, he resented the lingering daylight; the sun seemed motionless in the sky. He pointed at it, and complained:

> *When I talk with a happy friend,*
> *The sun will soon westward descend.*
> *But today, when I am to meet my love;*
> *The sun seems glued to the sky above.*

He was chagrined to note that it was still only noontime. After another hour, he berated the Heavens again:

> *No cloud in the azure sky*
> *No fragrance drifting by.*
> *Who can shorten the day,*
> *Driving the sun away?*

Then he struck him that perhaps Heaven was offended with him, and had stopped the sun in its tracks deliberately. So he changed his tactics. Bowing skyward, he prayed, "Oh Heaven! You give everything to everyone. Why won't you give me a single day? Oh Sun! Please go down quickly!" He went back to the library, sat at a desk, and tried to read. The minutes dragged by one by one. Finally the sun began to sink in the west. Frowning at it for its tardiness, Zhang recited:

> *The sun's a golden crow*
> *In Heaven's palace high.*
> *I'd shoot it with a bow*
> *Down from the western sky.*

At last, the drums and bells announcing nightfall brought this welcome news to Zhang's eager ears. Gulping down his supper, the young man hurriedly changed his clothes, closed the door of the library and ventured forth to meet his lover.

CHAPTER SEVEN

Repudiation

ON HER WAY back to her young mistress's room, Rose was wondering how she should report what had happened with Zhang. "If I tell her the truth, " she reasoned, "she will be too shy to keep the appointment, and Zhang will be very disappointed. But since she did not tell me the truth, I will simply suggest that she burn incense in the garden, and watch her reaction when the young man appears."

Oriole, meanwhile, was on tenterhooks, wondering what Zhang's reaction to her letter had been. She was hoping that he had not revealed their illicit love to Rose. Just then, Rose entered the room. Oriole looked carefully at the girl, trying to guess if she knew how matters stood between her and Zhang. But Rose showed no sign of having become privy to any secrets.

"Oh, you're back, Rose," said Oriole, feigning nonchalance.

"Yes, I am."

"Have you been to the library?"

"Yes."

"Did you give my letter to Master Zhang in person?"

"Yes."

"Did he read the letter?"

"Yes."

"Did he say anything?"

"Nothing much. And he didn't shed any tears either. I told him that you wanted him to regard you as a sister, as you told me. He seemed quite content with that idea."

At this, Oriole felt relieved. She let Rose go to attend her mother, while she prepared her make-up.

After Rose returned, she started to prepare the supper, knowing quite well what was in her young mistress's mind on noticing her dressed and made up for a lovers' tryst.

Overwhelmed with anxiety, Oriole pushed open the window, to find the sunset clouds gone and the land covered in darkness. Already the moon was high above the eastern wall.

"What a beautiful evening for burning incense in the garden!" exclaimed Rose.

Oriole had been thinking long and hard of an excuse to go to the garden to meet Zhang, but didn't want Rose accompanying her. Nevertheless, she couldn't very well order the girl to stay behind without arousing her suspicions. So she pretended not to want to go to the garden, protesting that the night dew was bad for her health.

At this, Rose played her part excellently. "Miss, you have prayed to the full moon for many years without fail," she reminded Oriole. "You should not break your rule today. Besides, the incense table and burner, along with the incense sticks, are already prepared."

Oriole had no choice but to comply.

As she proceeded to the garden of the Western Bower, she found the zigzag path hard to negotiate. The dewy moss was slippery under her feet. She gave a start as her jade hairpin caught in the grape trellis, and her heart leapt into her mouth when the ducks in the pond woke with an ear-splitting cackle at her approach. Rose set the incense table under the poolside rockery in a grove of poplar and willow trees. With the excuse of catching glowworms, she walked to the other side of the rockery to open the side door linking the monastery with the garden. She stepped through the door, and looked around. There was no sign of Zhang. She gave a low whistle, which was answered from nearby. Instantly, a man in a black silk headdress appeared from behind a tree and swept Rose up into his arms in a tight embrace. "My darling, how I have longed for this moment!" he panted.

Rose squealed, "Let me go, you idiot, I'm Rose!"

Stunned and mortified, Zhang dropped Rose as if she had been a hot brick. He jabbered a thousand apologies.

"Get a grip on yourself, sir," Rose urged. "My young mistress is over there in the garden burning incense and praying to the moon. But are you sure that she asked you to come here tonight? If not, I fear that I will be punished for letting you in."

"Didn't I tell you that I am a master at solving romantic riddles? So I am sure to captivate her. Now, don't delay me any longer, Miss Rose."

Rose felt relieved upon hearing this. She then said, "Don't go through the door, or my young mistress will say that I have let you in. You must climb over the wall, using that old apricot tree over there. Isn't it a beautiful night for a lovers' meeting?"

Zhang bowed to the girl. "Thank you very much for your help, Miss Rose," he said.

"But I have something else to tell you," Rose said.

"I am listening with respectful attention."

"My young mistress is a pure maiden. You must be gentle and use sweet words. You must not take her for a flaunting flower!"

"Don't worry about that, Miss Rose," the young man assured her. "How could I treat the most beautiful creature in the world with anything but the gentlest consideration?"

Then Rose closed the side door and went back to the poolside rockery.

At midnight, all was quiet. A light cloud veiled the bright moon, causing everything to be bathed in silvery candlelight. With Heaven as a quilt and the earth as a bed, the world seemed to be changed into a huge bridal chamber.

After she finished praying to the moon, Oriole paced back and forth, restless and whimsical. Her heart was beating fast. Suddenly she heard the shaking of tree branches, and the thud of feet on the grass. Before she had time to think, the ardent Zhang was standing before her. He took Oriole in his arms. But to his consternation,

Oriole struggled free in an instant.

"Have you no shame, sir?" she cried. "If my mother finds out that you have trespassed in the Western Bower like this, and thrust your attentions upon me, we shall both be ruined for life!"

This took Zhang completely by surprise. He was flabbergasted at this cold reception, and thought, "The young lady has changed her mind."

Rose, who was hiding behind the rockery, was outraged at Zhang's impetuous behavior. "What a bad memory you have!" she fumed inwardly. "You have forgotten everything I told you. You're too rude and too eager. Why don't you tell her that it was she who invited you here?" At this moment, Rose heard Oriole call to her: "Rose, there is an intruder in the garden."

Rose, pretending to be flustered and alarmed, hurried to her young mistress' side. "Who is it? Who has dared to sneak into the garden of the Western Bower?"

"It is I, Miss Rose," Zhang said, appealing to Rose, as if he had found a savior.

"What is your business here, Master Zhang?" Rose cast a stern glance at him.

Afraid that Zhang would tell Rose that she had invited him, Oriole cut in: "Don't bandy words with him. Have him taken before my mother!"

But Rose said, "Don't be angry, Young Mistress. Master Zhang is not a stranger; he has saved our lives. If we drag him off to my mistress, it would ruin his reputation. Let me deal with him for you." Oriole said nothing. "Master Zhang, kneel down," Rose ordered.

Like a wooden image, Zhang knelt down in front of Oriole, with tears in his eyes.

Rose interrogated him: "Since you've studied the classics, you should be aware of ethical behavior. Why have you come to the garden in the dead of night? Tell me the truth!"

Zhang could not think of how to answer this question without implicating Oriole, so he simply knelt there dumbly, his eyes pleading.

Rose thought, "So you're still trying to protect my young

mistress, are you? Well, I'm going to give you a hard time!" She questioned the young man again. "Do you know what your crime is?"

Zhang, trembling all over, said, "No."

"You're a scholar who does not know how to behave in a delicate situation. Who told you to jump into our garden at midnight? You should be a distinguished guest, but now you are a man who wants to steal sweet flowers."

Rose then proposed that he be let off, as it was certain that he would never do such a thing again.

Oriole said, with a snort of contempt, "If it was not for Rose's sake, you would be dragged to my mother's place without leniency. Then how could you face your elders in your hometown? Stand up!"

Rose gave Zhang a push, motioning him to stand up. She said to Oriole: "Thanks to you, Young Mistress, his mistake has been pardoned for my sake."

"We are bound to repay your kindness for saving our lives," said Oriole icily. "But since we have become brother and sister, how can you have any further desire? What if my mother should get to know of this? Let this be a lesson to you." So saying, she stalked away.

Rose remained behind, and as soon as her young mistress had disappeared, said to Zhang, "I thought that you were supposed to be a master at the art of solving romantic riddles!"

Zhang seized Rose by the sleeve, and begged, "Please listen to me, Miss Rose. I want to write another letter to express my love for Oriole. I need your help just one more time."

But the girl shook him off. "Your amorous scheme has come to naught; my young mistress has no tender feelings for you. The road ahead for you is clear. You should concentrate on your studies from now on."

"But your young mistress will be the death of me," he wailed. "When I was sick yesterday, it was her letter which revived me. But I suffered such a rebuff today that I'm afraid that I will never recover."

There was nothing to do but to return to the library. Zhang slept not a wink all night, thinking how Madam Cui had prevented his marriage to Miss Oriole, how the most beautiful girl in the world had denied the sentiments in the letter she had sent him, how thoroughly wretched and miserable he was. At daybreak, he felt dizzy and could not get out of bed.

His page, who did not know what had happened the night before, got up early as usual. He carried a basin of water to the library for his master to wash his face. But when he lifted the mosquito net around the bed, he was alarmed at the sight of his master's pallid complexion and the tear stains on his cheeks. He found that Zhang's forehead was blazing hot. "Sir, what's the matter with you?" he cried.

Zhang groaned. With his eyes screwed tight, he grunted, "Boy, I'm dying." Then he fainted. His terrified servant rushed to the abbot for help. The abbot sent Fa Cong to report the matter to Madam Cui, and Hui Ming to fetch a doctor. Then he followed the page to the library.

Madam Cui was chagrined at the news that Zhang was very ill. She thought to herself: "This is terrible! That young man saved my family, but, after all, I had no choice but to stop the marriage from going ahead. I had planned to give him a large sum of money so that he would be in good circumstances to marry another girl. However the young man failed to appreciate my kindness, and continued to hang around the monastery. Now he is ill. What a bother! I'd better send Rose to see him." So she said, "Rose, go to the library and find out what is wrong with that young man and what medicine the doctor has prescribed."

Rose realized that Zhang had not been exaggerating when he had said that Oriole's rebuff would be the death of him. But she pretended to make light of the situation. "Oh, he's nothing but a shameless fellow who is trying to win your sympathy, Madam. I think you should pay no attention to him."

Madam Cui was annoyed at her brazenness. "Don't talk back. How dare you refuse my order?" she barked.

"It is just that I don't understand why he should be allowed to ensnare you with his nonsense, Madam, just because he saved our lives," Rose said, cunningly.

This was a sore spot with Madam Cui. Even more ruffled than

before, she ordered Rose to go to see Master Zhang right away. Rose then went straight to the Embroidery Pavilion, where Oriole was waiting.

"Rose, what did my mother want you to do?" Oriole asked.

Afraid that her young mistress would be worried, Rose said, "Nothing important. It seems that last night's intruder is dying, that's all."

This news struck Oriole like a thunderbolt. "It's all my fault," she thought to herself. "I must somehow go to comfort him. But it would never do for my mother to find out." Suddenly she hit upon an idea. She turned to Rose and said, "Rose, if Master Zhang is very ill I have an excellent prescription for you to take to him."

"No, no!" Rose shook her head. "You are at it again. My dear young mistress, you will be the death of him!"

"Rose, I do believe that I am the only person who can save his life."

Rose sighed, and said, "Well, as your mother has just ordered me to go there, I will take your prescription to him."

Oriole was delighted to hear this. She went straight to her desk, picked up a brush and began to write. When she finished, she handed the piece of paper to Rose. Now, the girl may have been illiterate, but she had seen medical prescriptions before, and this did not look like one. "I hope you haven't forgotten to include the medicine," she said archly.

Oriole's face turned red. "This prescription is just what he needs," she said.

"I'm sure it is," retorted Rose, looking not at all convinced. Tucking the prescription or whatever it was in her sleeve, she skipped off to the library. Just outside, she bumped into the abbot and a doctor coming out. Rose greeted them, and the abbot informed her that the doctor had diagnosed nothing more important than a severe chill, which would be easy to cure once Zhang's young servant returned with the medicine the learned physician had prescribed.

As they departed, Rose thought to herself: "What a charlatan that old quack is! Master Zhang is suffering from a malady that no doctor can cure." She pushed open the door, and saw Zhang lying in bed with his eyes closed and his face ashen. Rose coughed lightly.

Zhang opened his eyes. Seeing Rose, he said, "Oh, it's you, Miss Rose. Thank Heavens you've come!" And tears coursed down his hollow cheeks.

Rose bent over him and asked, "How are you feeling?"

Zhang tried to sit up, gave a groan, and fell back in a faint. Rose pounded him on the back, and he eventually recovered consciousness. He grasped the girl by the sleeve: "Should I die, Miss Rose?" he croaked. "You must be my witness at the tribunal of the King of the Underworld."

Rose too began to weep. "I have never seen such a tragic case of lovesickness," she sighed.

Zhang moaned, "It is all because of your young mistress. Both the mother and daughter are good at telling lies. Last night, when I returned crestfallen to the library, I burned with anger. How could a savior be wronged by the people he saved? An old saying goes that the maiden dotes, while the swain is unfaithful. But in my case the reverse is true."

"You should blame yourself," Rose retorted. "If you had concentrated on your studies and become the No.1 Scholar, you would certainly have a beautiful wife, and not found yourself in this grief-stricken state."

"There is only one Oriole on earth; I will never marry anyone else," declared Zhang.

Rose was glad for Miss Oriole. After so many troubles, the pathetic young scholar was still firm in his devotion to her. "Anyway," she said, "My mistress has sent me to see you and ask which medicine you, elder brother, are taking."

Upon hearing the words "elder brother", Zhang trembled with rage. "No doctor on earth can cure me, but Miss Oriole..."

Before he finished, Rose cut in sternly: "Don't talk nonsense! You should conduct yourself with dignity."

Discouraged, Zhang sank back, exhausted, against the pillows, weeping copious tears. Overcome with pity, Rose hastened to comfort him. "Master Zhang, my young mistress has written a prescription for you. She asked me to bring it to you."

Zhang sat up at once. "Where is it? Let me have a look."

repudiation

"Don't be impatient. Now listen to me." And she began to recite, "The laurel flowers cast their shadows when night is deep. The flowers should be soaked in Chinese angelica."

"But laurel flowers are warm by nature, and Chinese angelica is used to invigorate the circulation of the blood. How can the flowers be soaked in Chinese angelica?" asked Zhang.

"Hidden in the shade of the rocks by the poolside. It is very hard for you to find. If you can find it, you will recover after one or two doses," Rose continued.

This was all a mystery to Zhang.

Seeing his puzzlement, Rose chided him: "You say you are a master at solving romantic riddles. How is it that you can't understand my riddle? What 'The laurel flowers cast their shadows when night is deep' means that you may go to the garden to have a secret meeting with my young mistress. Hide yourself in the shade of the rocks by the poolside, and you may find your bride. I myself will be attending Madam Cui. Soon after you take my young mistress in your arms, you will recover." So saying, Rose took the prescription from her sleeve and handed it to Zhang. "Here is the prescription written by my young mistress for you," said Rose.

Zhang opened the letter, and read it. The letter's contents seemed to infuse new life into him, so that he was able to rise from his bed. Beaming with joy, he said in a rapturous voice: "Had I known that this was a poem from your young mistress, I should have received it on my knees. How happy I am!"

Rose was amazed at the sudden transformation in the young man's health, and even more amazed when she saw Zhang put on his shoes and start to dance.

"Miss Rose," he cried, "your young mistress has written a poem declaring her love for me!"

"It is a medical prescription, not a silly love poem," snorted Rose. "Don't get carried away again, I warn you!"

"You're wrong, Rose. It is a beautiful love poem. Listen."

And he read out the poem — for it was indeed a poem — that Oriole had written to him:

Trouble not your heart with trifles mere,

> *Nor extinguish your talent aglow!*
> *To keep my modesty without a smear,*
> *I knew not that it would bring you woe.*
> *To pay my debt, convention I slight*
> *But send a new verse to the Western Bower.*
> *I'm sure to bring fresh showers tonight*
> *For the long, long thirsting flower.*

Though Rose did not completely understand the nuances in most of the poem, there was no mistaking the purport of the last sentence.

"Well, I'll tell you one thing," said Rose. "Your miserable chamber is like a monk's cell. I just can't imagine my young mistress being willing to catch her death of cold by spending a night here!"

Zhang was impressed by Rose's honest and forthright manner. Though she had a sharp tongue, she was always considerate about other people. He bowed to the girl, and said, "Here are 10 taels of silver. Could you please procure some suitable bedding for me?"

"I have pillows embroidered with pairs of lovebirds, and a coverlet of turquoise blue. But why should I lend them to you?" Rose said.

Zhang said, "If you can help me fulfill my love tonight, I will never forget your kindness."

"I don't want anything from you. Let bygones be bygones. I don't want white jade or yellow gold from you. If you have a suitable store of ambition, you should succeed in the imperial civil service examinations, and make my young mistress an honored official's wife."

Zhang was overcome with gratitude. But then it occurred to him that perhaps Madam Cui would not allow Oriole to come out into the garden that night.

When he mentioned this to Rose, she dismissed the idea. "It all depends on my young mistress," she said. "If she is willing to come out to meet you, Madam will not be able stop her even if she guards the door day and night. She will find a way to meet you."

As an old saying goes: "Once bitten by a snake, one shies at a coiled rope for the next 10 years." Likewise, Zhang was still worried. "But what if what happened last night happens again..."

"You have only yourself to blame for what happened last night," Rose said. "If my young mistress comes tonight, it will be up to you to consummate your love. You don't need anyone to teach you, do you?" Then Rose took her leave.

Rose went to the Rear Hall to report on Zhang's state of health to Madam Cui before returning to the Embroidery Pavilion, where Oriole was pretending to be busy with her embroidery work.

"Get my bed ready, Rose," she told the girl. "I will retire early tonight."

"Oh, really?" exclaimed Rose. "He will be disappointed!"

"Who will?" asked Oriole, guilelessly.

"You know perfectly well who," said Rose. "If you keep secrets from me I will go and inform my mistress that you told me to arrange a rendezvous for you with Master Zhang."

"You little cat!" cried Oriole indignantly. "I simply asked you to take a prescription to him. What's all this nonsense about a rendezvous?"

"You wrote, 'I'm sure to bring fresh showers tonight.' What are 'showers'? I have never heard of a herbal medicine called 'showers'."

Oriole blushed to the roots of her hair.

Without more ado, Rose helped Oriole to dress herself like a bride, and the two of them set off for the garden. Rose carried with her a brocade coverlet and a pair of pillows embroidered with love-birds. As they entered the gate, Oriole quickened her pace. Following behind, Rose thought, "You were shy a moment ago, and were hesitating whether to go or not. Now, the Fairy Queen is hastening to meet the Fairy King, who is waiting for her with dreams of spring."

CHAPTER EIGHT

The Tryst

AFTER TIDYING UP the library, Zhang waited for Oriole. The first watch of the night was already over, but there was still no sign of her. He was worried that she would play false with him again. In the bright moonlight, the wind stirred the bamboo groves, and the flowers danced. Zhang walked out of the library and, standing in front of the door, recited a verse: "The beautiful night on earth is silent far and nigh. When will the beautiful lady come from on high?" He thought to himself: "Since I first caught sight of Miss Oriole, I have been lovesick for her. But Oriole does not know how much I long for her. Had I foreseen that I would be obsessed day and night, I would have been afraid of meeting such a beauty. Perhaps she cannot escape the eagle eyes of her mother? There again, she may be sick."

Zhang was as restless as an ant on a hot pan. It was already the second watch, and Miss Oriole still had not shown up. He went back to his room and lay down on the bed, thinking: "If she is willing to come, it is only a short distance between her chamber and the library. Why is it so hard for her to come?" Just as he was thinking of how much he had suffered over the previous six months, there came a knock at the door.

Zhang jumped up from the bed as if at the sound of a fire alarm. He scurried to the door, opened it, and found himself face to face with Rose. "Has Miss Oriole come?" he gasped eagerly.

"Take her coverlet and pillows please. My young mistress is right behind me. How will you thank me, Master Zhang?"

The young man took the coverlet and pillows, and put them on the bed. Then he turned round and made a deep bow to Rose. "Miss Rose," he said, "words fail to express my feelings at this moment, but Heaven knows that I will be forever in your debt."

"Go to meet my young mistress. And remember to mind your manners, or you will frighten her," said Rose.

"But where is she?"

"Open your eyes wider. Who is the lady standing by the rockery?"

Zhang was about to set off at a run, but Rose stopped him.

"What a bad memory you have! The last time you acted rashly too, and my young mistress was angry. Don't be so impetuous!"

"You're right, of course. But what shall I do then?" asked Zhang.

"You stay here; I will bring her in."

"Whatever you say."

Rose returned to the rockery and whispered to Oriole: "Master Zhang has been waiting for you for quite a long time."

Upon hearing this, Oriole covered her face with her sleeve, and was too shy to say anything. They walked towards the library slowly. Rose opened the door for Oriole, closed it after her, and remained outside.

Seeing Oriole standing in front of him, Zhang knelt down and said: "How fortunate I am to be favored with your visit. Am I in a dream?"

Oriole lowered her head and asked shyly: "Please get up. Are you feeling better now?"

"The very sight of your Heavenly countenance would banish every ailment," Zhang replied gallantly.

Oriole stretched out her hand to help him get up. Zhang took this opportunity to embrace her willow-slender waist. Her fragrant body was as light as that of a swallow. He carried her gently to the bed and examined her exquisite form closely under the light of the lamp. Zhang untied the silken belt that held her robe. Oriole felt soft all over, allowing Zhang to do whatever he wished. They made love to each other. Overwhelmed with ecstasy, they felt as happy and free as a pair of fish swimming in the sea.

Soon the moon sank in the west. In the lamplight, Zhang took a look at red blood on the white silk under their bodies.

Zhang said while gazing at Oriole: "I have won your virgin purity. I have completed my happiness tonight."

Oriole got up to put on her clothes. "I must leave now," she said, "lest my mother discover my absence."

Zhang had no choice but to get up and put his own clothes on. "I'll see you off, my dear. Tonight, we have met behind the gauze bed-screen, but when shall I again untie your green belt?"

Oriole was too shy to say anything. They held each other tight. When they opened the door, they found Rose waiting outside. "Congratulations, Master Zhang," she said. "Now, how do you intend to thank me?"

"Miss Rose, I'm very grateful to you. I'll never forget your kindness."

"I should hope not," Rose said with a smile. Then she turned to Oriole: "Young Mistress, let's go back right away," she urged.

Zhang, who was reluctant to part from Oriole, said, "Please come earlier another night."

Oriole nodded slightly. Rose then led her away in the moonlight.

At this moment, there was a fragrant dew on the earth, the wind soughed over the lonely steps, and the moon shone its rays into the library.

CHAPTER NINE

A Handmaid in the Dock

SOON THE MID-AUTUMN Festival came. Madam Cui noticed that her daughter seemed absent-minded and preoccupied these days. Moreover, her figure appeared different, with protruding breasts and a bulging waist. "What is the matter with her?" she wondered. The Mid-Autumn Festival, which falls on the 15th day of the eighth lunar month, is a day for family reunions. Madam Cui expected Oriole and Rose to arrive early in the evening to eat moon cakes and enjoy the full moon together with her. However, when there was no sign of Oriole and Rose after dusk had fallen, Madam Cui thought that something very odd indeed must have happened.

"Mother, I have something to tell you," piped up Merry Boy, who was standing near.

"What is it?"

"That night before last, after you had gone to bed, I went outside and saw my sister and Rose burning incense in the garden. Later, I heard that they did not come back until daybreak."

Madam Cui was astonished to hear this, and immediately her suspicions were aroused.

"Call Rose here right now!" she ordered the boy through clenched teeth.

Off the boy went on his fateful errand.

"What does she want?" asked Rose, when she heard the summons.

"Oh, she wants to know what you and Oriole were up to in the garden of the Western Bower the other night, that's all," answered the boy.

These words pounded Rose like hammer blows, but she managed to retain her composure, and said to Merry Boy: "Well, you run along now, and tell my mistress that I will be with her soon."

"You'd better hurry up; she's in a bad mood." So saying, he skipped back the way he had come.

Rose ran into Oriole's bedroom and blurted out, "Young Mistress, I think your mother has found out about your affair with Master Zhang! She's sent for me, and I'm sure she's going to interrogate me about it."

Oriole was devastated. With tears in her eyes, she begged, "Dear Rose, you must not breath a word about it!"

"I kept telling you to be more discreet," said Rose. "I knew that the way you and Master Zhang were carrying on sooner or later someone would find out about your affair."

Oriole burst into a flood of tears. "What can we do? What can we do?" she cried. "Rose, you must be very careful when answering my mother's questions."

"You are the one who should be punished, Young Mistress, but instead I know that the blame will fall on me. While you two were snug and warm in your love nest, I was shivering outside all night. But anyway, I suppose that is the lot of a handmaiden. I will try to explain away your behavior, and if I cannot I am prepared to take the blows that should be directed at you." So saying, Rose left the Embroidery Pavilion, holding her head high. Her reception by Madam Cui was just as she had expected.

"Get down on your knees, you little wretch!" were her mistress' first words.

Obediently, Rose knelt down and lowered her head.

"Now confess your guilt!"

Rose raised her head and opened her eyes wide, "Your humble maid knows of no guilt to confess," she protested.

Madam Cui said, gnashing her teeth: "How dare you deny it! If you tell the truth, I will pardon you; if not, I will beat you to death, you little minx! Who told you to take your young mistress into the garden at midnight?"

Rose said: "Since her childhood, my young mistress has had the habit of praying to the moon. You always let me go with her on those occasions."

Madam Cui flew into a rage. "There was no moon the night before last, you impertinent slut!" she yelled. "Now, tell me: What were you doing in the garden?"

Rose realized that she was trapped, and if she had any more inclination to prevaricate, it vanished as soon as she felt the sting of a bamboo cane across her thin shoulders.

Rose explained: "One evening, when we had finished our sewing, we started to talk about her elder brother's plight. His health was becoming worse and worse. Alone there in the library, there was no one to take care of him. We felt sorry for him, and decided to inquire after his health without telling you."

"Bah! You're shameless! Then you went to the library?"

"Yes."

"What did the young man say?"

"He said that you had gone back on your word, returned evil for good and turned his joy into grief. He hates you because you stood in the way of his marrying Oriole."

"Oh, what an exaggeration!" cried Madam Cui. "What else did he say?"

"He told me to leave, but said my young mistress should remain."

Madam Cui's eyebrows shot up. "How could an unmarried maiden remain there unchaperoned?" she exclaimed. "I never heard of such a thing!"

"Well, I thought she was simply going to administer some healing medicine," explained Rose. "And then, before I knew it, they were spending every night together. There was nothing I could do about it, really Madam!"

Madam Cui trembled all over with anger. Pointing an accusing finger at Rose, she thundered, "This is all your fault. If you hadn't acted as the go-between this would never have happened."

"It is neither I nor Master Zhang nor Miss Oriole who is to blame, Madam. The fault lies with you yourself."

"What? Such impertinence! How can it be my fault?" Madam Cui yelled indignantly.

"It is fundamental for a man to keep faith. One who does not has no worth," said Rose, quoting *The Analects of Confucius*.

"Well, I never!" thought Madam Cui to herself. "I always thought that this girl was stupid, but although she is illiterate she knows how to pick up bits and pieces of wisdom from her young mistress's lessons and throw them in my face!"

"Why did you say I have not kept faith?" she asked aloud.

Rose said, "When the monastery was surrounded by the bandits, you promised to give your daughter as wife to anyone who could make them withdraw. If Master Zhang had not been an admirer of the beauty of my young mistress, would he, an outsider, have proposed a plan to rid us of the bandit plague? But when the bandits were routed and you were left in peace, you went back on your word. Was this not a breach of faith? If you found it impossible to consent to the match, you should have rewarded him with money and let him go far, far away. It was playing with fire to allow him to stay in the library near the young mistress's quarters in the Western Bower. Now what is done can't be undone. What is the use of blaming me? If you do not cover up this scandal, in the first place, the family honor of the late prime minister will be compromised, and in the second place, you will wrong Master Zhang, our benefactor. The best course for you to take is to keep the promise you made to unite them as man and wife. The young man has a bright future ahead of him, and your daughter is a radiant beauty. Besides, why make an enemy of a good friend who sent for the White Horse General to rescue you and your family when they were in distress? Why turn a benefactor into an enemy and bring disgrace to your own family?"

While listening to Rose, Madam Cui wrestled with mixed feelings of sadness, anxiety and anger. She thought: "Against innumerable hardships I struggled to bring up my daughter. I wanted her to marry my nephew, Zheng Heng, so that I could rely on them in my remaining years. To my surprise, my daughter has done such a disgraceful thing! But what this little chit of a handmaiden said makes sense after all. If the case were brought to the court, it would bring disgrace on our family." After pondering deeply for a while, she said, "There's no help for it but to sacrifice my beloved daughter to this unscrupulous schemer! Rose, go and tell Oriole to come here!"

"Yes, Madam," said Rose. She stood up, rubbed her knees and ran out of the Middle Hall. When she reached the Western Bower she saw that Oriole had been waiting on tenterhooks for her return.

Oriole was surprised and relieved to see that Rose was smiling after her ordeal of being interrogated by Madam Cui. She rushed to seize the girl by the hand. "Was it very terrible, Rose?" she asked solicitously.

"At first, yes. But after I gave her some straightforward advice, she came round to my way of thinking. She has agreed to let you and Master Zhang become man and wife. My mistress wants you to go to her straight away, together with Master Zhang, so that you can be married this very day. Congratulations, my dear young mistress!"

Oriole could not believe her ears. "Is it true?" she asked, grabbing Rose by both hands tightly.

"Absolutely true! Let's go to your mother now," replied Rose.

But suddenly the thought of facing her mother filled Oriole with dread. Flushed with shame, she lowered her head and twisted a handkerchief in her hands, in an agony of indecision. "Oh, Rose, how dare I stand in front of my mother face to face?"

"Young Mistress, what you did was for the sake of true love. You can hold your head high in front of the whole world, and not just in front of your mother," said Rose. With this, she half coaxed, half dragged Oriole towards the Middle Hall.

As soon as Oriole appeared in the doorway, Madam Cui started to berate her: "You wicked and unnatural daughter!" she cried. "How could you have been so deceitful?" She then dissolved into a flood of tears. Finally, she recovered sufficiently to gasp, "But there is nothing else for it; a scandal would bring intolerable disgrace on our family. Rose, go and fetch that villainous young man here!"

Zhang had been used to nightly trysts with Oriole, escorted by Rose, so when he saw Rose approach in the daytime he was filled with a sense of foreboding.

"Why are you calling on me, Rose?" asked Zhang.

"Your sneaky affair has been discovered. My mistress wants to see you right away," said Rose, with a grave look on her face.

Dumbfounded, Zhang was at a loss what to do. He appealed to the resourceful Rose: "This is terrible! How can I get out of this difficulty?"

Rose burst into laughter. "You look like a frightened schoolboy," she said. "As a matter of fact, it is probably not a bad thing that this secret liaison has come to light after all. You couldn't go on forever meeting furtively, now could you? Anyway, you don't need a go-between now."

"What do you mean?" Zhang was puzzled.

"I had no choice but to tell Madam Cui the whole truth once she got wind of what was going on. But I also told her that the only way to avoid any hint of disgrace to the family was to let you and Miss Oriole get married. And so she has agreed that you two should be wed this very day."

It took Zhang a long time to realize that he was not dreaming. When he did so, he made a deep bow to Rose, and said, "Thank Heaven! And thank you, Rose. The day I have looked forward to for so long has finally come!"

"Well, don't dillydally on this of all days," Rose urged. "Let's go right now."

When Zhang still hesitated, obviously too ashamed to face Madam Cui, the girl said, "You were brave enough when you climbed the tree and jumped over the wall that night. What are you afraid of today? Let's go."

Following Rose sheepishly, Zhang presented himself before Madam Cui in the Middle Hall. Bowing deeply, he said, "I, Zhang Gong, pay my most profound respects to you, Madam."

Madam Cui shot a glance full of venom at him. "A fine, upright scholar you turned out to be! It seems that I have nursed a viper in my bosom! All the time I thought that your service for our family was pure and disinterested, you were harboring shameful thoughts, it seems."

Zhang was so overcome with remorse that he could find no words with which to excuse himself.

Madam Cui continued, "If I were to hand you over to the judicial authorities — which I have every right to do — it would be the end of your career and all your fancy hopes and dreams. However, it would also bring disgrace on the late prime minister's name and the rest of his family. So I have concluded that the only way out of the mess you have got us all into is for you to marry my daughter."

Oriole, Rose and Zhang were overjoyed to hear these words, notwithstanding the fact that the preliminary part was far from flattering. Oriole was wild with joy, because she was to become the wife of a man with a brilliant career ahead of him. Rose was glad, because her efforts over the past half year to unite the lovers had not been in vain. And Zhang of course was deliriously happy to realize that his most fervent wish had come true. He threw himself on the ground at Madam Cui's feet: "Your humble son-in-law pays his heartfelt respects to his…"

But before he had chance to finish his gush of gratitude, Madam Cui cut him short: "Wait, let me finish. You must remember that for three generations our family has never had a son-in-law without an official rank. So the first thing you must do is hasten to the capital to take the civil service examinations. I will take care of your future wife in the meantime. If you pass the examinations with honor, come back and marry my daughter. If not, never darken our doorstep again. Do you understand?"

Upon hearing this, Zhang was nonplussed. He now knew perfectly well that Madam Cui still did not approve of the marriage between him and Oriole, and was looking for another excuse to prevent it. If he passed the highest imperial examinations, he could marry his lover. If he failed, he would lose Oriole. He thought to himself: "I am determined that I will never marry anyone but Oriole. So I am determined to be the nation's No. 1 Scholar and become a top official. Then I will come back to claim my bride."

"I hear and obey your command, Madam," he said humbly. "I will leave for the capital first thing tomorrow. I hope you will take good care of my future wife."

Oriole's eyes filled with tears when she heard her mother's harsh conditions. In her mind, she said to herself: "I am already, in fact if not in name, Master Zhang's wife. Mother, if you care about my reputation, you should let us get married before Master Zhang leaves for the capital. Why are you in such a hurry to drive him away? What you really want is to separate us. You attach great importance to the family's status, but I do not care for such things. A devoted married couple deserves the highest acclaim." Seeing that Zhang was determined to obey Madam Cui and leave the next day, Oriole was so upset that tears ran down her cheeks.

Rose, who cursed Madam Cui in her heart, said to Zhang: "Sir, your decision is a wise one. We look forward to the day when you return, having won the highest honors in the examinations. Then you two lovebirds will be joined for ever."

"What Rose said is right," said Madam Cui. "You'd better pack your luggage and prepare for your journey right away." Then she turned to Rose: "Give orders for wine and fruit to be prepared," she said, "and invite the abbot. We will see Master Zhang off at the Pavilion of Parting tomorrow and give him a farewell feast."

"Yes, Madam," Rose said. Then Rose, Zhang and Oriole left.

Alone in the hall, Madam Cui was lost in thought: "My husband died, leaving me alone in the world. Then this unexpected scandal happened. How can I face my husband in the nether world? Nothing would have happened if Sun the Flying Tiger had not besieged the monastery. But Oriole does not understand my dilemma. My beloved daughter is too naive. What's done can't be undone. They are deeply in love. Well, it's no use trying to separate them by force, so I think my decision was for the best. If they had got married here in the monastery, we would have become a laughing stock."

Zhang left the Middle Hall and returned to the library. When his Page asked why Madam Cui had called him, Zhang did not know what to say, so he remained silent, and the page was too tactful to pursue the matter.

CHAPTER TEN

A Tearful Farewell Feast

WHEN MADAM CUI promised her daughter's hand to Zhang, the lovers were overjoyed. But later, when she told the young man that he must first leave for the capital to take the civil service examination right away, both Oriole and Zhang were devastated.

Returning from the Middle Hall, Oriole lay listless on her bed behind the mosquito net, sighing and moaning. She did not sleep the whole night. Though Rose did her best to comfort her, Oriole could not stop weeping. At midnight, hearing leaves rustling in the wind, Rose pushed open the window, and realized that it had started to rain. "Good!" she cried. "Since it is raining, Master Zhang will certainly not start on his journey tomorrow." Oriole thought, "Heaven has had pity on us, a couple of lovers who are about to be parted, so it sheds tears for us. I can't wait to go to the Western Bower to say good-bye to my dearest. But now that our affair has been discovered, my mother will take strict precautions. On this cool autumn night, my lover has to sleep alone. He must be sad and shedding tears all night. How foolish you are, my love! You should not agree to leave for the capital tomorrow. I am already yours, so we should get married before you leave. What can I do if you fail in the civil service examination? If you pass the examination, and become an official, I hope that you will not marry the daughter of a high-ranking official in the capital, and then abandon me like an old fan..."

Before daybreak, it stopped raining. When morning came, Oriole still lay on the bed and did not want to get up. It was only after Rose had urged her time and again that she arose and began her toilet. Sitting in front of her dressing table, she gazed at her disheveled hair and red-rimmed eyes in the mirror. Suddenly she heard Zhang's voice: "Miss Rose, I'm leaving. Please say goodbye to Miss Oriole for me, and tell her I shall come back as soon as possible. I hope she will take good care of herself." He spoke loudly, hoping Oriole would hear him.

Oriole was devastated as she listened to the sounds of the preparations for Zhang's departure.

"Why haven't you made yourself presentable yet, Miss?" asked Rose. Oriole did not answer, but she thought, "Dear Rose, how can you know the torment in my heart? How can I not feel grief and anguish? How can I rouge my cheeks and powder my face, and assume winning charms and graces? All I want to do is bury my head deep in the bedclothes and weep."

Finally Oriole dressed and made up her face. She and Rose then went outside, to find Madam Cui, Zhang, the abbot, the page and Fa Cong mounted on carriages ready to go to the Pavilion of Parting, where a farewell feast was to be held for Zhang.

It was late autumn; clouds floated high in the sky and the wild geese were flying south in the chilly wind. As the carriages rumbled along, Oriole gazed at the enchanting scenery, and recited a poem:

The cloudy sky frowns grey
Over the yellow-bloom-paved way.
The western breeze does bitterly blow,
As north to south the wild geese go.
Like a wine-flushed face are the leaves so red,
Dyed in the tears that parting lovers shed.

a tearful farewell feast

Wiping away her mistress's tears, Rose coaxed her: "Don't be too sad, Young Mistress. In half a year, he will come back with an official rank. Then you can be formally married."

Oriole did not answer; she was too wrapped up in her own distressful thoughts.

Madam Cui, Oriole and Rose arrived at the Pavilion of Parting just after Zhang and his page.

The young man noticed that Oriole had become wan and sallow overnight. She seemed to be wasting away. The sight reminded him of the story of Wu Zixu, an official in ancient times, who was so worried when crossing Zhaoguan Pass that all his hair turned white overnight. "Worry can really be the death of a person," he thought to himself. He felt as if a knife were piercing his heart, and he felt on the verge of tears.

At Madam Cui's bidding, Rose set out the wine and dishes on the stone table in the pavilion.

Madam Cui invited the abbot to be seated first. She herself sat next to him. Oriole took the seat on the left of her mother, and sat there with her head bowed in modesty and sorrow. Zhang was the last to be seated, on the other side of the abbot. He wanted to call Madam Cui "mother-in-law", but he did not have the courage to do so.

Madam Cui looked at Oriole and Zhang while saying, "Since I have promised to marry my daughter to you, you must go to the capital and prove yourself worthy of our family by winning the top place in the examination."

Zhang was not happy to hear this. He thought: There are a great number of scholars in the country, but only one can become the No.1 Scholar. She has promised me her daughter's hand in marriage, but she is really scheming to put us asunder. She is playing the same old trick again in front of the abbot. "Thanks to your encouragement, Madam Cui," he said. "I am sure that I will have no problem gaining the highest honor in the examination."

Madam Cui thought, "This young man is talking wildly. He does not know how high the sky is or how deep the earth is. How can he face me if he fails to win the position of No.1 Scholar?"

Abbot Fa Ben, who thought that Master Zhang had been

presumptuous, said, "Talented young men are often over-confident, Madam, but I am sure that Master Zhang will be a credit to you and your esteemed family." He then proposed a toast to her future son-in-law.

Oriole detected the sharp edges to the voices of her mother and lover. She was alarmed by Zhang's boastful words, and thought, "If, after all your fine talk, you do not win the top place in the examination, I fear that you will be too ashamed to return. And then you will abandon me."

At the same time, Madam Cui was thinking, "The young man is getting carried away with his reckless ambition. That fits in neatly with my plan!" Icily calm, she ordered Rose to fill the wine cups.

Rose did so for the abbot, Madam Cui, Zhang and Oriole, one by one.

Madam Cui raised her cup and toasted Zhang, fulsomely wishing him success in the examination. Zhang returned a few words of appreciation.

"My child, you should present a cup of wine to Master Zhang," said Madam Cui to Oriole.

Rose poured the wine and gave the cup to Oriole. Oriole held the wine cup with trembling hands. She stood up and presented the cup of wine to Zhang: "Please!"

Zhang glanced at Oriole and drank the wine in one gulp.

Madam Cui then told Rose to present wine to Zhang. Rose did as she was bidden, and the young man drained this cup too.

Knowing that her mother wanted to finish the farewell feast as soon as possible, Oriole felt resentful. "Oh, Mother," she said to herself, "you are so heartless. Since Master Zhang and I are soon to be separated, you should at least let us have a few minutes to ourselves. But since you continue to sit here we cannot have the chance of exchanging a few parting words of love." There was nothing she could do but sit motionless, gazing upon the face of her beloved.

Rose whispered in her young mistress' ear urging her to have a bite to eat. But it was all in vain; Oriole refused to touch either the food or the wine. Instead, she thought, "For fame as worthless as the horn of a snail, and for profit as trifling as the head of a fly, my mother has torn us two lovebirds apart!"

a tearful farewell feast

At this moment both Oriole and Zhang heaved sigh after sigh.

Madam Cui was both sympathetic and annoyed. Since her daughter was unhappy, she was too. But as the daughter of later prime minister, she had no right to throw herself away on a penniless upstart like Zhang. "Well, anyway," she thought, "out of sight, out of mind. She'll forget him after a while, and if he doesn't come top of the list in the examination — which he won't — he'll be too ashamed to show his face to her again." Comforted by this thought, she ordered the carriage to be prepared for departure, and told Oriole and Rose not to be long following her. With that, she rose and left the pavilion.

Zhang took this as his cue to continue his journey to the capital. He stood up and made a bow to Fa Ben: "Thank you very much, Abbot, for coming to see me off."

Stroking his beard, Fa Ben said: "I hope you will be successful in the civil service examination, so that I can preside at your wedding ceremony. During your long journey, you must take good care of yourself."

"Thank you very much for your invaluable advice, Abbot," said Zhang.

"I will wait for the first spring thunder and expect good news from you. I will take my leave now." So saying, Fa Ben left with Fa Cong.

After Madam Cui and the abbot had gone, Oriole went up to Zhang to hold his hand and say good-bye. The young man said with ardor: "I'm determined to win the highest literary honor, and then come straight back and make you my bride."

"Don't swear you won't come back unless you win the highest honor!" said Oriole. "I don't care if you become the No.1 Scholar or not; I only hope that we can be together day and night for the rest of our lives. Now it is late autumn, and the weather is growing chilly. Take care of your health on your long and arduous journey. Before your arrival at the capital, you must get used to the harsh climate. Make sure you eat properly and sensibly."

Zhang nodded, but said nothing.

Oriole continued, "I will wait for you forever. But I fear you may give up your old and faithful lover and find a new one who is more glamorous in the capital, once you have achieved success."

"My dear Miss Oriole! How could I bestow my love on anyone else but you? No one in the world can compare with you. Make yourself easy on that score. I must bid you farewell now."

Holding back his tears, Zhang mounted his horse and left. Surrounded by mountains east and west, he flicked his whip and proceeded along the sunlit road. Seeing his form disappear at a bend in the road, Oriole recited, tearfully: "To Heaven should I wail? Oh, to what avail? My tears would make the Yellow River overflow; and my grief would make the mountain peaks bend low."

The sun was sinking behind a green hill, and the birds were returning to their nests in the forest when Zhang came to a thatched-roofed inn by a bridge, over 20 miles east of Puzhou City. He dismounted and called for the innkeeper, who soon appeared and ushered him inside, promising him the best room.

Zhang straightaway lay down on the bed, saying, "I do not want anything to eat. I only want to sleep."

The innkeeper left, and the page, after stabling Zhang's horse, lay down on another bed and fell fast asleep. Tired as he was after his long ride, Zhang found that sleep would not come. He tossed and turned, all the time thinking of Miss Oriole. He heard the autumn insects buzzing all around. Reclining on his lonely pillow, he found his coverlet too cold and thin.

Suddenly, it seemed that in a dream he heard someone knocking at the door. Startled, he thought: "Who would come to this country inn at midnight? Maybe it's a ghost?" In a quavering voice, he called out, "Who's there?"

"It is I," replied a gentle voice. Zhang got out of bed, and peeped through a crack in the door, to find a young lady standing outside under the cool moon and stars. "If you're human, assure me of the fact. But if you're a ghost, be gone this instant!" he called out, with more courage than he felt.

"Master Zhang, my dear, don't you know me?"

Zhang was overjoyed. He flung open the door, and took Oriole in his arms. "My dear, why have you pursued me like this?" he asked.

"I realized that I could no longer live without you by my side," the girl explained. "So, as soon as my mother and Rose were fast asleep, I slipped out of the Salvation Monastery to accompany you to the capital."

Oriole's clothes were in disorder, and she looked exhausted by the journey she had made. Zhang carried her into the room. "Oh, my dearest love, you have worn yourself quite out."

"I think the saddest thing for the human heart is to be torn away from the object of its love," said Oriole. "My dear, I am not afraid of this long journey. I do not want a valiant hero, nor a man rich and proud. I am willing to share with you a bed in life and a grave in death."

Zhang held Oriole tightly, crying: "My dear wife!"

At this moment, there was a commotion outside the inn. Somebody was shouting about an intruder and calling for lights. Zhang embraced Oriole tightly. "What shall we do?" he gasped.

Oriole, looking fearless, said to him: "My dear, stand behind me. Let me open the door and speak to them." So saying, she opened the door.

Outside, there was a crowd of bandits, headed by Sun the Flying Tiger, mounted on a horse. At the sight of Oriole, Sun, guffawed evilly: "You see, you cannot escape me, my girl!" he snarled.

Oriole defied the ruffian. "You had best make yourself scarce, you loathsome bandit," she cried. "The White Horse General is coming to make mincemeat of you at this very moment."

This only made Sun roar with laughter. At a nod from him, his men seized Oriole, and carried her off.

His own anguished cry woke Zhang from this horrible nightmare. His heart was thumping, and his whole body was drenched in sweat. Afraid of falling asleep again, he took a walk in the bright moonlight. The morning star was just rising. The wall of the inn yard was half hidden by green willow trees. Withered leaves occasionally fell from the branches in the gentle breeze. Leaning against the door of the inn, Zhang could not help giving a long sigh. It was indeed like:

The twittering of swallows on the branches heard
Has broken the dream of union of a lonely
lovebird.

CHAPTER ELEVEN

The Wedding

AFTER A LONG and weary journey, Zhang finally arrived at the capital. On the day the civil service examination began, scholars from all over the country gathered at the examination hall. Thanks to his exceptional talents, Zhang won the highest honor.

Suddenly, he was famous. The emperor himself invited him to a banquet at the imperial palace, where he was asked to write an inscription for the Goose Pagoda; high-ranking officials were eager to pay him courtesy calls, one after another; he paid a visit to his teacher; and his friends came to express their congratulations. Though the young man was eager to return to Mid-River Prefecture to be reunited with Oriole, he had to stay at the Hall for Gathering Talented People, waiting for the emperor to bestow an appointment on him. One day, when gazing at the plum blossoms in the courtyard, he thought poignantly of Oriole. "I met Oriole last spring, when the flowers were in full bloom," he thought, "and I left her when the sere leaves were tumbling from the trees. I have been parted from my dear for half a year; Oriole must be worried about me. I shall send her a letter at once." So thinking, he picked up a writing brush, and wrote a letter. As soon as he had done so, he dispatched his page to deliver it to Oriole at the Salvation Monastery.

Since Oriole had parted from Zhang at the Pavilion of Parting in the late autumn of the previous year, she had been in low spirits, showing no interest in her appearance. Her normally slender waist had grown thinner, so that all her clothes were too big for her. Whenever she went to the Embroidery Pavilion by herself, she could see only desolation all around, with trees hidden in mist, and withered grass in the distance.

She waited for news from Zhang day and night, in a constant state of anxiety. Her old worries were like the undulating Zhongtiao Mountains, and her new worries, like the flowing Yellow River. Spring came again, with red flowers blooming everywhere. Bees were busying collecting honey and pairs of birds sported in the sky. But for half a year, there had been no news of her lover. Oriole's eyes were misting with tears, when she heard Rose coming into the room, chuckling. "Rose," Oriole cried, "what on earth are you so happy about?"

Her face wreathed in smiles, Rose gabbled excitedly: "Good news, Young Mistress! Master Zhang has won the highest honor in the examination!"

Thinking Rose might be making fun of her, Oriole pulled a long face, and said, "That is not a joking matter. I do wish you would learn to act in a more responsible way."

Still smiling, Rose retorted, "It's true! I'm not joking, Young Mistress. It is true that Master Zhang has passed the imperial examination and is now the country's No.1 Scholar. His page has just brought a letter containing the good news. He has reported to Madam, and now is waiting to see you."

As if in a dream, Oriole said to herself: "The day I have been so looking forward to has finally come!" Then, as if waking from the dream, she said hurriedly: "Quick, let him in!"

As soon as Zhang's page entered, Oriole bombarded him with questions. When the latter had satisfied her curiosity, he handed Zhang's letter to her. With trembling fingers and eyes dimmed with tears of joy, the girl tore the letter open. The first thing she noticed was tear stains on the paper. Obviously, her lover had wept as he wrote it.

The letter read:

"I, Zhang Gong, pay my deepest regards to my dear wife-to-be. Since we parted in the late autumn of last year, half a year has elapsed. Thanks to the fortune of my ancestors, and your own matchless virtue, I have won the highest honor in the examination. I am now staying at the Hall for Gathering Talented People, awaiting an appointment. I have dispatched this letter to assure you and your esteemed mother that there is no need for you to worry about me. Though I am far away from you, my heart is always with you. I am not a man who regards academic honor as being worth more than love."

After reading the letter, Oriole fell into a reverie. She thought to herself: "Dear Master Zhang, I never imagined that you would win the highest honor in the imperial examination when you climbed over the wall to meet me and gave your love to me in the Western Bower. But it seems that my house is destined to become an official residence."

With mixed feelings of both happiness and sadness, Oriole ordered Rose to arrange refreshments for Zhang's page, while she wrote a reply to her true love's letter.

Together with the reply, Oriole handed to the messenger a set of fine clothes, a zither, a jade hairpin and a bamboo flute, saying, "Make sure you deliver these things safely to your master."

The other was puzzled. "Pardon my inquisitiveness, Madam," he said, "but my master is now a very important person, and these things are quite ordinary. I suppose they have some special meaning?"

"You're right," replied Oriole. "These garments are the ones he wore when we first fell in love. Incidentally, wearing this pair of socks he will be reminded not to go to any place he should not go."

"Master Zhang already has a zither; I don't think he needs another one."

"You don't understand. This is the zither which he played when he recited a poem he had composed specially for me last year, when he first tried to attract my attention."

"What is the significance of the jade hairpin and the bamboo flute?"

"The jade hairpin will warn him not to forget me now that he has won the highest academic honor in the land. The flute is made from bamboo growing at the foot of Jiuyi Mountain. In ancient times, Consort Xiang and Emperor Shun were deeply in love. Consort Xiang wept so much when the emperor was away that her tears dropped onto the bamboo and remained as spots. Hence spotted bamboo is sign of longing for one's absent lover."

She then ordered the messenger to hasten on his way, admonishing him to be most careful with the precious letter and love tokens.

Meanwhile, soon after the page had left for the Salvation Monastery, Zhang had received an imperial edict appointing him to the post of editor of historical records at the Imperial Academy. However, despite the prestige attached to this important position, Zhang found himself unable to concentrate on his duties. He missed Oriole so much that he could neither eat nor sleep, and before long he fell ill. An imperial doctor came to see him, but Zhang, who knew well what his malady was, refused to be treated. The doctor, however, being well versed in the human condition, diagnosed the problem at once. Shaking his head, the physician said, "There is only one ailment in the world which it is beyond my powers to cure, and that is lovesickness. Even if Bian Que (a famous doctor in ancient times) himself were to treat you, he could not effect a cure. I can only exhort you to take care of yourself."

Zhang wondered if he was about to die pining for Oriole, when just at that moment the page he had sent to the monastery returned. Eagerly snatching the letter from the man's hand, Zhang tore it open. It read:

"Your humble wife sends her deepest regards to you, my dear husband. In the long months since you left, my deep love for you has never waned, even for an instant. Your letter restored me to life. I am sending to you by your page some love tokens which I am sure you will understand and know how to cherish."

After reading the letter and checking everything mentioned in it, Zhang was overcome with admiration for Oriole's talent and affection for him. Examining the love tokens she had sent, Zhang suddenly felt well again. His appetite returned, and after a good night's sleep he was back to his normal self. At this moment, an imperial edict was issued, appointing him prefect of Mid-River Prefecture. Zhang immediately set off to go to his post, returning to Oriole in glory.

Now, that would have been the end of the story if it had not been for a strange coincidence. As Zhang was making his way to the Salvation Monastery, unbeknownst to him somebody he had forgotten all about had arrived before him. It was none other than Zheng Heng, Madam Cui's nephew. His father, Madam Cui's elder brother, served as the Minister of Rites. However, Zheng Heng was by no means a credit to his illustrious sire, being a frivolous and snobbish fop who had long abandoned himself to dissipation. At the instigation of his parents, he and his cousin Oriole had been engaged, but it happened that before the wedding ceremony could take place Prime Minister Cui had died, delaying the nuptials until the end of the lengthy mourning period. Delayed in Mid-River Prefecture by the bandit disturbance, Madam Cui had written to Zheng Heng asking for help, but the cowardly Zheng Heng had been loath to leave the comforts of the capital, especially at a time of danger. Later, when he learned that Madam Cui had promised Oriole to Zhang in gratitude for his saving them from the bandits — and that the bandits had been driven off — he determined to hasten to the Salvation Monastery to reclaim his fiancée.

On arrival in Mid-River Prefecture, Zheng Heng decided to make no rash moves without finding out the true nature of the situation from Rose. So he put up at a local inn and sent one of his henchmen to inform Madam Cui of his presence and ask her to send Rose to meet him at the inn. It suited Madam Cui too to have Rose act as go-between until she found out what Zheng Heng's intentions were.

Zheng Heng greeted Rose warmly when she arrived at the inn

the wedding

escorted by his follower, and asked her about the situation with Madam Cui.

"Your aunt, sir, is somewhat put out because you did not hasten to pay your respects to her as soon as you entered the district," Rose replied.

Zheng Heng sighed. "The fact is that I'm too embarrassed to face my aunt," he said. "So I want to talk to you first. You see, when my uncle was alive, Oriole was betrothed to me. And now that the period of mourning for him has expired, I expect your mistress to choose a date for our wedding. Then it will be very convenient for me to accompany them to the cemetery in Boling for the interment of the ex-prime minister. If you can convince my aunt for me, I will give you a handsome reward."

"Sir, please don't mention that any more. My young mistress has been betrothed to another man," Rose said.

"Nonsense!" Zheng Heng shouted, his brow as black as thunder. "A horse cannot have two saddles, and a girl can not be betrothed to two men. When my uncle was alive, Oriole and I were engaged, but now that he is out of the way, my aunt is trying to break the promise he made. This is really outrageous!"

"Master Zheng," Rose protested, "where were you when Sun the Flying Tiger surrounded the monastery with his band of 5,000 cutthroats? If it were not for Master Zhang, Oriole would have been carried off by Sun the bandit, and the rest of us would all be dead now."

"Master Zhang is only a poverty-stricken scholar. I am a much better match for Oriole than he. I come from a rich and honored family. In addition, I and Oriole are cousins, and our marriage was approved by my late uncle," Zheng Heng yelled.

But the spirited Rose was not impressed by his boasting. "Sir, despite your claims to prestige and honor, it seems that you do not understand the rules of propriety," she retorted. "You talk about marrying my young mistress as if it were a foregone conclusion. But where are the matchmakers, and the gifts of lambs, geese, gold and silk? I am afraid that you overrate yourself, sir."

"I don't believe Zhang could defeat those bandits all by himself. It is just a threadbare ruse to deprive myself of my rightful bride," sneered Zheng Heng.

"Believe it or not," said Rose. "Sun the Flying Tiger rose in rebellion, and he and his 5,000 men burned, killed and looted wherever they went. They surrounded the monastery, and Sun demanded that Oriole be handed over to him. In that desperate plight, and after seeking the abbot's advice, our mistress declared that if anyone in the monastery, priest or layman, was able to induce the bandits to withdraw, she would present her daughter to him as his wife and give him a handsome dowry. Then Master Zhang wrote a letter to his friend, the White Horse General, asking him to come to the rescue. When the general did so, Madam Cui formally betrothed her daughter to Master Zhang."

"But he's a nobody compared to me," Zheng Heng snorted. "How could my aunt throw her only daughter away like that?"

Rose retorted, raising her brows: "Master Zhang is a learned man. He constantly quotes the classics, and his poems are as good as those written by the famous poets. He speaks and acts with decorum. Madam Cui has kept her promise, and so it seems to me that there is an end to the matter."

"I am the scion of an aristocratic family," blustered Zheng Heng, "while he is only a poor scholar; such people are ten a penny. We cannot be mentioned in the same breath."

"Master Zhang relies on his teachers, friends and noble character, but you take advantage of your father's and brother's power to bully people," Rose counter-attacked. "You are so proud of your official family, but you should remember how many generals and prime ministers throughout history came from poor families!"

Zheng Heng lost patience with the waspish Rose. With a wave of his hand, he said, "I can't be bothered arguing with you any longer. It is the abbot who has caused me this trouble, I'll be bound. I'll get even with him tomorrow."

"The abbot is a kindly old monk who helps others. He never causes trouble for anyone. In my opinion, this 'trouble', as you call it, was brought about by your own weakness of character," Rose said with scorn.

"It is my duty to carry out the behest of my late uncle," replied Zheng Heng, smiling unctuously. "I will follow the traditional procedure, and pick an auspicious day. On that benevolent and blessed morning, I will take gifts of sheep and wine to the monastery, to set in train the time-honored nuptial rites that will lead to Oriole and I being united in wedded bliss."

"Bah!" cried Rose, stamping her foot in fury. "You are not like a son of Minister Zheng, but a bandit like Sun the Flying Tiger. Your shameless ways will bring you to a disgraceful end!" Whereupon, without taking her leave, Rose turned and stormed off to report the outcome of this unsatisfactory interview to her mistress.

Watching her go, Zheng Heng allowed his face to twist in death. Suddenly he made a sinister smile, as a cunning scheme entered his head.

When Madam Cui learned from Rose what had passed between her and Zheng Heng, she was overcome with remorse. "However," she thought, "the way things turned out I had no choice but to break Oriole's engagement to my nephew. For one thing, the situation was a life-and-death one when we were besieged by the bandits. If it had not been for Zhang, Oriole would have been carried off and lost forever. Then again, when I found out that Oriole and Zhang had already become intimate, what else could I do but make sure that they were engaged to be married as soon as possible? No doubt Zheng Heng will come here tomorrow, so I must have a feast prepared, and try to reconcile him to the situation."

Late in the morning of the following day, Zheng Heng did come to the Salvation Monastery. Prostrating himself at Madam Cui's feet and weeping copious tears, he greeted his aunt: "Your unworthy nephew Zheng Heng pays his humble respects, Madam."

Madam Cui, who had always been fond of her nephew, was touched by his wretchedness. "My dear child," she said, "why didn't you come to see me as soon as you arrived?"

Zheng Heng wailed, "I was too ashamed to face you, dearest relative, now that my darling Oriole has been wrenched from me and given to another man."

Wiping her tears, Madam Cui said, "Listen to me, my child. When Sun the Flying Tiger surrounded the monastery with his army and you failed to come and rescue us, I had to promise to give

Oriole to whoever could save Oriole from a fate worse than death. Zhang was the one who saved her, as well as the rest of us, and so I had to betroth Oriole to him."

"Who is this Master Zhang fellow?" asked Zheng Heng, with a grimace.

"His full name is Zhang Gong, or Zhang Junrui. He's from Luoyang."

"Oh, him!" Zheng Heng cried in astonishment. "He won the highest honor in the imperial examination. His name was top of the list of successful candidates. I saw him parading through the streets of the capital. He is about 24 or 25 years old. So that's how it is!"

"So he did succeed in becoming the No. 1 Scholar!" Madam Cui was overjoyed at this news. But just then a crafty thought entered Zheng Heng's head.

"Oh, but I am sorry to inform you, Madam," he said, with a mournful shake of his head, "that a misfortune has overtaken that man. As he was parading through the streets in triumph, the daughter of Minister Wei threw an embroidered ball at him — that's the way the daughters of that powerful family choose their husbands, you know. Anyway, the ball hit Zhang, and he was dragged into the minister's residence, despite his protests that he was already married. It caused a sensation in the capital, I can tell you. Now Zhang and Miss Wei are already married. Moreover, Minister Wei insisted that Oriole can only be Zhang's second wife." He heaved a hypocritical sigh.

Madam Cui flew into a rage. "I knew no good would come of Oriole's infatuation with that bungling bookworm!" she stormed. "Well, no daughter of mine — and of a late prime minister, may I add — is going to play second fiddle to some little minx in the capital, with all her airs and graces. So, since Master Zhang is already fixed up with a wife, you, my dear nephew may pick an auspicious day to marry Oriole, in accordance with your late uncle's behest."

Zheng Heng was overjoyed to hear this, but he maintained his composure. "But aunt," he asked, "what if Zhang comes to claim Oriole for himself, claiming that you have broken your promise? He's a powerful figure now, you know."

the wedding

"You just leave Master high-and-mighty Zhang to me," Madam Cui replied, her jaw set grimly. "Well, what are you waiting for? Off you go and pick an auspicious day for the wedding ceremony!"

Thanking his aunt profusely, and scarcely able to conceal his glee at her gullibility, Zheng Heng left to do as she had bidden him.

Now let's turn to Zhang. He arrived at Mid-River Prefecture soon after Zheng Heng's interview with Madam Cui. He met the local dignitaries, including the abbot, at the Pavilion of Parting, and then headed directly for the Salvation Monastery. There he fell to his knees before Madam Cui, and announced, "The new No.1 Scholar and recently appointed prefect of Mid-River Prefecture Zhang Gong pays his respects to his mother-in-law."

The other's response stunned the young man. "No more of your impudent nonsense!" snapped Madam Cui. "How dare you? The whole world knows that you've broken your promise and that you're someone else's son-in-law."

Dumbfounded, Zhang thought, "I know that the Cuis have not let a man without official rank marry into the family for three generations. But now I have won the highest honor in the imperial examination, my name is on the roll of the Imperial Academy and I have been appointed a prefect. Madam Cui cannot say that I am not worthy of her daughter's hand. And, besides, what on earth did she mean by 'breaking my promise' and being 'someone else's son-in-law?' "

He raised his head, and pleaded, "I beg that you will explain, Madam. I don't understand your words at all. You said that if I became the No. 1 Scholar I could return and marry Oriole. Well, here I am."

"I will not allow my daughter to be the second wife of anyone, even if he is the No. 1 Scholar. And I certainly will not have her at the beck and call of the stuck up daughter of Minister Wei!"

At this, Zhang was even more mystified. "Who told you all this?" he cried in a fit of anxiety.

At this moment, Rose came in. As a matter of fact, she had been suspicious of Zheng Heng's story right from the start, but she decided to test Zhang before committing herself to his side.

"Well, well," she chirped, "if it isn't the new No.1 Scholar! How is your new wife? Is she more beautiful than my Young Mistress?"

Zhang was indignant. "Miss Rose," he said reproachfully, "how can you make cruel jokes when you know perfectly well how much I have suffered for love of her? Somebody has been making mischief to try to tear us apart. When I find out who that person is, he — or she — will rue the day he or she was born! You mark my words."

These bold words convinced Rose that Zhang had not proved unfaithful, and, fearing that if she hesitated to reveal the truth, Madam Cui might give Oriole to Zheng Heng and so bring about calamity for the two true lovers, she hastened to explain that it was Zheng Heng who had spread the lie about Zhang marrying Minister Wei's daughter. She then turned to Madam Cui. "Madam," she said, pleading with tears in her eyes, "I believe Master Zhang is a sincere person who would never abandon Oriole. Please let her come and interrogate him. Then we will find out the real situation."

"Very well, bring her here, Rose," said Madam Cui, with a decisive nod.

Oriole's pallid, gaunt features and wasted body informed Zhang as clearly as any words that the girl had been devastated by the wicked lie spread by Zheng Heng. He felt his heart ache with pity, and tears ran down his cheeks.

"Young Mistress, ask Master Zhang to his face if there is any truth to the claim that he has married the daughter of Minister Wei," Rose urged.

"My cousin Zheng Heng reported this ghastly news to my mother," said Oriole. "I have no choice but to trust the word of such a near relative."

Zhang turned to Rose: "Tell me, Rose, have you been delivering letters between your young mistress and Zheng Heng?"

"How dare you, sir?" the indignant Rose cried. "Zheng Heng is a good-for-nothing. I serve no one but the prime minister's family, an honored official family for generations. I would have nothing to do with that sinister wretch!"

Zhang wilted under this barrage, and Rose, calming down somewhat, felt a pang of remorse. "I'll tell you what," she said. "Why don't we get Zheng Heng himself to come here, and confront him with Master Zhang himself?"

At this moment Abbot Fa Ben was announced. He too had heard the rumor that Zhang had married while he was in the capital, and was consumed by curiosity to know if the story was true or not. So, on the pretext of expressing his congratulations to Madam Cui on the happiness Zhang's success must have brought the family, he came bustling in. On this occasion his curiosity got the better of his accustomed diplomacy, and after a cursory greeting, he asked if it were true that Zhang had really married Minister Wei's daughter. This caused a great deal of embarrassment all round, which was changed to astonishment when the abbot announced that the White Horse General had arrived and was waiting outside the monastery.

Madam Cui was not happy to hear this, as Zhang's friend was a powerful figure who could force her to give Oriole in marriage to Zhang even if it turned out that the latter had married Minister Wei's daughter after all.

"Take your young mistress back to her room," she ordered Rose.

As soon as Rose and Oriole left, Fa Cong came bustling in. "The White Horse General Du Que is impatient to greet Master Zhang," he announced excitedly. Zhang could contain himself no longer, and dashed outside in the company of the young monk and the abbot.

The two old friends were overjoyed to see each other again. General Du explained that he had come as soon as he heard of Zhang's success in the examination, and was eager to be present at his wedding with Oriole. He frowned when he heard about the dastardly trick Zheng Heng had played on his dearest friend, and said, "Don't worry about that villain. I will deal with this matter, if you will be so kind as to procure an audience for me with Madam Cui."

Thereupon, Du Que, Zhang and the abbot went to see Madam Cui.

After exchanging conventional greetings with the dowager, Du Que said, "Madam, I have learned that a minor problem concerning Brother Junrui's marriage has occurred. I think it is most regrettable. Junrui is the son of the minister of rites, and now he has won the highest honor in the imperial examination. The marriage between Junrui and Oriole is ideal in terms of social and economic status. They are a perfect match. But now I hear that you want to break off the engagement, all because of some wild rumor. Do you not think this rash?"

Madam Cui looked embarrassed. "General Du, when my late husband was alive, he betrothed my daughter to my nephew, Zheng Heng. It was only because of our desperate situation when the bandits threatened to carry her off that I promised to betroth her to any man who would save her. I kept my promise. But when I heard that Zhang had married in the capital, I was forced to break off the engagement. You see, my late husband would never have consented to Oriole's being a junior wife, even to the daughter of a minister. It is utterly impossible. She must marry her original fiancé."

At this moment, they heard strains of celebratory music outside, and Zheng Heng, dressed in his holiday best, walked in, beaming all over his face.

"Zheng Heng, you have come at the right time," said Madam Cui haughtily. "Let me introduce you to the White Horse General Du Que, who is in charge of Puguan Pass. Of course, I don't need to introduce this other man to you."

"He must be..." Zheng Heng spoke evasively, his eyes glittering with sullen hatred.

"He is Zhang Gong, alias Zhang Junrui, the new No. 1 Scholar, and newly appointed prefect of Mid-River Prefecture. You said that he had married Minister Wei's daughter. Is this true?"

Zheng Heng was taken aback at Madam Cui's change of attitude towards him. He stammered out a few words of greeting.

"Why have you come, Zheng Heng?" asked Zhang.

"Er... I learned that the No. 1 Scholar had done the Cui family the honor of paying a courtesy call, and so I came to express my congratulations to you," said Zheng Heng, groaning inwardly.

"You're a scoundrel! Why did you cook up that story, and try to steal the girl destined to be Zhang's wife?" said Du Que sternly. "If I report this sordid matter to the emperor, he will have you executed."

"Oh sir, the fact of the matter is that I and my cousin were engaged at the express behest of my late uncle. I am the one who has been wronged."

"If you continue to babble nonsense I'll have my men arrest you," the general barked. "Take him away!"

This scared Zheng Heng almost out of his wits. "That won't be necessary!" he shrieked. "I confess that I fabricated the story about Zhang and the daughter of Minister Wei. I am willing to break off my engagement to Oriole right now."

Madam Cui stepped into the fray. "I see it all now," she declared. "He is a shameless rascal. Drive him away from here, and let us put an end to this distressing episode."

"Very well, Madam," said General Du. "Get out, and think yourself lucky to escape with your life."

Shamefaced, Zheng Heng staggered out and along the road. Coming across a flourishing apricot tree, he raised his head to look at it, and sighed deeply. "I have lost face thoroughly today," he groaned. What's the use of living any longer?" So saying, he closed his eyes, and dashed his brains out against the tree.

A passing monk witnessed this last desperate act of the wretched Zheng Heng, and lost no time reporting it to Madam Cui, who together with the others rushed to the fatal spot. Madam Cui could not help weeping sadly, but after a while she thought to herself: "He was the author of his own undoing. By trying to force himself on Oriole and slandering Zhang he embarked on a road of no return."

She then gave permission to Abbot Fa Ben to allow Fa Cong and Hui Ming to bury the body.

Returning to her quarters, Madam Cui began to feel remorse for the way she had tried to thwart the course of true love when she had schemed to put obstacles in the way of Zhang and her daughter. "Anyway, all's well that ends well," she reminded herself. "After all, there can be no better match for Oriole than the No. 1 Scholar, and a court-appointed official to boot!" Looking around, she said out loud: "Since we have General Du and Abbot Fa Ben to act as matchmakers, let us prepare a wedding feast and celebrate the marriage of Zhang and Oriole right now!"

Everybody cheered. Zhang bowed to Du Que and the abbot, "Without Brother Du and the abbot's help, this happiness would not have been possible today. If you had not laid bare Zheng Heng's lies, I would have been separated from my true love forever."

Rose ran to the Embroidery Pavilion to report the good news to Miss Oriole.

With tears of joy coursing down her cheeks, Oriole said, "Rose, I owe everything to you! It was you who steered me right through troubled times and have remained with me until this wonderful day, on which I shall be married."

That night, the Salvation Monastery was decorated with lanterns and colored streamers, and the air was filled with the deafening sounds of gongs and drums. All the officials of Mid-River Prefecture came to express their congratulations.

Supported by Rose, Oriole, wearing a phoenix coronet and red cape, emerged. She and Zhang made a bow to thank the emperor for his kindness. Then they bowed in turn to Heaven, Earth, Madam Cui, General Du, the abbot and all the other people at the ceremony. Everyone agreed that they were a perfectly matched pair.

Rose said to Zhang in a low voice: "Brother-in-law, don't you need to bow to someone else?"

Zhang was mystified at first, but soon understood what she meant. Pulling Oriole by the hand, he tried to get both of them to bow to Rose. But Rose said, "I was only joking. Now it's time for you to go to the bridal chamber."

The bridal chamber was lit by tall red candles. The new couple recalled their first tryst, waiting for the moon in the wind, the exchange of verses, expressing love through letters, and parting at the Pavilion of Parting. They had had to overcome many difficulties before they were finally united in matrimonial bliss. An old saying goes: "A brief parting is as sweet as a honeymoon." Three days later, Zhang took leave of his mother-in-law, and went to the Mid-River Prefectural office to take up his duties.

This love story of Zhang and Oriole has been handed down from generation to generation, and the pair have become symbols of perfect fidelity and affection.

Zhao the Orphan

	About the Original Work	123
Chapter 1	Remonstration in the Peach Garden	126
Chapter 2	Chu Ni Dashes His Brains Out	149
Chapter 3	The Slaughter of a Family	173
Chapter 4	Cheng Ying Saves a Child	191
Chapter 5	An Episode of Sterling Devotion	218
Chapter 6	The Noble Death of Gongsun Chujiu	235
Chapter 7	Taking Up Residence in the Tiger's Lair	247
Chapter 8	The Day of Reckoning	260

About the Original Work

THE DRAMA ZHAO *the Orphan* by Ji Junxiang (also known as Ji Tianxiang) is a tragedy steeped in Chinese folklore. The plot is a somewhat simplified version of a tale that can be found as far back as in the *Zuo Zhuan*, written over 2,000 years ago. Other classic works, such as Sima Qian's *Records of the Historian*, and the *New Annals* and *On Garden* by Liu Xiang, also contain versions of the same story. The details contained in these works laid the foundation for the plot of the drama. The historical background of the story has been considerably altered in this version: the setting was shifted from the reign of Duke Jing of the State of Jin to that of Duke Ling. Other details have also been altered: for instance, Zhao the Orphan does not conceal himself in the palace, but is instead smuggled out in a medicine box by Cheng Ying; the boy does not grow up deep in the mountains, but in the home of his adoptive father Tu'an Gu; Han Jue does not ask for an estate for Zhao the Orphan, but dies a righteous death to get Cheng Ying expelled from the palace; and the retainers of the Zhao family, Cheng Ying and Gongsun Chujiu, have become a humble physician and a fellow court official of Zhao Dun, respectively. These changes serve to render the clashes and antagonisms of the play sharper and more vivid, and thus strengthen the dramatic impact.

The theme of *Zhao the Orphan* is the conflict between "loyalty" and "treachery", both inside and outside the court of the State of Jin, during the Spring and Autumn Period. Throughout, the focus of the struggle against oppression is the theme of *Zhao the Orphan*. Woven around this is the heart-stopping hunt for and rescue of the orphan boy; as the hunt gets closer, various measures are taken to save him. When the search reaches the palace, the princess sacrifices her life to save him; at the palace gate, Han Jue dies a chivalrous death to save him; and when the hunt becomes nationwide, Cheng Ying gives up his own son and Gongsun Chujiu his own life to save him. One after the other, these loyal ministers and heroes go nobly to their deaths, and make tragic sacrifices for the sake of Zhao the Orphan.

The dastardly Tu'an Gu exercises absolute power with arrogance once he has the muddle-headed ruler of Jin under his thumb. As a result, righteous people who dare to oppose him face danger and oppression, a situation that permeates the whole drama with an aura of tragedy. But at the same time, a thread of hope runs through the story: at the end, the orphan is saved, and brings justice and extirpates the evil. In the midst of all the lamentable martyrdom, there is a stirring sense of righteousness, which inspires the protagonists with faith that good will always triumph over evil. At the same time, there is a sense of dramatic irony as the wicked minister weaves a trap in which will eventually ensnare himself. There is a distinct folk flavor about this aspect of the plot.

The drama successfully portrays a range of lofty-minded tragic characters who are individually delineated, the most outstanding of whom are Cheng Ying and Gongsun Chujiu. Following the massacre of the Zhao clan, the former risks his life to save Zhao the Orphan. In addition to this heroic act, Cheng Ying has to undergo the terrifying interrogation at the gate of the palace, the heartbreak of having to substitute his own son for the orphan, the anguish of witnessing the deaths of both his infant and his friend Gongsun Chujiu, and twenty years of humiliation and insults. These ordeals underline the sublime integrity of Cheng Ying. The latter character, Gongsun Chujiu, has always despised wickedness, and refuses to participate in government dominated by degenerate ministers. He goes to his death in an awe-inspiring display of rectitude. Besides these two, Han Jue's selfless heroism, Ti Miming's self-sacrifice for his master, and Ling Zhe's decision to carry the carriage on his shoulder are well described in the tale. Although the scenes are merely sketches, they highlight the heroes' distinct personalities.

The tale of *Zhao the Orphan* has circulated both inside and outside China for thousand years. Within China, every form of dramatic tradition has adapted it for the stage. In the 18th century, it reached France and England, where it was translated and published in book form. It was also adapted for the stage in Germany and Austria.

This present version has preserved the unadorned style of language of the original text, and is basically faithful to the original plot. However, we have taken the liberty of adding some minor details and psychological depth in the two scenes—the first scene describing the licentious antics of Duke Ling and the brutalities of Tu'an Gu, and second scene depicting the psychological tension between Cheng Ying and Gongsun Chujiu in Taiping Village when the latter meets his end. In this new version of *Zhao the Orphan*, we have striven to make the plot well-knit and the pathos vivid. We have tried to make the psychological mechanism finely detailed, and the language flowing and elegant, in order to make it more readable than the original poetic drama form.

The original drama presents the clash between Zhao Dun and Tu'an Gu as a conflict between civil and military court officials. This tends to obscure the more important conflict between good and evil, and so we have tried to highlight the latter.

We hope that with this endeavor, we have made a contribution to the popularity of classical Chinese drama.

CHAPTER ONE

Remonstration in the Peach Garden

IT IS SAID that Duke Ling of the State of Jin during the Spring and Autumn Period, who came to the throne as a child, was a petulant youngster of unstable temperament. But, fortunately for his realm, the influence of his benign forebears, dukes Wen and Xiang, still lingered, and the people were content and industrious. In addition, there were able and loyal ministers and generals, such as Zhao Dun and Han Jue, at court, ensuring that Jin stood undefeated amid the incessant wars between the various states of China in those days.

As the years went by and Duke Ling attained manhood, his nature became even more depraved. His extravagance knew no bounds, and he plundered the people mercilessly to pay for an orgy of construction of palaces and pleasure domes. He held human life in complete disregard; if anything irritated him, he would unleash a whirlwind of executions of innocent people. The warnings from upright officials such as Zhao Dun fell on deaf ears, and provoked only resentment. Now Zhao Dun was the son of Zhao Shuai, who had accompanied Duke Wen, the previous ruler of Jin, on his 19-year exile, and who had done much work to restore the fortunes of the state. Zhao Dun had also served Duke Wen. In addition, he was a man of noble character and high prestige, so that Duke Ling treated him with a mixture of hatred, respect and fear.

As dynasties rose and dynasties fell, just as there appeared loyal and honest ministers, so also crafty and scheming courtiers mounted the political stage from time to time. A prime example of the latter, Tu'an Gu, had the ear of Duke Ling at this time. Tu'an Gu came from a military family. He was a hefty individual, with a nose as hooked as a hawk's claw and narrow eyes. His very forehead exuded guile and wickedness. Having practiced martial arts from an early age, he was immensely strong, and so had come to the notice of Duke Ling, who appointed him head of the palace guard. Tu'an Gu was as cunning as a fox and an accomplished flatterer, as well as being adept at reading a person's thoughts. He soon had the ordinary court officials eating out of his hand, and as for Duke Ling, manipulating him was child's play for Tu'an Gu. The duke, in turn, doted on his chief bodyguard, who never left his side. If perchance, Tu'an Gu happened to be absent on any occasion, Duke Ling was as distressed as if he had lost his right arm.

Early on perceiving that Duke Ling cared for nothing but satisfying his appetites, Tu'an Gu used all his guile and flattery to wheedle out of the duke what he most desired. Then he had a park constructed in the eastern part of the royal palace in Jiangyi City, the capital of Jin. Crystal-clear streams and shady paths meandered around lofty halls, terraces and pavilions. Rare and exotic plants were brought from all over Jin and planted in the park, so that fine trees were in bloom all the year round, and lush lawns breathed their fragrance. Of all the flowers that bloomed in their turn, those of the peach trees were the most numerous. Everywhere the eye turned, it alighted on the peach blossoms. In the season when the buds started to ripen, the air seemed to be filled with a rosy mist hovering over the rows of emerald-green buds, giving the park the aspect of an embroidered and perfumed picture. Shimmering in a warm breeze, the peach blossoms had a fairyland-like quality about them and their scent wafted for miles around. For this reason, the park was given the name the Peach Garden.

With the opening of the Peach Garden, Duke Ling was overjoyed. He cast aside all thoughts of state affairs, and flung himself into an endless round of pleasure — sometimes carousing in the Flowery Pavilion, sometimes dicing in the Jade Hall, sometimes shooting at birds in the trees, and sometimes romping naked with his harem. There was no excess he did not indulge in. Both in the palace and in the streets, whenever the duke's name was mentioned, heads would shake and groans would be heard: "He's not like a ruler at all!"

Tu'an Gu's scheming knew no bounds. Seeing his master abandoned to riotous dissipation, he not only did not censure him, but went so far as to devise a way to sink him further into debauchery. He secretly summoned master craftsmen from all corners of the land, and instructed them to build a terrace three storied high by the entrance to the Peach Garden. Atop the terrace was erected the Crimson Cloud Tower. This tower was most magnificently appointed, with soaring eaves and flying buttresses, carved beams and decorated rafters, bright red pillars and jade-green steps. On all four sides it was surrounded by intricate painted rails and balustrades. The tower commanded a panoramic view; the whole of the capital city and its inhabitants came under the gaze of the viewer from its height. Duke Ling was transported with joy to receive this unexpected present from Tu'an Gu, and straightaway concluded that his chief bodyguard was the most devoted, loyal and capable of all his subjects.

One fine spring day, Zhao Dun, as was his custom, led a group of his subordinates outside the city to encourage the farmers with their work. Duke Ling, meanwhile, just like village scamp playing truant from school or a rascally servant lad dodging his master, had decided to devote the next few days to another round of pleasure. Rising early, he retired with his retainers to the Peach Garden. There the duke went into raptures at the sight of the peach trees adorned with blazing red and the emerald-hued willows, among which orioles and swallows chirped and sported. Desiring to be entertained with stage performances, he told Tu'an Gu to summon a troupe of actors to the Crimson Cloud Tower. Now the tower was adjacent to the busiest street in the capital. Even on ordinary days, not to mention holidays, this street was filled with people, and when the news that performances were to be held in the Crimson Cloud Tower ran through the crowds, young and old flocked to the foot of the tower. As Tu'an Gu gazed down at the mass of bobbing heads, a dastardly thought suddenly occurred to him. Smiling obsequiously, he murmured to the duke: "Your Majesty, see there below! That mass of people who have gathered outside the Peach Garden to get a glimpse of the performances — why, they are more numerous than the beasts in the wilds outside the capital!"

Hearing this, Duke Ling, who took a fiendish delight in the sport of hunting, suddenly had exciting visions of deer and hares pursued. "My dear commander," he burbled, "I have a wonderful idea! Let's pretend those people are animals, and each shoot balls into the crowd. Hitting an eye will count as the top score, hitting the body will count as second place, and a miss calls for a fine of a jug of wine. How about it?"

Tu'an Gu clapped his hands in approval, and laughed in delight: "A capital plan, Your Majesty!" He cried, and straightaway ordered his aides to bring catapults.

Duke Ling, scarcely able to contain his delight at this new game he had just thought up, said, "I'll shoot into the right of the mob, Commander," he cried, "and you shoot to the left. No slacking, now!"

Tu'an Gu made a great show of bowing to his master. "Of course, Your Majesty!" he gushed.

As the two of them prepared for the contest, attendants brought refreshments and the prize wine jug. The duke and his chief bodyguard then began to take turns shooting balls into the crowd of people below. Every time the cry "A hit!" was raised from atop the terrace, an agonized scream rose from multitude.

At first, the throng at the foot of the terrace did not realize what was going on; most of the people assumed that the screams, mingled with the din made by the musicians on the terrace, were the customary cries of appreciation for the ongoing performance, and continued to press forward in their ignorance. Not until a dozen or more of them had fallen transfixed by balls did the crowd begin to panic. Pushing and shoving, they stampeded in all directions, trampling children, the weak and the old, and ignoring their pitiful moans. This horrifying scene served only to send Duke Ling into further raptures, and, carried away by this new sport, he forgot about the contest as such, and called to his attendants: "Those of you who can use a bow, come and shoot a few balls with me!"

The duke's lackeys scrambled to obey. In a twinkling, a hail of balls whistled through the air, lodging in the skulls, bodies, eyes, mouths and ears of those unfortunate enough to be unable to get out of the way in time. The street below the terrace was turned into a bedlam of wails and pounding feet. Up on the terrace, Duke Ling howled with laughter, and slurped down a goblet-full of wine. Casting the goblet from him, he guffawed, "What excellent sport! I've never had such a good time!"

From this time on, people avoided the street below the Crimson Cloud Tower, and preferred to make long detours rather than traverse that ill-omened thoroughfare. This incident too planted bitter seeds of resentment against Duke Ling in the hearts of the populace of the capital. A satirical verse began to circulate:

> Don't look at the tower on high.
> Down from it deadly darts fly.
> You'll go for a festival gay,
> But groaning you'll come away.

But let us leave this grim scene, and seek out Minister Zhao Dun.

The minister was deeply worried at the antics of his ruler. Since the completion of the Crimson Cloud Tower, Duke Ling had abandoned all semblance of attending to state affairs. On the pretext of illness, he had stopped holding court; instead he spent night and day in revelry. What was worse, he was aided and abetted in his debauchery by Tu'an Gu, who stuck to the duke like a shadow. If things continued like this, what would become of the State of Jin? Zhao Dun was racked by anxiety. Seeing his master so distraught on this fine morning, his servant Zhao Yi urged the minister to take a walk in the back garden to try to ease his troubled mind.

Zhao Dun's residence was situated to the south of the royal palace, and was known as the Lower Palace. It had been built by the late Duke Wen for Zhao Dun's father, Zhao Shuai, as a reward for the latter's loyal services during Duke Wen's long exile. The mansion of the senior minister was inferior only to the duke's palace, the Upper Palace. The back garden was particularly charming, being endowed with crystal streams, ponds and rockeries. Zhao Dun had had little time to enjoy the garden's splendors, however, as he was a conscientious man, busy supervising government business, most of which had fallen on his shoulders since the duke had started to shun his responsibilities. On this day, he was feeling particularly vexed, and so his servant's suggestion was a welcome one. "Yes," he agreed. "Perhaps a stroll is just what I need."

Zhao Yi hurriedly made the arrangements, and the two of them went into the back garden, where they walked at leisure past pavilions and ponds, ornamented with quaint stones and creepers, until they came to the Piercing Clouds Pavilion. There they saw a wall made of red mud, and a cottage thatched with rice stalks. Over the wall hung the branches of peach trees, ablaze with fiery blossoms. Behind the cottage was a row of mulberry and willow trees, casting a mantle of green shade. Beside the trees was a well, with a well sweep and a pulley. On the left was a fenced-off vegetable garden, giving the area a genuinely rustic atmosphere. "Why don't you rest here for a while, sir?" urged Zhao Yi, with a winning smile. "It seems to be just the place for you to read and relax."

Zhao Dun sighed. "A few days of relaxation is exactly what I need. It's just that, these days..."

He cut short what he was going to say. Zhao Yi, knowing that something was preying on his master's mind, dared say nothing further. Zhao Dun paused for a moment, and then said, "Although this place was built by men's hands, it is extremely beautiful to gaze at. Some day, when affairs of state are straightened out, I would like to retire to this cottage and live the life of a hermit." At this point, he suddenly let out a gasp, as if he had just remembered something important. "I recall I have a most urgent matter to attend to," he muttered. "If I had not come on a stroll in the garden today, and cast my eyes upon this rural scene, it would have slipped my mind completely."

Zhao Yi, who regularly attended his master at court and was thoroughly acquainted with his duties, suggested, "Perhaps, sir, you are referring to your annual excursion to encourage the farmers?"

"That's exactly it!" Zhao Dun cried. "As the saying goes, 'Food is the everything to the people, and farming is the foundation of the state.' There is nothing of greater importance."

Now that the subject of encouraging the farmers had come up, a cloud of gloom overshadowed Zhao Dun's mind. Traditionally, at spring plowing time, generation after generation of rulers had gone to the suburbs in light carriages and accompanied by few retainers to bring comfort and encouragement to the farmers diligently working in the fields, and admonish the lazy ones. In this way, they showed how much importance was put on agriculture by the state. Dukes Wen and Xiang had been particularly scrupulous in carrying out this duty — to the extent of grasping the plow handles themselves and cracking the whip over the ox to plow a symbolic furrow. In their days, there had always been bumper harvests of the five grains, the state had been at peace and the people had been content. When Duke Ling had come to the throne and been too young to understand such matters, Zhao Dun himself had carried out the formality of encouraging the farmers. But now that the Duke had come of age and should have taken on this responsibility, he did not give it a thought, but instead spent all day in the Peach Garden pursuing his giddy pleasures. Moreover, Zhao Dun recalled, in recent years, many of Jin's venerable statesmen and able ministers, dismayed at the duke's wayward life style and his utter disregard for right or wrong, and alarmed at the increasing numbers of venal and dastardly officials who were creeping into positions of power at the court, had one after the other retired from public life. Some kept their mouths shut, and quietly slunk away with their tails between their legs; others, overawed by Tu'an Gu's might and influence, sought safety by throwing in their lot with him. Although Zhao Dun was the

remonstration in the peach garden

most senior minister at court, he alone could not stop the rot that threatened to destroy the whole state.

As these distressing thoughts filled his mind, Zhao Dun could not suppress a long sigh. Suddenly he was no longer in the mood for viewing scenery. He ordered his servant to prepare his carriage for a drive to the suburbs to encourage the farmers.

Learning that her husband was intending to go out, Zhao Dun's wife did not try to stop him, as she knew full well his stubborn nature. Instead, she made haste to order his official robes brought and servants to attend to him. But Zhao Dun said, "Besides, encouraging the farmers, my purpose is to sound out the feelings of the people. But I am afraid that if I appear before them dressed in my official attire, they will be reluctant to speak their minds frankly."

"Do you mean, My Lord, that you wish to travel incognito this time?" his wife asked, and upon receiving an affirmative reply, ordered her servant girl to bring plain robes.

Zhao Dun and his entourage, dressed in nondescript garb, left the city by the west gate, and headed for the suburbs. Their way was lined with peach and apricot trees in fiery-red bloom, and emerald-green reeds. The fields beyond them stretched as far as the eye could see, intersected by sparkling clear irrigation ditches. Partridges and cuckoos piped their sweet notes, and the whole of the countryside was vibrant with the vigor of spring. Zhao Dun found his heart lightening. He smiled, and said, "Since we have been blessed with such magnificent spring weather, excellent for plowing and planting, there is no excuse for slackening in the fields. If I find anyone not pulling his weight, I will come down hard on him. Mark my words."

Scarcely had he finished, when he spied a group of peasants carrying farming implements and entering a field. Among them was a white-haired old woman, shabbily dressed and with haggard, careworn face. Zhao Dun ordered his driver to stop the carriage, and, bowing humbly to the old woman, said, "Pardon me, but may I enquire as to your age, and the circumstances of your live?"

The old woman could see from Zhao Dun's entourage that he

was a noble from the capital. She answered, "I am 65 years old, Your Honor. Last year, my only son died while on military service, and there is no one left at home to support me. So I have to work in the fields myself in order to keep body and soul together." As she said this, tears started to flow from her eyes.

Zhao Dun found the old woman's words distressing. He reflected that the constant warfare between the feudal lords of the various rival state in recent years had caused the common people untold suffering. Just then, another peasant standing nearby, noticing the pensive expression on Zhao Dun's face, uttered a groan of sympathy and said, "Although we've had good harvests in the past few years, Your Lordship, the official taxes are crushing the life out of us."

So saying, he took out his lunch from a bamboo basket, and showed it to everyone. It consisted of a coarse bran cake together with a few scraps of wild vegetables.

Zhao Dun immediately understood the peasants' plight: the spring plowing and sowing season was one in which the winter stocks of grain had been used up, while the new harvest was still some months away. This realization tore at his heartstrings, and turning quickly to his attendants, he ordered them to give the peasants some relief silver. As he drove away, Zhao Dun was too preoccupied with worry to pay any heed to the peasants' cries of gratitude and blessing. Nor did he notice any longer the sparkling water gurgling in the irrigation ditches or the warm breeze that caressed his cheeks. Suddenly, from high in the air he heard a cawing sound. Raising his head, Zhao Dun spied a chevron of wild geese winging towards the north. Looking to left and right, he discovered for the first time that the tops of the hills were bare of their usual greenery; all that remained of the forests that used to clothe them was stumps. This, he realized, was the result of the frenzy of building that had been going on in the capital.

Seven or eight days passed, and Zhao Dun's depression deepened. The field work was going well enough; the peasants were working diligently, and there were no signs of any slackers. Zhao Dun consoled himself that a bumper harvest was assured that year. Nevertheless, that evening as he drove back to the capital, his mind was haunted by images of the old peasant woman's despairing eyes, the crude bran cake from the bamboo basket, the sighing of the water in the irrigation ditches and the denuded mountain slopes. Over and over again, the question popped up in his mind: "How can I get Duke Ling to abandon his dissolute ways and return to the proper path of a ruler?"

His attendants were as morose as he was on the journey back, and uttered not a sound. So the entourage proceeded in silence, until they reached the eastern gate of the capital. There they saw a dark mass of humanity blocking the road. The carriage driver reined in his horses with a sharp cry. Taken unawares, Zhao Dun was thrown heavily forward.

"What's the matter?" he muttered angrily.

"Sir, there a crowd of people kneeling in the road and blocking our progress," the driver replied.

Zhao Dun clambered down from the carriage, and saw that indeed there were people kneeling in the roadway, young and old, men and women, and with some white-whiskered seniors in the forefront. He perceived also that some of the crowd bore wounds, with bandaged eyes or limbs, bruised noses and swollen faces.

It was the very day upon which Duke Ling had shot balls into the crowd below the Crimson Cloud Tower for sport. Some of the victims in fact had died of their injuries. While the people were giving vent to their rage and frustration, one elder had suggested that they take their grievance to Zhao Dun. "He's the only upright man at the court," the man said. "Let's beg him to curb the duke's wantonness."

This met with general approval, and the people marched straight to Minister Zhao's mansion. Learning that the minister had gone to the countryside to encourage the farmers, the petitioners then went to the eastern gate to await his return. They had been there for three long and bitter days when Zhao Dun's carriage finally drove into view. Immediately, a great wail arose from the people.

Zhao Dun was shocked to the marrow when he learned of Duke Ling's wickedness. "From ancient times," he said, unable to disguise his feelings of outrage and pain, "enlightened rulers have shared their pleasures with the people. There have been, it is true, mediocre rulers who have indulged only themselves. But in all my sixty years on this Earth, I have never heard of a ruler who took pleasure in inflicting suffering on his subjects."

Abandoning all thought of going home that night, Zhao Dun ordered that relief silver be distributed among the suppliants and that the wounded be taken care of. He thereupon drove straight to the Peach Garden.

By this time, the whole city was enfolded in darkness, except for the Crimson Cloud Tower, which was ablaze with light, for in his pursuit of entertainment Duke Ling cared for neither night nor day. Gazing at the gaudy sight from afar, Zhao Dun said to himself: "I will confront the duke right there in the Peach Garden about this matter, and see what excuse he comes up with to justify his outrageous conduct."

His attendants had never seen their master so angry, and so not one of them dared to open his mouth all the way to the Peach Garden. When the carriage arrived there, the gate was locked tight, and there was no attendant to be seen. Zhao Dun was livid. He hammered on the gate with his fists, but all that was heard in return was the sound of stringed instruments wafting in the night breeze. Seeing that Zhao Dun was beside himself with rage, and fearing the consequences if he went as far as to break into the Peach Garden, the attendants sprang forward and pleaded with him: "Your Lordship, it is already late. Please come away. You will have the opportunity to chastise the duke tomorrow at the morning audience."

Seeing that his furious rapping on the gate had brought nobody to open it, Zhao Dun resigned himself to going home for the night. He had scarcely entered his gate when he was informed that Minister Shi Ji had called on him.

Zhao Dun was well acquainted with the minister, who was renowned for his upright character at court. The two of them worked in perfect harmony on matters of state. So, Zhao Dun reasoned, if he has come to see me so late at night, it must be a matter of some importance. "Bring the minister to see me," he ordered.

As soon as the two men were seated, Shi Ji came straight to the point. He gave Zhao Dun a succinct account of the day's atrocity, making a point of how incensed the common people were. "You really must persuade the duke to mend his ways, and devote himself heart and soul to his governmental duties," he urged. Zhao Dun, did not reply for some time, but sat deep in thought. He was fully aware that getting Duke Ling to give up his life of dissipation would be an enormously difficult task. He finally breathed a long sigh, and said, "I should have known long ago that a day like this would come!" And before his eyes floated a scene from twenty years ago.

It had been a dark and stormy afternoon. Zhao Dun and other senior ministers were suddenly summoned to the palace, where Duke Xiang lay on his deathbed. The duke raised his eyelids with a great effort and gasped weakly: "Following in the proud footsteps of my father, I defeated the Rong and Di barbarians time after time, and chastised the powerful State of Qin, never slackening in my zeal. But there is no prevailing against the will of Heaven, and now I am about to depart this life. The crown prince, Yi Gao (Duke Ling), is but a babe in arms; he is only two years old. My ministers, you must do your utmost to help him rule. Keep the peace with our neighbors, and preserve Jin's position as leader of the alliance of states. If you fail to do so, I will never be able to close my eyes when I have descended to the netherworld." With this, Duke Xiang relaxed his grip on this life, and died.

That had been a time of turmoil for Jin. Two wars had been fought, with the State of Qin and the Rong and Di barbarians, respectively. Tension and hostility mounted daily, and the ministers over and over again discussed the problem of their leaderless state. Most of them were for putting a prince of mature years on the throne to be a focus of the people's loyalty and ensure overall stability. Some recommended Prince Yong, who at that time resided in the State of Qin; others were in favor of Prince Yue, who was living in the State of Chen. The result was endless bickering.

At last, Minister Shi Ji said, "The ancients had a saying: 'Elevate the good, and stability results; respect the elders, and things go smoothly; serve one's parents, and filial piety prevails; but for safety, maintain old ties of friendship.' Prince Yong is noble-minded, experienced and prudent. He is sure to win the hearts of the people. Besides, he is a kinsman of the ruler of Qin. By making him our duke, we will get rid of a lot of the enmity that has built up between our two states. That would be killing two birds with one stone. Now, as for Prince Yue, he resides at the court of Chen, which is a weak state and comparatively distant. He would not hold the reins of power long here, I fear."

Zhao Dun, as the most powerful minister, was in a quandary. On the one hand, he had to admit that what Shi Ji said made sense; but on the other, to appoint Prince Yong the new duke would be to betray the final wish of the late Duke Xiang that the infant prince rule. In the end, he sent envoys to Qin to invite Prince Yong to return and take the throne, at the same time making arrangements for the funeral of the late duke. On her way back from the funeral, Duke Xiang's widow, Mu Ying, with the young Yi Gao in her arms, confronted Zhao Dun. "What offense did the late duke commit?" she demanded. "And, what is more, what crime is this innocent babe, his lawful heir-apparent born of his proper wife, guilty of, that you should cast aside the royal flesh and blood, and seek a stranger in a foreign land to be the ruler of Jin?"

Zhao Dun replied, "This is a high matter of state. It is not my personal whim."

But Mu Ying was not to be put off so easily. After that, every morning when the court assembled she would appear, with the infant heir-apparent in her arms, and throw tearful tantrums. "This is the late duke's own son," she would shriek at the ministers. "Why have you ridden roughshod over him and chosen that Prince Yong to be the ruler of Jin in his place?" Her ranting put the court officials completely out of countenance. What was worse, after court was dismissed, she would hasten to Zhao Dun's mansion, and there she would remind the chief minister that her late husband, on his deathbed, had entrusted his son to Zhao. "If you put someone else on the throne, with the late duke's words still echoing in your ears and his corpse not yet cold, you will commit a grave act of betrayal. In that case, I and my child will have no recourse but to seek death!"

She said this with a conviction that made it seem that she was bent on self-destruction. This provided ammunition for those officials who had been in favor of enthroning Yi Gao in the first place, and they gave Zhao Dun no peace thereafter. One day, Mu Ying appeared before the harassed Zhao with her hair disheveled. Her eyes filled with venom, she screeched, "Zhao Dun, make no mistake about it. Until the new duke is installed, I, as the late duke's widow, have the power to dismiss you from office."

Zhao Dun trembled upon hearing this. If this were to happen, he fretted, not only would his father's achievements come to naught, but disaster would come upon his entire family, and the State of Jin would be plunged into chaos. He had no choice but to clench his teeth in resignation and make the decision to put Yi Gao on the throne. At the same time, he dispatched a messenger to recall the mission he had already sent to Qin to invite Prince Yong to take the throne of Jin. In the meantime, he made arrangements for a lavish enthronement ceremony for Yi Gao. However, no sooner was all this completed than a commander arrived from the frontier to announce that the State of Qin had sent an armed force to escort Prince Yong to Jin. This force had already reached a place called Hexia.

Zhao Dun was thrown into a panic. He thought to himself: "With Prince Yong as the ruler of Jin, our state would have friendly relations with Qin. If not, Qin will be our enemy. But Yi Gao is already seated on the throne, and it's too late to offer an apology to Qin. In fact, Qin would probably not only refuse to forgive us, but would use this as an excuse for mounting a military campaign against Jin. Truly, once one has mounted the tiger, one dare not alight!" Arriving at this point, Zhao Dun realized that the only way out of his dilemma was to launch a pre-emptive strike at Qin. He lost no time mobilizing the army against the advancing Qin troops.

The Qin ruler, meanwhile, Duke Kang, had been delighted at the news of Jin's invitation to Prince Yong. Rubbing his hands with delight, he had declared, "On two previous occasions the rulers of Jin have come from Qin. This time, Jin's ruler will also come from Qin!" Thereupon, he sent the Central Army, under Bai Yibing, to escort Prince Yong as far as Hexia, where it set up camp and waited for the expected Jin envoys.

But instead of envoys coming to welcome Prince Yong, the Jin army was advancing to make a surprise attack on the Qin forces. Arriving in the vicinity of Hexia, under cover of darkness the Jin troops sharpened their weapons, fed their horses, had one last meal, and hastened to attack in complete silence so that no voice should alert the enemy. In the dead of night, just as the glittering stars of the Milky Way were slipping westward, a command rang out, drums and horns raised a frightful din, and the whole of the Jin army dashed headlong at the completely unprepared and sleeping Qin camp, howling their war cries. Bedlam erupted among the Qin troops. With time to neither saddle their horses nor snatch up arms, their troops scurried around in a panic, pursued by the ferocious Jin attackers who hacked them down relentlessly. Prince Yong perished in the carnage, and Commander Bai Yibing just managed to escape with his life. Utterly routed, the remnants of the Qin forces limped homeward as best they could.

This victory for Jin, while it removed the immediate danger from Qin, sowed the tragic seed of future chronic hostilities between the two states. But more of this later.

In the meantime, ever since he had installed Yi Gao as the ruler of Jin, Zhao Dun had devoted himself to assisting the new duke with the utmost devotion night and day. But Duke Ling did not turn out like a head of state should. He was interested only in feasting and entertainment, paying no heed to matters of government. There was little that Zhao Dun could do about this state of affairs: on the one hand, he was afraid that if he admonished the duke, other ministers would speak ill of him to curry favor with the latter, and on the other, he feared that the rulers of other states would take advantage of internal discord in Jin to attack. All he could do was to try to handle all matters of state himself, which he found a great strain. As the years went by, Duke Ling's behavior became more and more outrageous; the government grew chaotic, and the plight of the common people grew more desperate by the day. All Zhao Dun's attempts at advice and censure fell on deaf ears, and he himself, weary and heartsick, from time to time found himself on the brink of despair...

Disturbed by Zhao Dun's repeated sighs, Minister Shi Ji offered his friend a word of advice: "The duke's conduct is sure to bring disaster on our heads. As the prime minister, you have worked hard all your life. Now, in your later years, it is difficult for you to right these calamitous wrongs. Surely this is the time for you to make a bold decision to choose honorable retirement. That way, you would preserve the dignity of your family. Moreover, the duke is of an erratic temperament; I am afraid he may be inclined to do you some harm. And that is not all. That fellow Tu'an Gu is a wily rascal, and although at the moment he himself may be powerless to act against you, he has the duke's ear. There is no way you can influence the duke in these circumstances, and if Tu'an Gu gains the upper hand at court, do you expect that he will tolerate the presence of a loyal and upright prime minister like yourself?"

These words caused a shiver to run down Zhao Dun's spine. He mused: "All because I wavered on one occasion twenty years ago, when I made the mistake of putting Duke Ling on the throne, this present calamity has descended on the State of Jin and its people." A distressing sense of remorse clouded his mind, but he stiffened his back, and said, "Well, now that things have come to this pass, they can't get any worse. I have brought my troubles on myself, and I am determined to devote what few years I have left to serving my country, come what may!" As he said this, he could not hold back the tears that trickled from his eyes.

The sight of Duke Ling idling and carousing was like a knife twisting in the heart of the honest Shi Ji. He agonized over the fate of Jin. For Tu'an Gu and his cronies, Shi Ji felt a deep and burning enmity. But, as a low-ranking official, his words carried little weight, and his frequent admonitions had no more effect on Duke Ling than the autumn breeze murmuring in his ears. Day after day, Shi Ji gazed on his fellow officials with cold and disdainful eyes. He saw some senior ministers afraid to speak out against abuses, and others cynically safeguarding their own positions with mild words and diplomatic manners. Only Zhao Dun preserved his integrity, daring to rebuke the fatuous ruler, who held him in some awe, to his face. As soon as he had heard of the duke's shooting at the people, egged on by Tu'an Gu, Shi Ji was outraged. In a state of extreme agitation and distress, he sought out Zhao Dun to discuss a joint censure of Duke Ling. Now, seeing that Zhao Dun was preparing for a showdown with the duke for the sake of the state, heedless of his own safety, Shi Ji too gave way to tears.

And so it was that in the dead of night, hands clasped and gazing into each other's eyes, the two of them poured their hearts out to each other.

Zhao Dun muttered in distress: "What the duke has done this time is a heinous crime that even a dyed-in-the-wool tyrant would flinch from. If such atrocities are allowed to continue, how can the State of Jin escape its ruin?"

His friend was more circumspect. "It seems to me," he said, "that although the duke is wild and outrageous, his follies are more those of youth and inexperience. An old saying goes: 'He who touches rouge will be stained red, and he who touches ink will be stained black.' If only we can keep the duke away from wicked people like Tu'an Gu and his cronies, and get him to turn over a new leaf, there may be hope for Jin yet."

Zhao Dun pondered these words, and had to admit to himself that there was reason in them. When he reflected on how he had rushed to the Peach Garden and hammered on the gate in a frenzy, it seemed to him that he had been acting somewhat rashly. He sighed, and with a bitter smile said, "There is sense in what you say. From now on we must act in concert. We must urge the duke to associate only with worthy officials, and avoid the scheming courtiers — and then perhaps the affairs of our state may take a turn for the better."

The rhythmical cadence of a night watchman's clapper disturbed their deliberations. Dawn was not far off, and so they parted to refresh their spirits with sleep for a short while before attending court, at which they were to bring the duke to book.

At first light, all the court officials lined up in two rows before the throne, military functionaries on the left, civilian ones on the right. After a while, Duke Ling sauntered in, together with a flock of attendants and sycophants. As soon as he had plumped himself down on the throne, and before any of the officials could present a memorial, he dismissed the court with a wave of his hand. "I am not feeling my best today," he drawled. "If any of you has any business to bring to my attention, keep it for some other time." He then rose, and scurried out of the throne room.

The officials gazed at each other, speechless. Shaking their heads and sighing, they dispersed and went their ways. Zhao Dun and Shi Ji, who had gone virtually without sleep the whole night, were dismayed that they would not have a chance to remonstrate with the duke after all. Distressed, they left the palace and wandered to a secluded pavilion to discuss what to do next. But before they had a chance to say anything, they spotted two palace servants sneaking out of a side door of the palace, carrying a large bamboo basket. As they proceeded, their eyes looked carefully right and left. Zhao Dun's suspicions were immediately roused, and he commanded the pair to halt. "Hey, what are you two up to?" he demanded. "And what have you got in that basket?"

The servants pretended not to hear, and attempted to scurry off round a corner. But both Zhao Dun and Shi Ji barred their way. The other two had no choice but to stop and put the basket on the ground.

Upon Zhao Dun's asking them again what was in the basket, the servants turned ghastly pale and gave no answer. Eventually, one of them stammered, "We dare not say, Your Honor. Please deign to look yourself."

Zhao Dun gazed at the basket. There was nothing unusual about it from the outside; it was an ordinary bamboo basket covered with cabbage leaves. But when he lifted the leaves, he was appalled to find that the basket contained the bloody pieces of a dismembered corpse. Recoiling in horror, he questioned the servants: "Who was this man, and who chopped him up like this?"

The servants dithered, mumbled and pretended not to know anything about the affair, until Zhao Dun, in a towering rage, threatened to have both their heads lopped off. Only then did the truth come out.

The previous evening, the guards in the eastern quarter of the capital had noticed the crowds of people who had gathered in the road waiting to pour out their complaints about the duke's devilish target practice to Zhao Dun on his return from encouraging the farmers. The news was straightaway brought to Duke Ling, in the midst of his usual debauch in the Peach Garden. Befuddled as he was, the duke knew quite well that Zhao Dun would lose no time in condemning him to his face right there in the Peach Garden. He was rescued from his dilemma by Tu'an Gu, who whispered in his ear advising him to have the gates of the Peach Garden locked, and all visitors barred from entry. "Otherwise, he could spoil our fun, Your Majesty," Tu'an Gu explained blandly. The duke gave the necessary orders without delay. The result, as we have see, was that Zhao Dun knocked on the gate in vain, and had to return home defeated for the time being. But somehow, the mood of the evening had been spoiled for Duke Ling. He was somewhat in awe of his senior minister, and he knew well that he faced censure the next morning, when Zhao Dun would no doubt come stalking into the court to denounce his evil deed of that day. Before long, he called a halt to the revels, and with his entourage returned in a sullen mood to the palace. In the meantime, Tu'an Gu sent an urgent message to the palace kitchen to prepare the duke's usual late-night snack.

Now Duke Ling was inordinately fond of bear's paws, a gourmet dish, and this was what the palace chef was used to preparing for him every evening. However, on this occasion, as the duke had decided to go home early, the bear's paws were not properly cooked by the time he arrived. The royal waiter, trembling with fear, had no choice but to rush the dish to the duke just as it was.

Duke Ling was already in a foul mood when he raised a morsel of bear's paw to his lips, but when after chewing it a couple of times he found that it had the taste and consistency of cowhide, he flew into a towering rage. Flinging his elegant ivory chopsticks to the ground, he thundered at the cook, who was in attendance: "You insolent villain of a cook! How many heads have you got that you can risk having one chopped off for serving your sovereign uncooked bear's paws?"

The cook was beside himself with fear, and his knees knocked like clappers. He threw himself full length at the duke's feet, where he remained prostrate with his forehead beating the floor ceaselessly. At this, the duke became even more incensed. Grabbing the first missile that came to hand, which happened to be a heavy brass flagon, he flung at the unfortunate's cook's head. Blood and brains spurted from the smashed skull, and the cook died instantly. The horrified attendants stared, as speechless as wooden chickens. But the duke's wrath had not subsided yet. He drew his sword, and proceeded to chop the corpse of the cook up into little pieces. Then he stalked off to his bedchamber, grunting with satisfaction.

As soon as he had disappeared, Tu'an Gu ordered the others: "Wait until after the morning's court has been dismissed, and there is no one around. Then take the remains of the body and bury them in some obscure place. Don't say a word to a soul about this. Any slipups, and you'll pay for it with your lives!"

On hearing the servants' story, Zhao Dun was filled with anger. Stamping his foot, he cried, "This wicked ruler, who treats human life as if it were no more than straw, will be the ruin of our state! I fear its demise is imminent. We must both go and take this tyrant to task. If he rebuffs us, we must commit suicide right there in the palace."

Shi Ji shook his head. "May I venture to say that this is not a suitable course of action? If the duke refuses to listen to us, there will be nobody else ready to admonish him. I think it would be better if I tackled him first, and then, if the duke remains adamant, you can then bring pressure to bear on him. Perhaps that would be better?"

Zhao Dun realized that the other's plan was a good one, so he let him enter the palace first, while he himself waited outside.

When a servant announced that Shi Ji requested an audience, Duke Ling knew quite well on what errand Shi Ji had come. But there was no offending off this visitor, so he sighed and ordered that Shi Ji be shown in. Shi Ji paced the long hall up to the throne, under the eye of the duke the whole time. He knelt, kowtowed the customary number of times, and began, "Your Majesty?" But before he had a chance to continue, the duke, determined not to listen to a tiresome complaint, interrupted him: "You can save your breath, Minister. I know perfectly well that I am at fault. From now on, I have turned over a new leaf." With this, he turned to his attendants and ordered that the cook be given a solemn funeral, to appease his relatives.

Hearing this, Shi Ji hastily kowtowed, and said, "Who is without fault, sire? But there is nothing more laudable than correcting one's transgressions. If Your Majesty really does turn over a new leaf, the state will surely prosper. Then, how happy will we your servants be!"

Thereupon he withdrew, and reported all that had happened to Zhao Dun, who commented, "If the duke is resolved to become a reformed character, this should be reflected in his actions from now on."

As they were talking, there arose a hubbub at the doorway of the palace, as orders were given for a carriage to be got ready to take Duke Ling to the Peach Garden. Zhao Dun's face stiffened with indignation. "A fine sort of repentance," he cried, "to be so soon plunging into frivolity once more!" Without more ado, he mounted his own carriage, and hurried off to the Peach Garden. He was waiting at the gate of the pleasure ground, determined to give the duke a good talking to, when the royal party arrived.

The duke, meanwhile, was feeling very pleased with himself for having managed to get rid of Shi Ji with a shallow excuse, and was looking forward to a day of carefree pleasure with a bevy of beauties from his harem, when he perceived the stony-face Zhao Dun barring his way to the Peach Garden. There was nothing for it but to confront his accuser, and so, with a sickly grin, he said, "I have no business today, Minister, so I did not summon you. Perhaps you would care to join me in a little relaxation?"

Zhao Dun kowtowed before the duke's carriage. "Your unworthy servant," he said, "ventures to have something to inform you of, Your Majesty. I hope you will have the magnanimity to indulge me. I have heard that a virtuous ruler uses music to gladden the hearts of the people, while a ruler who lacks virtue uses music only to gladden his own heart. From ancient times, it has been the practice of rulers to take their pleasure either within the palace with their courtesans and servants or abroad hunting and sightseeing. Never has it been heard that an upright ruler kills people for sport. Such atrocities as setting savage mastiffs on or shooting harmless passers-by and dismembering a cook for some trifling misdemeanor are unheard of even from unrighteous rulers. But Your Majesty has been guilty of all these things! Human life is a gift from Heaven. If you spill blood so promiscuously the common people will rebel and the other feudal lords will invade our state, and then the disasters attendant upon the fall of the tyrants Jie of the Xia Dynasty and Zhou of the Shang Dynasty will befall Jin! It is because your humble servant cannot bear to sit by and watch the ruin of our country that I dare to risk death by speaking so bluntly. I beseech Your Majesty to turn your carriage around, return to the court and mend your ways by devoting yourself to affairs of state. No more frittering away day after day in petty pleasure-seeking, and no more taking of innocent lives! Only then will Jin be pulled back from the brink of disaster, and Your Majesty follow in the footsteps of the sage kings Yao and Shun. At such a time would I die without regret." Having said this, he kept kneeling in front of the duke's carriage.

Duke Ling, although he was muddle-headed and tyrannical, still had a spark of shrewdness left in him. Besides, he held Zhao Dun somewhat in awe. So when the latter reminded him of righteousness, a sliver of remorse touched his heart. But his heart was set on a day of carousing and cavorting, and nothing was further from his mind than court business. With a dismissive wave of a sleeve, he said, "Minister, you go back first, and leave me to one more day of relaxation. I promise you that after that I will heed your advice."

The sight of the duke, apparently in a state of abject contrition and whimpering like a child, dispelled the towering rage that had been bursting inside Zhao Dun's breast. The prime minister did not know whether to laugh or to frown. He felt like a negligent father facing his wayward son; indignation and affection, shame and regret struggled within him. Then, remembering his authority, he stood in front of the gate to the Peach Garden, resolutely barring the way for the duke.

Tu'an Gu had always resented the power that Zhao Dun wielded, his way of speaking out fearlessly, and especially that fact that he had many times denounced Tu'an Gu as a petty and evil man. He had long awaited an opportunity to trap the prime minister, but up until now none had presented itself. Today, however, perceiving that Zhao Dun had put Duke Ling in an embarrassing situation, Tu'an Gu butted in with insinuating words: "I am sure Your Honor has the best of intentions in blocking the gate and remonstrating with the duke. But you must take cognizance of our ruler's position. Here His Majesty is, already at the gate to the Peach Garden; if he were to heed your words, and turn back, how could he not become a laughing-stock among the rulers of the other states? Besides, your own duty to assist His Majesty to govern must occupy you with weighty matters of state. How is it that you allow yourself to be vexed over such a trifle as this?"

These words angered Zhao Dun. Drawing himself up to his full height and glaring at Tu'an Gu, he said, "The duke is young and inexperienced. He fritters away his time in idle pleasures. We, his ministers, have the duty guide him on the path of righteous conduct, not encourage him in his frivolity with base flattery! Do you not realize that this trifle, as you call it, is the sort of thing that could lead to the very downfall of our state?"

At this, Tu'an Gu gave a mirthless smile. "Oh, I see. So the prime minister is suggesting that His Majesty consult him about every little thing he wishes to do, I suppose! It is my humble opinion that the prime minister should calm down for the time being, and unblock the gateway. If the prime minister has any matter to bring up with His Majesty, it will surely not be too late to do so at tomorrow morning's court audience, will it?"

So saying, Tu'an Gu turned and gave Duke Ling a sly glance. This put new heart into the duke, who hastily interjected, "Yes, yes. That's right. I will summon you first thing tomorrow, Prime Minister!"

Zhao Dun had no choice but to stand aside and allow the duke and his entourage to enter the Peach Garden. His heart was full of rage and bitterness. As he glared at the retreating back of Tu'an Gu, he ground his teeth, and muttered to himself: "A blockhead of a ruler, and a doomed country — all because of that rascally official!" A surge of hatred filled his heart.

CHAPTER TWO

Chu Ni Dashes His Brains Out

WITH THE CONNIVANCE of Tu'an Gu, Duke Ling had managed to get back into the Peach Garden for another session of merrymaking. But Zhao Dun's intervention had dashed all his hopes of enjoying himself. The duke's temper became very sour indeed, until everything he looked at became loathsome to him. He stepped into garden, where the peaches and apricots were ripe in abundance, and the branches of the poplar and willow trees brushed the ground, as always. But this pleasant sight could not dispel the fury burning in the duke's breast. He drew his sword and began to slash savagely at the grass and trees beside the path, leaving heaps of red and green ruin to mark his passage. Tu'an Gu at his side fanned the flames of the duke's anguish by saying, "Your Highness, please curb your wrath. If the prime minister should hear of this he would be sure to upbraid you for it."

These words, as they were meant to, goaded the duke into a paroxysm of fury, as they reminded him of how Zhao Dun had defied him. Just at that moment the duke and his retinue happened to arrive at a rockery beside a pond. The craggy stones were set off by fantastic plants and trailing creepers, some dangling from the top, and others wrapped around the foot of the ornamental stones, in a wispy fragrant green veil. The delicate artistry of the rockery did not please the duke's jaundiced eye, however. "What idiot put that pile together?" he bawled. "Green leaves have always, since time immemorial, been used to set off red flowers. How is it that this thing has green creepers and vines straggling all over it? Bring that damned gardener here to me at once!"

With glee, Tu'an Gu perceived that his carefully timed words had had the desired effect. He lost no time sending soldiers to fetch the gardener, who was given a sound beating with clubs on the spot and thrown into the bushes, no one caring whether he was dead or alive. The duke let out a melancholy sigh. In truth he was beginning to feel somewhat better after this, and a trace of a smile could be detected on his face.

When the Peach Garden had been constructed, a channel had been chiseled to let in water, which gathered in a lotus pond in the southeast corner. In the height of summer, the pond was covered with bright red and green lotuses, a most delightful sight. The banks of the pond were lined with poplar, willow and locust trees, affording a deep and welcome shade from the sun. Within this arbor was a pavilion, with flying eaves and soaring corners. Inside were placed bamboo couches for the duke and his harem to sport upon. It was known as the "Pavilion of Joy". Now mid-spring was upon the place, and bright red fallen leaves floated upon the clear waters together with emerald lotuses. Fishes of many hues darted and glided in the ripples, now appearing, now vanishing. Duke Ling paced heavily to the edge of the pond. He summoned the courtesans he had brought with him, and began to embrace and fondle one and then another. In the midst of his lascivious slobbering and groping, the duke suddenly noticed a pair of mandarin ducks nestling up to and feeding each other by the margin of the pond. An idea for a new type of amusement arose into his mind, and he chortled, "I think I'd like to have a bath with you, my dears, just like these mandarin ducks." Everyone was startled to hear this, especially Tu'an Gu. He hastened to advise the duke against such foolishness: "Your Majesty should not risk your precious health," he begged. "The pond water is far too chilly for Your Majesty's delicate constitution. Why not order one of your servants and a palace maid to have a bath together instead, and you can watch them from the bank. Wouldn't that be much more interesting?"

The duke was pleased with this suggestion. "All right," he said, "it shall be as you say."

Duke Ling's lecherous nature knew no bounds, and he kept hundreds of courtesans for his own exclusive pleasure. One of these was particularly delicate and charming beauty, with skin as soft and white as snow. By nature she was bewitchingly charming as a fox, and the infatuated duke's nickname for her was "Fox Lady." Her amorous skills kept the duke in raptures. Now he ordered her and one of his close courtiers to imitate the mandarin ducks. The man knew well his master's evil nature, and dared not refuse to engage in this charade. So he doffed his garments and entered the water. But Fox Lady, pinning her hopes on the duke's previous affection for her, was loath to undress, anxious to escape the indignity. But a gruff command from the duke dashed any hope she had on that score. At once, his attendants rushed forward, howling like animals, stripped Fox Lady naked and hurled her into the pond. As she struggled in the water, she was grasped tightly by the courtier, and at the duke's direction the two were forced to imitate all the amorous cavorting of a pair of mandarin ducks. This sight caused Duke Ling extraordinary delight. He applauded heartily, and called out, "That's right, you're as good as a real pair of mandarin ducks!"

Although it was spring, the water in the pond was quite cold, and before the pair had been in it for half an hour, they were chilled to the marrow and quite purple in color, and were shivering from head to foot. But the duke showed no sign of tiring of the spectacle. Clapping his hands and laughing, he said, "You've shown me a proper spectacle today. I'll give you two a big reward tomorrow."

But Fox Lady could stand the cold no longer. "I'm freezing to death," she cried, and pushing away her companion, she struggled for the shore. But as soon as she placed her hands on the stone path surrounding the pond, Duke Ling's mood suddenly turned nasty, "Why, you ungrateful slut!" he cried. With that, and before anyone could stop him, the duke raised his sword and swung it down savagely, cleanly severing at a stroke the exquisite lily-white hands placed on the bank. Fox Lady slipped back into the pond, struggling in desperation as an ominous red stain darkened the limpid water.

The watchers on the bank were frozen with horror. One of the palace ladies, who had been jealous of the way Fox Lady had used her coquettish wiles to win the duke's favor, could not suppress a scream when she witnessed this brutality, and was poised for flight when the duke whirled round upon her.

"Oh, so you want to run away, do you, you bitch?" he snarled. And, without more ado, he ordered his bodyguards to chop off the unfortunate girl's legs.

This was done, following which a shocked silence fell upon the whole company on the margin of the pond, broken only by the moans of the two dismembered girls as they thrashed about in agony. The duke stretched lazily. "That's enough fun for one day," he yawned. "Now, up to the pavilion for some wine!"

Leaving the dying girls, the assemblage retired with the duke to the Crimson Cloud Tower. Watching them with glazed eyes was the courtier who had played the part of a male mandarin duck, his body rigid with cold. As the duke's retinue disappeared from view, so did he — into his watery grave. Three lives had been snuffed out in an instant, all because of a whim of the evil Duke Ling.

The feasting and merriment in the Crimson Cloud Tower continued until it was time for the lamps to be lit. Duke Ling and Tu'an Gu exchanged toast after toast. Harem girls snuggled up to the duke, giggling and teasing. But the shadow of the frightful deeds of that morning hung over the rest of the duke's attendants, and they stood round in silence, hardly even daring to breath heavily. Outside the tower, the guards too stood like statues, too oppressed with horror to utter a sound, so that the hubbub in the tower was strangely pervaded with a hush redolent of death.

Duke Ling's face flushed with wine, began to feel light-headed. There was a twinge of disquiet in his mind. Then rage started to bubble up inside him when he remembered the way that Zhao Dun had upbraided him over the death of the cook. But the thought of how powerful his prime minister was made him feel uneasy. Nonplussed, he glanced at Tu'an Gu, and immediately perceived that his crony knew what he was thinking.

Tu'an Gu was the eldest grandson of Tu'an Yi, a general who had served Duke Hui of the State of Jin. Tu'an Yi was a man of immense strength and courage and during a campaign against the State of Qin, Tu'an Yi wielded a huge iron halberd in a duel with the renowned Qin general Bai Yibing. The contest was a close one, as the earth rocked and the heavens resounded to the clash of the two champions. Tu'an Yi was struck by a treacherous arrow, and died on the spot. The Qin army, however, was defeated, and fled taking the sorely wounded Bai Yibing with it. Safe in his home state, Bai vomited gallons of blood, and only recovered from his ordeal half a year later. But ever afterwards, whenever the name of Tu'an Yi was mentioned, he turned pale and trembled.

Moved by Tu'an Yi's valor and his sacrifice in laying down his life for his country, Duke Hui bestowed lavish honors on his family, and made his son Tu'an Kui lord of a populous and productive estate. By the time Tu'an Gu was born, the Tu'an family was at the height of its prosperity. Tu'an Gu was also robust, and followed in the family tradition of studying the 18 martial arts. However, by nature he was degenerate, and perverted the qualities of heroism, loyalty and devotion that he had inherited from his forebears into treachery, viciousness and evil intent. With the demise in succession of Jin's senior ministers Luan Zhi, Xian Qieju, Xu Chen and Zhao Shuai, Tu'an Gu's star gradually rose at court. He had spent the previous several years worming his way into the good graces of Duke Ling, until he could get the latter to do anything he wanted. As he came to realize how simple-minded the duke was, Tu'an Gu began to covet the throne for himself, but as he perceived that the time was not yet ripe, he refrained from acting on his ambition. As he mulled his plan of action, he came to recognize that Zhao Dun was the main stumbling block to his schemes, and decided that somehow the prime minister must be removed. But, unfortunately the good-for-nothing duke feared Zhao Dun, and seeing how Duke Ling had cowered beneath his prime minister's tongue-lashing that morning, Tu'an Gu was convinced that only by getting rid of Zhao Dun first could he achieve mastery over the duke and then seize control of the whole State of Jin. At this point, he noticed that the duke had paused his cup midway to his lips. Duke Ling seemed to be distracted by something, and Tu'an Gu knew that his mind was troubled because of Zhao Dun. The wily Tu'an Gu then made a show of knitting his brows and sighing.

Duke Ling stared dully at Tu'an Gu's woebegone countenance for a while, and asked, "Minister, why are you not joining in the merriment? Sitting there sighing like that, you're spoiling my fun."

The other replied, "Who wouldn't want to join in the merriment, Your Majesty? It is just that I am worried for your sake, sire. I fear that after tonight there will be no more of these lavish entertainments."

The addle-brained duke fell into his minister's trap straightaway. "What do you mean?" he asked.

"Tomorrow, the prime minister will surely censure you, Your Majesty," Tu'an Gu explained. "Do you think he will ever allow you to come here again to enjoy yourself?"

The duke became crimson with fury, and was on the point of giving vent to his rage, but he thought he had better calm down. Tu'an Gu seized this opportunity to say, "Today he had the audacity to try to prevent Your Majesty entering the Peach Garden, and tomorrow he will try to prevent you leaving the palace. I myself was the object of his censure today, and so I fear that I will no longer dare accompany Your Majesty on pleasure jaunts here."

Hearing this, Duke Ling turned purple with anger. "What on earth do you mean?" he spluttered. "It has always been the rule that ministers obey their rulers' commands. I've never heard of a ruler being under the thumb of one of his ministers. This Zhao Dun keeps popping up and lecturing me. I'll never have any peace while he is alive. Tomorrow I'll have him impeached and his head chopped off! Just see if I don't!"

Perceiving that his master was beside himself with rage, Tu'an

Gu was secretly delighted, but said soberly: "May I be so bold as to venture to say that Your Majesty is being somewhat rash. How can you have Zhao Dun executed openly? Apart from the fact that the common people of Jin would be outraged, Your Majesty's other ministers would never consent to it. Besides, I am afraid that when the rulers of the other states heard of it, they would raise a great cry about 'righting an injustice' and use this as an excuse to invade Jin. Then there would be uproar both at home and abroad. How could Your Majesty enjoy yourself in those circumstances? Besides, the Zhao clan is numerous and powerful, and Zhao Dun himself has served two rulers and acted as regent during Your Majesty's minority. The Zhaos might depose you and set up another ruler."

A pall of gloom descended on the duke as these words sank in. "Then there's nothing I can do about him, it seems," he muttered.

Tu'an Gu saw that the time was ripe for the next step in his scheme. He gave a dry cough, and whispered, "Your Majesty, I have a suggestion. But I don't know whether or not…"

The duke leaned forward eagerly, his eyes popping out as big as bronze bells. "Come on, tell me!" he ordered. "I'm all ears."

For the moment, Tu'an Gu said not a word, but gestured for the officials, servants and palace ladies to leave. Only when the two of them were alone did he bend towards the duke's ear. "Your humble servant has a retainer whose name is Chu Ni. He entered my employ to escape destitution and is devoted to me. If I order him to, he will sneak into Zhao Dun's mansion and assassinate Zhao without anybody being the wiser. Of course, it goes without saying that there will be no way that Your Majesty will be implicated. Would not that be a convenient way of removing this nail from Your Majesty's eye, this thorn from the royal flesh?"

Duke Ling was overjoyed. "I'll leave it all to you, Minister," he burbled. "And when the deed is accomplished, I will see that you are handsomely rewarded."

With the plot in place, the duke mounted his carriage, and returned to his quarters.

That night, Tu'an Gu secretly summoned Chu Ni to him. He told his hireling that Zhao Dun had been plotting against the duke, for he had his eyes on the throne. Chu Ni, who spent all his time on duty in Tu'an Gu's mansion, knew nothing of the goings-on at court or of state affairs, and his master's poisonous words stirred indignation within him against this treacherous prime minister known as Zhao Dun. When Tu'an Gu informed him that it was the will of the emperor himself that Zhao Dun be dealt with, Chu Ni assented readily. "I have for many years been the humble recipient of Your Lordship's bounty," he said. "And I have long been ready to lay down my life for you. I will go straightaway and make that rascally Zhao Dun perish under the knife, and rid our country of a subversive and overweening minister!"

Seeing that his sinister plot was working, Tu'an Gu was delighted, but his faced showed no sign of his pleasure, being clouded with feigned worry. "But Zhao Dun's mansion is closely guarded. There is no assurance that your bold attempt will succeed. Please reconsider."

But Chu Ni retorted indignantly: "My Lord, I am determined to carry out my resolve, both to rid our country of an evil man and to repay you for your kindness. Even if I die in the attempt I will have no regrets."

Tu'an Gu forthwith ordered wine to be brought, and shared three toasts with Chu Ni. The matter being settled, and dawn being not far off, the assassin bowed low to his master and took his leave, a dagger strapped to his waist. Nimbly vaulting walls and scuttling over roofs, in no time at all he gained access to Zhao Dun's mansion.

The prime minister lived alone in secluded courtyard quarters. In the courtyard stood a Chinese scholar tree one hundred years old. It was still vigorous, and its foliage was thick and luxuriant. As a result, it cast deep shadows. Chu Ni knew about this tree, and as soon as he had infiltrated the building, he made straight for the courtyard and hid in the branches of the scholar tree. His plan was to wait for Zhao Dun to emerge, and then perform the dire deed. The sound of a watchman's clapper told him that the night had advanced to the fourth watch. The glimmer of a candle informed him that Zhao Dun had arisen from his bed. Chu Ni slipped to the ground, and tiptoed to the window in which he saw the gleam. Through a chink in the lattice work he saw the figure of an official dressed in court robes seated bolt upright on the bed and holding a ceremonial tablet in both hands before him. A snow-white beard hung from the man's chin, and his eyes were half-closed. His whole bearing was one of solemnity and dignity. Zhao Dun was just as Tu'an Gu had described him. Chu Ni guessed that he had awoken early, and being afraid to fall asleep again and be late for court, he had donned his ceremonial garb, and was sitting there waiting for dawn.

Now Chu Ni was at heart an upright man. It was only because he had been the recipient of Tu'an Gu's bounty that he had listened to his insidious words, and ventured forth on his murderous errand. But, seeing Zhao Dun sitting there in all serenity, it struck Chu Ni that he was the very image of a loyal minister, and unwittingly a feeling of admiration for the old man arose in his heart. He thought to himself: "This does not look like the villainous Zhao Dun who was described to me by my master. It seems that my master and the foolish Duke Ling have deceived me into making an attempt on the life of a loyal minister. That would be the sort of crime that I could not atone for even with one hundred deaths!" He thought for a while, and then concluded, "In my youth I studied the martial arts and the ways of chivalry. I learned to be true to my word and to repay kindnesses. Good faith and loyalty, I learned, were the principles a true man must live by. If I now kill by mistake an upright minister at his post of duty, that would be a treacherous act. On the other hand, if I disobey the order of my sovereign and my master, that would be an act of disloyalty. Either way, I would not be able to face the world again! The only way to save my conscience is to take my own life."

At this point, he made up his mind to commit suicide. But it occurred to him that if he simply did away with himself, Duke Ling and Tu'an Gu would find another way of harming Zhao Dun. So he had to do it in such a way as to put the prime minister on his guard. He thereupon stood a few paces from the tree, and facing Zhao Dun's bedroom, he called out, "My name is Chu Ni. Last night I received an order to assassinate you. However, impressed by your dignity, Prime Minister, I am unwilling to slay such a paragon of loyalty, and am resolved to fulfill my mission with my own death. But I fear that after my death others may come. Prime Minister, beware!"

With that, he bent at the waist and charged at the scholar-tree, splitting his skull and splattering blood and brains over its trunk. Hearing the noise, Zhao Dun and his household rushed out to see what the commotion was, and stared in horror when they beheld the gory scene. Later generations recited a verse about this event:

> *The assassin's blade was turned by Zhao Dun's dignity.*
> *The virtue-embracing killer found salvation at the tree.*

After the first shock of the gruesome discovery had worn off, there was pandemonium in the Zhao mansion. After a while, Ti Miming, Zhao Dun's carriage bodyguard, burst through the panic-stricken throng, and said to his master: "My Lord, it is better that you not attend court this morning, now that this incident has taken place!"

Zhao Dun replied, "Yesterday, the duke specifically charged me to appear before him this morning. It would be a breach of protocol to be absent. Besides, life and death are ordained; there is no need to be alarmed."

So saying, he gave orders for Chu Ni's corpse to be buried beneath the scholar-tree. Shedding tears, Zhao Dun bowed in reverence to the assassin's remains, mounted his carriage and left for the court.

Meanwhile, Duke Ling, confident that the evil scheme he had cooked up with Tu'an Gu had gone as planned, retired for the night and slept like a log. The following morning, as he mounted the throne to receive his ministers, he was in an ebullient mood. He was looking forward to good news. But there, right before him, he saw Zhao Dun safe and sound! In his palpitating heart he cursed Chu Ni, but outwardly he managed to keep a rigid countenance as he allowed the prime minister to approach with his petition.

As soon as Chu Ni had left the previous evening, Tu'an Gu had dispatched a trusted henchman to follow him. When the next day dawned and Chu Ni did not return, he was waiting with a sinking feeling for the spy's report. When the latter came running back with the account of the failed assassination attempt, and the suicide of Chu Ni, Tu'an Gu did not have the nerve to face Duke Ling. He excused himself from attendance at court that morning on the pretext of illness.

The fact that Zhao Dun was unharmed, coupled with Tu'an Gu's absence, sent palpitations of fear through Duke Ling. He became tongue-tied and agitated. Furthermore, someone had reported to Zhao Dun what the duke had done the previous day in the Peach Garden. With his face set as hard as granite, he heard the duke stammer that he should present his remonstrance, and then he said in a voice filled with wrath: "I have heard that Your Majesty cruelly punished a blameless park keeper yesterday in the Peach Garden . You then watched a disgusting display of 'mandarin ducks sporting in the water'. After that, you cut off the hands and legs of two palace ladies, finally causing the deaths of three people. Is all this true?"

Zhao Dun was seething with anger, and his strident voice caused Duke Ling's severe fright. To make things worse, Tu'an Gu was not present, and the other officials just stood there in grim silence. Not a single one stepped forward to defend their sovereign. The duke was at his wits' end. Finally, he jabbered, "I, er, I was just shooting at some birds, when I accidentally hit the park keeper by mistake..."

At this point, his voice faltered, and he made as if to scuttle off to his palace quarters. But Zhao Dun was too quick for him, striding forward and seizing the duke by the collar. The prime minister bowed, and in a voice full of pain said, "What Your Majesty has done even the tyrants Jie of the Xia Dynasty and Zhou of the Shang Dynasty would not have stooped to. If you do not mend your ways, I am afraid that the State of Jin is doomed!"

Duke Ling struggled, but could not free himself from Zhao Dun's iron grip. Panic seized him, and he broke out in a torrent of sweat. A nervous murmuring arose from the assembled officials, aghast at the sight of Zhao Dun remonstrating with the duke at the risk of his life. Filled with awe and admiration, they eventually said, with one voice: "The prime minister is right. Please heed his words, Your Majesty!"

Duke Ling, realizing how deeply he had offended his officials, then tried to wriggle out of his predicament by saying, "I beg you not to say any more. I promise that from now on I will never enter the Peach Garden again. I will lock myself away and ponder my misdeeds. Moreover, I will hand over court affairs to the prime minister to handle."

And so, for the next few days Tu'an Gu kept away from the court, still pretending to be ill, and Duke Ling buried himself deep in his palace quarters. Much relieved, Zhao Dun ordered that the Peach Garden be locked, severely reduced the number of palace ladies, and forbade all performances of music and dancing. At the same time, he purged the ranks of officials, rewarding the honest and punishing the venal. He also stiffened the training of the army and beefed up the state's defenses. All this, together with encouraging the farmers and relieving the common people of their burdens, kept Zhao Dun busy night and day, leaving him little time to eat or sleep. But he was content to see the State of Jin increasing in prosperity before his very eyes.

However, his carriage bodyguard Ti Miming was extremely worried that his master's hectic round of state affairs was undermining his health. Ti was a man of integrity, who was honest and straightforward in his dealings with others. He was intensely loyal to his friends, abhorred wickedness and had tremendous physical strength. He had long served Zhao Dun with the utmost fidelity. In recent years, he had watched with growing disquiet how Tu'an Gu had been becoming ever more outrageous in his plotting, cruel deeds and wild ambition. He perceived that Tu'an Gu posed a danger to his master. He had guessed immediately that Tu'an Gu had been behind the botched assassination attempt, and the latter's skulking at home ever since only confirmed his suspicion.

One day, Zhao Dun came home early from the court. Ti Miming had made up his mind to tell his master of his foreboding, and broached the subject in his usual blunt and honest manner: "My Lord, the duke is dimwitted, but Tu'an Gu is crafty and scheming.

You really must be on your guard!"

Zhao Dun, however, had his mind on governmental matters, and as everything had been going smoothly recently, he paid little heed to the warning. Smiling, he said, "Ti, you worry too much! The duke is determined to become a reformed character. And, as for Tu'an Gu, well, it's difficult to clap with only one hand, you know. So what can he do, eh?"

Ti Miming saw that the preoccupation with affairs of state had pushed all thoughts of his personal safety to the back of the prime minister's mind. He realized that it was incumbent upon himself to keep a high state of vigilance and guard his master at all times.

Meanwhile, Duke Ling, who had been used to living in a giddy whirl of pleasure, was finding life cooped up in his silent chambers with only his thoughts for company unbearably tedious. Some ten days had passed, and he was on the brink of collapse. Needless to say, his crony Tu'an Gu never showed his face; the only people he saw were Zhao Dun and the rest of his court officials, who came round every day preaching at him to forsake the company of petty men and eschew pleasure. He often thought of going out to relieve his boredom, but he never dared to open his mouth on the subject.

It was the height of the summer. The flowers were blooming and the grass formed a thick carpet in the duke's private courtyard. Flocks of orioles flitted here and there. After breakfast one morning, the duke dismissed all his attendants and sat listless and alone in the Pavilion of Celestial Attainment in the courtyard. Before long, drowsiness overcame him, and he slumped over the table in a doze.

Through a haze he heard a muffled voice: "You have a wicked heart, Your Majesty," it said. "You chopped off your favorite's hands and left her to suffer agonies. You cast her off heedlessly, and now that she is gone she will never return."

An icy blast seem to buffet the duke's face, and his eyes opened wide. He saw Fox Lady standing in front of him, holding out the bleeding stumps of her arms and with tears rolling down her cheeks. Duke Ling looked closely at her. Her fine eyebrows, sparkling eyes and peach-like complexion were even more bewitching than ever. But her face wore an expression of the deepest sorrow, and her stare was full of tragedy and hatred. Terrified at this apparition, the duke croaked, "But, aren't you dead? How did you come here, to this place?" Fox Lady wailed, "I died an undeserved death, and so cannot rest. I have come to condemn you." So saying, she thrust the gory stumps of her arms forward and threw herself at the duke. The latter shrieked in horror ... and woke up bathed in cold sweat. He glanced around, and saw that the sun was still shining as brightly as ever. It had been a bad dream, that was all. But the memory of it lingered, and sent icy shivers all over his body. After sitting staring gloomily into space for a long time, Duke Ling suddenly felt that he couldn't stand his seclusion any longer. Come what may, he had to get out of this dreadful place. He sent for Tu'an Gu.

Ever since the failure of his scheme to assassinate Zhao Dun, Tu'an Gu had been brooding over more sinister schemes. Under the pretext of illness, he had been lying low at home and watching how the situation developed. When he heard that Duke Ling had succumbed to pressure from Zhao Dun to turn over a new leaf, and that Shi Ji and the other officials were backing Zhao Dun in his efforts to put the government in order, he realized that if this continued, his dream of seizing the throne for himself would never be a reality. Moreover, he might be hard pressed to preserve his own life!

So when the summons came from the duke, he leaped with joy, ordered his carriage and dashed off to the palace. He congratulated himself on slipping away without being seen.

Seeing Tu'an Gu again, Duke Ling was as delighted as if he had been visited by an auspicious phoenix bringing good tidings. "My dear minister," he cried, "I've been dying of boredom since you have been absent at court."

While Tu'an Gu was pouring out profuse greetings to the duke, he was slyly taking stock of the other's countenance. He was struck by how lonely and dispirited the duke looked, and guessed that this was the result of the pleasure-loving duke's enforced stay in his now dreary quarters. Immediately Tu'an Gu had an idea for reversing their misfortunes. He thereupon seated himself and assumed the expression of a loyal servant who is distressed by his master's trouble. "Since ancient times," he said, "what has always made a ruler respected and honored has been his ability to enjoy the full pleasures of life. But now Your Majesty's bells and drums hang mute, singing and dancing are banished, the palace halls stand empty and the Peach Garden is locked. Gloom pervades Your Majesty's quarters. Lacking diversion, and with time lying heavy on your hands, I am afraid that Your Majesty will fall prey to illness!"

This little speech cheered the duke up. Immediately he felt that Tu'an Gu was a man who really understood what his feelings were. He exclaimed, "My dear minister, that is exactly why I summoned you. Quickly, I beg, think of a way out of this dilemma for me!"

Perceiving that his plan was working right from the start, Tu'an Gu hastened to add, "Since Your Majesty is temporarily confined to the palace, why not order a search to be made far and wide to fill these echoing chambers with the most beautiful girls in the land? They can be trained to sing and dance, and you can have a wonderful time!"

Upon hearing this, the duke immediately lost every scruple he had ever had about keeping his promise to Zhao Dun and his other officials. He chortled with glee: "My dear minister, that is exactly what I want! Please take care of the matter right away. Search high and low city girls, country girls, whatever, so long as they're pretty. Bring me as many as you can find. I expect you to report back in three days."

Tu'an Gu had never expected that, just when he thought that he was at the end of his tether, such a glorious road to salvation would suddenly open up. Galvanized with energy and excitement, he lost no time issuing an imperial decree, and mustering men and horses. This retinue scoured the capital, going from door to door and dragging off all the most comely maidens and putting the whole populace in a panic. After a few days, quite a few girls had been seized, but none that were really "fit for a king". To make up the numbers, Tu'an Gu had to force himself to abduct some girls who were only so-so at the most.

On the way back with his prizes to the duke, the despondent Tu'an Gu, together with his retinue, was passing through the eastern suburbs of Jiangyi, when he noticed by the side of the road a particularly stately large courtyard house, over the gate of which were the words, "Happy Abode". It was apparently the residence of some official. Tu'an Gu was filled with curiosity, and he examined the place carefully. He could see that the courtyard was not extensive, but it was exquisitely arranged. A row of large buildings faced the gate, and there were side rooms to the east and west. The main building was discreetly tucked away behind, adorned with crimson balustrades and embroidered curtains, and in front of it was a sequestered courtyard with tall pines and elegant cypresses, grotesque rocks and rare plants. Nestling among them were dainty pavilions. In the main courtyard, young male and female servants flitted back and forth.

After he had taken all this in, Tu'an Gu made inquiries in the neighborhood, and learned that the house had belonged to a rich merchant, who had died three years previously, leaving a widow and an infant son, as well as a huge fortune. The household continued the merchant's lavish lifestyle, and had an army of servants.

Tu'an Gu was particularly surprised to learn that the widow, although she was nearly thirty years old, was surpassingly graceful and charming. Her sparkling eyes, in particular, were supposed to be able to bewitch men at a glance, and so the local rakes had given her the nickname Laiji, meaning "Bedroom Eyes". Widowhood had left Laiji restless. Laiji had a favorite maid, Qiuhong, who was pretty and flirtatious and very sympathetic to her mistress's love intrigues. Qiuhong often acted as a go-between for her mistress. The two of them had a tacit understanding, and often engaged in outside liaisons together.

Learning all this, Tu'an Gu had an idea, and he marched straight up to the gate as if he were a visitor. The gate was opened by a smart and pretty serving maid. As soon as she saw that the caller was a high court official, she hurriedly ushered him and his attendants into the main hall. Before long, Laiji herself came to greet them, wearing her most elaborate gown and adornments. At first glance, Tu'an Gu thought that he had set eyes on an angel who had descended to Earth. He had seen Duke Ling's extensive harem of beauties, but not one of them compared to Laiji in sheer attractiveness. His eyes gazed her in admiration. Laiji dropped a curtsey, and said, "Sir, we are unaccustomed to such distinguished company here in the wilds. Please forgive the lack of proper courtesy."

Her voice was as sweet as the echoing twitter of young orioles in a mountain gorge, or like fledgling swallows returning to their nest; not like a woman approaching middle age at all. The longer Tu'an Gu stared at her, the more difficult he found it to think of something to say. Finally, he blurted, "I ... er ... I was out hunting when I ... er ... I ... you know ... just happened to be passing. I took the liberty to approach your gate in order to rest for a while. Please forgive the intrusion."

Laiji smiles, and said, "You are most welcome, sir, most welcome indeed. You honor my humble home." As she said this, she signaled for her servants to fetch tea.

Tu'an Gu continued, "It is said that the landscape in your mansion's rear courtyard is superb. May one be so bold as to ask to take a glimpse of it?"

Laiji beamed. "I was just about to ask you to be so kind as to deign to view it. Please allow me to change my clothes, and then I will accompany Your Honor."

So saying, she curtseyed once more, and was escorted by her maid into the inner quarters. Shortly afterwards, she returned. She had shed her outer robe, and was clad only in flimsy garments, under which her body gleamed like pear blossoms in the moonlight and plum flowers in the snow. At the sight of her magnificent figure, Tu'an Gu could not help gasping out loud and swallowing painfully. He followed Laiji into the rear courtyard, to a square pond by an artificial hill. The pond was just over three meters across, the water was a limpid blue, and the pebbles on the bottom, among which fish darted, could clearly be seen. Flowers and grass presented a riot of color on the banks, and gave off a heady perfume. Laiji had already arranged for wine and delicacies to be made available in the courtyard to entertain the guests visitors. This was just what Tu'an Gu needed after his tiring days kidnapping maidens, and he sat himself down in the refreshment pavilion, by the pond. Laiji encouraged her guests to drink wine, and after a few rounds she and Tu'an Gu began to lose all sense of decorum. Tu'an Gu stared at Laiji as if spellbound, while she in turn cast coquettish glances at him. It was not long before Tu'an Gu was befuddled with drink as well as besotted with his beautiful companion.

When his head cleared, Tu'an Gu found himself in bed snuggling up to his hostess. Suddenly remembering the mission he had been sent on, he leapt out of bed, flung on his clothes and bade a hasty farewell to Laiji. Whipping his horse furiously, he galloped straight to the palace. There, he described his discovery of the fascinating widow to Duke Ling, taking care, of course, to omit the details of his own sampling of Laiji's charms.

The duke was doubtful. "But, isn't she a bit old?" he inquired. "I mean, she must be fading by this time, mustn't she? As they say, 'like a peach blossom in late spring,' hmm?"

"I have gazed on her beauty with my very own eyes, Your Majesty," Tu'an Gu rejoined. "It is truly beyond description. Not only that, Your Majesty; they say that her skill at the arts of the boudoir would make a man think that she was an 18-year-old virgin!"

Duke Ling beamed. "Well, then, bring her to me, quickly!" he cried.

But Tu'an Gu balked at this. "Ah, well, Your Majesty," he said, hesitatingly. "Bringing her here would be easy enough. It's just that I am afraid of what the prime minister might say. You know that he is dead set against Your Majesty enjoying himself!"

This mention of Zhao Dun punctured Duke Ling's ebullience, and he looked crestfallen. Tu'an Gu, however, had an ace up his sleeve. "The Happy Abode is located outside the capital, sire," he explained. "And although it can't compare with the Peach Garden, it is quite scenic. Now, recently, the prime minister has been preoccupied with government affairs, and if Your Majesty were to say that you has not been feeling well of late, and wishes to partake of the fresh country air. I am sure that the prime minister will not object. You can go straight to the Happy Abode and have a rendezvous with the ravishing widow. Isn't that the best way to do it?"

This suggestion sent Duke Ling into raptures. He clasped his hands and explained, "What a brilliant idea! Tomorrow, we'll go together to the Happy Abode. How about that?" As he said this, he grinned with an almost simian glee.

And so, the next day, according to plan, at the morning audience the duke complained to Zhao Dun of feeling somewhat under the weather of late. He added that he felt like taking a short jaunt out to the suburbs to get a breath of fresh air, with Tu'an Gu as his escort. Neither Zhao Dun nor any of the other court officials suspected what the wily duke really had in mind, so the pair set off without more ado.

The whole way, Duke Ling never stopped looking about him, fidgeting and shuffling his feet in agitation and excitement. He was as light-headed as a bird that has just been let out of its cage or a fish taken from a pond and returned to the river.

When they arrived at the Happy Abode, and Laiji was informed that the duke himself had come calling, she gushed with effusions of welcome. Duke Ling, for his part, was transported with delight when he saw that Tu'an Gu had not exaggerated the lady's appeal. Unlike his companion, the duke was not a person to beat about the bush. Utterly entranced, he jabbered, "Madame, as I gaze upon your beauty, the 3,000 damsels in my harem have suddenly become as repulsive to me!"

During the subsequent welcoming banquet, Laiji plied the duke with wine. The potent brew quickly went to the duke's head, and it was not long before he was sitting rigid in a drunken daze. Tu'an Gu thereupon discreetly slipped away, and Laiji went to bathe and await the duke's summons.

When Duke Ling came to his senses, the first thing that he saw was the maidservant Qiuhong standing before him, holding a bowl of soup. Through his bleary eyes, the lascivious duke noticed how pretty she was; in fact, she looked somewhat like his late favorite Fox Lady. As if by instinct, he made a grab for her. But the girl was too quick for the befuddled oaf. Dodging nimbly to one side, she said, with a tinkling laugh: "Your Majesty, I think you had better drink this hangover soup first."

Realizing that she was neither Fox Lady nor Laiji, the duke took the bowl. The very first sip filled his mouth with a deliciously sweet and sour fragrance. The liquid then produced within him an overwhelming sense of well-being as it seeped into his innards.

"What kind of soup is this, and who made it?" he asked.

"This soup, Your Majesty, is a special tonic for those who have over-indulged in wine," the girl replied. "It is called sour plum soup."

"Well, my dear," rejoined the duke, "you can certainly make a very fine soup. But I wonder if you can do something else for me. Could you be my go-between in a very serious matter?"

Qiuhong replied archly: "I am but a servant here, Your Majesty, and busy all the time with household chores. Would you be referring to some specific person by any chance?"

"To tell you the truth, my dear, it was your mistress I came here specially to see."

"Oh, Your Majesty," Qiuhong cried. "My mistress is far too plain and humble in status to be worthy of your exalted notice, I'm sure."

Fascinated by the girl's wiles, the duke pulled her towards him, and started to fondle her, saying, "Well, never mind about your mistress, then; it's you I want now."

By this time, dusk had set in. Qiuhong, bearing a candle, led Duke Ling through winding corridors into the inner quarters of the mansion. There, Laiji had arranged brocaded coverlets and embroidered pillows for the expected tryst. Even before Qiuhong had a chance to retire, Laiji had flung her arms around the duke. She heaved him behind the bed curtains, where they both undressed and began to cavort on the bed. In the dim light of the lamp, Duke Ling observed that Laiji did indeed have tender skin like a virgin's. In addition, her store of lascivious tricks and blandishments made him feel that he wanted to melt into her body. He congratulated himself on meeting with this sublime opportunity.

From this time on, there was no softening of Duke Ling's vicious and sadistic nature, and his lecherous appetites grew apace. Every few days he would find some excuse to rush off to the Happy Abode with Tu'an Gu, and, as time went on, these expeditions and the goings-on gradually became the scandal of the capital.

Zhao Dun and the other court officials, meanwhile, were having their own suspicions about the duke and his mysterious disappearances. At the morning court audiences he was weary and inattentive, and on two occasions excused himself altogether on grounds of illness. When questioned about their master's comings and goings, his attendants were afraid to speak the truth. When the prime minister himself questioned them, Tu'an Gu suavely interrupted, and successfully obscured the issue.

One morning, as the officials were assembled for the court audience, the duke arrived in his carriage, as if from a journey. The officials' first thought was that he had been out hunting the day before and had spent the night away from the palace. Such behavior in itself deserved a reprimand, but Duke Ling simply brushed aside their anxious enquiries with a few brusque words, and with an airy wave of his hand dismissed the court, saying, "Unless you have some important business to broach, you may all retire. I have something to discuss with Tu'an Gu."

The officials had no choice but to withdraw, but as they did so, they made an implicit pact between them to wait just outside the door listening to what was said inside the court chamber.

Thinking that he was quite alone with his crony, Duke Ling threw all inhibitions to the winds. Turning to Tu'an Gu with a smile, he said, "My dear minister, rest assured that I will reward you handsomely for finding for me that tasty morsel."

With a fawning smirk, the other replied, "A servant's duty is to lighten, if he can, his master's burden. How would I dare to covet such a thing as a reward?"

"Be that as it may," said the duke, still smiling, "I was thinking more along the lines of you sharing your master's pleasure — tasting the morsel, if you see what I mean. Now wouldn't that be a far better reward than things like gold, silver and jewels?"

Hearing this, Tu'an Gu felt a rush of a guilty-conscience and turned a bright crimson. But, glancing at his master, he realized that he could speak freely about what had taken place between himself and Laiji. Again, he assumed an obsequious smile. "I hope Your Majesty will not be angry," he said in an oily voice, "but your humble servant has already sampled the morsel, to make sure that it was fit for Your Majesty's palate. I dared not risk its being displeasing to you."

Duke Ling roared with laughter. "I thought so!" he said. "Yes, Minister, you were quite right to do so."

Tu'an Gu joined in his master's merriment. The duke went on, "So, you were swifter than your master in grabbing that delightful dainty. And what token did she present to you?"

As he said this, he produced from his waistband blood-red handkerchief, and waved it in front of Tu'an Gu's nose. The latter gaped with glee. "I have a present from the same lady," he said, "but it does not compare with that granted to Your Majesty." Whereupon, he produced a perfumed pouch on which was embroidered a pair of mandarin ducks. The duke guffawed, "It seems that you and I have both received love tokens. I propose that the two of us go to the Happy Abode tomorrow and enjoy ourselves with our hostess all together in the same bed."

Their salacious conversation continued in this vein, becoming coarser and cruder as their voices became more strident. They were unaware that every disgraceful word was being overheard by the officials who were hovering outside in the ante-chamber. At last, Zhao Dun could endure it no longer. He stamped his foot and groaned. Then, straightening his robes and holding his tablet of office rigidly in front of him, the prime minister marched back into the court, followed by the rest of the state officials. The duke nearly jumped out of his skin when he saw them suddenly reappear. The prime minister did not stand on ceremony, but came straight to the point. "Your servant has heard," he intoned, "that a certain decorum should be maintained between a ruler and his ministers; also that propriety demands strict separation of the sexes. If a ruler casts aside all sense of purity and shame, then it is easy for unchaste women to disorder the state. Now, right here in the hallowed seat of government of the State of Jin, we find the sovereign and his servant abetting each other in lewd pursuits. Such undermining of proper conduct and morality will surely lead to rampant lechery, disorder, chaos and the ruin of Jin!"

Duke Ling reddened and paled in turns at this verbal onslaught. Thoroughly disconcerted, he stammered an excuse: "Oh Prime Minister, it was just a slip on my part. An aberration, nothing more, I assure you. From now on, I will definitely start to live a regular life, just as a proper ruler ought to."

Zhao Dun, assuming that the duke had recognized that his behavior was unacceptable, felt loath to berate him further. Instead, he turned to Tu'an Gu, and said, "When a ruler's actions are righteous, his servants should encourage him in such courses. But when a ruler's actions are base, his servants have a duty to bar him from continuing in his degeneration. Who should bear this responsibility more than you, Tu'an Gu — you who are His Majesty's chief bodyguard? Yet you even go so far as to lure your master into debauchery, exulting in your wickedness right here in the very seat of sovereignty! If the nobility and gentry were to learn of this, it would shake the very foundations of the state. Aren't you deeply ashamed?"

Tu'an Gu could say nothing to defend himself, but stood with bent head, gnashing his teeth, like a whipped cur. Fuming with righteous indignation, Zhao Dun turned on his heel, and swept out of the court chamber, the rest of the officials close behind him.

The duke and Tu'an Gu gazed at each other for a while through narrowed eyelids, at a complete loss what to do. Then, Tu'an Gu said, weighing his words carefully: "From now on, Your Majesty, I think you had better keep away from the Happy Abode, in order to avoid the wrath of the prime minister."

With this, he glanced slyly at the duke, who said in a voice full of chagrin: "I suppose there's nothing to stop you chasing off to the Happy Abode, is there?"

Tu'an Gu's ambiguous reply was: "The prime minister, sire, blames your servant for leading you astray, I am afraid. But, so long as I no longer escort Your Majesty, the prime minister will not care where I go."

This sly barb found its mark, and Duke Ling exploded in fury. "I don't care if that doddering old fool Zhao Dun doesn't like it," he yelled, "I positively refuse to be deprived of the delights of the Happy Abode, so there!"

Tu'an Gu saw that the time was ripe for adding fuel to the flames. Simulating distress at his master's resolution, he said, "Oh, Your Majesty, that would be most unwise! The prime minister would never countenance it. I implore Your Majesty not to provoke

Zhao Dun into coming here again with his harsh words!"

Duke Ling was hopelessly addicted to debauchery, and the idea of eschewing the pleasures of the flesh was inconceivable to him. Hatred for Zhao Dun seethed within him. Grinding his teeth, he growled, "That sharp tongue of Zhao Dun's grates on my nerves. If only I could stop it wagging! Do you, minister, have any idea as to how that might be accomplished?"

With venom, Tu'an Gu's replied. "The only way to stop Zhao Dun's mouth is with his death."

This sinister note was echoed by Duke Ling: "Right. When he is a dead man, let's see if he can keep interfering with my pleasure!" The two then put their heads together, and plotted the disposal of Zhao Dun.

CHAPTER THREE

The Slaughter of a Family

DUKE LING AND Tu'an Gu were plotting how to get rid of Zhao and resume their carefree and debauched lifestyle. Tu'an Gu brooded for a while, and then he said, "I have a plan, Your Majesty. I know how to get rid of Zhao Dun with no risk to yourself at all."

"What is it? Quick, tell me!" cried the duke eagerly.

Tu'an Gu bent towards his master's ear. "You must think of a pretext for inviting Zhao Dun to a banquet at the palace. Have a dozen armed men waiting in ambush. Then, when the wine cups have gone round a few times, ask him to show you the sword he wears at his waist. He will have no choice but to draw it in order to show it to you. At that point, I will shout, 'Zhao Dun is threatening the duke with his sword. Help, save our master!' The men-at-arms will then spring from their hiding-place, seize Zhao Dun and execute him on the spot. Everybody will then think that Zhao Dun was plotting an insurrection, and brought his death upon himself, and you, Your Majesty, will escape censure for his slaughter. Nobody will be able to protest. What do you think of this plan?"

173

Duke Ling clapped his hands in delight. "Splendid! Splendid!" he cried. "My dear minister, please put your plan into execution as speedily as possible!"

The other then added, "But to make sure that nothing goes wrong, I need to borrow Your Majesty's Terrible Hound."

At this point, we must explain about the Terrible Hound.

A few months previously, the Western Rong tribe had sent a fierce dog to Duke Ling as tribute. It was a huge mastiff with bright red bristles, giving it the appearance of a glowing piece of coal. Its handler explained, "This dog is utterly loyal to its master. It has an uncanny sense of people's intentions, and is good at discerning both upright and wicked natures. If any of your entourage is plotting against you, Your Majesty, this dog will sniff the villain out."

Duke Ling had been very pleased with this gift. "Excellent!" he commented. "In the ancient days of the sage emperors Yao and Shun, there was said to be a magical animal with an unerring sense for identifying evil. Who would have thought that the State of Jin during my reign would have an animal with supernatural powers too? Haha! Let's see who dares to plot against me now!"

Duke Ling had been pleased with this beast and had doted on the dog, appointing a full-time keeper for it and even giving it an official rank. He stopped holding court in the court chamber, and made the officials wait on him in his quarters. He paraded the dog before them, and if anything in their reports or petitions displeased him he would order the dog to bite the luckless man. The Terrible Hound was so powerful and savage that a single bite was enough to leave the victim lifeless. As a result, everyone in the royal household, whether a minister, clerk, servant, member of the harem or palace maid, was kept in state of constant terror. When the duke went out hunting, he ordered the dog keeper to bring the Terrible Hound along on a golden chain. The citizens of the capital too, would flee in terror when they saw the duke with the Terrible Hound at his side. Zhao Dun several times upbraided the duke about this, but his words just went in one ear and out the other. The prime minister would then sigh and say, "He alienates his people for the sake of an animal! Apart from being fierce, what use is the creature?"

Now the duke was always fond of novelty, and soon tired of familiar things. And so, before long, he grew bored with the Terrible Hound too. He dispatched it and its keeper to a rear courtyard, and he himself more or less forgot all about it. But now that Tu'an Gu had requested a loan of the animal in order to rid him of the bane of his life, Zhao Dun, he was only too willing to comply. "Of course! Just tell its keeper to take it to your mansion. But how will the beast recognize Zhao Dun, and know that it is supposed to bite him?"

Tu'an Gu's reply was a mysterious one. "I don't want to bother you with the details, Your Majesty, but I have a plan to overcome that little difficulty."

The duke, relieved, asked, "When will you accomplish what I most desire in all the world?"

"Please be patient for a few days, Your Majesty," replied Tu'an Gu. "When I have everything arranged, I guarantee the plan will work perfectly."

Duke Ling was content to let him have his way.

The Tu'an family was an illustrious one in Jin, and had produced several generations of famous generals for the state. It was this reflected glory that had secured for Tu'an Gu the position of chief of the duke's bodyguard. He lived in a sumptuous mansion with extensive grounds and crowds of servants. Like all scions of the Tu'an family, Tu'an Gu had trained in martial arts as a youth, and in the parklands of his estate there was a drill ground, with archery targets and apparatus for practicing various weapons exercises.

Tu'an Gu had the Terrible Hound shut up in an empty room, and gave instructions that it was to be given no food or water for several days and nights. Then, a straw figure dressed in court robes and holding a tablet of office before it was set up on the drill ground. When seen from a distance, the figure was a close likeness of Zhao Dun. When these preparations had been completed, the following morning Tu'an Gu ordered that the Terrible Hound be released.

The ravenous beast darted out of the room where it had been kept, like a mad thing. It looked around, desperate to find something to eat. It soon spied in the middle of the drill ground what looked to it like a living man. With the speed of an arrow, it bounded towards it, uttering a low growl. At a signal from its keeper, it leapt through the air and pounced on the straw figure, and began to rend it savagely with its mighty fangs. Tu'an Gu had instructed that the entrails of a sheep be placed inside the figure, so that the smell of blood from the entrails should madden the animal. In no time at all the straw figure had been torn to shreds, and the Terrible Hound had gulped down the entrails.

The dog keeper was unaware of Tu'an Gu's real intention, but he dared not be slack in carrying out his master's orders, and so this charade was repeated four or five times. Thus, the Terrible Hound came to associate the sight of a figure in the prime minister's court robes with a delicious meal. No longer did it await its keeper's signal, but as soon as it was let out of the room it opened its cavernous jaws and straightaway fell upon the straw figure, tearing it to shreds and feasting on its innards.

But Tu'an Gu was still not satisfied. Early one morning, he had the dog brought to the front of the palace gate. As soon as the Terrible Hound saw Zhao Dun passing by it bared its teeth and claws, and if it had not been restrained by its chain, it would have attacked the prime minister there and then. Tu'an Gu then knew that the time was ripe to put his dastardly scheme into practice. He sent the dog keeper and the Terrible Hound back to his mansion, while he himself went into the palace to report to the duke. "Your servant has completed the necessary arrangements," he said. "Your Majesty may summon Zhao Dun to a banquet tomorrow, and I guarantee that from thenceforth you will be able to enjoy yourself to your heart's content. That interfering dotard will trouble Your Majesty no more." He laughed loudly in anticipation of his success.

Ever since he had consulted Tu'an Gu on how to get rid of the prime minister, Duke Ling had worried from time to time that news of the plot might leak out, and Zhao Dun might take countermeasures and overthrow him. At the same time, he was looking forward to putting Zhao Dun out of the way for good and resuming his carefree debauched life style. So, agitated and impatient, he felt as though he were sitting on needles, and time dragged by slowly. Now everything was ready. The following day, as the morning audience came to a close and Zhao Dun was withdrawing, Duke Ling suddenly addressed him: "I have been blessed with the unstinting assistance from you, a worthy and loyal servant. You have advised me on numerous occasions, and caused me to mend my careless ways and concentrate on governmental affairs. As a result, the state is prospering as never before, and the common people live and work in contentment. This is all owing to your wholehearted carrying out of your official duties. Today I have prepared a little reception in my quarters for your refreshment, and I hope you will attend."

Zhao Dun was a loyal subject and a good-natured person at heart. Seeing what he took for an expression of gratitude and sincerity on the duke's face, he was pleased. He bowed to the duke, and said, "Your servant's duty is to devote his utmost energies to the service of the state, diligently attend to governmental affairs and assist Your Majesty. Having received the royal summons, your servant begs leave to retire and attend to some pressing affairs first."

Thereupon, he left the court chamber, and after having given some instructions concerning urgent matters to his subordinates, prepared to return to join the banquet. Ti Miming, bowing low, impeded his progress, saying, "Your Honor, the duke has always been tyrannous and vicious. Although recently he has shown himself somewhat milder in disposition, it will be difficult for him to change his base nature. Now, even though he has invited Your Honor to a banquet, I feel that there is something fishy about it. I fear that he is hatching some dastardly plot. I beg Your Honor to make some excuse for not attending this so-called banquet."

The prime minister's attendants, too, agreed with Ti, and all entreated Zhao Dun avoid the banquet. But the latter dismissed their anxieties with a wave of his hand. "It would be an act of disrespect to refuse to accept my sovereign's invitation. Moreover, the duke has been sequestered in the palace for several days, mulling state affairs. How can I decline, when he expressed the wish to have me at his side to advise him at any time?"

So saying, he turned to enter the palace. Ti Miming, still uneasy, followed close behind. As the two approached the duke's quarters, they noticed that guards armed with pikes lined both sides of the staircase to the duke's quarters, standing stiffly to attention. Ti Miming, alarmed, stepped in front of his master, and whispered: "It is most unusual to have armed guards on duty at such a time. Please, sir, return to your home for the moment. Tomorrow you can make your excuses." But Zhao Dun was not to be put off like this. Loudly, he ordered Ti Miming out of the way, and walked straight ahead. Ti Miming had no choice but to obey. He was right behind Zhao Dun, until they reached the stairs to the duke's quarters, when the guard in front of the door boomed, "His Majesty summoned only the prime minister into his presence. No others may enter!"

Ti Miming watched like a hawk from the foot of the stairs as Zhao Dun ascended.

The ambushers, meanwhile, were concealed in the rear of the duke's quarters, and the Terrible Hound was held on a leash by its keeper on one side of the banqueting chamber.

Seeing Zhao Dun enter, Duke Ling rose to greet him and escorted him to a seat with the utmost courtesy and kindness. Even Tu'an Gu showed himself to be unusually affable and attentive, showering the prime minister with flattering words. The three of them shared a table; the duke was in the middle, with Zhao Dun on his right and Tu'an Gu on his left. Servants hastened up with wine and delicacies. The duke took the lead in offering toasts, and the three of them drank merrily as they chatted. Before he could take notice, Zhao Dun had downed three large beakers of wine. His head began to feel fuzzy, and, as if through a thick haze, he heard Duke Ling say, "Prime Minister, I have heard that you carry a most precious sword of exceptional sharpness. My I be allowed to examine it?"

Many years before this, when Zhao Shuai had accompanied Duke Wen of Jin in exile, they had sojourned among the Di nomads of the northwest. It happened that the Di captured two girls during a campaign against another tribe and brought them back as prisoners. They were exceedingly beautiful and magnificently dressed. One was named Shukui and the other, Jikui. Now the khan of the Di tribesmen recognized Duke Wen as a man of extraordinary character, and someone who was destined to accomplish great things, so he gave Jikui in marriage to the duke, and Shukui to Zhao Shuai. The son Shukui bore to Zhao Shuai was Zhao Dun. Later, as Duke Wen and his entourage were about to depart from the land of the Di, it was impossible for Zhao Shuai to take his wife and son with him. He said to her: "Wait for me here for three years. If you do not see me returning by that time, you may freely remarry."

Holding Zhao Dun to her breast, and with tears streaming down her cheeks, Shukui said, "I have born this child as the scion of the Zhao family; how could I marry another man? I have made up my mind to wait for you, no matter how long it takes."

So saying, she presented Zhao Shuai with a precious sword. The sword had been an heirloom for generations among Shukui's people. It glittered with a cold sheen, and was so sharp that it could slice through iron as if it were mud. Shukui continued, "Some day, when your master has regained his rightful place a ruler of Jin, and has accomplished mighty deeds, I beg that you will send for me and the child, so that the boy can inherit this sword."

From that time on, Zhao Shuai had worn the sword at his waist at all times. Seven years later, when Duke Wen had regained his throne, he made Zhao Shuai a senior minister and married his daughter, Junji, to him. Junji bore Zhao Shuai three sons — Zhao Tong, Zhao Kuo and Zhao Ying. Despite being born into privilege as a member of the royal family, Junji was virtuous, wise and faithful by nature. Moreover, she was unassuming and modest. Conscious of the fact that Zhao Shuai had a previous wife and a son, Junji sent for them to be brought to Jin, where Zhao Dun inherited his father's post. On his deathbed, Zhao Shuai called Zhao Dun to his side, and said, "The Duke of Jin has bestowed incalculable benefits on the Zhao family. After my death, it will be your duty to serve our sovereign with the utmost loyalty, while at the same time driving out wickedness, to protect the land of Jin." With this, he handed the sword to Zhao Dun. From then on, the latter was reminded of his father's admonition whenever he strapped it on.

Hearing Duke Ling's request, Zhao Dun struggled to his feet, tipsy with wine, and started to draw the sword. Watching from afar, Ti Miming was horrified, but there was no way he could intervene to prevent his master falling into the trap. All he could do was raise a warning cry. Hearing Ti Miming's voice, Zhao Dun immediately realized the danger, and his heart turned cold. But it was too late, Tu'an Gu seized the moment to shout, "Zhao Dun has drawn his sword! There is some treacherous plot afoot to harm the duke! Quick, to the rescue of His Majesty!"

The words were scarcely out of his mouth when the men-at-arms who had been concealed in ambush rushed into the banqueting hall, brandishing swords and pikes, and surrounded Zhao Dun. Seeing this from the foot of the stairs, Ti Miming was possessed with but one thought — that he must save his master at all costs. So, seizing a halberd, he sprang up the stairs and into the banqueting chamber. Fending off the attackers with his weapon, he pulled Zhao Dun towards the door.

As the ambushers reeled from the surprise and impact of Ti Miming's ferocious attack, Tu'an Gu ordered the dog handler to unleash the Terrible Hound. The beast had been starved of all nourishment for two days, and at the sight of Zhao Dun, whom it associated with the straw man and his delectable innards, entered the hall uttering a low and menacing growl. Up to this moment, its handler could barely restrain it. Now that it had been freed, it didn't wait for any order from its master but bounded as if in flight towards Zhao Dun, who had just reached the door of the hall. Perceiving the Terrible Hound bearing down on him, Zhao Dun was terrified, and tried to dodge behind a pillar. But the ravenous beast was not to be cheated of its prey; in the twinkling of an eye it had pinned the prime minister to the ground. Ti Miming, however, was just as speedy in coming to the rescue. With his head in fury and his hair standing straight on end, Ti Miming let out a roar, "You hellhound, how dare you harm my master!?"

And he seized the dog by the back legs, swung the huge animal in the air and dashed its brains out on the adamantine floor. Panting in its death agony, the Terrible Hound was past all evil doing, but just to make sure, Ti Miming seized the animal by the head, gave a tremendous wrench, and broke its neck, whereupon it expired on the spot. The throng of banqueters was struck dumb with awe at the sight of this feat of strength. As for Duke Ling, he was petrified with fear sand was frozen to his seat. Then, trembling like a leaf, he tried to flee to the rear of the palace, but his limbs would not obey. But Tu'an Gu, who was, after all, a soldier by training and had seen slaughter on the battlefield, had remained calm throughout the commotion and had the presence of mind to bellow an order: "Guards, seize that miscreant at once!"

As if waking from a dream, the men-at-arms dashed forward to grapple with Ti Miming. The latter, knowing that he was outnumbered and that he would be lucky to escape with his life if he stood his ground, hustled Zhao Dun outside the palace and urged him to flee, assuring his master that he would be right behind him.

As Zhao Dun tottered off, Ti Miming turned to bar the progress of Tu'an Gu's men. After a fierce battle, the outnumbered Ti Miming fell dead, covered in wounds. His enormous strength and supreme loyalty to his master inspired later generations to compose ballads about him, which were sung from generation to generation. He was likened to Jing Ke, the heroic assassin of the king of Qin. But this was later.

Thanks to Ti Miming's self-sacrificing act in delaying his pursuers, Zhao Dun managed to stumble out of the palace gate unscathed. As he reached his carriage, he saw his driver lying dead beside it. Moreover, two of the four horses had vanished, and the carriage was lying on its side with one of its two wheels missing. Zhao Dun looked around anxiously, but there was no sign of the attendants who had accompanied him to the palace. A cold shiver ran down his spine, as the prime minister realized what a desperate predicament he was in. He turned, and saw a husky soldier running towards him. Zhao Dun, straightened his back, faced his executioner and awaited his inevitable end.

But the soldier ignored Zhao Dun for the moment, and turned his attention to the broken carriage. He lifted it upright with one hand, saying in a low voice to Zhao Dun: "Prime Minister, never fear! I have come to repay a small debt by helping out of your difficulty. Please make haste and mount the carriage."

Zhao Dun was flabbergasted, but he realized that this was no time to start asking questions, and so he scrambled into the carriage. The stranger yelled at the horses to break into a gallop, while he himself supported the side of the carriage with the missing wheel on his shoulder and started to run. As the carriage rattled off through the city and out of the city gate, Zhao Dun, who had begun to recover from his fright, looked carefully at his savior. The man's shoulder by this time was rubbed raw and drenched with blood. A flicker of recognition stirred within Zhao Dun as he took account of the other's thick eyebrows, large eyes and robust frame. He wondered where he had seen the man before. When the carriage was well clear of the capital, and there had been no sign of pursuit for a long time, the stranger stopped for a rest. Zhao Dun stepped out of the carriage, straightened his dress, gave a low bow and addressed the soldier thus: "May I ask your name, sir, and why you have risked your life to save me, with whom you have no acquaintance?"

The other, who stood by the roadside panting heavily after his herculean exertions, hastened to raise the prime minister upright from his obeisance. He in turn made a bow to Zhao Dun, saying, "I suppose, Prime Minister, that you must have forgotten the starving man under the mulberry tree five years ago?"

Upon hearing these words, the mind of Zhao Dun was taken back five years...

It had been in the summer, and the day had been unbearably hot. Zhao Dun and his entourage were on their way back from a hunting trip to Mount Jiuyuan, when they came upon a delightful spot. With the mountains and stately trees as the background, the place was carpeted with wild flowers. Beside the road stood a mulberry tree. Its trunk was extraordinarily thick, and it was adorned with luxuriant branches and leaves, and crowned with green. Zhao Dun alighted from his carriage to rest for a while in the emerald shade. As he did so, he noticed a hulking figure stretched on the ground under the mulberry tree. Although the man's body was sturdy, his face was bony and pinched. His mouth was wide open, and he lay quite still. At first, Zhao Dun was alarmed at the thought that this fellow might be a villain of some kind. He instructed his attendants to find out who he was. They ascertained that the man was starving. He had no strength, and his eyes were dull and lackluster.

When Zhao Dun asked him how he had come to be in that emaciated condition, the man replied, "My name is Ling Zhe. Three years ago, I traveled to the State of Wei to study, and am now on my journey home. My pack is completely empty; not a morsel of food or a drop of drink have passed my lips for three days. I had thought to pick some of these mulberries to assuage my hunger, but I was afraid that the owner of the tree might take me for a thief. Rather than bring such disgrace upon myself, I decided to lie under the tree with my mouth open, on the off-chance that some of the fruit might fall into it. If no mulberries did fall, then I was resolved to die of hunger rather than be tainted with the foul name of thief."

Zhao Dun was touched by the man's story. He exclaimed with a sigh: "What a truly upright gentleman!" He then gave orders to his attendants to give some of the food and wine they had with them to Ling Zhe. When they did so, Ling Zhe did not immediately devour the victuals, but first took out a small bamboo basket, and put half of what he had been offered in it. That done, he ate the rest with great gusto.

Curious, Zhao Dun inquired, "Sir, the food and drink just now provided for you were scarce enough to allay the hunger and thirst of a man who has been starving for several days. Yet you actually put some aside. Why was that?"

Ling Zhe replied, "Your Honor, I have at home my old mother. She lives near the West Gate of Jiangyi, only a few *li* from here. During the three years I have been away, she has no doubt been living a hard life. So I put some of the food and drink Your honor kindly offered to one side to give to her to appease her hunger."

Zhao Dun uttered several deep sighs of admiration upon hearing this, and said, "Sir, you are not only a man of righteousness, but a filial son the like of whom is rarely seen!" He thereupon turned to his attendants, and told them to give Ling Zhe some more food to take to his mother. Later, a verse was written about this incident, as follows:

> *Returning from a rural ride, he rested as the sun set.*
> *Simple fare, a swig of wine revived the starving*
> *stranger.*

At this point in his reverie, Zhao came to himself again. He scrutinized Ling Zhe closely, and found that sure enough he was the man under the mulberry tree. Filled with compassion, he said, "I hope, sir, your aged mother at home is well."

Ling Zhe replied, "After receiving Your Honor's bounty on that day, I returned home. Alas, I found that my mother had already passed away. I had no choice but to offer Your Honor's gift as a sacrificial offering at her grave. Later, I was summoned to a post at the capital as a guard in the duke's palace. When it came to my attention that Tu'an Gu meant to harm Your Honor, I eavesdropped from time to time. It must have been Heaven's determination to save the life of a good man that guided you into my hands today!"

As the two stood there talking, the rumble of chariots and the pounding of horses' hooves were heard, and before long Zhao Chuan and a company of followers galloped up.

As soon as news of the commotion at the palace had reached the Zhao mansion, the company had hastened to the spot. There they beheld the bodies of Ti Miming and the driver, but there was no sign of Zhao Dun or his carriage. Making inquiries, they learned that a burly fellow had pushed the carriage out of the city, so they set off in hot pursuit. Zhao Dun told his brother all that had happened. Zhao Chuan said, "Elder Brother, it seems that this rascally Tu'an Gu has a deep enmity for you. On top of that, the duke is muddle-headed, and doesn't know right from wrong. I think you should take shelter somewhere for a few days and then decide what to do."

Thereupon, Ling Zhe chimed in with, "Sir, you are absolutely right. I beg to be allowed to escort the prime minister deep into the mountains, to some safe place."

Zhao Dun was loath to abandon affairs of state, but as he seemed to have no choice in the circumstances, he reluctantly acquiesced. So, instead of going home, he mounted Zhao Chuan's carriage, which Ling Zhe then drove away. As the verse goes:

Zhao Dun was in desperate straits; his carriage was missing a wheel.
But just in time, Ling Zhe came up, and repaid the gift of a meal.

Having ordered his guards to finish off Ti Miming, Tu'an Gu went in pursuit of Zhao Dun. But when he saw that the rest of the Zhao clan had reached the prime minister before him, he turned back to report to Duke Ling.

He found the dull-witted duke in high spirits. Although the plot to kill Zhao Dun had not succeeded, Duke Ling thought that as his importunate prime minister had been driven far away from the palace he would be no longer bothered by him. He chuckled, "Now that I've got rid of that nail in my eye, that thorn in my flesh, let's see who dares to play the busybody with me now!"

His officials, who had witnessed Zhao Dun's hairbreadth escape from assassination, stood as mute as frozen crickets. From then on, none of them dared say a word concerning the duke's behavior. The duke himself was as carefree as a lark, forgot all about governmental affairs, sent for Laiji and took her and a large contingent of palace ladies and guards to the Peach Garden, where he indulged himself in feasting, entertainment and all imaginable pleasures from morning till night.

Tu'an Gu, meanwhile, took himself off home. He was uneasy about the way the whole business had gone.

He woke up after a noontide nap, and wandered alone into his back courtyard. He pondered how his plans had gone awry: The sudden appearance of Ti Miming had spoiled his scheme to get the Terrible Hound to do away with Zhao Dun. And then there was that fellow Ling Zhe. Where had he suddenly sprung from? Tu'an Gu was troubled; it boded ill, he thought. Then an alarming scenario came into his head: What if Zhao Dun fled to another state, and there brooded on how to return and get his revenge? In the meantime, Zhao's son was married to Duke Ling's sister; in fact, the Zhao clan was represented all over the country, from the court down. There were a lot of them, and if they rose in sympathy with Zhao Dun returning at the head of another ruler's army —

it didn't bear thinking about! He himself had had so many clashes with Zhao Dun that they were now mortal foes. If Zhao Dun got the upper hand again, he would be finished!

At this point, Tu'an Gu was gripped with terror, as only a person with a guilty conscience can be. But he forced himself to analyze the situation rationally: "At the moment," he said to himself, "Zhao Dun is on the run. The dragon is headless, and so I have no rival at court. Why not seize the opportunity to strike now, clear away all my enemies, root and branch, and get rid of the source of future danger?"

Thus resolved, the very next morning after breakfast, Tu'an Gu hastened to the Peach Garden and demanded an audience with Duke Ling. The duke had spent the previous night frolicking with Laiji and the palace ladies. When Tu'an Gu called he was fast asleep with his arms round Laiji. But Tu'an Gu had always been on easy terms with the duke, so the duke's chamberlain did not hesitate to wake his master, who, when he heard who the visitor was, rubbed his bleary eyes and ordered that he be admitted.

Tu'an Gu marched straight into Duke Ling's bedroom. He made a perfunctory bow, and uttered a deep sigh.

"What's the matter, minister?" cried Duke Ling.

Tu'an Gu gave a mirthless laugh. "Your servant, sire," he said, "has something weighing on his mind. Surely you can't have forgotten that for many years Zhao Dun handled government affairs, and was plotting to seize the throne when the time was ripe. He has fled now, but where has he fled to — perhaps to the State of Qin, or the State of Chu? If so, then he intends to borrow forces with which to wreak his revenge, and raise supporters among local ruffians here to attack the capital. The Zhao clan is well represented at court, and it has powerful forces at its disposal. If they rise up in concert with an attack from outside our borders, you and I, Your Majesty, will be slaughtered out of hand."

The duke was appalled. "Quick, minister," he urged, "think of a good plan to remove this dreadful danger from me, so that I can go on enjoying life without a care in the world!"

Tu'an Gu gestured to Laiji to retire, and feigning a worried frown, said, "All my previous plans have come to naught, I am afraid, Your Majesty, and so I dare not speak incautiously. But, you are a man of wisdom, sire. In this matter I beg you to take decisive action."

The addle-brained duke had no idea what his minister was talking about. "My Dear Minister," he pleaded, "you are full of ideas. Please suggest a good one for me."

Seeing that Duke Ling was confused as to his intention, Tu'an Gu chose his words with care, slowly spelling out his scheme: "Now that Zhao Dun has fled, Your Majesty, the dragon is headless, so to speak. In order to get rid of the sources of future troubles, I suggest you decree the execution of the whole Zhao clan, all three hundred of them, high and low."

Now although the duke resented Zhao Dun for his irksome admonitions and for interfering in his pleasures, he did not harbor any deep-seated hatred of the man. He was well aware that Zhao Dun had served his father as well as himself, and had a reputation for loyalty to the country. Duke Ling balked at the idea of committing so a monstrous a deed as wiping out his whole clan. To overcome the duke's scruples, Tu'an Gu reinforced his argument. "I know that I deserve death for suggesting such a thing, Your Majesty, but if Zhao Dun returns with an armed force and conquers the capital, he will certainly depose you, and set himself up as ruler. And in that case, even if you manage to escape with your life you will surely be banished to some remote region where life will not be worth living. Every time I think of the fate which awaits Your Majesty, my heart breaks into little pieces and I cannot restrain my tears!" As he spoke, he squeezed two tears from his eyes. The alarming picture painted by Tu'an Gu sent the duke into a state of complete stupefaction, in the midst of which the only thought that came into his head was that he must protect his life at all costs. He blurted out, "Well, if that is the case, you must see that it is done at once, Minister. Your duty is to see that all future harm to me is averted!"

After conferring with the duke for a long while on the details of the massacre, Tu'an Gu went home in a buoyant mood. Just before dawn the following morning, he ordered some 1,000 of his guards to assemble. Under the personal command of Tu'an Gu, they surrounded the Zhao family's mansion, cutting off all avenues of escape.

Following the flight of Zhao Dun, the whole of the Zhao clan had been thrown into gloom and despair. They cursed the doltish duke bitterly, but they never suspected that he would move against them, much less consent to the massacre of the entire clan. And so, when the sudden assault on the mansion came, all 300 of the Zhaos were fast asleep and completely unprepared to defend themselves. Zhao Chuan and his attendants were startled from their slumbers to see soldiers armed to the teeth smashing their way into the mansion and hewing down all they encountered, young and old. In no time at all, the Zhao mansion was turned into a shrieking pandemonium, and corpses littered the floors. Zhao Chuan and his attendants were military men, and their first reaction was to draw their swords and rally everyone left alive to counter-attack. But they were doomed from the start. One after the other, Zhao Chuan, Zhao Tong, Zhao Kuo and Zhao Ying fell dead. Leaderless, the handful of survivors fled in all directions, only to be slaughtered by Tu'an Gu's men. Within less than an hour, the massacre was complete — the whole 300-member Zhao clan, high and low, had been butchered. Dawn found the Zhao mansion heaped with corpses and swimming with blood. Not a living soul was left alive inside its walls.

When the court officials, both civil and military, and the common people of the capital heard the shocking news, not a soul dared to utter a word about it, but everyone walked with downcast eyes, completely crushed in spirit by the bloodthirsty tyranny of Duke Ling and Tu'an Gu.

Worried that some member of the Zhao clan might have slipped through the net and survived to cause him trouble in the future, Tu'an Gu sent men to search through the piles of bodies one by one and dispatch anyone whom they might find still alive. In this way, he came to learn that Zhao Shuo, the duke's brother-in-law had escaped the assault on the Zhao mansion because he had been with the princess in the duke's palace the previous night.

Zhao Shuo was Zhao Dun's son. He held a high rank at court, and had married Duke Ling's younger sister. They were a loving couple who lived happily. At this time, the princess was expecting a child soon.

Learning that Zhao Shuo was still alive, Tu'an Gu was so alarmed that he broke out in a cold sweat. Zhao Shuo would be sure to seek revenge for the enormity visited on his family, Tu'an Gu thought to himself. Not only that, but the duke himself might protect his close relative by marriage, and then Tu'an Gu would never be safe. At this point, he gave a hideous cackle and ground his teeth fiercely. "Zhao Shuo, Zhao Shuo," he hissed, "you might have escaped my grasp this time. But you certainly will not the next time!"

He turned the matter over and over in his mind. He had to act quickly, before a complaint was lodged with Duke Ling. Tu'an Gu immediately led a dozen men-at-arms to Zhao Shuo's quarters.

Zhao Shuo had heard of the massacre early that morning. Burning with outrage and fury, he snatched up his sword and was ready to seek out Tu'an Gu there and then. But the princess restrained him, saying, "How can you face Tu'an Gu's men alone? They are as fierce as wolves or tigers. Moreover, that villainous Tu'an has poison in his heart. It is very likely that he is coming here to slay you at this very moment! You must flee for your life. In the eastern mountains you can foment an uprising and get your revenge."

At this moment, Tu'an Gu and his henchmen burst in. At the sight of them, Zhao Shuo's eyes blazed with fire, and he was on the point of lunging at the intruders, when Tu'an Gu waved a hand in deprecation. "Sir, please calm yourself. Your servant has come to deliver an order from the duke." So saying, he adopted a grave expression and intoned as follows: "The treacherous minister Zhao Dun, having plotted insurrection and fearing punishment, has fled. Zhao Shuo colluded with his father in his wickedness. As Zhao Shuo is kin to the royal person by marriage, he is excused by the rules of protocol from undergoing public execution, and is hereby granted leave to commit suicide. The princess must return to the royal palace to await a decision on her fate. Let this order be carried out without fail."

On hearing this, Zhao Shuo and his wife beat their foreheads and wailed in agony. Tu'an Gu interrupted their grief with words of uncertain import: "When the sovereign commands it, it is his servant's duty to die. Sir, it is an honor to die by one's own hand in such a case." Thereupon, he laid a dagger, a goblet of poisoned wine and a rope on a table.

Zhao Shuo was beside himself with rage and sorrow. Wiping away his tears, he cried, "For generations, we Zhaos have been paragons of loyalty in the service of our lords. And now we have descended to this!" So saying, he snatched up the goblet and drank its contents.

The princess turned pale with fear at the sight. She made a feeble attempt to snatch the goblet from her husband's hand, but she was too late. He had drained the poisoned wine to the dregs. The poison soon began its work. Zhao Shuo fell to the ground and rolled over and over in agony, his four limbs thrashing wildly. His face was a steely gray, and large beads of sweat streamed from it. Before long, a thick black spot appeared between his eyebrows, he fought desperately for breath. Watching this tragic scene, the princess, distraught with grief, threw herself upon her husband, wailing, "My dearest, if you die, I will have no reason to go on living. Please do not depart this world just yet, but wait for me to accompany you!" She then seized the dagger, and made as if to plunge it into her breast.

Zhao Shuo, despite being at his last gasp, was still aware of what was going on around him. He wrested the dagger from his wife's hand, and pleaded in a low voice: "Princess, you must not die! You are bearing the heartbeat of the Zhaos within you. Heaven has eyes, and if you give birth to a boy, he will inherit the duty of exacting revenge for the massacre at the Zhao mansion!"

With these words, he turned his eyes to Heaven, and fell back. His legs shook with convulsions, and after a little while he was dead. The heartbroken princess hugged his corpse and wailed piteously. Tu'an Gu, on the other hand, felt that a great weight had been lifted from his mind, and after mouthing a few empty words of condolence to the princess, secretly dispatched men to surround Zhao Shuo's quarters and keep it under tight surveillance. He himself then strode off, with a light heart, to report to Duke Ling.

CHAPTER FOUR

Cheng Ying Saves a Child

AFTER TU'AN GU got Duke Ling to order the massacre of the Zhao clan, and he himself deceived Zhao Shuo into committing suicide, he gathered the reins of power in his own hands. While making sure that everything was arranged to keep the duke fully occupied with merrymaking, leaving him no time to take any notice of governmental affairs, he set about forming a powerful faction, at the same time eliminating those who were not of like mind. This was all done to pave the way for usurping the throne. When Commander-in-Chief of Jin died of illness, Tu'an Gu, without asking Duke Ling's permission, took over his authority, and thus controlled both the civil and military power of the State of Jin. Tu'an Gu was now in a position of unassailable authority. Yet, dizzy with success as he was, he still had one worry: The princess carried within her spawn of the Zhaos! If he allowed the whelp to grow up, he would be unleashing a deadly enemy against himself. However, he did not dare move against the princess yet, as she was after all the duke's sister. He decided therefore to use the pretext of ensuring the princess' safety and station some of his most trusted men around her. Nobody else would be allowed near her, and when the baby was born it would be spirited away and killed.

As the princess' time grew near, Tu'an Gu arranged for a constant stream of gifts and ordered his men to enter the princess' quarters every day on the pretext of checking on her condition and escorting the presents. Then, as soon as the baby was born they would be in a position to snatch it away.

The princess had been brought up in the royal palace. She had been pampered and spoiled, and finally she had been married to the man of her dreams. But now, a terrible calamity had befallen her: Her husband's clan had been massacred, and her husband himself had drunk poison and expired before her very eyes. The princess had been devastated by the enormity of these events, and spent every waking hour in tears. One afternoon, as she was sitting alone by a window, she noticed that the sun was growing pale, and fallen leaves were being whirled by the wind. She felt a chill in her heart. Again, the tears started to fall. Suddenly, she heard the patter of cold raindrops. Raising her head, she looked out into the courtyard, to see that a thin mist had collected there. The rain was by this time falling in sheets, reminding her of her own pent-up grief. Depression and despair welled up inside her when she thought of how the 300 members of the Zhao clan had met their unnatural end. There had been no news from her father-in-law, Zhao Dun, since he had fled the capital several months previously. She recalled that her husband, just before he died, had urged her to brave the humiliation that was in store, and make sure that she gave birth to their child, so that the Zhao clan would have posterity. Now she was about to give birth; who knew whether the child would be a boy or a girl? Tears cascaded down her cheeks as she realized that Tu'an Gu had her chambers tightly guarded by his men, and he would never allow the child to live if it should be a boy. As dusk gathered, the rain abated somewhat, and the princess ordered her maid to bring her a light coverlet, and lay down fully clothed.

Suddenly, the door of her room opened, and her husband entered, with disheveled hair and covered in blood. The princess tried to sit up to welcome him, but found that she could not move. Zhao Shuo approached, lightly stroked her swollen abdomen, and said, "My dear, if you give birth to a boy, you must call him Zhao the Orphan. Nurture him carefully and raise him to manhood, so that he can wreak vengeance for the Zhao clan."

The princess was overcome with distress. She wanted to say something to her husband, but no coherent words would pass her lips. As she mumbled and moaned, Zhao Shuo vanished from her sight. In terror, she leapt to her feet, and rushed out of the door. There was no sign of her husband, but the sound of lamenting was heard. Staring wildly around her, the princess spied a multitude of people — some headless, some without feet, some with gaping chest wounds, some with their entrails spilling outside their bodies. They cried with one voice: "We are the ghosts of the 300 murdered members of the Zhao clan, calling for vengeance. Princess, you must take good care of yourself, and raise your child to be a man who will avenge our bloody slaughter!"

The princess was about to reply, when she heard a shout of command. In the twinkling of an eye, Tu'an Gu and a crowd of guards burst in, bearing sharp implements. Without more ado, they pinned the princess to the floor, with the intention of ripping open her belly and taking the child. As they did so, she heard Tu'an Gu gloat, "I tell you that I will exterminate the Zhao clan once and for all. Its seeds will never sprout again!"

A sharp pain tearing through her abdomen caused the princess to shriek in agony, but through the mist of pain she heard a voice: "Princess, wake up, wake up!"

The princess rolled over, and sat up. The room was dimly lit by the guttering remains of a candle. Her most trusted maid stood by her bedside. It had been a nightmare. But her screams had been real enough. A pain in her stomach caused her to cry out again. Then there was another, and then another. Her maid knew that the princess' time had come. "I'll fetch the midwife," she said.

But the princess urged her in a whisper: "Make not a sound! If that monster Tu'an Gu finds out that I am about to give birth, he will make sure the child does not survive!"

The maid understood the situation perfectly well, and lost no time preparing what was needed. Huge beads of sweat poured from the princess' forehead as the birth pangs tore through her. But, afraid lest anyone hear her, she clenched her teeth and smothered her groans. She had to endure this torture for nearly an hour, until a tiny cry was heard — she had given birth to a strapping baby boy! Fortunately, the night was far advanced, and everyone both inside and out was fast asleep. Nobody heard the baby's first cry. Moreover, strangely enough, after that first greeting to the world, the child did not utter another sound. Swiftly, the princess and her maid, trembling with fear and transported with joy at the same time, severed the umbilical cord, cleaned everything and fed the baby. When they had removed every trace of the childbirth, dawn was already peeping through the papered window. Exhausted by the exertions of the previous night, the princess fell into a deep sleep, with her maid guarding at her side. Halfway through the morning, the heavy tramp of feet was heard outside the window, startling the princess from her slumber. Instantly, she knew that it was an inspection by her captors. It was like:

The wild wind buffets the vulture on high
The cruel frost nips the withered grass roots.

Her maid paled in fright, and fell into a panic. But the princess maintained her composure. Taking the baby from her side, she concealed it in the wide crotch of her undergarment, and covered it with her outer clothing. On top, she spread the thin coverlet, and lay back as before, praying silently to herself: "Oh Heaven, if you do not wish the Zhao clan to perish, please do not let the baby cry. But if it is your will that the Zhaos disappear from the earth, then let it cry."

No sooner had she settled herself than there came a rap at the door. The maid went to open it. As she did so, a sergeant and a group of soldiers burst in. Straightaway, they searched the room, but did not find the baby. Seeing the princess lying there with a bulging stomach, they concluded that she had not yet given birth, and left to report to Tu'an Gu. The princess and her maid, sweating with fear, searched out the baby, only to find it sleeping sweetly, not a bit alarmed by the recent disturbance. This calmed the two women down a bit.

Receiving the report that the princess still had not given birth, Tu'an Gu snarled, "The little whelp can escape my clutches only just so long." He then gave an order that the princess' door be tightly guarded; that if anyone tried to smuggle the child out his whole family to the ninth degree of kinship would be beheaded; that anyone who tried to conceal the child would receive the same punishment.

He then gave a cold chuckle: "Why should I let someone else slay the little creature, anyway? The best way to accomplish my purpose is to slaughter it myself!"

When the guards had departed, the maid, seeing that the baby was unharmed, said to the princess: "Mistress, the guards are sure to come back after a while for more inspections. We can't hide the child for long in this place. You must think of some other way!"

The princess knew well that Tu'an Gu was determined to remove all sources of future trouble for himself, and would never allow the Orphan of the Zhaos to survive if he could help it. But he had already had notices posted that if anyone dared to hide the baby he would be killed. In addition, he had put a tight guard on the princess's quarters, and anyone bold enough to try to abduct or conceal the child would be arrested for sure. And no matter how hard the princess tried, there was no way to get a message to the outside. She was wrapped in distress, and could think of no way out of her predicament. Truly:

> Her heart churning with sorrow, tangled in skeins of sighs.
> Drowning in a sea of injustice, bitterness fills the skies.

Soon, it would be noon. The princess told her maid to hide the baby in a closet. She herself took a pillow, and placed it on her stomach in such a way as to convince a casual observer that she was still pregnant. At noon, as usual, the guards came bursting into the room to check the situation. Finding that there was apparently no change, they left to report. The princess and her maid knew that their luck was running out. If the child were to cry out while the soldiers were in the room on one of their regular inspections, all would be lost!

But Heaven never leaves no way out. Just as the princess and her maid were plunged into despair, they were informed that a doctor had called to see the princess. The latter was filled with dread and hope at the same time. This doctor, whoever he was, had not been sent for; he had come of his own volition. So he must have had some purpose in coming! As if she were drowning and clutching at a straw, the princess cried, "Quick, ask him to come in!"

The maid lifted the door curtain, and stood in the doorway, ready to repulse any unwanted intruders. The princess lay and watched, wondering who the visitor might be. A thin, bony man in his 40s was shown in. Three tufts of whisky beard hung down to his chest. He had a dark complexion, and his expression was grave. The princess recognized him immediately as a one-time member of the household of Zhao Dun; she had seen him often in the Zhao mansion. His name was Cheng Ying.

The princess was overjoyed. She could hardly believe her eyes. She gasped in delight: "Sir, aren't you Mr. Cheng who used to frequent the Zhao mansion?"

"Yes, I am," the newcomer replied with a courteous bow.

Let us pause here to explain the background of this man Cheng Ying. His family had dwelt in the suburbs of the capital, and had practiced as physicians for generations. Although his father had been taught by his father, and inherited the family skills, and indeed acquired quite a reputation as a doctor, he felt that medicine was but a petty trade, and longed to make a name for himself in history by serving his country. By the time Cheng Ying was 16 years old he had mastered his father's skills; indeed he had an encyclopedic knowledge of medicine. He had an almost magical healing touch, and was a wizard at the application of drugs. Seeing that his son was so intelligent, capable and meticulous, Cheng Ying's father laid the mantle of his own lofty aspirations on the young man's shoulders. He told him: "Nowadays, the world is divided and in confusion. Men of talent are sorely needed. My son, you should spend some years studying. If you can gain an important post you will bring glory on our house, which will be much better than following the example of your father and living your life in obscurity."

Cheng Ying was reticent by nature. Hearing his father's words, he said nothing, but only nodded his head. He chose an auspicious day for starting out, and journeyed to the State of Wei. There he studied for several years, and when he returned to his native Jin, his head was crammed full of knowledge. But his character was still introverted and taciturn, and he was slow to reveal his feelings.

Following his father's wishes, Cheng Ying forsook the practice of medicine, and sought his fortune in the capital. For many months, he sought employment in vain, but at last was recommended to the Zhao mansion as a retainer of the prime minister.

The Zhao clan had occupied official posts for generations, and their house was an illustrious one. There were over 100 retainers, well versed in all the arts both civil and military. Among such a distinguished company, Cheng Ying, with his dowdy clothes and homely appearance, went virtually unnoticed. Like a stone tossed into the ocean, he made hardly a ripple in the Lower Palace. Several years passed, and Cheng Ying was still a hanger-on in the mansion of the prime minister. In all this time, he could not fail to notice the upright and loyal nature of Zhao Dun, which made the desire to do something to repay the prime minister for his kindness burn even more fiercely inside him. And this yearning did not leave him even though he was not entrusted with any important task. In the meantime, his shy nature did not allow him to articulate his feelings.

Then one day, Zhao Dun's wife contracted some strange illness. Her pulse was irregular, her eyes were red and her face was puffed up. Moreover, her whole body itched, she could hold down neither food nor drink, and from time to time she would faint. The whole household was in a panic over this. Famous physicians were sent for, but all to no avail. When Cheng Ying heard about this, he plucked up courage to approach Zhao Dun, and explained how he had learned medicine from his father. He thereupon requested permission to try to cure the patient.

Zhao Dun looked Cheng Ying up and down. Although the latter had been in the Zhao household for several years, he had never been formally introduced to Zhao Dun, and so the prime minister looked at him as if he were being confronted by a stranger. However, as his wife's illness had baffled the best medical brains in the State of Jin, with a nod he gave Cheng Ying leave to examine her.

Cheng Ying entered the bedroom of Zhao Dun's wife. After completing the traditional diagnostic routine of viewing, listening, questioning and pulse-taking, it was not long before he had made up his mind what the problem was. He returned to Zhao Dun and asked him: "Midsummer, several years ago, sir, did your wife partake of ginseng by any chance?"

The prime minister turned to the attendants. A maid, after ransacking her memory, said, "Yes, Your Honor, for several years past Madame has suffered from summer heat disorder, with loss of appetite. One of the household physicians recommended that she take ginseng soup. Madame did so a few times."

With perfect composure, Cheng Ying said, "That must be the reason. The lady was originally not ill. But, you see, ginseng is far too nutritious, and she overdosed on it. In addition, taking it at the height of the summer heat brought her system into disorder. Two doses of herbal medicine will soon put her right." So saying, he hastened to make up a prescription.

Zhao Dun was not wholly convinced that Cheng Ying knew what he was talking about. However, he had no choice but to tell his people to concoct the medicine under the latter's supervision. Sure enough, after swallowing the first dose, color started to return to the cheeks of Zhao Dun's wife, and her spirits perked up remarkably. After the second dose, she made a complete recovery.

The prime minister was overjoyed. "Sir, you have a truly miraculous healing touch!" he exclaimed.

After this, Cheng Ying took up the practice of his old trade once more, becoming the physician-in-residence of the Zhao mansion. Naturally, Zhao Dun started to treat Cheng Ying with particular courtesy, and this in turn made the rest of the household see him with new eyes. Thus, it was by a complete fluke that his years of study and his encyclopedic knowledge finally stood him in good stead.

Years passed, and Cheng Ying remained a bachelor. Zhao Dun, ever mindful of the way that the doctor had saved his wife's life, determined to find a spouse for him. At his own expense, he arranged for Cheng Ying to marry a Miss Guo from Guo Shanren in the suburbs of the capital. He also bought a small courtyard house for the newlyweds. Cheng Ying then moved from the Lower Palace and practiced medicine in the capital.

He never forgot his old master's kindness, though, and often paid courtesy calls at the Lower Palace. And whenever anybody in the prime minister's household, no matter what his or her status, fell ill, Cheng Ying would hurry to offer treatment, as previously. He would usually stay at home, waiting for patients, but he also sometimes made house calls. In this way, his skill and knowledge increased greatly, and he gained the trust and goodwill of the people of Jiangyi. In addition, his reputation was enhanced by the fact that whenever a poor person came to consult him, he would often waive his fee and even provide him with medicines free.

More years elapsed, and Cheng Ying grew not only more skillful and famous, but richer too. His only regret was that his wife was frail in body, and although twice pregnant, had lost the baby both times. The childless couple grew sadder and more lonely as time went on. Then suddenly, at the beginning of the year Cheng Ying's wife found herself pregnant again. The two of them were overjoyed. Cheng Ying took the greatest care of his wife, dosing her with tonics, and the baby inside her grew. After a few months, her waist started to get thicker and her waistband to get tighter by the day. Her breasts swelled with milk, and her eyes took on a dreamy look. A few days later, she would give birth to a baby. Cheng Ying was beside himself with happiness: He would finally have a son, although he was over 40 years old. Now he stayed at home all day, looking after his wife. He no longer made house calls, and kept away from the Zhao mansion for a long time.

One morning, just after breakfast, Cheng Ying, having nothing to do in the house, went out to do some shopping. At the corner of the street, he bumped into an acquaintance known as Gaffer Zhao and engaged in polite small talk. Now this Gaffer Zhao was a sturdy and forthright character with somewhat of an old-fashioned air about him. It was said that his ancestors and those of the prime minister's clan had had some connection, but the relationship was so distant that he and the other Zhaos had little to do with each other. At one time, Gaffer Zhao's granddaughter, who was the apple of his eye, had fallen gravely ill. Cheng Ying had used all his skill, and had eventually saved the girl's life. Ever since that time, the grateful Gaffer Zhao had often visited Cheng Ying's house, and the two had become firm friends. Having been cooped up inside the house for several days, Cheng Ying was delighted to see Gaffer Zhao, and insisted on taking him into a tavern for a drink and a chat. Cheng Ying was surprised to find that his normally boisterous friend looked strangely downcast and worried. Refusing Cheng Ying's invitation, Gaffer Zhao pulled him round a corner, and, glancing right and left to make sure that nobody was listening, muttered, "Something terrible has happened at the prime minister's mansion. Perhaps you don't know?" Cheng Ying was seized with alarm, and gasped, "What's happened?" Gaffer Zhao then related in detail the stories of the flight of Zhao Dun, the massacre at the Lower Palace and Zhao Shuo's suicide by poison. His voice had barely died away when Cheng Ying asked, "But what about the princess? Is the baby she's expecting safe?"

Cheng Ying had examined the princess when she had first become pregnant, so of course he knew all about her condition. Gaffer Zhao exclaimed, in a rage: "They say that that dastardly Tu'an Gu will not dare raise a hand against the princess. But he has sent men to guard her quarters, and as soon as the baby is born, he is going to whisk it away and put it to death, in order to destroy every last future threat to himself." He added, with great disdain: "He is completely ruthless. And as for his lieutenant Han Jue, at one time he was a regular visitor at the Lower Palace, and was treated with great kindness by the prime minister. But now he aids and abets Tu'an Gu in his wickedness. He is the one who is in charge of the cohort of guards keeping the princess prisoner. Even if you are carrying as much as a blade of grass, they search you from head to toe!"

The blood drained from Cheng Ying's face. He bade Gaffer Zhao a hurried goodbye, and straightaway made for the Lower Palace. When he was only a street away from the mansion, he slowed his footsteps to a leisurely saunter. As he passed the place, he noticed that there were few people in the street, and they hurried on their way with their eyes fixed on the ground. The main gate of the prime minister's mansion was wide open, and the doors themselves were missing. The lofty steps still bore bloody traces of the massacre, although there was no sign of any corpses. Cheng Ying guessed that they had already been borne away and buried on the outskirts of the capital. Two men-at-arms lounging in the gateway bawled at Cheng Ying to hurry along.

Cheng Ying had seen enough. He went straight home, and told his wife all that he had heard and seen that day. "The Zhao clan have been loyal officials for generations, serving the country wholeheartedly. He has done this evil deed because he is scheming to seize the throne for himself. The State of Jin will be in turmoil until the day this scoundrel of a minister is eliminated!"

Now although Madame Guo was a woman, she had a sense of loyalty and justice, with which she quietly influenced her husband. Hearing Cheng Ying's grisly story, she burst out in indignation: "The ancients said that if a person receives so much as a drop of water in kindness, he should pay a well-worth of water back. Where would we be today, my dear, if it had not been for the prime minister's kindness? Moreover, how can we just sit back and do nothing when his family, which has been a pillar of the state, has been massacred? Can we allow the grievance of these good and loyal people to go unanswered forever? But Heaven has not turned its face from the Zhaos. Right now, the princess bears within her the seed of the Zhaos. If she can smuggle the baby out, you and I could look after it, and raise it, pretending that it is our own, so that in future this scion of the Zhaos can wreak revenge for the clan. It would not be too late for that even if we have to wait ten years. So long as the Zhao line is preserved, sooner or later they will be avenged."

Cheng Ying was surprised that his wife could speak out with

such a dignity, and could not help bowing to her in admiration. In a quavering voice, he said, "Please accept my humble appreciation, my dear. As a man with warm blood in his veins, how can I not distinguish between loyalty and treachery, and especially since the prime minister has been so benevolent to us? But you yourself are about to give birth. I must give all my attention to you."

His wife replied, "Do not worry about me, my dear. Tomorrow I will go to my mother's house. You must devote all your energies to saving the princess' baby. But that Tu'an Gu is a wicked man. You must be careful!"

Let us turn to General Han Jue. What kind of a man was he? A bold general of the State of Jin, he had once been a subordinate of Zhao Dun. He had a swarthy face and bulging eyes. His demeanor was forceful, and he had a deafening voice. He was known for being trustworthy and forthright, and when Zhao Dun had been promoted to minister, he had been transferred to the troops of Tu'an Gu, whom he served just as loyally as he had served Zhao Dun. But as Tu'an Gu began his evil maneuvers, bringing harm to good and faithful officials, and making it clear that he had his eye on the throne, Han Jue looked on with cold eyes. His heart was troubled by what he saw, but he kept his feelings to himself.

Cheng Ying had become acquainted with Han Jue in his days in the Zhao mansion. So he knew that the general had been trained under the benign gaze of Zhao Dun, and although he came under the command of Tu'an Gu later, he would never turn against his old master. Despite his bluff manners, Han Jue was not the sort of person to confuse black with white or blur the line between loyalty and treachery. In a crisis, he would not stoop to wickedness.

Cheng Ying was fairly confidant of Han Jue's upright character, and counted on him to allow him to dash into the princess's quarters as soon as the baby was born, and carry the child off to safety. But he reflected that there were two conditions necessary to ensure the success of his plan: One was ensuring the exact date of her giving birth, and the other was the attitude of Han Jue. If the commander refused to cooperate, having thrown in his lot with Tu'an Gu, then the whole enterprise would be ruined. Cheng Ying, being a doctor by training, was able to calculate accurately when the princess was likely to give birth. But as for Han Jue, he decided in the end that he could not take the chance of him turning traitor and denying him access to the princess and the baby at the crucial moment. Cheng Ying made up his mind to attempt his rescue alone. Having made this decision, he felt much easier in his mind. Thereupon, he made his preparations, and awaited the moment to act.

On the day that he reckoned the princess would give birth, he shouldered his medicine bag, and strode off with the stated purpose of going to take the princess' pulse. The guards were only interested in searching people coming out of the mansion, and not those going in, and after a few perfunctory questions allowed Cheng Ying to enter.

As soon as Cheng Ying came face to face with the princess, the two wasted no time on formalities, despite the difference in their social statues. To the princess, this unexpected visit was like that of a savior star fallen from Heaven. Without more ado, she asked, "Sir, have you come for the Zhao child?"

Cheng Ying nodded gravely. "I have," he said.

Hearing these two words, the princess could not hold back her tears. She said, "Sir, let me first thank you on behalf of the 300 aggrieved souls. I will never forget your kindness and virtue as long as I live. And you will surely be rewarded in the next life."

As she spoke, she bowed from the bed where she lay.

Cheng Ying bowed back in humility, and asked her when the child was due, assuming from her bulging abdomen that she had not yet given birth.

The princess hastened to inform the doctor that she had given birth to a baby boy the previous night. She also explained why she had given the child the name of Zhao the Orphan. She then told her maid to bring the baby for Cheng Ying's inspection. The doctor was overjoyed. "Wonderful!" he cried. "I can take him at once. Although I am a person of no account, I would struggle through fire and flood to uphold loyalty and justice. If my body were mangled and my bones smashed in the process, I would have no regrets." At this point, he paused, seemingly hard put to express something that he wanted to say next. The princess was astute enough to perceive this, and urged him to continue.

"If I am fortunate enough to save the child," he muttered, "that dastardly Tu'an Gu will for certain ransack this house. When he does not find the baby, he will dispatch his men to interrogate every member of your household, threatening them with the most dire punishments, and not even exempting yourself, princess. You may be unable to withstand their savage torture, and then divulge my name. Now, although the extermination of my whole family would be of little consequence, the real tragedy would be that our attempt to save the child would come to naught. Moreover, even if you yourself are as silent as a clam, how can we be sure that every one of your multitude of servants will remain silent?"

So saying, he cast a glance at the maid servant in the doorway. The princess gave him a wan smile. "Sir, allay your fears," she said. "Only I and my faithful maid servant there know that the child has been born. You may trust us to handle such a contingency. But there is just one thing that puzzles me: The walls around this mansion are high, and the moat is deep. Guards are stationed outside the gate. How will you, bare-handed, manage to carry the child out of this place?"

Cheng Ying pointed at his medicine bag. "I'll hide the boy in there," he said. "The commander of the guard is General Han Jue, who once served under the prime minister. He is an upright and loyal man. I am confident that nothing will go wrong."

The princess was greatly relieved to hear this. "Heaven has eyes to see, after all!" she cried. "It will not countenance the destruction of an honest and faithful family. There is hope that the wrong done to the Zhaos will be avenged!"

So saying, she cradled the baby in her bosom, as tears fell from her eyes. Cheng Ying, observing this heart-rending scene, did not have the heart to urge the princess to hurry. Eventually, the princess raised her head, and said, "Sir, please wait a little while, until I have suckled the child one last time. Then I will hand it over to you." She then went into a back room, fed the baby, and laid it on one side. Then she untied her waist sash, made a loop in it and attached the other end to the door frame. With tears cascading down her cheeks, she mounted a low stool. In a low voice, she said to herself: "My husband in the nether world, know this: I have entrusted the Zhao orphan to a righteous man. I now come to join you." She kicked the stool away from beneath her, and in no time at all the life had fled from her body.

Meanwhile, Cheng Ying waited for what seemed ages, and when he could hear no sound from the inner room, began to feel uneasy. When he finally hurried inside, it was too late. The maid servant, viewing the dreadful scene from the doorway, was seized with terror. She fell to her knees, and kowtowed over and over again to the dead princess. Then, turning to the doctor, she produced a pair of scissors from her bosom. With the scissors tightly clutched in one hand, she cried, "Sir, I beg you not to take this amiss. But my mistress was exceedingly kind to me, and now that Zhao the Orphan has been delivered to your care, my life has come to its end." So saying, she plunged the sharp-pointed scissors into her heart, and followed the princess to the netherworld.

With a solemn countenance, Cheng Ying bowed to the bodies of the princess and her faithful maid. Then he turned his attention to the baby. He laid it carefully in his medicine box, and spread medicines lightly over the child to conceal it. Although it was only a few paces to the gate of the mansion, the medicine box felt as heavy as if it contained the very lives of those 300-odd martyrs of the Zhao clan. By this time, it was almost dusk, and most of the gate guards had gone for their evening meal, leaving only two of their number at the gate. General Han Jue sat alone in a small guardhouse outside the gate, seemingly wrapped in thought. Seeing this, Cheng Ying felt a surge of hope, and said to himself: "Truly, Heaven has come to my aid!" However, the sight of the doctor emerging alone from the house, wearing only a thin robe and carrying a medicine box in his hands, roused the suspicions of the two guards. Before Cheng Ying had a chance to say anything, they challenged him: "Hey you! What's in that box?" they yelled. "Open it up, and let's have a look!" Cheng Ying replied, calmly: "Nothing but medicines, I assure you." But one of the guards barred his way with his halberd, while the other made to snatch the medicine box away from him. Cheng Ying, however, clung to the box for dear life, and a struggle ensued. Just at this moment, General Han Jue called out from the guardhouse: "Bring him here!"

I'll examine him myself."

Ever since he had been put in charge of guarding the mansion of the emperor's deceased son-in-law, Han Jue had been accustomed to supervising operations and dispatching patrols from the guardhouse, just outside the gate. But at the time that Cheng Ying had entered the mansion he himself had been leading a patrol, and did not know of his visit until later. When it was reported to him that a doctor had come to take the princess' pulse, a pang of disquiet stirred within him. As the doctor emerged from the house, he recognized him as the very Cheng Ying whom had had used to see often at the Zhao mansion. Then, he was convinced that something was fishy; and when he saw Cheng Ying struggling with the guard over the medicine box he was sure of it. At first, he was filled with doubt as to what he should do: On the one hand, he wanted to let Cheng Ying go. But if, as was likely, he was trying to smuggle the Zhao child out in his medicine box, Tu'an Gu would be bound to find out. Then, not only would Han Jue forfeit his life, but his whole family, young and old, would be executed along with him. On the other hand, if he examined the medicine box and found the child, he would have to hand it over to Tu'an Gu — and that would mean the extinction of the Zhao clan. Not only that, but Cheng Ying too would be executed. While he was suffering this agony of indecision, he saw the guard about to wrest the medicine box from the doctor's grasp to examine it. Han Jue hastily ordered the man to desist.

The two guards then escorted Cheng Ying to the guardhouse. The doctor calmly carried his medicine box to Han Jue, and stood before the general to await the outcome of this interview. The latter was in a predicament. He put on a show of bluster, barking, "Who are you, fellow? And what were you doing in the princess's quarters?"

Cheng Ying correctly interpreted Han Jue's harsh tone as a sign that he was pretending not to recognize him, and he knew that he had come to a life-or-death crossroads. Nevertheless, he stared fearlessly into Han Jue's fiercely bulging eyes, and said in a voice that was unwavering: "I am just an ordinary doctor, come to attend the princess."

Han Jue played for time. "What ails the princess? And what medicine have you prescribed for her?" he growled.

"The princess is about to give birth," Cheng Ying explained. "Moreover, she has suffered a tragic turn of fortune. As a result, there is a failure of blood to circulate properly in the pulse, and a slackening in the functions of the meridians and collaterals. I prescribed motherwort soup."

Han Jue glanced at the medicine box in Cheng Ying's hands. "What's in the box?" he asked.

"Medicine ... that's all, General." came the reply.

"You're not smuggling anything out in it, by any chance, are you?"

"Certainly not, General!"

The more bullying the questions, the more serene were the replies. Han Jue was at his wits' end. He couldn't decide for the life of him what to do. Seeing Cheng Ying standing before him, facing danger unafraid, he could not help secretly admiring the man's courage. At the same time, he felt somewhat ashamed of himself. All of a sudden, he made up his mind. With a dismissive wave of his hand, he said curtly: "All right, all right. Off you go!"

Hearing this, Cheng Ying gave a slight bow, and turned to go on his way. But he had proceeded no more than a few steps, when he was startled to hear Han Jue call out, "Cheng Ying, come back here!"

The doctor's heart began to palpitate, but he had no choice but to halt in his tracks. Slowly turning round, he inquired, "Yes, General. Is there something more I can do for you?"

Hesitation overcame Han Jue once more. Finally, he asked, "Er, what kind of medicines have you got in the box?"

"Oh, nothing but root of balloon flower, licorice and peppermint, that sort of thing."

Han Jue hesitated for a moment. Finally, he sighed, "Well, if that's all, you can go."

With an overwhelming feeling of relief, Cheng Ying hurried on his way. But again he was brought to an abrupt stop by Han Jue shouting, "Cheng Ying, you come back here!"

The doctor knew that Han Jue was suspicious of him but

couldn't make up his mind what action to take. So this time he walked back to the guardhouse, set the medicine box on a table and said, "General, please look for yourself, and stop harassing an insignificant fellow like me."

Han Jue stared meaningfully at Cheng Ying, and spoke deliberately: "You say you only have balloon flower, licorice and stuff like that in this medicine box. But if I find ginseng in there you'll suffer for it."

The hidden import of his words was not lost on Cheng Ying, ginseng being a root shaped like a human being. But he stubbornly replied, in a manner guaranteed to confuse his hearer: "The princess is suffering from excessive Fire in the Heart. There is no need to apply the Great Remedial. Therefore, what would be the point of carrying ginseng about with me?"

This exasperated Han Jue, who cried, "Cheng Ying, don't think you're so smart that I can't see right through you. You've got something concealed in this medicine box, and I'm going to have a look and find out what it is!"

Cheng Ying felt a solemn resolution rise in his breast. Stepping forward, he opened the medicine box. "I have something concealed in the box. It is the sole remaining heir of the Zhao bloodline. General, if you are the sort of person who clings to life at all costs, and wants to play the toady to the wicked and ruthless Tu'an Gu, then hand the child over to that monster. I have already put aside all cares about my own life or death. I only fear that you, having been a staunchly loyal and upright man all your life, might make one small lapse now and have your name cursed for generations to come."

Han Jue's mind churned in excruciating turmoil. This tongue-lashing from Cheng Ying had cut the ground completely from under his feet. Deliberately, he stretched out his hand, and parted the top layer of medicines in the box, and saw the baby, sleeping peacefully, blissfully unaware that he was facing a moment of life or death. Han Jue bowed his head and pondered deeply: If he handed Zhao the Orphan over to Tu'an Gu, he would be committing a treacherous and heinous act, as bad as assisting the tyrants Zhou and Jie in their savagery. Moreover, he would be regarded for ever as the worst villain in the State of Jin. The thought made his blood run cold.

Observing Han Jue deep in thought and with large beads of sweat pushing through the skin of his swarthy face, Cheng Ying knew that he was feeling the pricks of conscience. Now was the time to add fuel to the fire! He addressed the general thus: "Sir, do you remember the assassin Chu Ni, who preserved righteousness at the cost of his life? He killed himself by dashing out his brains against a tree. And then there was Ti Miming, who wielded his pike so bravely ... and Ling Zhe, who supported the carriage on his shoulder. They both acted in defense of that thing called righteousness. General, when I came here today, I did not expect to leave alive. My only hope was that, by trusting to divine chance, I might rescue Zhao the Orphan, so that a loyal minister might have posterity and his bloodline not be severed. Just before I left the mansion, the princess and her serving maid both committed suicide. They died as martyrs to righteousness, having enjoined me to 'save the orphan and preserve the Zhao clan'. I never thought that you, General, who have always been a man of uprightness and loyalty and in the past rendered valuable services for the prime minister, should today side with a scoundrel and prove weak and irresolute, or that a person with such a manly appearance should turn out to be no better than a woman!"

At this, all Han Jue's selfish thoughts vanished like a puff of smoke, and he was filled with a sense of boldness in the pursuit of justice. In a clear, ringing tone of voice, he said, "Cheng Ying, take your medicine box and depart! I will take care of everything here."

When the doctor showed no sign of leaving, Han Jue, puzzled, asked, "Sir, why do you hesitate?"

With a sardonic smile, Cheng Ying replied, "How do I know that the moment I have gone, you will not report what has happened, soldiers will not pursue me, and I will not fall into one of that villain Tu'an Gu's many traps?"

Han Jue raised his eyes to Heaven, and breathed a long sigh: "Sir, if you never put your trust in any man," he admonished the doctor, "how will you make your way in the world? Enough, enough! By letting you go I have endangered my own life. You may go with an easy mind, but I advise you to leave the capital with all speed. Wean this child, and raise him to manhood, and then I will not have died in vain!"

With a grave countenance, he called to the two guards to him. Not knowing the reason why they had been summoned, they hastened to obey. As the guards stood before him, Han Jue, as swift as lightning, drew his sword and slew them on the spot. Then he drew the razor-sharp blade across his own throat, which left a stream of crimson blood in its wake. The sturdy body of the general swayed and tottered, and crashed to the floor.

Cheng Ying kowtowed to the lifeless form of Han Jue, with tears in his eyes. Then he picked up his medicine box, and scurried out of the guardhouse. Fortunately, there was nobody in front of the mansion of the late royal son-in-law, and the doctor made his escape as fast as his legs could carry him.

Fearing that Tu'an Gu would mount a full-scale search of the capital for the infant and his rescuer, Cheng Ying did not dared to go home; instead, he hurried out of the city gate and headed for the village of Guojiazhuang.

Cheng Ying's father-in-law, Guo Shanren, lived in his ancestral village, supporting himself by farming. His wife had died four or five years previously, and there was only the old man and his daughter at home. Guo Shanren had become acquainted with Zhao Dun when the latter had visited the village to encourage the farmers. Later, the prime minister had acted as the go-between for the marriage between Guo's daughter and Cheng Ying. The old man was very fond of his son-in-law, and often visited the couple. A few days before, his daughter had arrived unexpectedly from the city with news of the massacre of the Zhao clan, and explained that Cheng Ying had remained behind to try to rescue Zhao the Orphan. The old man cursed Tu'an Gu bitterly, and at the same time was filled with anxiety for his son-in-law. Every day since then, whenever he had time he had gone to the entrance to the village to watch anxiously for the coming of Cheng Ying. That very morning, his daughter had been seized by stomach pains, and was apparently about to give birth, so he had stayed at home to look after her. In the afternoon, she had given birth to a healthy baby boy, to the old man's great delight. At midnight there had come an unexpected knock on the door. Opening it, Guo Shanren found Cheng Ying standing there with Zhao the Orphan.

He hastily ushered them in. Guo told his son-in-law the glad tidings that his wife had given birth to bonny baby boy that very day. Cheng Ying, in turn, related how he had saved Zhao the Orphan. When he told them of the suicides of the princess, her maid servant and Han Jue, his father-in-law and his wife sobbed uncontrollably. And so, weeping and laughing in turns, they chatted for hours. Cheng Ying took Zhao the Orphan from his medicine box, and laid him beside his new-born son. Gazing at them closely, it struck him that they were as alike as twins, both having fine eyes and eyebrows, straight noses and square cheeks. Guo Shanren was delighted. "What luck!" he cried. "If anybody asks, you can say that your wife gave birth to twins," he pointed out to Cheng Ying.

At that moment, they heard the neighbor's cock crowing. Dawn was breaking already, so the three adults went to bed. As soon as he arose the following day, Cheng Ying planned to go out to buy some nutritious food, such as chicken and duck, meat and vegetables, for his wife to help her recover her health and promote lactation. But Guo Shanren stopped him. "For one thing," he said, "over the past few days you have been dashing about, and have even plunged into the tiger's lair to rescue Zhao the Orphan. You deserve a bit of a rest. For another, Tu'an Gu will have men out searching high and low for the baby; if he gets wind of your whereabouts disaster will befall us all."

Cheng Ying saw the sense of this, and agreed to lie low for a while. "I'll leave everything to you, father-in-law," he said. "Please hurry back."

Taking some money with him, Guo Shanren went to the nearby market town to make the purchases. There he noticed that the place was not as tranquil and sleepy as it usually was. Groups of people stood here and there, with their heads together, whispering. Fear was written all over their ashen faces. Guo Shanren was curious, but he did not dare ask what the matter was. Before long, he came across a group of people gathered around a notice. Elbowing his way through the crowd, he saw large black characters on a white sheet of paper, which read:

Whoever has kidnapped and concealed Zhao the Orphan is hereby ordered to hand over the child to the authorities within five days. If that person fails to do so and is discovered, his whole family to the ninth degree of kinship will be beheaded. Anyone knowing of such a person and not reporting the matter will be treated as an accomplice, while informers will be handsomely rewarded. If the child has not been handed over within five days, every infant below the age of six months will be put to death, without exception.

The previous evening, not long after Cheng Ying had got safely away with Zhao the Orphan, the relief guards arrived at the gate of the mansion of the late royal son-in-law. To their horror, they found the bodies of General Han Jue and the two guards. Two of them rushed off to report to Tu'an Gu, while the others hurried into the mansion. By this time, darkness had fallen, and when they saw that no light gleamed in the house, they were filled with foreboding. Hastily lighting a torch, they entered the princess's quarters, where they found the princess hanging by the neck and her maid lying in a pool of blood. Both bodies were already cold. A careful search revealed nothing else suspicious. Another messenger was dispatched to report this further finding, and the rest of the guards remained at the mansion to await the coming of Tu'an Gu.

When the news reached Tu'an Gu he turned apoplectic with rage. "You useless blockheads!" he stormed. "The princess and her maid didn't kill themselves for nothing; someone must have stolen the Zhao whelp." Then a question crossed his mind. "But Han Jue and the two guards... How did they come to be killed outside the mansion? Did the kidnapper slaughter them as he fought his way out, I wonder?"

He had no time for further speculation, but hurried off to the mansion of the late royal son-in-law with a body of soldiers to inspect the scene for himself. He first examined the bodies of Han Jue and the two guards. He noticed that Han Jue still grasped a sword tightly in his right hand, and his neck had been slashed through to the vertebrae. Blood dripping from the mouths of the two guards indicated that they had been stabbed by someone. Suddenly it dawned on him: "Han Jue must have been in league with the kidnapper! First, he killed the guards, and then, fearing punishment, slit his own throat. The spawn of the Zhaos must have been spirited away." An examination of the princess's body showed that she was no longer pregnant, but there was no sign of a child anywhere. Tu'an Gu ordered the mansion sealed and a thorough search made of the city of Jiangyi. He himself remained at the scene of the bloodbath, to await news. It was not long before his messengers returned, and reported that nobody had seen a man carrying a baby leave through any of the city gates. The search of the city too had been fruitless.

Seized with a fit of uncontrollable fury, Tu'an Gu snatched his sword from its scabbard, and hacked frenziedly at the corpse of Han Jue. He then ordered that all the dead general's family be executed.

Having vented his spleen thus, Tu'an Gu returned home. He sat for a long while deep in thought, his mind greatly troubled. He thought of the man who had risked the extermination of his whole clan to enter the tiger's lair and make off with Zhao the Orphan and of Han Jue and the princess and her maid, who had willingly taken their own lives to cover up the plot and save the child. He realized that if Zhao the Orphan were allowed to grow up his very life would be endangered in the future. The more he pondered the matter, the more afraid Tu'an Gu became. He knew that he had to get rid of this threat somehow; but how? The State of Jin had a large population, so at any time there had to be lots of newborn babies. Searching every household would be like looking for a needle in a haystack. Besides, the child wouldn't have "Zhao" tattooed on its face, would it? If he let the matter rest, it would be like releasing a tiger into the wild — a potential source of untold calamities. Tu'an Gu fretted until he was almost distracted with anxiety, but finally a dreadful solution to his dilemma flashed into his ruthless brain: "It's better to risk killing the innocent than to let the brat escape. That's it! If Zhao the Orphan can't be found

I'll have every baby in Jin killed, and then we'll see where that accursed puppy can run to!"

Having made up his mind, Tu'an Gu called for his most trusted henchmen. "I want you to post notices all over Jin," he said. "The notices must say that Zhao the Orphan must be surrendered within five days. After five days, if the child has not been handed in every infant within the boundaries of Jin will be executed." His men forthwith attended to their master's order, and by the following morning the required posters were stuck up all over the country. They caused fear and consternation in all the people of the state, especially in those families with a new-born baby.

Guo Shanren, too, was petrified with horror when he read one of the notices. He stood in front of it for a long time, with his mouth agape and not knowing what to do. Finally, he backed out of the crowd massed in front of the poster, and made his way hastily homeward. When he reported what he had seen to Cheng Ying, the latter was stunned. The whole family, in fact, was stricken with panic.

As he gazed distraught at the two babies lying side by side in their bed, an idea came to the doctor. But he immediately shook his head, and dismissed the preposterous thought. But the more he worried about the problem facing them, turning one scheme after another over and over in his mind, the more he became convinced that this was the only way out. The realization that he could not tell his wife what he was thinking made the pain in his heart even harder to bear. Again he banished the thought from him. But it refused to go away, and in the end Cheng Ying could not help crying out in anguish.

His wife and father-in-law, who had been gazing intently at Cheng Ying, in the hope that he could come up with a plan, were startled out of their wits when he suddenly bawled in sorrow, his face contorted with pain. Little guessing the reason for his son-in-law's bitter wailing, Guo Shanren tried to console him by reminding him that the notice gave them five days' grace within which to think of a plan to save the child and themselves.

But far from bringing him any comfort, his father-in-law's

words only served to twist the dagger that seemed to be piercing Cheng Ying's heart. He tried to explain the reason for his agony, but no coherent words came out. His wife guessed that there was a deeper sorrow tearing at him, and urged him to speak out.

Calming down somewhat, and wiping away the tears, Cheng Ying said, "I have thought of a plan, and I beg both of you not to hate me for what I am about to say." Before either of them had time to say anything, he continued. "I know that Tu'an Gu is as vicious as a viper or a scorpion, and that he would stoop to any foul deed. His threat to slaughter all the newborn infants in Jin is no idle one. If we do not hand over Zhao the Orphan, we will bring a terrible calamity upon thousands of innocent families. The plan I have thought up will not only save Zhao the Orphan; it will also save the lives of all the babies of Jin. We can do this by surrendering our own child to Tu'an Gu…"

He could not continue, and tears cascaded down his cheeks. After sitting in silence for a few moments, as if she had been struck dumb, Cheng Ying's wife screamed, "You heartless beast!" and abandoned herself to a paroxysm of weeping. Guo Shanren rubbed his hands in agitation, but said nothing.

Cheng Ying waited for his wife to recover her composure, and then said, "My dear, please don't hate me. We are both nearly forty years old, and only now have we been blessed with a son and heir. The idea of having to part with him tears at my heart just as much as it does yours. But I am afraid that there is no other way to save Zhao the Orphan. Besides, remember how kind the prime minister has been to us both. Think of the massacre of the 300 blameless members of the Zhao clan, and of how the duke's son-in-law committed suicide by drinking poison. Remember how the princess, just before she died, entrusted Zhao the Orphan to me. Then there were the upright Chu Ni, Ti Miming, General Han Jue and the princess' serving maid — they all gave their lives in the cause of loyalty and righteousness. After all these noble sacrifices of lives and sufferings to save him, if we simply hand over Zhao the Orphan we will be no better than curs or swine. Then how could we face the prime minister again in this life, or his aggrieved ghost in the next? Besides, if we refuse to hand a child over to Tu'an Gu, he will barbarously slaughter all the infants in Jin, and both Zhao the Orphan and our own baby together with them! Then our whole venture will come to naught. Please, my dear, think carefully: Is there not reason in what I say?"

Before his wife could reply, her father said to her: "You were the only person I had in the world until the prime minister kindly found a fine son-in-law for me. And now I have a grandson, whom I love dearly. When Cheng Ying talks of sending the child to his death, of course every fiber of my being cries out against it. However, your husband is right. Put yourself in the place of others, and think of how many families in Jin will be left without heirs if that fiend Tu'an Gu carries out his threat. We will not be the only ones to suffer."

Choking back her tears, Cheng Ying's wife replied, "I may be only a woman, but I understand what is right. Yes, it is better that my baby be sacrificed than that the hated Tu'an Gu should murder all the infants in Jin. Nevertheless, I cannot face the consequences of this cruel decision. For if my husband surrenders our child to Tu'an Gu, I am afraid that that wicked monster will kill both of them. How could I bear to lose both my child and my husband in the same day, and end up as a wretched woman alone? How I loathe that evil Tu'an Gu, who has brought harm to loyal and good people, and massacred the innocent! I hate him so much that I could feast on his flesh and drink his blood!" As she spat the words out, her face turned a bright crimson, and her eyes looked as though jets of fire were about to spurt from them.

Cheng Ying bowed deeply to both his father-in-law and his wife, saying, "In order to save Zhao the Orphan, I have dedicated myself to the pursuit of loyalty and justice. To attain this goal, I would submit without rancor to being boiled alive. After I am gone, you must both care for Zhao the Orphan as if he were your own flesh and blood. Raise him to adulthood, so that he can exact payment in full for this awesome blood debt. Then, with my most cherished desire fulfilled, I will lie smiling beneath the ground."

He then picked up his child, and was about to leave the house, when Guo Shanren stretched out a hand to detain him. "Don't be so rash!" he cried. "Tu'an Gu is a cunning devil, and he is determined to get his hands on Zhao the Orphan. If you simply hand over a baby, how do you know that he will believe that the child is the one he is seeking? He may decide to kill not only you and your child, but all the other infants in Jin as well to make sure he has got rid of the right one. Then the two of you will have perished in vain!"

Cheng Ying saw the sense in his father-in-law's words, and stood dumbfounded, not knowing what to do. At this moment, Guo Shanren continued, "I think that what is needed now is another hero to act in concert with you. While one pretends to have kidnapped Zhao the Orphan, the other will pretend to denounce him. This charade might deceive Tu'an Gu. But where can we find such a stalwart partner?"

This scheme sounded feasible to Cheng Ying, and he stood deep in thought for a while. Suddenly the image of a man flashed before his mind's eye.

CHAPTER FIVE

An Episode of Sterling Devotion

WHO WAS THE man whom Cheng Ying thought of to accomplish his daunting task? His name was Gongsun Chujiu, and he was living at this time in Taiping Village, near Mount Shouyang.

Gongsun Chujiu had been a senior official at the court of Duke Wen of Jin, a position he continued to hold under Duke Wen's successor, Duke Xiang. But when Duke Ling came to the throne, he found his situation increasingly untenable, as the new ruler surrounded himself with sycophants and slaughtered innocent people. Seeing the morale at court deteriorating by the day, Gongsun Chujiu, had a noble and unbending spirit, and did not hesitate to rebuke Duke Ling with stern words. Eventually, however, seeing that the duke persisted in the path of folly, and Gonsun Chujiu resigned his post and retired to devote himself to farming. His wife, a woman of the Wei clan, was by nature indifferent to fame and gain, but when she saw her husband staunchly and boldly reproving Duke Ling for his wickedness, she was afraid that he would bring calamity upon himself. And so, she was greatly relieved when he made the decision to leave the court and go into seclusion in the countryside. With a handful of servants, the pair left the capital to look for a place where they could settle down in retirement, eventually settling upon Mount Shouyang.

Taiping Village was a charming spot, situated with its back to the mountain and facing water—an ideal configuration. Behind the village stood lofty peaks and precipitous ridges, with fantastic rocks piled one on top of the other. From the heights tumbled cascades and waterfalls, spouting pearly and jade-like beads of spray. In spring and summer, the mountain was clothed in lush foliage, with splashes of brilliant color from rare flowers and other plants. A crystal-clear stream flowed in front of the village. In the fields, mulberry and elm trees stood high, and the lotus blossoms opened up like the rosy rays of dawn. The very sight of Taiping Village was gladdening. The most impressive sight of all was the myriad pine trees, which clung to the crags. From close up, they seemed to form a huge green umbrella, and from afar like an emerald cloak thrown over the land. Whenever a breeze sprang up, verdant billows swept over the pine-covered hills, rolling into the horizon. In the still of the night, the murmuring in the pines filled the heart with gentle delight. As soon as he set eyes on this delightful spot, Gongsun Chujiu was overjoyed, and decided to settle down here.

The old couple did not have any children, but they had never missed not having a son or daughter. Gongsun Chujiu was an easygoing fellow. He had never paid attention to amassing property, and although he had served in a high official post for decades, he had not saved up enough money to buy a house with some land, and so he chose a spot between the mountain and the stream to erect a three-room cottage. Here he settled down, and together with his servants cleared some wasteland, upon which he planted rice and millet. Every day, as the sun rose, he would go out to work on the land, plowing and weeding, planting and reaping, and would not return until sunset. During his rare moments of leisure, he would read or play chess. All in all, he was quite content with this way of life. The village was located far from the capital, and no news of the court or of state affairs reached the ears of its simple, unspoiled inhabitants. Gongsun Chujiu made up his mind to spend the rest of his days there. But there were times in the dead of night when he would sit up, alone and sleepless, thinking back on the days when he had led the life of an official, wondering how things were going at court, and worrying about the destiny of the State of Jin. When he thought of how he had resigned his post and gone to live in obscurity, he found himself sighing. Truly:

> *Wakeful at midnight in my humble shack, I hear*
> *the soughing in the pines.*
> *By day, leaning on my rickety door, I count the*
> *wild geese as they pass.*

Several years passed in this way, and Gongsun Chujiu's wife died of illness. His servants, one by one, married and moved away, until he was left with only one boy. The days passed in a leisurely manner. In the early days of Gongsun Chujiu's retirement, his erstwhile colleagues at court had sent a messenger from time to time to inquire after him, but eventually such calls became fewer and fewer, until they ceased altogether, except for gifts of clothing and food from Prime Minister Zhao Dun. Like Gongsun Chujiu, Zhao Dun had served three generations of rulers. The two were alike in temperament and spirit, sharing the same deep feeling of loyalty to their country. Serving together, they had become fast friends. When Gongsun Chujiu resigned his position, Zhao Dun had done his utmost to get him to change his mind, but all to no avail. Just as they were about to part, Gongsun Chujiu said, "All my life, I have hated evil. So when I saw wicked villains pulling the strings at court, I did my best to put the situation right. However, I have proved powerless to do so, and my words have fallen on deaf ears. Now the only thing for me to do is to go far away. You, sir, are devoted heart and soul to the welfare of our country, but I must warn you to be on your guard day and night against plots and conspiracies against you." Zhao Dun, who viewed with alarm the attrition in the ranks of all those who were noble and good at the court, was profoundly saddened that his old friend was going away too. Grief-stricken, he could find no words to say, and the two bade a tearful but silent farewell.

At that time, Cheng Ying was living in the Zhao mansion, and got to know Gongsun Chujiu well. He heard the prime minister say that he and Gongsun shared the same ideals and were bosom friends. Now, in a great quandary, he thought of Gongsun Chujiu. He thereupon said to his father-in-law and his wife: "The prime minister formerly had a close friend who was a colleague of his at court, named Gongsun Chujiu. He was an upright man who hated evil. Several years ago, he retired to the countryside, to a place called Taiping Village at Mount Shouyang. I met him many times when I was living in the Zhao mansion. I felt that he was the sort of person who would not hesitate to help someone who was in trouble. So I think I should take Zhao the Orphan to Taiping Village and ask Gongsun Chujiu to look after him. Then I will go and surrender myself and my son to Tu'an Gu, letting him think that my baby is actually Zhao the Orphan. In that way, the real Zhao the Orphan will be safe and the infants of Jin will escape slaughter."

Cheng Ying's wife was overcome with distress when she heard this, and choked with sobs. But she knew that her husband's plan was aimed solely at saving the orphan, and so she stifled her grief and kept her tears inside her. Watching this heartrending scene, Guo Shanren was also overcome with sorrow, and very much affected by his son-in-law's high-minded selflessness. He uttered a few words of comfort to his daughter, and then burst into tears. The night was well advanced by this time, and as Cheng Ying intended to set out at daybreak, the three of them did not sleep, but made all the preparations necessary for his journey.

Before cock-crow, taking advantage of the fact that there would be few people about at that time of the morning, Cheng Ying hurried out of the house. As before, Zhao the Orphan was concealed in his medicine box. Guojiazhuang was some 110 *li* from Mount Shouyang on the ordinary road, but Cheng Ying decided to take a longer, mountainous route, for fear of meeting prying eyes or government troops. The journey was uneventful. He only met a few woodcutters on the path, and they displayed no curiosity about him. By noon, he had already covered 40 *li*. He rested beneath a shady tree by a stream. He fed the baby and himself, but did not dare to linger long. Soon he was on his way again.

It was mid-autumn. The path was lined with greenery and clear emerald streams. The nearer slopes of the mountains were fiery red, as the maple leaves were in all their glory at this time. On the higher parts of the mountains, the leaves of the smoke trees, clustered in mass ranks, had already been touched by the frost, and were changing color. Little brooks bubbled musically from crevices and flowed down, following the contours of the rocks. Among the trees and by the banks of the streams was a multitude of strange, nameless wildflowers. Impervious to cold, and even frost, they still blossomed gaily in their quiet abodes.

But Cheng Ying gave them no heed, as his mind was preoccupied with his mission. When he did notice the beauty of his surroundings, he felt a pang of anxiety. Retiring to a place like this, surely Gongsun Chujiu must be perfectly content, and his heart must be as pure as water, Cheng Ying thought to himself. Perhaps he was doing wrong to thrust such a dire and important task upon him? Cheng Ying's steps began to falter. But when he remembered Gongsun Chujiu's reputation for being an upright and justice-loving man, and a staunch friend of Zhao Dun, he decided that Gongsun Chujiu was the only person who could undertake this great responsibility.

And so, after much deliberation, he came to the conclusion that there was nothing else for it at this stage but to press ahead and meet Gongsun Chujiu. But as he did so, he noticed that the sun was setting, and dusk was gathering. He did not dare to continue by night, so he sought lodging at a nearby farmhouse. As luck would have it, the woman of the house was a nursing mother, and Zhao the Orphan had his fill of milk that night.

Early the next morning, Cheng Ying bade farewell to his host, and hurried on his way, reaching Taiping Village before noon. After making a few inquiries with the local people, he learned that Gongsun Chujiu did not live in the village itself, but in a hut at the foot of the mountain. He thereupon moved on quickly until he came upon a cluster of thatched dwellings on a south-facing slope. In front was a double fence, adorned with vines and creepers.

Cheng Ying hurried forward, elated that he had at last come

to the house of Gongsun Chujiu. He was just about to knock at the gate when caution overcame him: "This Gongsun Chujiu was a great friend of Prime Minister Zhao Dun in the old days," he thought to himself. "But what if his years of retirement here have made him too fond of peace and contentment to be willing to embroil himself in the perilous cause of justice? What if he refuses to accept Zhao the Orphan? Besides, it is of the utmost importance that this matter be kept as secret as possible. The fewer people who know about it the better. If he shirks the responsibility of looking after it, he may reveal the child's identity to others. I had better keep the baby hidden for the time being."

He then turned away from the gate, found a thick clump of bushes, and hid the medicine box, with Zhao the Orphan inside it, there. Then he straightened his clothing, walked up to the wicker gate, and knocked lightly.

The gate creaked open, and there stood a tall, well-poised old man. His eyes were clear and firm. His hair and sideburns were completely white, as was the wisp of beard that hung down to his chest. Cheng Ying recognized him at once as Gongsun Chujiu, whom he had not seen for many years. In spite of the fact that he was in his seventies, the old man seemed alert and in fine spirits. Cheng Ying hastened to step forward and bow, saying, "Sir, you have long been in retirement. I, Cheng Ying, have come especially to call on you."

Now, when the two of them had made each other's acquaintance in the Zhao mansion, they had got along very well together. So Cheng Ying's turning up on his doorstep like this, just as the old man was feeling the loneliness of many years living in seclusion, was as welcome to him as meeting a boon companion in a strange land. Moved, Gongsun Chujiu returned his visitor's greeting, and said, "I am honored by this unexpected visit, Mr. Cheng. Forgive me for not coming to greet you on the road. Please come in, and sit down." When they were both seated, Gongsun Chujiu ordered his servant boy to make some tea. Cheng Ying was both pleased and apprehensive about this reception, and was at a loss what to say at first. A thousand things were eager to spill forth from his lips, but he managed to say only: "I trust you are well, sir?"

Gongsun Chujiu smiled and said, "These past few years I have kept myself away from the hubbub. As a result, I have a good appetite and I sleep soundly, and I am never ill." He added, with a laugh: "I am afraid, doctor, that I can't give you any business." Then he said, eagerly: "Tell me, how are the court officials? Has there been any improvement in state affairs, I wonder? You see, moldering in retirement as I have been for such a long time, I hear no more news of the outside world than a deaf person."

Cheng Ying sighed, and said. "I am afraid, sir, that the situation at court has grown worse since you held you post. The duke is a dissipated dunce, evil officials hold the reins of power, and the government gets worse by the day."

Gongsun Chujiu interjected, "But, why don't the ministers censure the duke, and curb the excesses of the degenerate officials?"

"Rascals the like of Tu'an Gu have been known since ancient times," Cheng Ying replied. "Even the reigns of the sage kings Tang and Yu were disturbed by the Four Villains, and conspirators ran rampant."

Gongsun Chujiu's blood, which had been cool and calm for so long, suddenly began to boil and seethe. "But do you mean to tell me that Prime Minister Zhao Dun can do nothing about it?" he spluttered.

This mention of Zhao Dun gave Cheng Ying just the opening he wanted. He launched into a detailed account of how Duke Ling and Tu'an Gu had killed innocent people for sport, turned the palace into a den of lascivious wantonness, driven Zhao Dun into exile and massacred the Zhao clan. As he listened to all this, Gongsun Chujiu's eyes started from his head. In the end, he banged the table and leapt to his feet, saying, "If I were still at court, that blockhead of a duke and those reprobates of officials would not get away with such outrages!"

Cheng Ying was relieved to see that Gongsun Chujiu's old sense of righteous indignation had not withered during his lengthy retirement, and hastened to broach the purpose of his visit. "Fortunately," he said, "the princess was pregnant at the time these disasters struck, and she gave birth to a boy. However, Tu'an Gu, determined to uproot all possible causes of future danger to himself, put a heavy guard around the princess's quarters."

At this point, Gongsun Chujiu burst out, "Just let me go and bring that baby back to the mountains. I'll raise him until he is old enough to avenge the Zhao clan."

Cheng Ying cried, "Sir, calm yourself, I pray. The child has already been snatched from the jaws of death."

Gongsun Chujiu looked closely at his visitor. From the other man's calm and resolute expression, with shining eyes and keen glance, he began to sense that there was more to Cheng Ying's presence than just a courtesy call. Turning over in his mind what Cheng Ying had just told him, the purpose of the doctor's mission suddenly dawned on him. At once, his fury turned to elation. Clapping Cheng Ying on the shoulder, he said, "You're a splendid fellow, Cheng Ying. So, you wasted no time in performing the heroic deed of rescuing Zhao the Orphan, eh? Well, now I suppose you want to leave him here. Where is the baby now, by the way?"

"To tell you the truth, sir," replied Cheng Ying, "my purpose in coming here was to seek sanctuary for the child. Zhao the Orphan is not far from your gate."

Hearing this, Gongsun Chujiu jumped up and ran outside, closely followed by Cheng Ying. They lifted the medicine box from the bushes, opened the lid, and looked inside. There was the baby, fast asleep, its chubby face fair and plump. Gazing on Zhao the Orphan, Gongsun Chujiu felt a mixture of emotions surge through him as he contemplated the child's plight — joy, resentment and pain. He gently lifted it from the box, murmuring, "What a noble countenance you have, little one! Alas, while you were still in your mother's womb your clan was destroyed. No sooner had you been born than you were left without either father or mother. How pitiful is your condition! But when you grow up, and come seeking reckoning for that horrendous blood debt, I am sure that you will mow down your family's enemies like a scythe reaps the barley."

The two men took Zhao the Orphan into the house, and settled him comfortably. The Gongsun Chujiu said, "It's best if the child stays with me. I will raise him. That dastardly Tu'an Gu will never think of looking for him in this remote, mountainous region."

But Cheng Ying, although he was overjoyed to hear this, looked anguished as he explained, "Sir, I am afraid there is something you do not know. As soon as Tu'an Gu learned that the child had slipped through his fingers, he was so incensed that he ordered posters to be put up, saying that if Zhao the Orphan is not surrendered within five days every newborn infant in the State of Jin will be slaughtered."

Gongsun Chujiu's face turned steely-grey with anger. "That wicked monster!" he roared. "I will go straightaway and cast his evil deeds back in his teeth!"

He was so consumed with fury that his silvery whiskers trembled, and he would have rushed off to have it out with Tu'an Gu there and then, if Cheng Ying had not hurriedly stopped him. "Please calm yourself, sir," he urged. "The situation at court is not what it was. Tu'an Gu has gathered all power into his own hands. If you were to confront him alone, that would be tantamount to throwing yourself right into his net. It would be like trying to smash a rock with an egg. You would not only be helping the cause of preserving Zhao the Orphan, but on the contrary you would ruin the whole enterprise."

Gongsun Chujiu calmed down and reflected on the position they were in. It was true that he had been about to act rashly, but it was hard to suppress the anger in his heart. "But we can't let Tu'an Gu get away with this," he groaned.

Cheng Ying said, "Right now, the most important thing is to save Zhao the Orphan at all costs. I have discussed it with my wife and father-in-law, and we have formed a plan. But we need your assistance, sir, for it to succeed. It just so happens that a few days ago my wife gave birth to a baby boy — in fact, only one day after Zhao the Orphan was born. The plan is to pass this boy off as Zhao the Orphan, whom I smuggled out of the mansion of the royal son-in-law. Then you, sir, must hurry to Tu'an Gu, and denounce me as the culprit. You must tell him that I have the baby hidden. Tu'an Gu will have my house searched, and all my family will be executed. Tu'an Gu will then be satisfied, and all the newborn babies in the State of Jin will be saved — as will Zhao the Orphan. You can then bring up this child, who will avenge the Zhao clan."

Gongsun Chujiu stared at Cheng Ying in amazement and awe. "My dear fellow," he said, "are you really willing to sacrifice your own flesh and blood for the sake of Zhao the Orphan?"

Holding back his tears, Cheng Ying replied, "I will not deceive you, sir. In middle age I have finally acquired a son and heir. Of course, he is the most precious thing in the world to me. Not to mention, of course, the suffering and pain my dear wife has undergone, through many miscarriages, to produce a son. Naturally, the very thought of handing my baby over to Tu'an Gu tears at my heart. But the Zhao clan has served the State of Jin faithfully for generations. Their meritorious deeds have been magnificent. But now they have fallen into the snares of a villainous official, whose intention is to exterminate all the Zhaos, including the sole surviving male child. How can I just sit back and watch this happen? Besides, in the old days the prime minister was extremely kind to me, and enabled me to become what I am today. It seems to me that if Zhao the Orphan survives, there is hope that justice will be restored to the State of Jin. I will have no regrets about dying, together with my whole family, if I can serve my country on the one hand and repay my debt of gratitude to Prime Minister Zhao Dun on the other."

As he spoke, tears poured down his cheeks. He then sobbed out the stories of the noble deaths of Chu Ni, Ti Miming, Ling Zhe, Han Jue, and the princess and her serving maid. Wiping his eyes, Cheng Ying added, "As soon as I crossed the threshold of the mansion of the royal son-in-law, I consigned the fate of my family to oblivion. My only consideration was that if Heaven has eyes it will not allow loyal and good people to perish utterly. It was thanks to Han Jue, who drew his sword and used it to aid me, that I managed to escape death myself and rescue Zhao the Orphan. Little did I suspect that Tu'an Gu would be so cruel and vicious as to threaten to kill all the newborn infants in the State of Jin if he could not get his hands on Zhao the Orphan. But I don't care if my head is chopped off and my blood runs in streams. Zhao the Orphan must never be handed over to him! But it is because I cannot bear the thought of bringing tragedy to thousands of innocent families in Jin that I have devised this plan, and I hope you will cooperate with me, sir."

Gongsun Chujiu was moved to tears by this declaration. He said, with deep emotion: "This is a most lofty-minded decision. Although I am unworthy to assist you in this noble undertaking, I will raise Zhao the Orphan to adulthood, and instruct him in his destiny, which is to wreak vengeance for his clan." He then hesitated for a moment, shook his head and said, "No, I'm afraid it won't work; it won't work at all. You see, when I was serving as a minister at court I had frequent clashes with that reptile Tu'an Gu. If I suddenly turn up out of the blue with this story, he'll never believe it. I myself don't mind dying, as the price to pay for ruining a great enterprise. But if this plan to save Zhao the Orphan is scuttled, it will mean that you and your child will have died in vain, and that I will have betrayed the great hopes of General Han Jue and the other martyrs!"

This left Cheng Ying nonplussed. The two of them stood there for a while in silence, Gongsun Chujiu stroking his beard and deep in thought, and Cheng Ying wringing his hands in distress. Suddenly, Gongsun Chujiu asked his companion: "How old are you now, my friend?"

Puzzled at this abrupt inquiry, Cheng Ying replied, "Forty-five, sir."

"Excellent!" remarked the other. "You see, I am now 75 years old. If I am to raise the orphan until he is old enough to fulfill his destiny, that will take some 20 years. By that time, I will be 95. Who knows? If I die in the next ten years, the boy will still not have reached maturity, and will not be able to accomplish his task. But you, on the other hand, are much younger than I. Even after another 20 years, you will still not be as old as I am now, and you will be able to help him reach his life's appointed goal. Besides, you have never held a court position — in the old days you were just a client in the household of Zhao Dun. So Tu'an Gu doesn't know you. I, on the other hand, have served three rulers, and together with the prime minister assisted in the business of government for a long time. We were the closest of friends, and foiled Tu'an Gu's schemes many times. It is obvious that he would never believe me no matter what I told him. If you are willing to sacrifice your own son, bring him here to me. Then report to Tu'an Gu that I was the one who spirited away

Zhao the Orphan. He will send his men here to kill me and your baby, and that will be the end of the affair. You can then choose to live in some place where you can raise Zhao the Orphan, so that some day he will be ready to embark on his mission of vengeance."

Cheng Ying could not help but admire Gongsun Chujiu's exquisite reasoning. However, he was still inclined to stick to his original plan, until Gongsun Chujiu appealed top him, saying, "Please look at the matter this way: Each of us has his task to perform. Now, which is the most arduous — seeking death or raising the orphan?"

Cheng Ying pondered for a short while, and then said, "Death is quick, but raising the orphan will take 20 years. Of the two, I would say that seeking death is the easier option."

Gongsun Chujiu clapped his hands, and laughed heartily. "Well said," he chortled. "And since I have been moldering away up to my neck in the yellow soil, I'll choose the easier option. You have many years of life ahead of you, and you are still full of vigor, so you should take on the onerous burden. What do you say to that?"

Cheng Ying protested, "But, sir, you have being living in seclusion here in Taiping Village for many years, in peace and contentment, avoiding the mundane world of state affairs. I have not the heart to ask you to submit to death, while a worthless man like myself shoulders such a great responsibility."

But Gongsun Chujiu retorted, "What kind of talk is that, my friend? I have one foot in the coffin already. Death awaits me just around the corner anyway. Besides, if Chu Ni, Ti Miming, Ling Zhe and Han Jue could so generously lay down their lives for the Zhao clan, with whom they had no connection, surely the time has come for me to repay the prime minister for his close friendship with me in the old days."

Seeing that the other's mind was made up, Cheng Ying realized that he himself had a better chance of convincing Tu'an Gu, and thereby ensuring the success of their mission. Cheng Ying could not oppose the old man, but said with concern: "Sir, your resoluteness in upholding justice at the cost of your life will shine for evermore in the annals of history. But Tu'an Gu is a cruel and ruthless man. He may put you to the most excruciating tortures to try to extract from you the truth about how Zhao the Orphan was snatched away from under his very nose. How could a man of your advanced years withstand harsh interrogation and savage torture? If that fiend Tu'an Gu succeeded in breaking your spirit and extracting the truth, both I and my son would die in vain, and, what would be much more tragic, the effort to save Zhao the Orphan would be aborted."

But Gongsun Chujiu only laughed at this argument. "You may set your mind at rest," he assured his companion. "I may be old and decrepit, but a sturdy heart still beats in my breast. My pledge is unbreakable. No matter what tortures Tu'an Gu puts me through, he will not get a word out of me. I will resist till the end."

The trials and fatigues of the past few days as he strove desperately to rescue Zhao the Orphan, and the knowledge that finally he was to lose the baby son he had always longed for, were too much for Cheng Ying, and he abandoned himself to a flood of tears. Gongsun Chujiu also wept. They clung to each other in their grief for a long time, until the older man wiped his eyes, and spoke a few words of comfort to Cheng Ying: "Be assured that your fidelity and service to the Zhao clan, and as a noble benefactor of the State of Jin, will make your name splendid for all time to come."

Cheng Ying likewise wiped away his tears. "It is because I cannot bear to see wickedness run rampant, riding roughshod over the good and loyal, that I have devoted myself to serving the country's cause and repaying private kindness. Now, the help I have asked you for, sir, means you going to your death of your own free will. I will make sure that in twenty years' time you are repaid for your sacrifice."

Gongsun Chujiu replied, "To serve the country's cause and repay private kindness — that is my long-cherished wish. And today it has been fulfilled!" So saying, he sent his servant for wine, and he and Cheng Ying drank toasts to the day when Zhao the Orphan would grow to manhood and exact vengeance for the wrongs done to the Zhao clan. They drank to the day when all the treacherous officials would be beheaded; when sacrifices to the Zhao ancestors would be resumed; when Zhao the Orphan would reclaim his inheritance and wield power in the reformed court; and when the State of Jin would once more be a mighty power among the feudal states. Their spirits restored, they encouraged each other to face their trials with confidence.

It was evening when they had finished discussing their plans. Because time was pressing, Cheng Ying proposed traveling back by night to substitute the babies for each other, and bring his own to Taiping Village. Gongsun Chujiu did not try to dissuade him, but insisted on traveling with him.

So off these two stalwart men set. A crescent moon hung in the sky. A blustery wind blew from the mountains and made the pine trees moan. The hearts of the travelers thumped uncontrollably, and the blood roared in their ears. Rounding a mountain, they came to a high plain. Cheng Ying took leave of his companion there, and continued his journey in the moonlight. Watching Cheng Ying's form fade into the distance, Gongsun Chujiu found it hard to suppress a feeling of turmoil in his breast, as scenes from the days when he and Zhao Dun battled evil flashed before his eyes...

Gongsun Chujiu remembered the day that Duke Ling succeeded to the throne at the age of ten. Shortly thereafter, his mother had been seized by a sudden fit of illness, and died. Now the boy was by nature tyrannical and cruel, and of extraordinary behavior. With his mother gone, and no one else in authority to restrain him, his conduct became more and more erratic; he simply did as he pleased. All day he indulged himself in the pastimes of hunting and cock fighting, together with low companions. He was callous and had a brutal streak in him. The court officials observed this, and were fearful that when their ruler grew to manhood, he would turn out to be a tyrant who would care nothing for the welfare of the state. Minister Gongsun Chujiu, being an upright official, did not hesitate to confront the duke with his neglect of duty. At one morning audience, he told the duke: "Filial piety is the basis of a ruler's management of the state. Now that Your Majesty's mother has passed away, Your Majesty should be putting on a display of mourning which would set an example for the common people. So how does it come about that even before the late dowager's bones are cold, Your Majesty is devoting himself to frivolity. Even the common people strictly observe the mourning rites for a deceased parent; how much the more is it incumbent on Your Majesty to do so!"

The duke, who was used to a carefree round of pleasure, was stung by this rebuke, and would have retorted sharply had he not noticed that Zhao Dun and the other ministers were supporting Gongsun Chujiu. He did not want to incur the displeasure of the whole body of court officials. Besides, he remembered his mother telling him when he had first come to the throne that Zhao Dun had the power to depose him. So, for the time being he pretended to accept the criticism and to be prepared to mend his ways.

Following this incident, the more the duke thought about it, the more incensed he became. He was the sovereign of a state, after all, monarch of all he surveyed! How dare some petty official take him to task. If things went on like this, what would the world come to? Meanwhile, the cronies and hangers-on who surrounded the duke, seeing that their master was annoyed, seized the opportunity to ingratiate themselves with him by egging him on in his excesses. And before long the pack of them were scheming to get Gongsun Chujiu dismissed from office and facing criminal charges.

A few days later, when Gongsun Chujiu presented a memorial to the throne at a morning audience, Duke Ling deliberately picked out a slight imperfection in the wording, and accused him of disrespect for his ruler and defiance of the ducal authority. He straightaway gave orders to have Gongsun Chujiu stripped of his post and thrown in the dungeons. At this, there was a cackle of approval from the villainous sycophants surrounding the throne. But just as Gongsun Chujiu was about to be led away, Zhao Dun stepped forward from the ranks of the ministers. He had been watching the situation closely, and knew well that Duke Ling was getting revenge for his humiliation of a few days previously. Now he intervened, saying, "Your Majesty, as the lord of your people and the ruler of the state, it behooves you to set an example of filial piety by observing the rites and carrying out the ceremonies fitting to the memory of your recently deceased mother. But you seem to be completely untouched by grief, spending your days gallivanting and sporting to your heart's content. If you continue in this way, how can you gain the trust and sympathy of the common people? I appeal to you: Minister Gongsun is your loyal servant, who gives you honest advice. All for the sake of the State of Jin, he yearns to turn you from the crooked path onto the straight one. But Your Majesty, I am afraid, refuses to heed loyal words, instead lending an ear constantly to the treacherous urgings of base men, and heaping injustices upon true-hearted officials. I am very much afraid that you may be following in the doom-directed footsteps of the tyrants Jie of Xia and Zhou of Shang. The result will be the ruin of the State of Jin!"

Duke Ling blushed to the roots of his hair. He could find no words to reply to this diatribe of Zhao Dun's, and nor could his gaggle of cronies. The duke had no choice but to rescind his order, and there the matter rested and festered.

Gongsun Chujiu was overcome with gratitude for Zhao Dun's bold intervention, and the two men became the closest of friends from that time on. As the influence of Tu'an Gu over Duke Ling grew, Gongsun Chujiu and Zhao Dun worked in close coordination to denounce the duke's excesses. As a result, the two of them earned a wide-ranging reputation for virtue. But finally, seeing that his admonitions were all in vain and that Tu'an Gu's evil influence was growing by the day and unable to bear his indignation any longer, Gongsun Chujiu took the bold step of resigning his post and going to live in obscurity in Taiping Village. But he still had lingering regrets that he had not been as unyielding as Zhao Dun. Perhaps they could have curbed some of the wild excesses of Duke Ling and Tu'an Gu, and reined in their persecution of good men? But it was too late for regrets, Gongsun Chujiu now reminded himself. The only thing for him was to devote himself heart and soul to the saving of Zhao the Orphan, and in that way remain true to the friendship he had shared with Zhao Dun in the old days.

These old memories stirred a flood of noble sentiments in the breast of Gongsun Chujiu. He looked up at the waning moon. It looked like a sharp curved dagger. The fancy came into his head of plucking it out of the sky and plunging it into the breast of Tu'an Gu. The wailing of the wind in the pines seemed to become the roar of a lion shaking the forests and the gorges, and gradually become a fire of hatred blazing in Gongsun Chujiu's heart. He thought ahead to his thundering denunciation of Tu'an Gu, to his walk to death undaunted. This would be the way he would vent his rage, and leave behind a heroic name for all eternity.

As he stood there lost in thought, the moon dipped and the stars dimmed. Morning dew gathered on his clothing. Only then did he turn, and plod the lonely way back to his cottage.

CHAPTER SIX

The Noble Death of Gongsun Chujiu

CHENG YING WALKED all night, until he arrived at the village of Guojiazhuang. He lost no time explaining to his father-in-law and wife the ruse he had worked out with Gongsun Chujiu. He dared not linger too long, and so, after handing over Zhao the Orphan to his wife and putting his own baby son in the medicine box, despite his wife's great reluctance to part with her offspring, he set off immediately on his return journey.

Cheng Ying reached Taiping Village towards evening of the next day. As he caught sight of Gongsun Chujiu's dwelling, there came to his ears the clear twang of a zither. Knowing that the performer must be Gongsun Chujiu, he stopped to listen. At first the notes were like the murmuring of a hidden brook, or the trickling of a stream across a sandy bed. Before long, the strings sent forth a more lively sound: reminiscent of the gurgling of waters in spring or the waves rippling across the surface of a pond. Then came the crescendo, the shattering of silver bottles and the spilling of liquid, the springing forth of cavalry and the clash of swords and lances — the discordant sounds of battle. Finally, all the strings sounded in harmony, making one think of a bright moon reflected on the emerald waves of a calm sea. An old saying goes: "The sound of the zither arouses elegant thoughts." According to another: "The zither reproduces the sounds of the heartstrings." The notes of the zither told Cheng Ying that Gongsun Chujiu had made up his mind to face death. The thought filled him with unbearable sorrow. Without more ado, he rushed into the house. The two of them exchanged words of comfort, mindful of the deadline on the Tu'an Gu's notice. Cheng Ying then deposited his own son comfortably in Gongsun Chujiu's cottage, ate a hasty breakfast, and set off for the capital of Jin.

Having accepted the baby boy, Gongsun Chujiu began to reflect on the situation: First of all, if he allowed Tu'an Gu to find the baby too easily, it would arouse that cunning fox's suspicions. It would be better to lay a bit of a false trail in order to fool him. At noon the next day, calculating that Tu'an Gu must be drawing near by this time, Gongsun Chujiu climbed a high hill to watch for his approach. Sure enough, before long he espied in the distance a troop of several hundred horsemen. So, Tu'an Gu must have believed Cheng Ying's story, and had dispatched troops to recover Zhao the Orphan! He hurried back to the cottage, hid the child in a cave behind the house, and sat down to await events, to all appearances quite at leisure.

Meanwhile, after ordering the posters to be put up and dispatching spies all over the capital, Tu'an Gu had also been waiting. After a few days, when nobody surrendered Zhao the Orphan or denounced the kidnapper, and his spies returned with nothing to show for their efforts, Tu'an Gu came to the end of his patience. "Very well," he growled to himself, "if this wretched populace chooses to defy me, I'll put all their brats to death!" He thereupon ordered more posters to be made, and pasted up at the appropriate time. The decree read:

"Every infant below the age of six months, whether born to an official family or that of a private citizen, within the territory of the State of Jin must be handed over to the office of the commander of the palace guard within three days. Penalty for disobedience: Execution of the family to the ninth degree of kinship."

This done, he immediately sent men to search every house for children of the targeted age. Before long, one of his guards announced that a man named Cheng Ying had come to make a denunciation: "He says that he knows the whereabouts of Zhao the Orphan, sir!"

Tu'an Gu was as delighted as if someone had brought him a treasure. "Show him in at once," he ordered.

The person who was ushered into Tu'an Gu's presence was short of stature, had a swarthy face and bore a serene expression on his face. It was none other than Cheng Ying. Tu'an Gu put on a show of sternness. "Who are you?" he barked.

His visitor replied, "My name is Cheng Ying. I live in Guojiazhuang Village in the suburbs of Jiangyi. I am a physician by profession."

"You say that you have come to make a denunciation. Where is Zhao the Orphan?"

"The child is concealed in the house of Gongsun Chujiu, in Taiping Village, Your Honor."

Tu'an Gu was by nature suspicious, crafty and sly. His first reaction was to smell something fishy about this report. With a slight frown creasing his brows, he inquired, "How does a country doctor like you come by news of Zhao the Orphan?"

Unperturbed, Cheng Ying replied, "I often go to Mount Shouyang to pick herbs, Your Honor. I have met Gongsun Chujiu several times. Yesterday, while coming back from a herb-hunting trip, I happened to call in at his house for a drink of water. I was surprised to see a baby there, wrapped in a brocaded silk coverlet. Now I know that Gongsun Chujiu is over 70 years old, and his wife is deceased. Moreover, they never had children. So, I asked myself, where did that baby come from? I remembered seeing a poster that Your Honor had had pasted up, so I asked him point-blank: 'Is this the child they call Zhao the Orphan?' He turned pale with fear, and was speechless. And so from that I concluded that he was the one who had kidnapped Zhao the Orphan."

But Tu'an Gu was not so easily convinced. "You lying wretch! How dare you come to me with such a cock and bull story?"

"I assure you, Your Honor, that every word I have said is the truth. If you do not believe me, why not send men to Taiping Village to find out?"

A grimace crossed Tu'an Gu's countenance. "What I want to know," he said, "is why you are so eager to inform on Gongsun Chujiu, a man against whom you have never had a grievance in the past and do not have a grievance now. Perhaps the two of you are trying to pull the wool over my eyes, eh? Well, if you are telling the truth, all right. But if you are not, I have a sharp sword with which to deal with the likes of you." So saying, he drew his sword from its scabbard with a menacing swoosh, and brandished it under Cheng Ying's nose.

Cheng Ying was prepared for this kind of reception. He knew that Tu'an Gu would bluster and try to frighten him. So he pretended to be intimidated, and whined, "I beg Your Honor not to be angry with me, but to hear me out. It is true, sir, that I have no grievance against Gongsun Chujiu. But I read a notice that Your Honor had had posted, to the effect that if Zhao the Orphan were not found, then all the infants in the State of Jin would be put to death. Now, for three generations there has only been one son in my family. I am now in my 45th year, and have at last managed to produce a son and heir, who is not yet one month old. My wife, who is of a frail disposition, carried him for ten months, and it was a difficult birth. Naturally, she regards him as a precious treasure. If I comply with Your Honor's command, it would no longer mean the extinction of the Cheng line. So my reason for informing on Gongsun Chujiu is not to save the lives of the other babies of Jin, but to ensure the continuity of my family tree."

As he spoke, Cheng Ying remembered the fate that awaited his child, and tears of grief accompanied his last words.

This display of anguish, together with the plausible explanation he had heard from Cheng Ying, more or less convinced Tu'an Gu. He said, "In the past, Gongsun Chujiu was a colleague at court with Zhao Dun. The two of them were as thick as thieves, and constantly ganged up against me. Having learned of the massacre of the Zhao clan, I suppose he was anxious to raise Zhao the Orphan himself. But he has been in retirement for many years. Without inside help, how could he manage to get the child away?"

As he spoke, he fixed an accusing gaze on Cheng Ying. But the latter was unperturbed. "That I don't know, Your Honor," he replied. "But, as the saying goes: 'The longer the night the more the dreams.' I am afraid that if you delay, Your Honor, the bird may fly the coop."

"All right," said Tu'an Gu. "You lead the way. I'll arrest that old fellow Gongsun first, and decide what to do later."

He thereupon gave the necessary orders, and before long a troop of several hundred mounted men, with Tu'an Gu in full armor at their head, was trotting down the road towards Taiping Village, banners flying and swords and pikes gleaming. As they passed, the bystanders averted their eyes in fear.

At their head was Cheng Ying, riding a donkey led by a servant of Tu'an Gu's household. He doggedly led the way, not daring to betray an inkling of the pain and anger in his heart. Reaching Taiping Village after noon, Tu'an Gu ordered his men to put a tight guard on Gongsun Chujiu's house, and then to go in and find Zhao the Orphan and bring Gongsun Chujiu before him.

The soldiers smashed down the gate, and poured into the cottage. Before long, they dragged Gongsun Chujiu out, tightly bound. Their captain went down on one knee before Tu'an Gu, and reported, "Sir, we only found this old man in the cottage. There was no sign of Zhao the Orphan."

Tu'an Gu motioned to the soldiers to fall back. He gave a sinister chuckle. "Well," he said to Gongsun Chujiu, "even at your advanced age you are impatient to meddle in affairs which don't concern you, eh? Do you know what crime you have committed?"

Gongsun Chujiu answered, "I have been living in seclusion, Your Honor, with only the forests and mountains for company. What crime could I have committed? I really don't understand why you have mobilized this great armed force to arrest a harmless old fellow like me."

"Old man," said Tu'an Gu, "you have played a sly trick right under my very nose. Tell me. In the days after the posters were put up by the court, and a search was being made throughout the State of Jin for the orphan, and the country was in an uproar, why did you set yourself up against me and hide Zhao the Orphan?"

Gongsun Chujiu uttered a mirthless laugh. "So it's Zhao the Orphan you are after, is it?" he cried. "I really can't help you there, I'm afraid. Even if I ate the heart of a bear and drank the bile of a leopard, I would still not have the courage to kidnap Zhao the Orphan."

The old man's dignified denial of any wrongdoing enraged his captor. His eyes bulging with fury, he roared, "It seems that you need a good beating before you'll confess." Then, turning to his guards, said, "Come here you men, and give this doddering old fool a sound thrashing!"

His minions rushed to do his bidding. Throwing Gongsun Chujiu to the ground, they started to beat him with clubs. Just then, a squad of soldiers who had been searching the cottage and its surroundings returned to report that no trace of the baby could be found.

This only increased Tu'an Gu's frustration, and he ordered that Gongsun Chujiu be beaten even harder, until he revealed the whereabouts of Zhao the Orphan.

As he did so, he gave Cheng Ying a suspicious sideways glance. The latter felt a shiver of fear run through him. He looked furtively at Gongsun Chujiu, and saw that the old man was withstanding the beating stoically. Suddenly, he had an idea. Turning to Tu'an Gu, he said, "Your Honor, this is a region of high mountains and thick forests. Perhaps the old man has hidden the baby somewhere in the vicinity?" This made sense to Tu'an Gu, and he immediately dispatched men to search the countryside round about.

While they were doing so, Gongsun Chujiu said nothing, despite the savage beating he was receiving, but "If you think I have hidden Zhao the Orphan, tell me: Who was it saw me do so?"

Whereupon, Tu'an Gu sneered, "It was Cheng Ying here who informed on you."

A look of indignation came over Gongsun Chujiu's face, and he yelled at Cheng Ying: "You infamous villain, Cheng Ying! How many times have I shown you hospitality? Have I ever done anything to harm you? And this is how you repay me for my kindness! With vile slander, you cur!"

Cheng Ying endured this condemnation with lowered head. Not a word did he utter, putting on a show of embarrassment. Gongsun Chujiu kept on pouring out a stream of invective.

In the meantime, Tu'an Gu was getting more and more impatient. He muttered, "If this stubborn old dotard doesn't confess soon, I'll die of apoplexy." He whirled round on Cheng Ying, who was standing mute nearby, and suspicion stirred within him once more. Frowning, he thought of a new tactic. In a crafty tone of voice, he said to Cheng Ying: "This situation has come about because of your report. Now you beat the old man, and if he doesn't confess, you will bear the blame."

Cheng Ying gazed at Gongsun Chujiu's torn and bleeding flesh. The idea of inflicting even more pain on his friend, by his own hand, horrified him. In a panic he appealed to Tu'an Gu: "Your Honor, I am only a poor country doctor. I am physically weak — why, I don't even have the strength to truss a chicken! Besides, my disposition is to do good. How could I beat somebody? I beg you to rescind your order, and think of some other way."

But Tu'an Gu was unmoved. "Cheng Ying, if you are squeamish about hurting Gongsun Chujiu, I will have to think that it's because you are afraid that he will point an accusatory finger at yourself," was his bland response.

At this, Cheng Ying realized that Tu'an Gu was suspicious of his own role in the affair. There was nothing for it but to steel himself to beat his friend. "Very well, Your Honor," he said.

Picking up a thin stick from the ground, he stepped forward. But Tu'an Gu snorted. "I see that you are careful to choose a club no thicker than a chopstick. So you must be afraid that he'll denounce you if you hurt him!"

Cheng Ying then put the thin twig down, and picked up a thick cudgel. However, the paranoid Tu'an Gu snarled, "Aha! So that's it! You picked up the thin one, hoping that if you did not hurt him he would not betray your complicity in his crime. Now you pick up a thick one, hoping to kill him with it, so that he can't reveal your guilt!"

Cheng Ying was flabbergasted. "Your Honor," he cried, "if the thin one was no good, and the thick one is no good, do you want me to beat him or not?"

"Cheng Ying, stop dithering!" was the reply. "Choose a stick which is neither too thin nor too thick, and get on with it."

Cheng Ying did as he was ordered. Suppressing his distaste for what he was about to do, he began to beat Gongsun Chujiu. The old man, knowing how distressful this must be to Cheng Ying, thought of a ruse to remove Tu'an Gu's suspicions. Pretending to swoon with pain, when he came to he cried out, "Oh, that was the worst beating I have had to endure so far. Which devil is beating me now?"

Delighted, Tu'an Gu informed him that his tormentor was the man who had informed on him, Cheng Ying.

Gongsun Chujiu raised his head, and glared at Cheng Ying. "There is no quarrel between us, so why are you beating me so savagely?"

Cheng Ying retorted, "You had better confess quickly, Mr Gongsun, to save yourself more suffering."

"Don't talk nonsense," said Gongsun Chujiu. "Why are you trying to pin all the blame on me when you know perfectly well where Zhao the Orphan is?"

Cheng Ying was terrified when he heard these words, and began to tremble from head to toe. He hastily stammered, "The old man has had all his brains beaten out of him, talking like that."

Seeing that not even the prospect of death would make Gongsun Chujiu confess, Tu'an Gu lost all patience. He seized a club himself, and belabored the old man with it. With a pitiful cry, Gongsun Chujiu swooned. Some of the guards fetched a bucket of water, and doused Gongsun Chujiu's head. This revived him somewhat. He mumbled incoherently: "The two of us, ... together..." Then he lost consciousness again.

Cheng Ying's heart skipped a beat. The alarming thought came to him that Gongsun Chujiu had been beaten so badly that he was talking in a delirium. If that was so, then he might blurt out the truth, and their plan to save Zhao the Orphan would be wrecked."

He blenched at the prospect, and, noticing the doctor's sudden confusion, Tu'an Gu became convinced that some trick was being played on him. "Old man Gongsun's stubbornness has finally been broken. He is ready to tell us who his accomplice is, I think."

Thereupon, he bent down, and shouted in Gongsun Chujiu's ear: "Old man, just now you said something about 'the two of us together'. Who's the other one? Tell the truth, and I'm prepared to let you live."

The corners of Gongsun Chujiu's mouth twitched. The words came haltingly: "I ... I ... two of us ..."

The terrified Cheng Ying hastened to interrupt him before he said anything more: "Mr. Gongsun," he cried sternly, "everyone is responsible for his own actions. Don't try to shift the blame onto someone else."

Tu'an Gu gave a hollow chuckle, turned to Cheng Ying, and said, "I think you must be the other person involved, Cheng Ying. Otherwise why are you quaking in your shoes like that?"

With an ingratiating smile wreathing his face, Cheng Ying said, "The old man has been beaten so badly he doesn't know what he is saying, Your Honor."

At this point, Gongsun Chujiu revived again. "What do you have to be afraid of, Cheng Ying?" he asked. "I wasn't implicating you."

Tu'an Gu yelled at him: "If Cheng Ying wasn't one of the two people you mentioned, who was the other one?"

"You have had me beaten so severely, Your Honor, that I hardly know what I am saying," was Gongsun Chujiu's reply. "I don't remember saying anything about two people."

Infuriated, Tu'an Gu drew his sword. Bellowing, "You old reprobate, how dare you trifle with me?" he was just about to chop Gongsun Chujiu's head off when one of his men came running down the mountainside, carrying a baby.

"Sir," he cried, "I found this boy child in a cave on the hillside behind the old man's cottage. I think it's that Zhao the Orphan."

On the spot, Tu'an Gu's anger turned to joy. He grabbed the infant, and thrust it before Gongsun Chujiu's face, saying with a wicked smile: "Well, Mr. Gongsun Chujiu, do you still deny any role in this affair? Since there is nobody else living around here, I wonder who could have concealed the child if not your good-old self, eh?"

The old man uttered a piercing cry. A fire seemed to be raging in his breast. He berated Tu'an Gu in thunderous tones: "You evil miscreant of a court official. You trained that savage hound to attack an honest servant of the court, and drove the prime minister far away. Then you forged a royal decree, and deceived the duke's son-in-law into committing suicide. You slaughtered over 300 members of the Zhao clan, and caused the princess to hang herself. Now, you are going to deprive this orphan — not even ten days old — of his life. Surely the world knows few villains as black-hearted as you!"

This indictment cut Tu'an Gu to the quick. In a towering rage, his face contorted like that of a ravening wolf, he hissed, "Gongsun Chujiu, you know not what enmity you have stirred within me. And now, you are going to have the privilege of watching me cut Zhao the Orphan into three pieces. Then, I will deal with you at my leisure."

So saying, he raised his sword on high. As it flashed in the sunlight prior to its deadly downswing, which would end the life of his only son, Cheng Ying felt a pain like a knife twisting in his heart. He could not bear to watch, and closed his eyes. But unexpectedly, Tu'an Gu sheathed his sword. A baleful grin twisted his features as he said, "Cheng Ying, you performed a singular service for me by denouncing Gongsun Chujiu. Now I have a further task to trouble you with. Slay Zhao the Orphan, and I will reward you handsomely upon our return to my mansion."

Cheng Ying was aghast. His whole life had been devoted to healing the sick and saving lives; he had even brought people back to life. How could he take a life, especially the life of his own baby boy? He hastened to make an excuse. "Your Honor," he pleaded, "I am a physician, and the highest aspiration of a physician is the saving of life. I have never taken the life of a living creature in all my long career. Besides, I am unworthy to aspire to Your Honor's rewards."

Tu'an Gu glared at Cheng Ying with malevolent eyes. "Your feeble prevarications suggest to me that you wish this spawn of the Zhaos to live. If it lives, it will grow up, and if it grows up, it will kill me eventually, won't it?"

Cheng Ying had been backed into a corner. He feared that if he delayed obeying Tu'an Gu's order any longer, he would arouse the latter's suspicions again. Hardening his heart, he walked over to the baby, and picked it up with trembling hands. He raised the child above his head, and with all his strength dashed it against a rock. The poor infant, not having been in the world ten days, was reduced to a pulpy mass. Cheng Ying turned, and with his eyes tightly closed to hold back the flood of tears that threatened to come rushing out. His heart felt as though it were being boiled in oil.

Gongsun Chujiu struggled forward, and cradled the child's body in his arms. At the same time, he cursed Tu'an Gu: "You heinous monster," he cried, "your wicked deeds make the very skies tremble. The Lord of Heaven will never forgive you. After my death, I will become a ravenous ghost, who will pluck out your black heart and tear out your liver. You will suffer a hideous death!"

But Tu'an Gu stood there with a frightful leer as he said this. Then he said, "Be that as it may, but first I will show you how the brat should have died." So saying, he drew his sword, and chopped the little body into three pieces.

With the blood pumping in his heart, and his eyes swimming with tears, Cheng Ying turned to Tu'an Gu. Furtively wiping his eyes, he said, "I trust in Your Honor's wisdom. Now that Zhao the Orphan has been disposed of, the other infants in the State of Jin are cleared of any taint, and so I take it that I will no longer have to worry about my progeny?"

Gongsun Chujiu took his cue perfectly on time. "You shameless wretch," he shouted at Cheng Ying, "You care not which innocent and good dies as long as you and yours live! Well, don't be too sure of your triumph. In another 20 years' time Zhao the Orphan will come back to life, and then he will be a grown man. Then he will wreak vengeance upon evil ministers, and then will my heart's desire be fulfilled."

Cheng Ying knew that Gongsun Chujiu was hinting to him that he must endure humiliation and the heavy burden that had been placed upon him of fostering Zhao the Orphan so that eventually justice would be done. He turned to the old man, and covering an imperceptible nod of the head with a sneer, he said, "Old man, you are facing death. How can you still find time to curse me?"

Gongsun Chujiu understood the hidden meaning in Cheng Ying's words. All his worries were at an end. While the attention of the guards was distracted, he suddenly smashed his head against a large rock. His skull cracked, and blood poured out, and his soul fled from his body. Seeing this, Tu'an Gu laughed out loud with approval.

Turning to Cheng Ying, he said. "This affair has turned out well for you. When we get back to may residence, you will be richly rewarded, I assure you."

Cheng Ying's mind was a whirlpool of conflicting emotions: He was devastated with grief over the death of his beloved son, and at the same time he was elated at the knowledge that Zhao the Orphan was now safe.

Right at this moment, a tempestuous wind began to blow. It caused the mountain pines to roar like a boiling ocean. Tu'an Gu and the others could not withstand the bone-chilling blast, and made their way back to the capital with all speed.

The corpses of Gongsun Chujiu and Cheng Ying's child — one old, one young — lay exposed on the mountain slope, their blood shed in a just cause. The green-clad mountains stood as solemn witnesses, and the clear waters poured forth a lament. Even the sun suddenly started to dim. It was as if they were mourning over the tragedy that had taken place in Taiping Village and will be commemorated for all time to come. And it was not long before news of this atrocity — that had "frightened Heaven and Earth, and made even ghosts and spirits weep"— spread through the whole of the State of Jin.

CHAPTER SEVEN

Taking Up Residence in the Tiger's Lair

AFTER HIS HECTIC few days, in which he snatched Zhao the Orphan from the jaws of death, and witnessed the murder of his own son, Cheng Ying's mind was in such turmoil that as soon as he reached home in Guojiazhuang Village, he collapsed on his bed, worn out by fatigue and with a great feeling of relief. That evening, he developed a fever. His whole body boiled, and he babbled in delirium, frothing at the mouth and oblivious to what was going on around him. Guo Shanren and his daughter were in a panic, and towards dawn sent for all the doctors in the neighborhood. The doctors all said that all seven emotions in Cheng Ying's body had suffered harm. On top of that, he had over-exerted himself, and this had brought the ailment to a dangerous stage. All that could be done was to administer a couple of doses of medicine, and wait and see. Guo Shanren hurried off to the nearest town, procured the medicine, prepared it and fed it to his son-in-law. The fever started to subside immediately. Needless to say, this was a trying time for the household, what with Cheng

Ying's wife, who had given birth less than a month previously, having to look after Zhao the Orphan and at the same time attend to her sick husband, and Guo Shanren having to dash around summoning doctors and fetching and administering medicine.

After 20 days or so, Cheng Ying had recovered. But although his mind was clear, his limbs were weak and flaccid, and his body seemed drained of strength. He knew that he had been at death's door, and that he needed to rest and calm his mind. His wife prepared special nourishing tonics for him every day. She was constantly in attendance at his bedside, whispering words of comfort.

A month or so passed, and winter set in. Cheng Ying felt fully recovered from his illness, but strength was still lacking in his body. One day, seeing that the winter sunshine was warm and bright, and that there was no wind, he expressed a desire to take a stroll outside. His wife thought that this would do him good after lying in bed for two months, so she wrapped him up in warm clothes and saw him off, with an admonition not to go too far and to come back soon.

Cheng Ying assented, and went for a leisurely walk. At the eastern edge of the village, he saw a dilapidated temple. The surrounding wall had crumbled in several places. There were also two neglected pavilions, which reminded Cheng Ying of something that his father-in-law had told him. It seemed that the people of Guojiazhuang Village had erected a temple with two pavilions in honor of Jie Zitui, who had lived in the time of Duke Wen. They had not been repaired for many years, with the result that they now lay in ruins. This must be the place, he thought, and he quickened his pace. Entering the temple grounds, he startled a flock of jackdaws, which flew away from the tangled grass that was their nesting place. He saw ancient vines and creepers, and a pond of clear water, now frozen over. A feeling over desolation crept over him. He followed an overgrown path. The main door to the temple was missing, and inside the building he could make out the shape of a statue, which he guessed was that of Jie Zitui. The body of the statue was delicately carved, and its posture was relaxed and at ease. Before it was an offering table, heaped with ashes and stubs of candles and incense sticks. As he stood gazing at this scene, a myriad thoughts crowded into his head. He reflected on the rare people who scorned fame and fortune. Jie Zitui had followed Duke Wen into exile, suffered every kind of hardship for 19 years, and when he finally returned home, unlike the other exiled ministers, he had refused both reward and rank, and gone to live in obscurity, looking after his mother deep in the mountains. He was truly a man to revere and admire, thought Cheng Ying.

But his long illness had taken its toll of Cheng Ying. He was still not strong enough to walk far, and this sudden burst of emotion made him feel dizzy. His head swam, and his feet felt as heavy as lead. Turning to leave, he found that he could hardly put one foot in front of the other. He groped his way to a clean stone bench in one of the pavilions. But no sooner had he slumped onto it than he fainted.

In the blink of an eye, Gongsun Chujiu floated into the pavilion. In a stern voice, he addressed the doctor: "Cheng Ying, your mission has not yet been accomplished. What do you mean by dawdling in this place?"

Cheng Ying felt an urge to rise and greet his old comrade, but in a flash, Gongsun Chujiu vanished. He tottered a couple of steps, when there suddenly appeared before him a faint vision of the naked form of his baby son, covered in blood and wailing. He tried to focus his eyes on the vision, but it was enveloped in dismal clouds and mist, and he could not see it clearly. Then he awoke in a frenzy of terror. He soon realized that he had had a dream, but his mind remained troubled. When he got home, he told his wife about the dream, and said that he had decided that he should go back to Taiping Village, and there give the remains of Gongsun Chujiu and his son a decent burial, with a proper grave mound for each. His wife, however, was horrified at the suggestion. "Are you out of your mind?" she gasped. "That cunning Tu'an Gu is still suspicious of you. While you were ill, he sent people to summon you, saying that he had something to talk to you about. But since you were still unconscious, they left it at that. If Tu'an Gu finds out that you have been back to Taiping Village, there will be hell to pay! Not only will all your sufferings have been in vain, but it will be hard to keep

Zhao the Orphan safe. Besides, Gongsun Chujiu and our child will have died for nothing."

Cheng Ying saw the wisdom in her words, so he shelved his plan. Nevertheless, he could not dispel the uneasiness from his mind.

As the pair were talking, there came the noise of the arrival of men and horses. Several soldiers came barging into the house, saying that they had orders to take Cheng Ying to Tu'an Gu.

Cheng Ying and his wife exchange a glance full of silent trepidation.

Having, as he thought, got rid of one big problem with his murder of Zhao the Orphan, Tu'an Gu, upon his return to the capital began plotting: He started to gather both the governmental and military power of the State of Jin into his own hands, so that he could usurp the throne. But he realized that he had no able men among his subordinates, only base flatterers unfitted for any great enterprise. He thereupon recruited client henchmen from far and wide, to build up his power and raise a revolt when the time should be ripe. To his disappointment, the response was poor. The few men who answered his call were of low caliber, or wretches who wanted free food. For a long time, he brooded on this problem, when all of a sudden he thought of Cheng Ying. After he had killed "Zhao the Orphan" and returned from Mount Shoushan, he had invited Cheng Ying back to his mansion to receive a reward. Cheng Ying, however, had steadfastly refused to take any reward, saying that the only reason he had informed on Gongsun Chujiu was to save the infants of Jin, including his own child. At that time, Tu'an Gu accepted this with equanimity, and let Cheng Ying go home. Now Cheng Ying sprang to mind again: Wouldn't he make a good addition to his band of clients? For one thing, it would be a way to reward him for his services. For another, ever since Cheng Ying had denounced Gongsun Chujiu and led him to Taiping Village, he had never been able to get rid of a lingering doubt about Cheng Ying; if he could get him into his household, he could keep an eye on him. Moreover, although Tu'an Gu had three wives and six concubines, they had produced no children for the 50-year-old Tu'an. He could adopt Cheng Ying's baby son as his own, and when he grew up, the lad could perform great feats for him. That would be killing a whole flock of birds with one stone!

The more he mulled over this plan, the more he liked it. So he wasted no more time, and sent men to summon Cheng Ying from his home in Guojiazhuang Village. Unexpectedly, they came back and reported that Cheng Ying was ill in bed, delirious with fever. Tu'an Gu had no choice but to let the matter rest there, but after about another month, judging that Cheng Ying would be recovered by this time, he sent men with a carriage to fetch him. Just before they set out, Tu'an Gu gave secret instructions to their captain to look closely for signs of anything suspicious about Cheng Ying, and if he noticed any to bring the whole household before him in chains.

Knowing nothing of Tu'an Gu's schemes, Cheng Ying and his wife feared that their part in the Zhao the Orphan affair had been discovered. So they were flabbergasted when they heard the captain of the guards say, "In recognition of your help in the execution of the orphan, the commander-in-chief wishes to raise you to the status of a member of his household. Not only that, but he also wishes to adopt your son. All three of you will move into his mansion, and in due course, his adopted son will succeed to his position."

The prospect of being installed in the "tiger's den" appalled the pair: Zhao the Orphan would have to treat Tu'an Gu as his father, and every minute of the day they would have to be on their guard, for one slip would mean disaster for them all. But Cheng Ying dared not refuse the offer, for fear of stirring Tu'an Gu's suspicions. He well knew that the ruthless Tu'an was capable of having him and his family slain on the spot, and that would be the end of their attempt to preserve the Zhao line. As Cheng Ying hesitated, his quick-witted wife said, before her husband could blurt out something disastrous: "We thank the commander-in-chief for his great kindness."

Tu'an Gu's men were well pleased with the alacrity with which

251

she accepted the offer, and considered their errand accomplished.

Cheng Ying was thereupon forced to pretend to be delighted, and he too accepted, saying, "I never thought that a humble fellow such as I would be the beneficiary of the commander-in-chief's bounty." But while his face blandished an obsequious smile, as if he were conscious of receiving a great favor, his heart was in torment. After gathering up some things they needed, Cheng Ying and his wife, with the baby, mounted the waiting carriage and were taken to Tu'an Gu's mansion.

They found Tu'an Gu himself waiting for them in the main hall. He rose and came forward to greet them. Tu'an Gu's beaming face seemed to shoot ten thousand arrows of loathing and distress into Cheng Ying's heart. He dared not reveal one iota of his real feelings, however, but kowtowed and said, "Many thanks for your boundless kindness, Commander-in-Chief. My wife and I will never forget your goodness."

"Sir," said Tu'an Gu, "you rendered me a great service in helping me get rid of that Zhao whelp. I was most impressed that you refused any reward. As a retainer in my household, I trust that you can be of more service to me in the future. Moreover, I am now nearing my fiftieth year, and have no children. So I propose to adopt your son, and bequeath to him my house and rank so that he can carry on my line and inherit my position. I would like to hear your own opinion on the matter."

Flustered, Cheng Ying replied, "Your Honor, I am a man of humble origins, living in straightened circumstances. My wife, myself and our child are lucky indeed to be the objects of your munificence."

Thereupon, Cheng Ying and his wife bowed repeatedly. This pleased Tu'an Gu excessively, and with a smug smile, he said. "Not at all, my dear fellow. You have put my mind at ease. With your help, we shall both come to enjoy wealth and honor." He then took the baby, and asked, "Have you given him a name yet?"

Cheng Ying replied, "Yes, Your Honor. It's Cheng Bo."

Tu'an Gu said, "From now on, in my presence he shall be called Tu'an Cheng, while you may continue to call him Cheng Bo in private. When he gets older, I shall train him in the martial arts, while you teach him his letters. That way, he will grow up accomplished in both civil and military arts, and will surpass all others in his grasp of strategy. When that time comes, he and I will have the State of Jin in the palms of our hands, will we not?"

So saying, he let out a roar of laughter, and his hideous face quivered. Despite his feeling of loathing, Cheng Ying could not but chime in with, "Just as you say, Commander-in-Chief. And it will all be because the little one has had the good fortune to meet Your Honor."

From this time on, Cheng Ying and his wife lived in a small courtyard house in the mansion compound. The courtyard was dainty and the house comfortable. Poplars and willows brushed the eaves, and magnolias caressed the steps. Outside the window were two flower beds, with exotic blooms of all kinds. As spring turned into summer, the flower beds became a riot of color. To one side was a trellis of roseleaf raspberry which was adorned with dappled snow-white blossoms every summer, like a myriad stars winking in the sky. Tu'an Gu had arranged a study for Cheng Ying, the bookshelves of which were filled with complete editions of the classics. It also contained a large desk with writing brushes, and ink stone, in short, everything needed for the education of young Cheng Bo.

As the courtyard was in an obscure part of Tu'an Gu's mansion, Cheng Ying and his wife seldom saw any of the other residents; indeed, they did their utmost to avoid them, in case they should let slip anything that might bring calamity on their heads. And so, they passed their days peacefully enough. But in the stillness of the night, when there was nobody about, their thoughts could not escape the image of the noble martyrs and their own dead child. They were tormented by sorrow, and a feeling of desolation. During the day, when they met Tu'an Gu or other members of the household, they were careful to assume expressions of glowing satisfaction and engage naturally in conversation. Needless to say, this kind of life was a great strain on them.

For several years, Cheng Ying acted as the household physician, going out occasionally in the summer and autumn to gather herbs. His wife attended to the baby and did needlework. Cheng Bo grew up a healthy child, who loved to run around and play in the courtyard. Tu'an Gu was immensely pleased to see this, and in order to keep him in a good mood, the whole household fawned on Cheng Bo.

The tragedy that had taken place a few years before at Taiping Village by now was known to everyone in the State of Jin. The people venerated Gongsun Chujiu for the high-minded way he had gone to his death; at the same time, they despised Cheng Ying as a base scoundrel, and were torn with pity for Zhao the Orphan who, they thought, had died a tragic death at such an early age. Scholars exercised their imaginations, and produced fanciful tales relating to the incident. Ordinary people too, despite having little learning, made up ballads on the same theme, which were passed from mouth to mouth. Peddlers and other travelers sang the praises of the staunch defender of justice Gongsun Chujiu, who had laid down his life in a righteous cause; and even babes scarcely out of their mothers' arms were taught to excoriate Cheng Ying, who had betrayed his friend to save his own skin and reap a rich reward. When it became known that Cheng Ying was aiding and abetting the evil court officials as a hanger-on in Tu'an Gu's household, he was loathed even more intensely. Nobody knew the pain in his heart.

One day, when Cheng Ying happened to step out into the street, he noticed that all the people he knew avoided him, casting glances of open contempt. It was clear that they wanted nothing to do with him. As he passed them, they would gather in groups and point at him behind his back. Hurrying on with head bent, he happened to see his erstwhile friend Old Zhao coming towards him. But when he hastened to greet Old Zhao, the latter simply spat on the ground and strode away. As he stood in the street, he suddenly heard from behind him cries of "It's that villain Cheng Ying!" He turned, to see a crowd of children taunting him. The children then started to throw mud balls and sand at him, and before long he was splattered from head to foot. Cheng Ying had no choice but to flee back to Tu'an Gu's mansion. There he broke down in tears as he related to his wife what had happened. Heartbroken, his wife was worried that this incident might depress her husband so much that he might fall ill again, and she uttered what words of comfort she could. In this way, the weary days dragged by for Cheng Ying and his wife, as they suffered in silence the contempt and insults heaped upon them.

Tu'an Gu, on the other hand, was pleased to see that the pair seldom strayed outside, and had cut themselves off from their old acquaintances. His suspicions concerning them finally died down.

One day a message came from Guojiazhuang Village, to the effect that Guo Shanren had fallen seriously ill, and could die at any minute. He wanted his daughter and son-in-law to come home at once.

When Tu'an Gu raised no objection, Cheng Ying and his wife, together with little Cheng Bo, hastily mounted a carriage and hurried to Guojiazhuang Village. There they found Guo Shanren on his deathbed. The old man was unable to speak, but he pointed at the child and gasped. Cheng Ying understood what he meant, and assured him: "Put your mind at ease, Father-in-Law. We will raise him so that someday he will do mighty deeds." Guo Shanren nodded, and his eyes shone brightly for a moment. Then he turned his head, and died. His daughter threw herself on her father's corpse, and wept inconsolably. Cheng Ying too shed copious tears.

It was arranged that the driver would take the carriage back to the Tu'an mansion, leaving Cheng Ying and his wife to attend to the funeral arrangements. The following day, with the help of neighbors, they put Guo Shanren in his coffin and carried it to the grave. The funeral rites completed, they set about tidying the house. As they did so, the grieving Cheng Ying suddenly thought of his son. He had a few quiet words with his wife, and at the crack of dawn the next morning set out for Taiping Village. Now although Cheng Ying had visited the nearby mountains several times searching for herbs, he had avoided Taiping Village for fear that Tu'an Gu might have sent spies after him, or that he might meet somebody who knew him. This time, he felt that he could not pass up the opportunity, and so, choosing obscure paths, he traveled to the village, arriving at Gongsun Chujiu's old cottage the following day. On the mountain slope behind the dismal and dilapidated house were two grave mounds, one large and one small, long since overgrown with grass. Cheng Ying guessed that they were where the villagers had buried the bodies of Gongsun Chujiu and the baby

He wept silently at the sight, and then, throwing all caution to the winds, wailed and mourned aloud. He dared not remain there long, and was soon on his way back, looking around him all the time. Fortunately, it was a remote spot, and he encountered no other person until he was safely clear.

Back at Guojiazhuang Village, he collected his wife and the baby, and returned to the Tu'an mansion. From then on, every few months, on the excuse of going to the mountains to look for herbs, Cheng Ying would sneak off to Taiping Village, to tend the graves and conduct mourning rites. In this way, he found some outlet for his grief. He was so discreet about this that no one in the Tu'an household was aware of his trips, apart from his wife.

One frosty, blustery autumn night, Cheng Ying lay awake, feeling too cold to sleep. Seeing his wife and Cheng Bo deep in slumber, he slipped out of bed, dressed and went out into the courtyard. There he stood gazing up at the cloudless, moonlit sky, in which the Milky Way glittered. Crickets were chirping in the grass and trees. Cheng Ying felt a sense of desolation creep over him, and a sadness that he could not dispel. An autumn breeze sprang up, making the leaves rustle and fall. The chilly air pierced him to the marrow. He shivered, and went back inside. Still, sleep would not come. He paced his study, and then sat deep in thought. The rustling of the paper in the window, stirred by the autumn wind made the room dreary. Cheng Ying suddenly began to compose a poem:

The west wind teases the window blinds,
Stirring the curtains and chilling the sheets.
Donning a doublet, I gaze on the moon,
And sorrowing grieve for my lost little child.

But he found his heart no lighter for the effort. He recommenced pacing the study floor, and before he knew it, the eastern sky had paled, and dawn came peeping through the window. Abandoning all thoughts of sleep, Cheng Ying gently wakened his wife and told her that he intended to go once more to Taiping Village to pay sacrifice to the souls of Gongsun Chujiu and his poor deceased infant son. He thereupon hurriedly packed a few things, and with his medicine box on his back, he left the house. At the gate of the mansion he came across Tu'an Gu marshaling some of his men in preparation for a hunting trip. When he explained that he was going to the mountains to pick herbs, Tu'an Gu airily waved him on his way, and told him to hurry back.

Cheng Ying was very familiar with the way to Taiping Village by this time, and he arrived at the grave mounds in good time. Burning paper money there, his heart was again pierced with grief. But, when he had opened his heart to his departed friend, he felt somewhat better, and left the place with red and swollen eyes.

In the meantime, Tu'an Gu had headed for the eastern suburbs of the capital. As the arrogant procession clattered along the road, with banners flying and armor gleaming, everyone it passed growled in disgust. In the eastern suburbs was a broad flat plain, which made an ideal hunting ground. It was also the perfect season for hunting, being early autumn. The sky was high and the breeze was bracing, the grass was lush and the horses plump. Tu'an Gu, who had devoted all his thoughts and energies during the previous few years to ensnaring loyal and good men, and grabbing more power, found himself unusually refreshed and elated on this fine morning. At their master's order, the men-at-arms, each eager to show off his prowess, dashed to form a wide circle. The driver of Tu'an Gu's chariot put his horses through their paces, making them gallop at full speed back and forth and round and round. Then bows twanged, and arrows fell like rain, as the bowmen showed their skill. Hawks and hounds sprang frenziedly at their prey, while foxes and hares raced away in panic. The well-aimed shafts soon left heaps of dead animals where they fell, and filled the air with whirling feathers and tufts of fur. Viewing this scene of bedlam, Tu'an Gu felt his spirits soaring. He himself tried his hand at notching an arrow or two. He whooped with glee, as he made his quarry scatter in all directions. Meanwhile, the circle was tightening, and frenzy seized the animals trapped inside. Tu'an Gu laughed uproariously. But at the height of his joy, disaster struck. From a clump of bushes crept a leopard, its thick fur dazzling in the sunlight. While the nearby men-at-arms stood dumbfounded, the beast, swift as lightning, sprang through a gap in the circle and made straight for Tu'an Gu. As his men yelled frantically: "Kill it! Kill it!" the leopard sprang, and bore Tu'an Gu to the ground, before anyone could stop it. Tu'an Gu's military training had prepared him for this emergency, for he instinctively rolled along the ground, and sprang to his feet with his sword drawn. A desperate battle then ensued. Finding itself challenged on all sides, the leopard fought desperately. Time and again Tu'an Gu lunged with his sword, only to stab thin air. Finally seeing an opening, the beast sprang at Tu'an Gu with a blood-curdling roar. Tu'an Gu was no longer young, and his body bloated from overindulgence, so could not able to dodge the attack. He only managed to jerk his head to one side, and the leopard sank its teeth into his left shoulder, bearing him to the ground. Luckily for him, his men had run up by this time, and killed the leopard before it had time to finish off their master.

While his attendants were binding Tu'an Gu's wounds, an order was given to call off the hunt and return to the Tu'an mansion. What had started off as an exhilarating day had ended in disaster. Tu'an Gu managed to stagger to his feet, and totter back to his chariot. He felt humiliated and angry, but there was no way for him to vent on this occasion.

When he got back home, the whole household, having heard the news that their master had been mauled by a wild animal, came crowding around him. Tu'an Gu petulantly waved them away, saying that he only wanted to talk to Cheng Ying. The summons sent a shiver of fear running down Cheng Ying's spine, but he had no choice but to attend Tu'an Gu on his sickbed. In due course, the latter coughed, cleared his throat, and said in solemn tones: "In the past few years I have been feeling my vigor ebbing away. I am not as nimble as I used to be, and today while out hunting, I was injured. I have to face the fact that I am getting old, as we all must some day." He sighed deeply as he spoke. Cheng Ying, seeing him so gloomy, uttered a few words of comfort, whereupon, Tu'an Gu uttered a scornful laugh. "Please don't be polite. I remember that at the time I adopted your son and named him Tu'an Cheng, you were given the task of teaching him his letters, while I undertook to train him in the martial arts. The boy is now ten years old, while you and I are growing older by the day. He must be made to master the two branches of learning without delay, or it will be too late." So saying, he glanced at Cheng Ying.

Now the sufferings he had undergone had steeled Cheng Ying's temperament, and the burden of bringing up the orphan while living in the lair of his worst enemy had inured him to insult and degradation. He lived in a state of constant terror of his secret being found out. All these afflictions and pressures had reduced his already frail body to skin and bone. His complexion was pale and sallow, and white hairs had appeared at his temples. He had aged beyond his years.

Cheng Ying could read in Tu'an Gu's eyes that the latter regarded him as old and doddering. He could not suppress a wan smile, thinking to himself: "I long ago started to teach Cheng Bo his letters, but I fear that he has received no training in the martial arts as yet. Now that this villainous Tu'an has raised the subject of giving Cheng Bo an all-round education encompassing both the civil and the military arts, he has unwittingly voiced my own heart's desire, for he is simply hastening his own death." Then, out loud, he said, "Your Honor, I will do my best to accomplish this worthy plan. I simply await your orders." This response pleased Tu'an Gu, and he explained that as soon as he recovered from his wound, he would personally instruct Cheng Bo in the martial arts during the day, while Cheng Ying would teach the boy his letters in the evenings.

From then on, Cheng Ying and Tu'an Gu worked diligently hand in hand for the education of Zhao the Orphan. The youngster was diligent at both branches of study, and grew up robust and dignified, attracting the admiration of all around. Every day, as he gazed on this grand young man, Tu'an Gu was filled with delight, thinking that he was raising a hero whom he could depend on the support him in his twilight years. Little did he know that he was digging his own grave.

CHAPTER EIGHT

The Day of Reckoning

TEN YEARS PASSED. Cheng Ying was now a white-haired, decrepit old man. Truly:

The days hurry on old age, and time prods youth aside.
But a myriad wordless yearnings in our hearts still abide.

The balmy spring returned to the world, and the flowers began to bloom again. Zhao the Orphan was a grown man by this time. Being possessed of exceptional intelligence, he had profited from the tutorship of both Cheng Ying and Tu'an Gu, and emerged a person of all-round talents in both scholarship and the martial skills. He was praised by everyone who knew him, and there were many both at court and outside it. However, their admiration was tempered by the knowledge that he was, lamentably, the adopted son of Tu'an Gu.

Contemplating his adopted son's accomplishments, Tu'an Gu felt his ambition swell inside him, and when he was alone he would often

the day of reckoning

boast to himself: "Sooner or later, my plan will mature, and I will then slay the duke and seize the throne and hand it over to my son Tu'an Cheng. And then my lifelong aim will have been achieved."

Needless to say, while Tu'an Gu was nursing his wicked scheme, Cheng Ying was growing ever more anxious. His intention had been to relate to the youth the whole sad story of who he was and what had happened to his clansmen and their friends. Now that he was a grown man and adept at both learning and martial prowess, it was time for Zhao the Orphan to exact retribution from Tu'an Gu. But as he watched the young man practice his physical exercises during the day and study in the evening — blissfully unaware of his grim history — he reflected that there was a strong possibility that Cheng Bo would scoff at his tale, since Cheng Ying has not mentioned the bloody history for the past twenty years. He could also see how Tu'an Gu doted on his adopted son, and feared that a strong bond of affection might have developed between them, so that even after he had learned the truth, this might prompt him to stay his hand. Another consideration was the fact that Tu'an Gu was a crafty and ruthless man. If Cheng Bo got to know the truth, and then made some rash mood, his adoptive father would be alerted to his danger, and would not hesitate to strike first. Then all 20 years of Cheng Ying's painstaking efforts would be wasted. The upshot was that Cheng Ying was at a loss how to tell Zhao the Orphan of his destiny. He was in such a state of agitation that he spent every day either pacing the floor in agitation or slumped in his study buried in gloomy thoughts. One night he was sitting in his study, brooding by candlelight and still unable to come to a decision. Suddenly a wave of tiredness swept over him, and he fell asleep with his head resting on the desk in front of him. He seemed to see the candle flare up and then go dim again. As the flame sputtered, Gongsun Chujiu floated into the room, his snow-white beard hanging down to his chest. The old man boomed, "The orphan has become a man, and still his task is not fulfilled. Why the delay? You must inform him of his mission of vengeance without more ado, and report the good news to me." He repeated this over and over again, but just as Cheng Ying was struggling to reply, Gongsun Chujiu vanished.

Cheng Ying awoke with a violent start, unsure whether he had had a dream or not, the experience had been so vivid. He sat there for a long time, his mind blank. Then he put out the candle and went into his bedroom. He woke his wife, and told her of his dream. Then he explained, "Recently, I've been very troubled about this matter. I am already 65 years old, and my days are a torment to me, and I feel as if I am almost eighty. If anything should happen to me and you are left alone, I am afraid that our noble mission would fail. When I see how completely unaware of his background the youth is, and how close he is to that dastardly Tu'an, I don't know how to broach the subject of his earth-shaking task. I am vexed almost to death!"

His wife replied, "You are right to be worried, my dear. This matter brooks no delay. It seems to me that what you should do is to paint a picture containing the main strands of the story. Leave it somewhere he is bound to see it, and let it awaken in him a sense of righteous indignation. Then you can tell him the whole truth, and act at the opportune time."

His wife's words were a revelation to Cheng Ying. He nodded several times in agreement, feeling that a great weight had been lifted from his mind. The very next day, he got his wife to search out a sheet of white silk, and set to work painting. For several days in a row, in the dead of night, the two of them painted feverishly. When it was finished, they rolled it up carefully, and left it in a suitable spot.

The next day, Cheng Bo rose early to go to the drill ground. Cheng Ying was sitting alone in his study, his cheek resting on his hand, deep in sad contemplation. Outside the window, willow trees trailed their golden branches, their buds an emerald green. Peach trees, ablaze with blossoms gave off a heady perfume. A warm breeze wafted through their branches, making the petals shower down like raindrops. But Cheng Ying scratched his hoary head, and sighed. "Time flies, and man's life is bitter and short, like a glimpse of a white colt galloping past a chink in the wall!"

He then unrolled the scroll. The tragic scenes of 20 years flashed before his eyes, scene by scene. Tears cascaded down his cheeks as he thought of all the fine ministers and noble heroes who had gone to their deaths to save Zhao the Orphan, and of the bitter end of his son, not even ten days old. After a while, he rolled the scroll up again and laid it on the desk. Then he took up a zither. The instrument seemed of its own accord to choose notes redolent of pent-up grief and rage, like the dropping of tears or cries of accusation. Then the tempo picked up, and became impassioned, fading finally away into a limitless abyss of bitterness.

At this moment, Cheng Bo returned from his martial exercises. He had heard the plaintive music of the zither as he approached the house. He hurried inside, and found Cheng Ying still cradling the zither. Alarmed at the sight of the old man's tear-stained face, he hastened to ask him: "Father, why are you so upset? Has somebody acted in a high-handed way towards you? Tell me, quickly, and I will make him answer for it!"

The young man's words woke Cheng Ying from his brooding. Startled, he brush away the tears, and with a forced smile, said, "Oh, it's nothing. You go and have your morning meal." But as he turned away he could not help sighing.

Cheng Bo was taken aback by this reception. He thought to himself: "Usually my father is all smiles whenever he sees me, and is eager to chat. Why is he so cold and distant today? Moreover, he has been weeping, that's obvious. And why did he sigh like that?" Thereupon, he asked again: "Father, have you and my adoptive father had a quarrel?"

Annoyed at this interrogation, Cheng Ying answered sharply: "I have not been quarreling with anybody. If I told you what is in my heart, I'm afraid you would disown your father and mother. Now run along; you must be hungry."

Shaking his head and sighing, Cheng Ying rose and went into the rear chamber. As he did so, his sleeve brushed the scroll from the desk onto the floor. Puzzled at Cheng Ying's bad temper, Cheng Bo picked up the scroll. Out of curiosity, he unrolled it and examined it intently.

There were nine pictures painted one after the other on the white silk. They contained a large number of images of people, depicted in a vivid and lifelike manner. The pictures seemed to be telling a story, and the young man followed the sequence with interest. In the first picture there was a man dressed in a red robe letting loose a fiercely snarling dog. Its fangs and claws bared, the dog was about to leap at another man, dressed in a purple robe. In the second picture, a stalwart figure had rushed forward to save the man in purple, and was tearing the dog in two. The third picture showed another sturdy man. This one was whipping a horse and lifting a carriage with one hand. The carriage, strangely enough, had only one wheel, and the figure of a man clad in a purple robe could faintly be seen seated in the fore part of it. In the fourth picture too, there was a husky figure, clutching a wicked-looking dagger and pounding his head against a large tree.

Looking at these pictures, Cheng Bo was baffled. He could not even guess what they meant. He puzzled over them for a long while, but couldn't figure out what story they portrayed. He then looked at the fifth picture. It showed a general facing the viewer and in front of him are a bowstring and a short sword. Also in his hand was a wine cup that had just been drained. The young man wondered aloud: "Why on earth would this general wish to kill himself?"

In the sixth picture was a man dressed as a physician, carrying a medicine box on his back. He was receiving a baby from the hands of a woman. In the seventh picture, the same woman had hanged herself in a room, while outside the door was a general cutting his own throat with a sword. The longer he gazed at the pictures the more incomprehensible they seemed to him. Curiosity spurred him on to look at the eighth picture. In it was the red-clad man he had seen in the first picture. He was beating a white-haired, white-bearded old man mercilessly. He was also chopping a baby into three pieces. The last picture showed several hundred corpses of both men and women, old and young, lying in pools of blood in the courtyard of a large mansion. They looked as if they had all been killed at the same time.

Although even when he had examined all the pictures, Cheng Bo still did not understand their meaning, his natural sense of justice and hatred of evil made him boil with righteous anger at the sight of the man in red unleashing a savage dog upon a victim, savagely beating an old man and murdering a baby. He even cried aloud, "That heinous monster in red! If he fell into my hands, I'd dispatch him with my sword on the spot!" Then he continued, "Which depraved fiend massacred all those people, I'd like to know? His mind must be infested with evil!"

Cheng Ying, who had been eavesdropping around a corner, knew when he heard this that the young man had viewed the paintings. After a while, he called out through the doorway: "You are perfectly right, my son. Those murders were committed by a black-hearted villain indeed!" Cheng Bo hurried in to confront the old man. "Father," he demanded, "tell me, what story do the pictures relate? And who is that wicked scoundrel?"

His eyes filled with tears, Cheng Ying replied, "The story recounted in that series of pictures is connected with you yourself. I have been nursing it in my heart for twenty years, not daring to tell anyone else."

Cheng Bo stared at him in astonishment. "What can this story have to do with me, Father? I beg you to explain exactly what it all means."

Pointing to the first picture, Cheng Ying said, "The man in red and the man in purple were once ministers of the same court. But they were as unlike as fire and water — one was loyal and the other was treacherous. The latter schemed to bring about the downfall of the former."

Cheng Bo interjected, "How did he manage to do it?"

Cheng Ying then drew the other's attention to the picture of Chu Ni's suicide. "The villain in red," he said, "first sent an assassin, a man of honor as it turned out, called Chu Ni. But the would-be assassin was so moved by the loyalty of the man in purple that he could not bring himself to commit a deed that would be an affront to Heaven. But to return with his mission unfulfilled, would have meant certain death for him. So he dashed his brains out against a tree."

At this point, the young man remarked, "You said the name of this upright man was Chu Ni, I think."

"That's right," said Cheng Ying. "Remember that name."

Cheng Bo nodded his assent. Cheng Ying next pointed again to the first picture, saying, "This hound had been sent as tribute from the kingdom of Western Rong. It was terribly fierce. The man in red obtained it from the duke, dressed a straw dummy up in a purple robe, and trained the mastiff to attack and rend it. When it had been fully trained to do so, he took it to the court. There, as soon as it saw the man in purple, it thought that he was the dummy, and it sprang at him. This galvanized a brave man standing by into action. You see him in the second picture."

Pointing at the figure who had just slain the hound, Cheng Bo said, "Oh, you mean him? What was his name?"

"Yes," said Cheng Ying. "His name was Ti Miming. When he saw that terrible dog leap at the loyal minister in purple, he was so furious that he tore the beast in two. Sadly, he was pursued and killed by the palace guards. Are you beginning to understand now, my son?"

Again Cheng Bo nodded. "I will remember," he said, "that this hero's name was Ti Miming. He then pointed to the third picture, and asked, "Who is this big fellow driving the carriage? And how did it come to have only one wheel?"

Cheng Ying explained, "It's a long story. The man in purple used to go to the suburbs every spring to encourage the farmers. One year, he spied a stalwart yeoman lying on his back beneath a mulberry tree, with his mouth wide open. When he asked the man what he was doing, the reply was that his name was Ling Zhe, and that he hadn't eaten anything for days and was weak from hunger. However, as he was loath to steal somebody else's mulberries, all he could do was lie under the tree with his mouth open and wait for mulberries to fall into it. The honest minister in purple was impressed with the man's integrity, and ordered that he be given food and wine. Later, fleeing from the court after being saved by Ti Miming from the hound, he found that two of the horses had been unhitched from his carriage by the red-robed villain's men and one wheel had been destroyed, to make it impossible for him to escape. But in the nick of time Ling Zhe arrived. Supporting the carriage on his shoulder and managing the remaining horses with his right hand, he conveyed the righteous minister to safety outside the capital."

At this point, Cheng Bo interrupted. "Father, I recognize that

the day of reckoning

Ling Zhe, in requiting the chance kindness he had received from the minister in purple, was a true man of honor. But what was the name of the wicked knave in red, and who was the upright minister in purple?"

Cheng Ying looked at him, and nodded. "Very good, my boy," he said. "You know well how to distinguish loyalty from treachery. At the moment I am not able to tell you the name of the one in red. But the loyal minister in purple was named Zhao Dun. He used to be the prime minister of Jin — and there is a connection between you and him."

Cheng Bo said, "I have heard people mention Prime Minister Zhao Dun. But what connection can there be between us?"

"Let me continue," replied Cheng Ying, "and you will come to understand." As he said this, he pointed to the picture of the massacre. "When the man in red realized that Zhao Dun had escaped, he took out his fury on the rest of the Zhao clan, slaughtering the over 300 people in the Zhao mansion."

Cheng Bo cried aloud in outrage and horror at hearing this.

Cheng Ying simply continued, "Only one of the Zhaos remained alive in Jin. His name was Zhao Shuo, and he was married to the duke's sister. The man in red forged an order from the duke that Zhao Shuo commit suicide, offering him a choice of a rope, a sword and poisoned wine. Zhao Shuo drank the poisoned wine. Just before he died, he named the baby in the princess's womb Zhao the Orphan, and his last wish was that the orphan should grow up and avenge the deaths of the 300-odd members of the Zhao clan."

Having reached this stage in his narrative, Cheng Ying felt a pang of grief stab his heart, and he could not hold back his tears.

"But did the orphan manage to avenge the Zhao clan, by killing the villain in red?" asked the young man.

Instead of answering, Cheng Ying pointed to the sixth picture. "Having got rid of Zhao Shuo," he continued, "the man in red dispatched General Han Jue to tightly guard the royal son-in-law's mansion, so that as soon as the princess gave birth to Zhao Shuo's child, it should be taken from her and put to death. Now, there had been a retainer at the Zhao mansion, a doctor from the countryside called Cheng Ying..."

"Father, that's you!" cried Cheng Bo.

Cheng Ying realized that he had made a slip of the tongue, and hurriedly tried to cover up his mistake. "Oh, er, well, there are lots of people with the same name in this world," he stuttered. "This was another Cheng Ying."

But Cheng Bo was not convinced. "A man called Cheng Ying, who also happened to be a doctor," he mused. "Of course there are many people with the same name, but this seems to be too much of a coincidence. Almost certainly, that man was my father!" However, he did not say this aloud, but urged Cheng Ying to continue with his story.

"This doctor went to the mansion of the royal son-in-law. There, the princess handed the newborn child to him. She then hanged herself. The doctor was intercepted and searched by General Han Jue as he tried to smuggle the child out of the mansion. Fortunately, the general was a man of loyalty and integrity. He was burning with indignation at the way the evil red-clad court official had attempted to destroy the loyal prime minister, and allowed the physician to escape. He thereupon cut his own throat, and died on the spot."

Cheng Bo let out an exclamation of awe: "So many loyal and good people died for this Zhao the Orphan!"

Cheng Ying took up the tale once more. "But the villain in red did not take the loss of the orphan lying down. He issued a decree demanding that the person who had spirited the baby away hand it over to him; otherwise he would seize every infant under the age of six months within the territory of the State of Jin and chop it into three pieces. In that way, he would be sure that Zhao the Orphan would not escape. Now it just so happened that the wife of the doctor who had abducted Zhao the Orphan had just given birth to a son herself. What the doctor did was to pretend that his own son was the orphan, in the meantime handing the orphan over to Gongsun Chujiu — the old man with white hair and a white beard in that picture there. The original plan was for Gongsun Chujiu to denounce the doctor, and fool the red-robed villain into executing the doctor and his newborn baby. Gongsun would then raise the orphan to manhood so that he could wreak revenge for the Zhao clan."

"Who, in fact, was Gongsun Chujiu?" asked the young man.

Cheng Ying said, "Gongsun Chujiu was originally a fairly high-ranking official who served at court along with Prime Minister Zhao Dun. They were bosom friends. He told the doctor: 'I am advanced in years, and could die at any time. I am afraid I will not be able to raise the orphan until he reaches adulthood. It would be better if you handed your own child over to me, and denounced me as the kidnapper. When that red-garbed monster has executed both me and your son, you can raise Zhao the Orphan, so that he will eventually avenge his wronged clan. And so, the physician gave his own child to Gongsun Chujiu, and then went to the villain in red and denounced Gongsun Chujiu as the person who had stolen Zhao the Orphan. The villain in red, together with a great troop of men and horses, seized Gongsun Chujiu and the child. He submitted the old man to fearsome torture to try to get him to reveal who his accomplice was, but the stalwart old man uttered not a word to incriminate the physician, even though he knew he was threatened with death. Gongsun Chujiu finally killed himself by dashing his brains out on a rock. The wicked fiend then forced the doctor to beat his own son to death." The remembrance of his infant son's tragic end was too painful for Cheng Ying to continue his tale for a while, and he abandoned himself to a flood of tears. Cheng Bo took this opportunity to ask, "How could the doctor bear to kill his own son? "

Wiping away his tears, Cheng Ying replied, "To save the life of Zhao the Orphan, he would have been willing to sacrifice his own life, let alone that of his child."

Cheng Bo stiffened, and his eyes blazed with rage. "That red-robed villain is so depraved and will stoop to any wickedness!" he cried. "I beg you, Father, to tell me his name, so that I can help Zhao the Orphan to avenge the wrongs done to him and to his clan. I will chop that red-wrapped renegade into ten thousand pieces!" So saying, he drew his sword and fixed his gaze on Cheng Ying.

Instead of replying directly, Cheng Ying, holding back his tears recited the following:

> *Why tarries the strapping hero, master of civil and*
> *martial skills?*
> *His grandsire has fled in a carriage, his household's*
> *cruelly killed.*
> *His mother, imprisoned, hung herself, his father,*
> *blameless, was slain.*
> *A strange hero indeed is he who neglects to avenge*
> *his family's pain.*

He then uttered a long sigh, and said, "I have long been afraid that you would not understand when the day came for me to explain all this, my son. But that Zhao the Orphan is now twenty years old. He, in fact, is as far away as the horizon and at the same time right under my nose."

Cheng Bo heard these words in a state of growing agitation, as the connection between Zhao the Orphan and himself began to dawn on him. He cried out, "Father, tell me the truth! Don't leave me groping in the dark any longer!"

Cheng Ying drew a deep breath, and intoned, "The man is red is Tu'an Gu. The man in purple is your grandfather. The royal son-in-law was your father, and the princess was your mother. I myself am that Dr. Cheng Ying who sacrificed his own son to save Zhao the Orphan."

"Is that true?" cried Cheng Bo, aghast.

Cheng Ying was too choked by sobs and tears to reply in words. He simply nodded vigorously. Cheng Ying's wife, who had crept in unnoticed and had heard these last words, then announced her presence. She uttered a strangled gasp, "My ... my ...Oh my poor ... child!" Cheng Bo could refuse to recognize the truth no longer. With a cry of "So I am Zhao the Orphan! This anguish is too much to bear." He fell down in a swoon.

Cheng Ying and his wife rushed to help him, and after a flurry of distraction on their part, the young man gradually revived. The first thing he did upon regaining consciousness was to rave that he was going to have it out with Tu'an Gu. But Cheng Ying managed to calm him down by saying, "Please don't be rash. If you are to avenge the deaths of your clansmen, the three of us must lay long-term plans. If that black-hearted villain Tu'an Gu gets wind of what is afoot, he will not hesitate to strike first. In that case, my twenty years of agony will all have been for naught, and the sacrifices of your real father and mother, as well as those of the other martyrs in your cause, will all have been wasted."

Hearing this, Cheng Bo realized that he must bide his time. He looked carefully at Cheng Ying and his wife, and noticed how worn out with age they were, with wrinkled skin and white hair. They looked, he thought, as frail as worn candles flickering in the wind. When he recollected how they had given up their own child to save him and had devoted themselves to bringing him up, he was overcome with emotion, and there and then he fell to his knees and kowtowed to them, begging them to accept this gesture of his reverence.

Cheng Ying and his wife could control themselves no longer, as the memory of their twenty years of bitterness and hardship welled up inside them. The three of them clung to each other, weeping. Fortunately for them, the courtyard was tucked away, and no outsider witnessed this scene.

That night, while all the rest of the household was asleep, Cheng Ying, his wife and Cheng Bo held a whispered discussion. The upshot of their deliberations was that the following day they would approach the duke and reveal to him who Cheng Bo really was, and ask him for soldiers to help the young man to arrest the rascally Tu'an Gu and wreak vengeance for the massacre of his clansmen. When this had been decided, Cheng Bo declared, his hair standing stiff on his scalp and his eyes glaring: "When we have denounced that blackguard to the duke and had him arrested — his seal of office removed and his official robes stripped from his back — I shall tear out his tongue and pluck out his eyes, and then chop him into ten thousand pieces. I'll make him suffer all the agonies he inflicted on others. But even when I have had my blood vengeance, it will still not be enough to appease the sense of injustice I feel in my heart."

Early the next morning, Tu'an Gu, as usual, went with a troop of soldiers to summon Cheng Bo to the drill ground. But Cheng Ying intercepted them, telling them that the young man had caught a chill the previous night, and was ill in bed with a headache and a fever. "He begs to be excused from practice today," he informed them. Tu'an Gu, suspecting nothing, assented and departed.

As soon as they had gone, Cheng Ying and Cheng Bo hurried to the palace to request an audience with the duke.

Duke Ling had died many years before, worn out by a life of debauchery. He had left no heir, and the senior ministers had made Cheng the duke. Cheng had been of a weak constitution, and had also passed away after a short reign. The present ruler was Duke Dao, who, although not a man of great talent or vision, was devoted to the welfare of the state and its people. For some time he had been appalled by the tyranny and arrogance of Tu'an Gu, and harbored an anxious desire to have him removed from power. But, in consideration of Tu'an Gu's hold on the military forces, his mastery of the bow and his large band of diehard followers, Duke Dao had no choice but to bide his time and wait for the right moment to strike.

On this morning, right after the customary audience, as the duke was scanning official documents, alone in the royal quarters, his attendants announced that "Zhao the Orphan" wished to see him.

The duke was puzzled, and asked who "Zhao the Orphan" was. When he was informed that he was Tu'an Gu's adopted son, a feeling of disquiet came over Duke Dao, but he ordered that the young man be admitted to his presence.

After Cheng Bo had finished kowtowing, the duke noticed that he was a fine figure of a man, with a dignified bearing. Yet he had an air of great sadness about him, and his eyes were red and puffy. Duke Dao said, "I heard that your original name was Cheng Bo, and that as Tu'an Gu's adopted son you go by the name of Tu'an Cheng. Why today do you call yourself Zhao the Orphan?"

The young man wailed, and collapsed on the ground, weeping copious tears. "Your Majesty," he cried, "there has been an injustice done which cries out to Heaven for redress! My grandfather was a senior minister of Jin, named Zhao Dun. He and Tu'an Gu were as unlike as fire and water. Whereas he personified loyalty, Tu'an

Gu personified treachery. Tu'an Gu hatched an evil plot to have a savage mastiff attack Zhao Dun. My grandfather was forced to flee, and no one knows where he is now. Pouring slanderous lies into the ears of Duke Ling, that ruler allowed Tu'an Gu to slaughter all the 300-odd people in the mansion of the Zhao clan. He also drove my father, Zhao Shuo, to suicide. Moreover, in order to remove all future danger, he imprisoned my mother, who was pregnant with me at the time, and caused her to hang herself. The Zhao line was only saved from extermination by the fortunate intervention of a loyal hero who sacrificed his own son to save me. This good person raised me to manhood. Now I have come to beg Your Majesty to champion the cause of the Zhao clan and have that scoundrel Tu'an Gu arrested. Only with his death will the souls of the murdered Zhao clansmen be avenged."

Duke Dao had heard of the Zhao affair, but he had been unaware that the orphan still lived. Now he was overjoyed to hear Cheng Bo's testimony, realizing that this was just the charge he needed to bring about Tu'an Gu's fall. He asked in a low voice: "Do you have evidence for what you have stated?"

Cheng Bo replied, "The man who raised me, Cheng Ying, knows all about this affair. He is outside the palace at this moment, awaiting your summons, Your Majesty."

Duke Dao ordered that Cheng Ying be brought in. After making the ritual obeisance and greetings, Cheng Ying stood up and unrolled the painting scroll, and explained in detail Tu'an Gu's crimes against the Zhao clan. When he had finished, the duke, with a brow like thunder, roared, "Ten thousand deaths would not atone for that villain's crimes in leading his ruler into the ways of wickedness and reducing the state to disorder!" Then he assigned General Wei Jiang and 500 men to assist Cheng Bo in the execution of Tu'an Gu.

Outside the palace, Cheng Bo and General Wei Jiang discussed how best to go about their mission. Cheng Bo said, "When Tu'an Gu returns from the training ground every day, he has to pass the Eastern Market. You can leave soldiers in ambush there, to separate him from his guards as they pass by. I will then dash out and seize him when he least expects it. That is the safest way to ensure that he does not have the chance to raise a rebellion."

The general agreed to this with a nod, and stationed his men in ambush in the vicinity of the Eastern Market. Meanwhile, Cheng Bo, armed with a sword and with a determined scowl on his face, stood waiting at a nearby crossroads.

It was nearly noon when Tu'an Gu returned from the drill ground. With his usual arrogant pose, he rode at the head of a group of a couple of hundred guards. As the gaudy procession drew near, and Cheng Bo spied his foe, his eyes blazed with crimson fire. As swift as an arrow, the young man stepped in front of Tu'an Gu's steed, his blade glittering like autumn frost. Tu'an Gu was dismayed at finding his path blocked thus by Cheng Bo, with drawn sword and a countenance made fearsome by anger. "Tu'an Cheng, my boy!" he cried, "What are you doing here?"

"What do you mean, Tu'an Cheng?" growled the young man. "I am Zhao the Orphan! Twenty years ago, you massacred all the rest of my clan. Now I have come to take your worthless life, and make you repay the blood debt!"

These words struck Tu'an Gu like thunderbolts. For the moment he was at a complete loss what to do. Then he suddenly heard a commotion behind him. Turning round, he saw General Wei Jiang and his men close in and cut him off from his retinue of men-at-arms. He was surrounded, but he tried to brazen the situation out. "My boy," he cried, "don't be foolish. Who has lured you into harming your adoptive father?"

"Cheng Ying has revealed the whole truth to me. Don't try to wriggle out of it, you dastardly villain!"

Hearing this, Tu'an Gu's face turned ashen. He realized that he had made a terrible mistake in raising a tiger cub, which was now fully grown and had turned on him. With Cheng Bo and his sword blocking his way forward, and General Wei Jiang's men blocking his retreat, Tu'an Gu knew that he would have to fight to the death with the young man. However, there was a slim chance that he might come out of this alive, he thought. So he flung a challenging sneer in Cheng Bo's face: "So, you wretched whelp, you skulked in my house for twenty years, did you? How blind I was to raise a little viper like you! But today is not too late to kill you!" So saying, he made to draw his sword and close with Cheng Bo.

But the young man was too quick for him. Cheng Bo leaped lightly forward, and dragged Tu'an Gu from his horse onto the ground. What with being startled out of his wits, as well as being old and portly, Tu'an Gu was no match for Cheng Bo. Moreover, the tumble had stunned him. It was too late now to repent of his wicked life, during which he had killed people like flies. All he could do was to sit there helplessly, awaiting execution.

Seeing their chieftain captured, Tu'an Gu's men threw down their weapons, and fled in panic. Before long, they had all been rounded up by General Wei Jiang's soldiers.

General Wei and Cheng Bo brought Tu'an Gu, bound hand and foot, before Duke Dao. The latter pronounced sentence: "This monster's heinous crimes are too well known to warrant special investigation. Take him immediately to the market place for execution!" General Wei and Cheng Bo thereupon escorted Tu'an Gu to the market place, where they made preparations for the execution in a clear space. When news of the death sentence passed on Tu'an Gu spread through the capital there was not one person who did not clap with glee and run around to tell others. The whole populace flocked to the execution site.

With General Wei's soldiers standing guard all round, Tu'an Gu was brought forward. The general addressed him thus: "Tu'an Gu, today you have been arrested for slaughtering loyal and good people. As you face death, do you have anything to say?"

Tu'an Gu was degenerate to the core. Even though he knew there was no escape from death this time, he was unrepentant. "Win, and you become a king," he snarled. "Lose, and you're regarded as a bandit. My only regret is that I did not exterminate that Zhao brat, but let him live to bring ruin upon me. Well, seeing as it's come to this, kill me and be done with it!"

Hearing this, Cheng Bo was suddenly filled with fury. "So, you fiend, you want to die quickly, do you? Well, you will not have your wish!"

General Wei Jiang then gave a command: "Nail the criminal to the wooden donkey. Then slowly apply the three thousand cuts.

When his flesh is all stripped away, cut off his head!"

At this point, Cheng Ying and his wife appeared, just in time to see the sentence being carried out. First Tu'an Gu's ears were sliced off; then his eyes were gouged out; his tongue was torn out, and bit by bit the flesh was stripped from his body. Tu'an Gu screamed in torment, neither alive or dead. The bystanders clapped and cheered, feeling that only now was their sorrow appeased. Finally, after two hours, when Tu'an Gu had suffered all possible pain, his head was cut off and his chest ripped open. Truly:

> It's been 20 years, since those wicked deeds were done.
> But a tyrant's been beheaded, and justice has finally won.

Joy spread throughout the State of Jin as people learned of the execution of Tu'an Gu. As General Wei Jiang and Cheng Bo made their way back to the palace, they were met by a group of ministers, with Shi Ji at their head. At the court, Duke Dao announced, "Tu'an Gu deserved ten thousand deaths for murdering loyal and faithful people, and throwing the government into chaos. I declare all his property confiscated, and sentence his whole household to execution — not even a chicken or a dog must be spared. In addition, Zhao the Orphan may use his real surname once again, and I give him the name Zhao Wu. He shall succeed to his grandfather's rank at court, and have command of the army. Moreover, he shall have the Lower Palace as his dwelling. As for Cheng Ying, who sacrificed his own child to save Zhao the Orphan, I grant him ten acres of land, and he shall be supported in his old age by Zhao Wu. As Han Jue lay down his life for righteousness, I grant his descendants the rank of general. For Gongsun Chujiu, who showed an inspiring devotion to justice as he faced death, I will have a tomb mound raised and a stele placed before it recording his merit. And the heroes Ling Zhe and Ti Miming will be bestowed with honor and praise."

Everybody present kowtowed in gratitude, and cried, "Long live the duke!" The people of Jin were delighted when they heard about the duke's munificence. They all agreed that Tu'an Gu had deserved his execution for his murderous career, and that Cheng Ying was a model of selflessness and lofty virtue for all time.

Zhao Wu, having succeeded to his rightful title, repaired the Lower Palace and went to live there together with Cheng Ying and his wife. Despite his youth, Zhao Wu was experienced in the ways of the world and prudent. In both the literary and martial arts, he was outstanding among his generation. Every day he combined the training of the soldiers with the handling of state affairs. Returning home, he would chat and joke with the old couple, and attend to their needs as if he were their own son.

Strangely enough, after he was awarded a farming estate and moved into the Lower Palace, Cheng Ying became morose and taciturn. Whenever he had spare time, he would sit by the window deep in thought, occasionally shedding a tear. Seeing him so withdrawn and distracted, his wife and Zhao Wu tried to cheer him up, saying, "We three have been through so many trials and tribulations together that now we should revel in our good fortune. Why are you so depressed?" But Cheng Ying simply fended them off with the excuse that he was getting old. He preferred solitude, he said. The other two were content to leave it at that, and inquired no further.

Dear readers, what do you think was on Cheng Ying's mind? Well, the fact was that even after Zhao Wu had executed Tu'an Gu, and got his revenge, and after Cheng Ying had been awarded a grant of land, and had started to live in the Lower Palace, clothed in silks and satins, the latter could not help constantly casting his mind back 20 years. Whenever he did so, he felt both proud and remorseful. He was proud of the fact that for 20 years he had endured shame and humiliation in order to raise Zhao the Orphan to manhood so that he could get revenge for the injustice that had been visited on his clan. But he felt remorse that so many upstanding and loyal officials had lost their lives in the course of those years, while he alone survived, living in the lap of luxury. It pained him to think of his only son, not yet ten days old, whom he had beaten to death with his own hands. It pained him to think of his old friend Gongsun Chujiu, whose bones were lying alone in a remote grave and whose soul had gone alone to the netherworld. At such times, he would murmur, "I should have died 20 years ago. The only reason for me living on for all those years was to make sure that Zhao the Orphan grew up and fulfilled his duty of vengeance. But now that the evil minister has been beheaded and the fortunes of the Zhao clan restored, how could I face Gongsun Chujiu and all the other loyal worthies if I continued to live in this world?" After much contemplation, he came to a decision.

One day, Cheng Ying told his wife and Zhao Wu that he intended to journey to Taiping Village to offer a sacrifice at the grave of Gongsun Chujiu and let him know that Zhao the Orphan had accomplished his task of wreaking vengeance. When Zhao Wu expressed the intention of accompanying him, Cheng Ying said, "No, my boy. You must stay here and continue your daily training. It is sufficient if I go alone." His wife's pleas were likewise brushed aside, and the following day he set out, with his medicine box on his back.

When he reached Taiping Village, he noticed that two stone tablets had been set up in front of the large and small grave mounds, respectively. On the offering tables, there was fresh fruit and burning incense. Sitting in front of the tombs, Cheng Ying felt a wave of sadness flow over him, and he burst into tears. Pulling himself together, he stood up, took a small knife from his medicine box. Facing the mounds, he slit his throat and fell down dead. When the local people discovered the body, they sent the news to the capital with the utmost speed. Zhao Wu was at first dumbfounded, and when he had recovered from the shock, he started to weep. Cheng Ying's wife, too, was so stunned that she fainted several times.

Early the next morning, Zhao Wu reported the tragedy to Duke Dao, and asked for leave to go to Taiping Village to give the man who had raised him a decent burial. The duke, in admiration of Cheng Ying's adherence to righteousness even at the cost of his life, gave permission for him to be interred in the same tomb as Gongsun Chujiu on Mount Cang.

Zhao Wu hurried off to Taiping Village, where he gathered the bones of Gongsun Chujiu and re-buried them on Mount Cang, together with the body of Cheng Ying. Around the tomb mound, he planted fir trees and cypresses, and in front erected an inscribed tablet. Later generations called it the "Tomb of the Two Worthies".

After he had observed the customary three years of mourning by the tomb of the man who had been a father to him, Zhao Wu devoted himself to looking after Cheng Ying's widow for the remainder of her days, as if she were his own mother. When she died, he set up a shrine for her, at which he offered sacrifices for her every spring and autumn, year in and year out. To this day, in the region east of the Yellow River, when members of the Zhao clan perform rites for their ancestors on the main festival occasions, they always include sacrifices to the Two Worthies Cheng Ying and Gongsun Chujiu.

Zhao Wu's descendants continued to hold high offices, including those of general and prime minister. Eventually, the State of Jin was divided by its powerful clans into three parts. The Zhao clan set up the State of Zhao, which lasted for over 100 years in the area of present-day Shanxi and Hebei provinces, as one of the seven powerful states of the Warring States Period (475-221 BC).

Snow in Summer

About the Original Work   282

Chapter 1   Eternal Parting   285
Chapter 2   Widow Cai Meets with Misfortune   298
Chapter 3   Inviting Wolves into the House   310
Chapter 4   Zhang the Dog Dies at the Hands of His Son   319
Chapter 5   Evil Plotters   332
Chapter 6   A Confession Extracted Under Torture   349
Chapter 7   Appeal to Heaven on the Execution Ground   362
Chapter 8   The Emperor's Inspector   378
Chapter 9   A Ghost Appeals for Justice   388
Chapter 10   An Injustice Avenged   400

About the Original Work

SNOW IN SUMMER is the master work of the illustrious Yuan Dynasty (1279-1368 AD) *zaju* playwright Guan Hanqing. The embryo of the story comes from an ancient folk tale known as "The Filial Daughter of the East Coast". The earliest written accounts that are similar to the story appear in *On Gardens* by Liu Xiang of the Western Han Dynasty and in Ban Gu's *History of the Han Dynasty: Biography of Yu Dingguo*. It emerges in clearer form during the Jin Dynasty in Gan Bao's *In Search of Ghosts*, upon which the *zaju* playwrights Wang Shifu and Liang Jinzhi based their work *The Prestigious Duke Yu*. But these works have no critical point of view, apart from *In Search of Ghosts*, which uses street anecdotes to make the point that "the gods are not deceived", and underlines the girl's filial constancy by stressing her spirit of resistance. Guan Hanqing's accomplishment was to fuse the accounts in the historical records with the folk tradition and to draw from other *zaju* plays of his own time and thus embellish the tale with life-like cameos of Yuan Dynasty society. His talents produced a classic tragedy, *Snow in Summer*, that has continued to move audiences deeply.

The play reveals the seamy side of Yuan Dynasty society and is a scathing indictment of corrupt officialdom and the cruel oppression of ordinary people by petty local tyrants. Through the suffering of the heroine Dou E, Guan Hanqing gives voice to the ordinary people's spirit of stubborn resistance. The three appeals Dou E makes to Heaven just before she is to be put to death not only underline the terrible injustice that has been visited upon her, but challenge the whole traditional ruling class. This cry for justice has resounded through the ages, and is the real reason why *The Injustice Done to Dou E Moves Heaven and Earth* has remained a favorite of theatre-goers for 700 years.

It was Guan Hanqing's misfortune to be born in the early years of the Yuan Dynasty, when intellectuals were oppressed and despised, and their status was on par with the dregs of society. It was as a result of this that he gained a deep understanding for and sympathy with the sufferings of the laboring people. As a consequence, he took delight in articulating the hopes and aspirations of the oppressed. This impulse, in fact, was what moved him to write this great tragedy, which catapulted him into the ranks of the "four great playwrights of the Yuan Dynasty". Guan Hanqing is also one of China's most admired dramatists.

The Injustice Done to Dou E Moves Heaven and Earth has been adapted into a wide variety of literary forms, and is probably best known today in the form of a novel. In our adaptation of this drama classic as a novel, we have endeavored to remain faithful to the original format, with reference to the Ming Dynasty version, known as *The Story of the Golden Lock*, for the sequence of the plot. However, the scenes of action and the protagonists' psychological development have been highlighted as is appropriate to the genre of the novel. In addition, the action has been somewhat fleshed out.

We sincerely hope that our adaptation has not done violence to the spirit of the original work, but has made the characters and their tribulations more vivid and believable, and the plot and the intrigue more vigorous and true-to-life. In this way, we hope to have produced a more insightful and thought-provoking work.

CHAPTER ONE

Eternal Parting

IT IS SAID that the founder of the Yuan Dynasty, the Mongol leader Kublai Khan, chose the name of the dynasty from a passage in the *Book of Changes*. In the 16th year of his reign (1279), the Yuan finally destroyed the Song Dynasty and united the country. China became a mighty empire once more. However, the Mongols were a proud, fierce and warlike people. From the moment that they entered the Central Plains, they showed contempt and hostility for the traditional culture of the Chinese people. They held Confucian scholars in especially low esteem, and slaughtered them indiscriminately. The result was that many scholars were reduced to the bottom ranks of society, and lived as destitute vagabonds.

One of these unfortunates was a graduate of the county level imperial examinations, named Dou Tianzhang. His ancestral home was Jingzhao, Chang'an City (present-day Xi'an in Shaanxi Province). Dou Tianzhang had devoted himself to Confucian studies from an early age. He was thoroughly acquainted with all the schools of thought, and excelled at the study of the law. But, being unlucky enough to live at the time when the Mongol hordes were pouring south, Dou Tianzhang could find no employment for his talents. Moreover, his education had left him with no head for business or the management of household affairs, and so, when his parents died and he had to manage on his own, he found himself in desperate straits. Fortunately, he found a wife with the help of a matchmaker. Now this wife came from a background so obscure that she did not even have a name. But she was virtuous and intelligent, and because she had floated into his life like a cloud, with no kin or friends, Dou Tianzhang gave her the name Cloud.

Dou Tianzhang was fortunate to have found a wife who was not only good at managing the house, but had deep respect for her husband's scholarly attainments. And so the couple lived in perfect harmony. Dou, however, paid no heed to whether there was rice for the pot or not, and spent his days with a book forever in his hand, reciting and mumbling. Finally, Cloud managed to persuade him to go out and cut firewood in the hills, and sell it in the market place. But even then he would take a book with him, and become so absorbed in his reading that, more often than not, he would look up from it to find that the market had closed and he hadn't sold so much as a single stick of firewood. Cloud then started going to the market place with her husband, and did the bargaining for him. Nevertheless, she did not utter a word of complaint. And so, they lived hand to mouth like this for three years.

In the third year of her marriage to Dou Tianzhang, Cloud gave birth to a baby girl. Her husband was overjoyed when he saw that the infant was the image of her comely mother, and he named the child Duanyun, meaning "just like Cloud". However, her poverty-stricken childhood had left Cloud with a fragile constitution, and the loss of blood occasioned by the birth proved too much for her. There was no money for a doctor, and she never again arose from her bed. For three years, she lingered on. It grieved her to be such a burden to her husband, who was at his wits' end bustling about here and there trying to run the house and feed his poor family. Whenever he had time, he would speak a few words of comfort to Cloud, and she would turn her back to him to hide her tears. She eventually decided that she could do her loving husband a favor by dying, and so she stopped eating and refused anything to drink. Before long, she was mere skin and bones, and her breathing grew shallow. Just before she left this world, Cloud clasped her baby girl to her bosom, and in trembling tones spoke thus to Dou Tianzhang: "My dear, I have brought nothing to our marriage but this child. You must bring her up properly; on no account must she be allowed to become a waif on the streets as her wretched mother did."

Dou Tianzhang took the two of them in his arms, and in a choking voice, said, "Please rest assured, my dear. I will indeed ensure her a proper upbringing and find her a respectable husband. As long as there is a mouthful of food left to me, she shall not go hungry!"

After Cloud passed away, Dou Tianzhang and his daughter looked after each other as best they could, but life became harder and harder. The final blow came when a fierce drought struck their region, the central Shaanxi plain. The earth was scorched brown; the bodies of those who had died of hunger littered the ground; and many people fled the district to seek succor from friends and relatives elsewhere. Dou Tianzhang thought to himself: "There is no telling how long this drought will last, and with no kinfolk to aid us, death by starvation seems certain for both me and Duanyun. I have heard that the region south of the Yangtze River is a 'land of fish and rice', populous and thriving. They say the scenery is magnificent there too. Since my wife died a long time ago, there is nothing to keep me here; I might as well try my look elsewhere. Who knows, this might turn out to be a blessing in disguise, after all?" He thereupon tied his meager belongings in a bundle, said farewell to his neighbors, and after paying his respects at Cloud's grave, he set off on his journey.

Jingzhao is a long way from the land south of the Yangtze, and Dou Tianzhang, carrying both his bundle and Duanyun, found it an arduous trek. With no choice but to travel on foot and sleep in the open, he plodded on day after day. The little silver he had brought with him was soon used up, and he was reduced to begging along the road.

After several months, they drew near to the city of Jinling

[present-day Nanjing], when Duanyun came down with a fever and they were forced to seek shelter for a few days. It happened that at this time the Mongols had forced a crossing of the Yangtze, and besieged Jinling in the teeth of fierce resistance from the Southern Song forces. When the enraged Mongols finally captured the city they engaged in an orgy of slaughter, causing a mass exodus of all the people in the surrounding area. From the refugees Dou Tianzhang learned of the fall of Jinling, and so he turned aside and headed for the city of Chuzhou [present-day Qingjiang City in Jiangsu Province]. As the countryside was being ravaged by the marauding Mongols and Duanyun had not yet recovered from her fever, father and daughter put up in the abandoned Town God's Temple, just outside Chuzhou, to wait for the girl to recover.

Having no acquaintances whatsoever in Chuzhou, Duan Tianzhang had to resort to begging again. But in those troubled times the local people, too, were hard put to make a living, and so there were many days when father and daughter went hungry. Fortunately for them, in the vicinity lived some old people, who took pity on the pair, and helped them with food and clothing. As a result of their kindness, Duanyun gradually recovered from her illness. Not only that, but one of their old neighbors, finding that Dou Tianzhang was a learned man, recommended him as a tutor to a certain Squire Li, who lived in the south part of the city. The squire immediately perceived that, in spite of his ragged and half-starved appearance, Dou Tianzhang was a man of no mean scholarship and took father and daughter into his household, where Dou was to act as tutor to his son. Thenceforth, Dou Tianzhang threw himself heart and soul into his teaching duties. Within half a year, his young pupil had made gratifying progress, and Dou Tianzhang rose further in the squire's estimation.

In this way two full years passed. Duanyun, now six years old, was a lovely, intelligent girl. She also displayed a gentle and refined nature. Every day, she studied the "Classic for Women" and "Tales of Exemplary Women" with her father and started to learn to write as well as read. Dou Tianzhang by this time had reached the age when the flame of ambition had begun to dull in his breast. Besides, as the Mongols were still rampaging throughout the south, seeking out and executing scholars who had served the now-defunct Song Dynasty, oblivious to the need to build a new civil administration. Dou Tianzhang resigned himself to spending the remainder of his days quietly as a private tutor.

But the ways of Heaven allow no man to rest easy for long. One night, Squire Li's mansion caught fire and burned to the ground. The squire himself, a kindly man who had devoted himself to charitable works such as building roads and bridges at his own expense, and helping those in need, was devastated by this sudden calamity. He railed at Heaven and cursed the earth, until he fell into a delirium, and not long afterwards died. With the passing of its head, the Li household was destitute. As the family could no longer afford to employ a tutor, Dou Tianzhang was compelled to move out and seek lodgings elsewhere.

He rented a room in the suburbs. But, no longer having employment and with no land to cultivate, the little money he had managed to save during the time he had been the Li household's tutor was soon spent, and father and daughter once more faced the specter of starvation. Dou Tianzhang spent many days worrying and sighing, until he heard from someone that in the neighborhood there was a widow named Cai, who supported herself and her seven-year-old son by lending out money from her late husband's legacy at high interest. Having nowhere else to turn, Dou Tianzhang borrowed 20 ounces of silver from the widow, assuring her that he would pay it back, together with 100% interest, at the end of one year.

Father and daughter lived frugally, but as Dou Tianzhang neither tilled the land nor gathered firewood, no matter how much money he borrowed it would sooner or later all be used up. And so, when the following spring arrived, Dou Tianzhang began to dread the knock on the door that would inform him that Widow Cai had come to collect the 40 ounces of silver. Sure enough, that fateful day came. The scholar begged for more time to pay. The widow was sympathetic enough, clearly aware that he had no means of earning a livelihood. But, after all, she couldn't just write off a huge sum like 40 ounces of silver, and so every few days she would be back, dunning Dou Tianzhang for the debt.

Every time, she was treated to wheedling words and tea — but not a cent was forthcoming. As she gazed round the bare walls of Dou Tianzhang's sparsely furnished room, the conviction began to sink in that she would never be paid. Then, one day, on another fruitless visit, her gaze alighted on the comely features of Duanyun. Without more ado, she offered to cancel the debt if Dou Tianzhang would allow her to take this pretty, gracious girl into her own home, to be raised as a future bride for her son. Now, Duanyun was the apple of her father's eye; moreover, he constantly bore in mind his wife's dying words. He adamantly refused Widow Cai's offer, and as a result, the usurer become more importunate.

One day, fearing another visit from the widow, Dou Tianzhang slipped out early in the morning, and wandered aimlessly into the city. Coming to a crossroads, he saw a crowd of people gazing at a notice. Curious, he elbowed his way through the throng. The object of attention turned out to be an imperial decree, announcing that the court had turned from war to the arts of peace. Furthermore, to recruit worthy persons to assist His Imperial Majesty in affairs of state an examination was to be held in the coming autumn.

When he finished reading the notice, Dou Tianzhang could not help a feeling of excitement. He thought to himself, "I am a learned man, and I have always cherished an ambition to be a person of renown. It's just that I have had the misfortune to have encountered troubled times, which caused me to wander far from home. This is a Heaven-sent opportunity. If I miss this chance, I will in all likelihood spend the rest of my life in poverty and misery. Besides, even if I cared little for fame and fortune, how could I condemn my child Duanyun to a life of cold and hunger? Surely, the best thing for me to do is to enter the examination. Then, if I'm lucky enough to pass, I will be appointed an official, and we will never again have to worry about having enough to eat and wear." Just then, a sobering thought struck him: Chuzhou was a long way from the capital, where the examination would be held. Where would a man who was already in debt to the tune of 40 ounces of silver get the funds to enable him to make the journey? Besides, who would look after Duanyun while he was away? His elation turned to gloom, and he trudged his weary way homeward.

Dou Tianzhang spent a sleepless night, worrying and sighing. When dawn came, he had still not thought of a solution to his dilemma.

The first thing that happened was that Widow Cai came marching in without waiting for an invitation. "I'm sick and tired of your excuses, Scholar Dou," she yelled. "You owe me 40 ounces of silver, and I'm not budging from here until I get it!"

Flustered, Dou Tianzhang urged her to take a seat, and commenced his usual litany of hardship stories, begging for a few more days to pay.

"A few more days?" the old woman exploded. "Let me tell you — as if you didn't know already — that my poor son and I depend on the interest on that loan to scrape a bare existence. If I give you any more time, I might as well smash my rice bowl — for I'll have nothing to put in it any more. A few more days or no few more days, how on earth do you intend to pay me back?"

Dou Tianzhang replied. "I have been suffering a bad run of luck lately. But, as soon as my ambition is achieved, I'll pay you back several times over, I assure you!"

"How do you expect to achieve your ambition, having drifted into a god-forsaken neighborhood like this?" she sneered. "I'll be in my grave long before you make anything of yourself. And I'm not interested in getting it several times over some time in the distant future. I only want my 40 ounces of silver, and I want them now!"

"Madam, you are too harsh on me," Dou Tianzhang protested. "From an early age, I devoted myself to study, and I have long nurtured a lofty ambition to serve the empire. For a man with my talents and drive, fame and fortune are there for the taking. When that time comes around, what will a mere 40 ounces of silver be to me?"

This riposte confused the old woman. "Has perhaps some change come about in your fortunes recently, sir?" she asked tentatively.

The other played his trump card. "As a matter of fact," he said, with an air of great self-satisfaction, "the emperor has announced that an examination is about to be held, for the purpose of recruiting men of talent for the court. I need hardly tell you, Widow Cai, that all I have to do is enter that examination and honors and riches will be showered upon me."

The old woman then thought to herself: "I have heard people say that this man Dou is indeed an outstanding scholar. If he goes to the capital, and takes the examination, the chances are that he will be rewarded with an official post. If I press him too hard now to pay the debt, he will certainly make life hard for me when he becomes a powerful figure in the government. I had better forget about the 40 ounces of silver, just to be on the safe side." She then wreathed her features in smiles, and gushed, "Of course, sir, everybody for miles around is well aware what an accomplished scholar you are. Now, may I inquire when you intend to leave for the capital, and what provision you have made in the matter of traveling expenses?"

A shrewd glance told Widow Cai that she had touched a sore spot. Dou Tianzhang hesitated in confusion for some time. At length, he stammered, "To be frank, madam, that is something I have not yet got around to arranging."

The old woman saw her chance, and took it. "Well," she mused, "that is a problem, isn't it? I mean, without traveling expenses you won't be able to get to the capital, will you? And without getting to the capital, you won't be able to take the examination. And then you won't get an official position, and all your ambitions will come to naught. What a pity!" She quickly continued, "But I have a plan to help you out, sir. I wonder if I might be so bold...?"

Dou Tianzhang made an eager bow to the widow: "Madam, please let me know what you have in mind."

"On my many visits here," Widow Cai explained, "I could not help but notice how lovely your daughter has grown. She is about the same age as my son, and so I thought she would make an ideal daughter-in-law. However, my approaches to yourself on the matter have met with no success. If you now wish to travel to the capital to take the imperial examination you're going to need funds for the trip. Now then: If you leave your daughter with me while you're away, to serve me as my daughter-in-law, I'll not only waive the 40 ounces of silver you owe me, I'll give you enough for

eternal parting

the journey. So you can be off to the capital without a care in the world. And then when you become an official, you can come back and be reunited with your daughter. That of course would be a great honor for me, and the arrangement would benefit both sides, don't you think? Otherwise, you'd end up making your way to the capital like a beggar — because you haven't got a penny, you know. And you'd be dragging a child along with you. Is that any way to approach the imperial examinations? I urge you to think it over carefully. But if you don't agree, you can just pay me the money you owe me, and we'll both go our separate ways. How's that?"

It was a very persuasive argument that the old woman had put forward, and Dou Tianzhang was speechless for a while. He pondered deeply, concluding, "I have no choice. If I don't take my chance in the imperial examinations, both Duanyun and I will starve to death for sure. The old woman will never let me take her with me without dunning me for debt every step of the way. And she's right — I would arrive in the capital like a beggar with this child! There's nothing else for it but to agree to Widow Cai's plan, and leave Duanyun with her for the time being. Then, when I've made a name for myself, I can come back for her." He was on the point of saying yes, when his wife's dying behest echoed in his memory. Through gritted teeth, he stammered, "Madam, I must admit that there is reason in your words. But, Duanyun is so young still that I could not feel easy leaving her behind. Besides, it would be just like selling her to you. How could I do such a thing?"

The wily old woman sensed that the scholar was beginning to waver. Secretly rejoicing, she put on a fawning smile and chose her words craftily: "Sir, if you agree to my proposal, that would be tantamount to our becoming kinfolk. Then your daughter would be as good as my own daughter-in-law. What would be so remarkable about helping a relative with something as trifling as traveling expenses? What's all this talk of selling your daughter? Once she is living in my house, like my own flesh and blood she certainly won't go cold or hungry, I can assure you!"

Dou Tianzhang thought the matter over once more, and

finally, with anguish in his heart, he turned his face to the sky, and groaned, "Very well. There is no alternative. I agree to do as you say."

"You have made a very wise decision, sir," cried the triumphant widow. "Your daughter will be as well looked after by me as if she were at your own side. You can start on your journey in the full knowledge that the girl will be completely safe from any ill treatment. Now, when will you send Duanyun to me?"

Dou Tianzhang replied, "The autumn examination is not far off, and it is a long way to the capital. I should not delay my departure, but I must first consult Duanyun, and obtain her consent."

"Oh, what can the child know about such matters?" protested Widow Cai. "What point is there in seeking her permission? As a matter of fact, I took the liberty a few days ago of consulting a soothsayer. And he said that the day after tomorrow would be a good day for starting out on a long journey. So it would be best if you were to send the girl to me on that day, and I will have your traveling expenses ready, and will see you on your way."

Dou Tianzhang agreed. "Very well," he said. "Tomorrow I'll pack my things, and the following day I will bring Duanyun to you."

Delighted with the bargain, Widow Cai took her leave. As he saw her out, the scholar noticed that Duanyun was playing by herself in the courtyard. He beckoned to her.

It was with some reluctance that he broke the news to the girl that he was about to depart on a long journey, and that he would be leaving her in the care of Widow Cai. At this, Duanyun uttered a loud wail, which pierced her father's heart like a knife. He hugged the girl to his breast, and father and daughter wept copious tears. Finally wiping his own eyes, Dou Tianzhang dried Duanyun's tears too. He patiently explained the situation to her, until she came to understand that her stay with the old woman would only be a temporary one, until her father had passed the examination and could return to fetch her.

Her reluctant consent lightened Dou Tianzhang's heart somewhat. "That's a good girl!" he said. "You're sensible enough to know what is right. That makes your old father much happier."

"I will do as you say, father," Duanyun said. "I will live with Widow Cai while I wait for you to return. Please come back as soon as you obtain an official post, and don't make me miss you for too long."

Dou Tianzhang assured her that the first thing he would do upon gaining a position would be to rush back to her. "And then we will never be parted again," he promised. "But while you are at Widow Cai's house you must be very careful to obey her in all things," he added. "Don't be always playing. And don't do anything to upset the old woman."

The girl assented. Thereupon, Duan Tianzhang got busy packing for his journey.

On the appointed day, the scholar presented himself at Widow Cai's door, a knapsack on his back and leading his daughter by the hand. The widow, who was already waiting for them, hastened to usher them into the house. Dou Tianzhang sat down, and said, "I entrust my daughter to you, Madam. I do not say she can serve you as a daughter-in-law, but I entreat you to look after her well."

Filled with satisfaction, Widow Cai gushed, "My dear sir, we are now as good as kith and kin! Your daughter is just like my own child. You may set your heart completely at ease." So saying, she produced the scholar's IOU for the money she had already lent him, and at the same time 20 ounces of silver. "Take this document back, sir," she urged him. "This little matter between us is now settled. And here is something to help you on your way. Seeing as we are now as close as family members, it's the least I can do."

Dou Tianzhang accepted the IOU and the money, made a deep bow, and said, "Many thanks, Madam. Some day I will repay you handsomely, you may be sure."

He rose to take his leave, whereupon Duanyun flung herself weeping into his arms and refusing to let him go. Dou Tianzhang addressed the old woman: "Madam, if there is anything amiss in my daughter's conduct, please have the goodness to overlook it, regarding it as my fault for neglecting her upbringing."

Widow Cai was affability itself. "My dear sir," she cried. "Such an instruction is completely unnecessary. You know well my affection for the child." As she said this, she took Duanyun from her father's arms.

After a few last words of instruction to his daughter, Dou Tianzhang went on his way. Duanyun gazed after him for some time, dry-eyed, and then followed Widow Cai into the house.

The old woman seated herself in the main hall, and summoned the child to her. Duanyun hurried forward and fell to her knees in front of her new guardian. "What orders do you have for me, Madam?" she inquired meekly.

The widow was even more pleased to see that her charge was so well-mannered. "Ah, it must be because you come from a scholar's family that you know how to behave!" she said, with approval. "Now, my child, you are living in my house, just like my own flesh and blood. So you must not keep crying and prattling on about your father."

"Yes, Madam. I understand."

"What is your given name?"

"Duanyun, Madam."

"Well, now that you are in the position of my daughter-in-law, such a name won't do, you know. Shall I give you a more suitable name?"

"I will accept whatever name you choose for me, Madam."

"All right. What do you think of Dou E?"

"From now on, Madam, I will be called Dou E, and Duanyun will only be my pet name."

The old woman was pleased with this exchange. "Well, so that's settled!" she announced. "You may rise now. When you grow old enough, you will marry my son Zongchang, and we'll spend the rest of our days together. From now on, you must not be lazy, and make me angry, you know."

Duanyun replied, "I will keep in mind all you have told me, Madam."

From this time on, the girl was known as Dou E. During the day, she helped Widow Cai with running the house, and at night they shared a bed. Although the old woman could not love the child as much as her father could, nevertheless, she was very fond of her and never mistreated her in any way. Besides, the Cai household was comfortably off, and Dou E had no worries about getting enough to eat and wear. Thus the three of them lived in peaceful harmony. Of course, at first, the girl still missed her father, and would often turn away to wipe away tears. On such occasions Widow Cai would utter some kind words of comfort, understanding that Dou E was still very young, and fully confident that as time went on the ache of separation would die down.

CHAPTER TWO

Widow Cai Meets with Misfortune

THE REASON WIDOW Cai had gone to all this trouble to get Dou E into her house was that she wanted her as a future bride for her son, whose name was Zongchang. At this time, he was just eight years old. The old woman's late husband had prospered in business, and had left her a tidy sum of money upon his demise. Widow Cai supported herself and her son by lending out the capital she had been left at high interest. In this way, the two of them were comfortably off. However, their prosperity incited envy among many of the neighbors, and some of the more rascally people took advantage of the helplessness of the widow and Zongchang to default on their loans. When the old woman pestered them for repayment they caught Zongchang playing in the street, and give him a beating, sending him running home crying to his mother.

Shocked at this, the old woman realized that without evidence it was no use complaining to the local magistrate; all she could do was to send Dou E out to buy some ointment and attend to the little boy's cuts and bruises.

This incident caused her to decide to leave Chuzhou and move back to her home village in Shanyang County. She thereupon sent a man to search out her relatives and give them a letter. But the man returned with a sorry tale. It seems that the Cai clan had in the meantime fallen on hard times, and its members had scattered; only a few of the widow's relatives remained, and they had no interest in renewing her acquaintance. Widow Cai was in a quandary: "If we stay in Chuzhou," she thought, "a helpless widow and a little boy, we are bound to keep running into trouble. Zongchang is the last of the family line; if anything happens to him, whom will I be able to rely on? We have no clan members in Shanyang who can help us out. So what is to be done?" Finally, deciding that moving to Shanyang was better for the time being than remaining where they were, she began to sell off the household possessions in preparation for the move.

She did not consult either Zongchang or Dou E, considering them too young to understand the predicament they were in. Within a few days, everything was settled, apart from a few outstanding loans that the old woman was too timid to chase up, and the three of them set off for Shanyang in a hired cart.

They moved into a spacious house in the eastern part of Shanyang County, which Widow Cai, with her shrewd bargaining powers, managed to buy for a reasonable price. However, because they were strangers, they kept themselves at home, and for the first few months hardly ever ventured outside. But eventually, the widow realized that living like this, and no matter how frugally, was bound to exhaust her stock of capital eventually, and she began to think of how she could secure an income. Aware that she had no talent for either farming or trade, she decided to return to her old occupation of money lending. But this time she made it a rule to lend only small amounts, such as ten or 20 pieces of silver, and only to people she could trust. This way, she wouldn't have to keep dunning her debtors, like before. This policy turned out to be a highly successful one, and Widow Cai became very popular in the neighborhood, with people constantly calling on her. The old woman now lived a life of leisure; apart from sallying forth to collect what was owed her, she spent most of the day instructing Dou E in the art of needlework.

In this way, ten years passed. Dou E had grown into a fine

young woman. Not only was she excellent with a needle, she was a fine cook too. Widow Cai thought that it was high time for Dou E to marry her son. Unfortunately, Zongchang, who had always been a sickly child, contracted consumption as he approached the age of 20. His mother spent a fortune on bringing doctors from miles around, but all to no avail. Dou E herself nursed the boy night and day.

One day, one of the neighbors called to advise Widow Cai that the only thing that could make Zongchang recover would be the happy event of his marriage. At her wits' end for any other solution, the widow agreed to try this straightaway. And so, an auspicious day was chosen, the wedding arrangements were made, and the couple were married. Dou E made no objection, but just went along with Widow Cai's wishes.

However, after the wedding, far from getting better, Zongchang's illness got worse by the day. In less than three months, he passed away. His mother and Dou E were devastated by grief. But there was no help for it: The coffin and grave clothes had to be bought, and a monk hired to recite the funeral service as Zongchang was buried in a public cemetery.

Dou E spent the required three years of mourning hardly able to eat, drink or sleep. At the end of this period she was thin and haggard, and her clothes hung on her. She could not help recounting her misfortunes bitterly to herself: "Since my father left, over ten years ago, I have had no news of him. I have been brought up in the Cai household, and finally married. But our marital bliss lasted a mere three months, before my husband passed away. I am now left alone at a tender age. All I can do now is devote myself to looking after Widow Cai with the utmost filial duty, scrupulously adhering to womanly virtue."

So from then on she took upon herself all the household duties, and attended to Widow Cai's every need, inquiring after her health first thing in the morning, and visiting her just before she retired at night, just like a daughter-in-law should. She made sure that there was enough food in the house, and if clothes were torn she mended them. She took the old woman's arm whenever she went for walks, and fluffed up the bedclothes for her at night. In short,

Dou E attended Widow Cai with the utmost devotion and respect. The money lending business, however, was still carried on by the old woman, as Dou E was too young to venture out alone in the streets. Widow Cai was content that the girl kept herself cloistered.

At the end of three years, Dou E doffed her hempen mourning garments. But the clothes she adopted were simple ones, nor did she use any kind of makeup or adornment. She kept the house in perfect order, which was a great comfort to Widow Cai, and excited the admiration of all the neighbors, who praised her for her filial piety and exemplary respect for her elderly mother-in-law.

Now it happened that there was a rascally bachelor by the name of Lu, who kept an apothecary's shop outside the south gate of Shanyang County. He had studied in his youth, but, being a dunderhead, he had only managed to memorize the words of the classics without understanding their meaning. However, as his family had money, they had managed to acquire for him the title of *xiucai*, signifying a person who had passed the imperial examination at the county level. This title stood him in good stead when his parents passed away and he was looking for a means of making his living. He borrowed enough capital to set himself up in business as an apothecary. But he knew nothing of the profundities of the art he practiced; when treating patients, he neither felt the pulse nor applied the techniques of acupuncture and moxibustion. Neither observing, listening, inquiring nor probing, he simply trying to match the symptoms with those described in medical books. As a result, he killed more patients than he cured. What was more ludicrous was that he was quite brazen when boasting of his skill, claiming that it surpassed that of the legendary physicians of the Spring and Autumn Period, Master Lu and Bian Que. The local people, disdainful of this quack's odious nonsense, gave him the nickname 'Sai Lu Yi'. meaning "Exceeding Doctor Lu", implying that he was superior to the great healer Master Lu. The apothecary, however, far from being abashed by this jibe, took it as a great compliment, and even had the words "Sai Lu Yi's Pharmacy" written on a signboard and hung over the door of his shop.

As Sai Lu Yi's appalling record for hastening his patients out of this world became known, his business went rapidly down hill, until he was reduced to selling nothing but rat poison. And, as there was little profit in rat poison, he soon had to resort to trying to borrow money to make ends meet. But, as most people in the area knew that his shop did little business, and that Sai Lu Yi himself was a good-for-nothing who was highly unlikely to pay back any money he borrowed, he could not find anyone to extend even a short-term loan. About one year previously, when Sai Lu Yi was in desperate straits, he had been most interested to hear about an old woman called Widow Cai, recently moved into the neighborhood, whose only son had just died and who lent out money in order to keep herself and her daughter-in-law. He wangled an introduction to Widow Cai, and borrowed ten pieces of silver from her. The old woman, by now well advanced in years and feeble in both body and mind, and not knowing about Sai Lu Yi's unsavory background, assumed that, as a man of business, his credit was good. Sai Lu Yi, however, had no intention of paying the loan — at 100% interest — back, and when the customary year was up fobbed off Widow Cai with a whole litany of excuses every time she came to demand repayment. When she saw how little stock the apothecary had in his shop and how sluggish his business was, the old woman realized that she had been tricked. Making inquiries locally, her worst fears were confirmed by the reports she heard about the slipperiness of Sai Lu Yi. But, as a helpless widow with only a young daughter-in-law to take care of her, she dared not create a disturbance, and so resigned herself with a heavy heart to the loss at any rate of the interest, and tried to get the principal back. Sai Lu Yi, however, had no way of returning even this much, and when Widow Cai's importuning got too much for him, devised a plan to strangle her with a cord he had prepared specially for this purpose.

One fine morning after breakfast, Widow Cai decided to make one more call on Sai Lu Yi, leaving Dou E to look after the house. The girl was worried that the old woman was taking a risk dealing with a rascal like Sai Lu Yi, and advised her: "Please don't argue with him. Just ask for the principal, and forget the interest."

"That's exactly what I have been doing," the widow replied.

"Don't worry."

Widow Cai made her way to the apothecary's shop outside the south gate. To her great surprise, Sai Lu Yi was all smiles as he rose from his seat behind the counter and hurried forward to greet his visitor.

"My dear madam," he gushed, "if I had only known that I was to be honored by a visit from you, I would have rushed out to greet you! Please come in, and take a seat."

Widow Cai perched herself on the stool the apothecary brought for her, but refused his offer of tea. "Don't bother," she snapped. "I won't be here long enough to drink it."

Nevertheless, Sai Lu Yi insisted on popping into the back room. The old woman had walked right into his trap by coming alone, and he was determined not to miss this opportunity of luring her to some lonely spot and strangling her. When he returned with the tea, he had a length of cord wrapped round his waist and concealed. "I'm so sorry for keeping you waiting, madam, but I had quite misplaced the tea caddy," he lied.

"It's not your tea I've come for," Widow Cai aid peevishly.

But Sai Lu Yi continued to lull the old woman into a false sense of security. "Madam, you are my benefactress," he assured her, as he poured the tea. "At a time when my business was not doing so well, you stretched out a helping hand, and rescued me virtually from ruin. Such kindness! Such amiability! This debt of gratitude I owe you must be repaid. Now, please, accept this tea to refresh yourself."

Somewhat mollified, yet puzzled, the old woman took a sip from the cup the apothecary pressed upon her. "Sir, since you claim to have been rescued from ruin, I suppose you have recouped your fortunes to some extent — enough at any rate to repay the money you owe me. The debt has been outstanding for long enough. Besides, I'm not as young as I used to be; it's not easy for me to come traipsing all the way out here, especially if it's on another fool's errand."

"I know I should have paid back the money long ago," the apothecary sighed. "And I am so ashamed to have caused you all this trouble. It is true that business has picked up somewhat lately, but you can see that my shelves are now empty, and I need to buy in more stock. If you will only deign to give me a few more days to pay, I promise that you shall have your money in full."

Widow Cai said, "I have heard that your business is slack, and so I won't press you for the interest. But you must realize that I have no other source of income. I need that money to buy food. So if you will just repay the principal, I'll let it go at that."

Sai Lu Yi thought for a moment. Then he said, "How very kind of you, madam! To forego the interest on the loan shows me that you are a person of magnanimity. I would be an ungrateful wretch indeed if I did not repay you here and now on the spot. But, the fact is that I don't keep that kind of money in the shop. I will have to fetch it from my residence, in a little village not far from here. Perhaps it would be too much trouble for you to accompany me?"

Tired as she was, the thought of getting the matter settled and washing her hands of Sai Lu Yi once and for all had a special appeal for Widow Cai. "Well, if it's not too far...," she faltered.

"We don't have far to go at all, madam, I assure you," said the apothecary, with confidence. "After this, you won't have all the bother of coming all the way out here again. It will also be a load off my mind."

Little suspecting what evil deed Sai Lu Yi was planning, the old woman preceded him out of the shop. Sai Lu Yi locked the door, and led the way, southward along the main road.

As they walked along, they frequently encountered other travelers, giving Sai Lu Yi no chance to carry out his foul plot. Eventually, Widow Cai noticed that there were no longer any villages by the side of the road. Footsore, she stopped. "How much further is it?" she asked, indignantly.

Sai Lu Yi glanced round in desperation. Spotting a path disappearing into a field of tall maize stalks, he pointed to it: "It's just down that path, madam."

The maize stalks on either side hid the pair almost entirely as they walked along the path. They had not gone far when the apothecary, having made sure that there was nobody in the vicinity, suddenly turned and said, "Is somebody following us?"

The unsuspecting widow turned to look behind her, alarmed by Sai Lu Yi's abrupt change of expression. "Where?" she asked.

Just as the old woman's attention was distracted, Sai Lu Yi whipped out the length of cord from around his waist, looped it round Widow Cai's neck, and jerked on both ends with all his might.

The old woman's strangled cry of "Help! Murder!" turned Sai Lu Yi's knees to jelly. But he could not back out now. The deed had to be carried to its horrendous conclusion. He heaved on the cord with all his might, muttering, "Try to scream if you can! Try to scream if you can!" Struggling furiously and gasping, Widow Cai struggled to loosen the noose that was choking the life out of her. Sai Lu Yi gave one more tug, and the old woman's hands dropped limp from the cord, and dangled by her sides. At the same time, her eyes rolled up into her head, until only the whites were visible, and her whole body went limp and still. Then, satisfied that his victim was dead, the apothecary loosened the cord, allowing the old woman to slump to the ground. He was just mopping his feverish brow, when he heard a sharp cry behind him:

"Murder in broad daylight! Hey you, stay where you are!"

Sai Lu Yi jerked his head round, to see two swarthy fellows, one older than the other, dashing towards him. Dropping his sweat-soaked handkerchief, Sai Lu Yi dived into the thickets of grain, and disappeared from view.

Who, dear readers, do you think these rough-looking newcomers were?

In fact, they were a father and son. They were surnamed Zhang. The father's name was Zhang Jun, nicknamed Zhang the Dog, and the son's name was Zhang Ji. They were notorious throughout Shanyang County for being hoodlums and blackguards. Zhang the Dog, in fact had never married, but for years had consorted with a prostitute, who had born him his son. The latter, an uncouth and villainous boor, had a repulsive long face like that of a mule, earning for him the nickname Zhang the Mule. Unable and unwilling to turn his hand to honest work when he reached manhood, Zhang the Mule had straggled along with the Mongol army, under a commander named Saputo, on its southward invasion, joining in with enthusiasm in its orgy of rapine and plunder. Following the fall of the Southern Song Dynasty, Saputo had been made commander of the Shanyang area, and so Zhang the Mule had wandered back to his hometown in Saputo's wake. Saputo was a fierce and brave commander, who had earned much merit in the field. Besides, he was a member of the imperial clan. So when he settled down in Shanyang he exerted absolute despotic power. Every official in the county was terrified of him. Zhang the Mule tried every means to toady up to his commander, but the latter knew that the young oaf was both unlettered and cowardly, and soon sent him packing. Zhang the Mule, virtually penniless and with no means of earning a living, then embarked on a life of blackmailing women, children and other helpless people, claiming close connections with Saputo, which was enough to silence anybody rash enough to protest.

As time went by, and the reputation of the two Zhangs was such that everyone in Shanyang gave them a wide berth, father and son were compelled to seek farther afield for someone to bully. And on this particular day that is just what they were doing, prowling the outlying villages in search of easy prey. Zhang the Mule's sharp ears had caught the strangled croaking of Widow Cai coming from the roadside field. "Did you hear that, Father?" he hissed to Zhang the Dog. "It sounded like a woman was being murdered. That's right up our street!"

So saying, he plunged off the highway, and hurried along the path that Sai Lu Yi and Widow Cai had taken, with his father close behind him. Zhang the Mule's intention was by no means to apprehend a murderer, but to blackmail a few pieces of silver from him. When Sai Lu Yi darted into the labyrinth of grain stalks, Zhang the Mule followed half-heartedly for a few paces, but then, having lost his quarry, returned.

He found that Zhang the Dog had propped Widow Cai up, and was rubbing her chest. Zhang the Mule pinched and slapped the old woman's face. Eventually, she drew a deep breath, and came back to life. Zhang the Mule whispered to his father: "Why would anyone want to murder this old woman, I wonder? She must have money at home, I'll bet, and someone had his greedy eyes on it. When she recovers fully, you try and find out from her if she's rich. And tell her that she owes us a few pieces of silver for saving her life."

Widow Cai slowly opened her eyes, and stared wildly at her two saviors. "Is this Hell?" she groaned.

Zhang the Dog quickly helped her to her feet. "We have just saved your life," he explained. "But who are you, and where are you from? And why was someone trying to kill you?"

Realizing that she had been snatched from the jaws of death, Widow Cai freely told the two strangers that her name was Cai, that her husband and son had died many years previously, and that she lived with her daughter-in-law, who was her only support. She then explained the dastardly trick that had been played on her by a debtor, and expressed her gratitude for the two Zhangs' timely rescue.

All this was music to the ears of Zhang the Mule, who whispered to his father: "If she's got money to lend out, she must have lots of it in her house. Not only that, but she's got a widowed daughter-in-law there too. She surely must be grateful to us for saving her life. Why don't you take the old woman, and I take the young one — and then we'll get all their wealth as well? We'll have wives and money too, with no effort at all! What could be better?"

Then, without waiting to find out what his father thought about this scheme, Zhang the Mule approached Widow Cai, and said, with a leer: "Madam, how do you intend to thank my father and me for saving your life?"

The young man's crafty smirk caused a pang of foreboding to strike the old woman's heart. She gabbled nervously: "As soon as we get to my house, I'll prepare a present of money for you two kind gentlemen."

Zhang the Mule bared his clenched teeth and shot Widow Cai a baleful glare. "Do you think we'll be satisfied with a few measly pennies?" he growled.

The old woman was mystified at this reply, and asked, "But if it's not money you want, what can I do to show my gratitude?"

Zhang the Mule glanced at his father: "You tell her."

The old man gave a dry cough, and explained, "You see, Madam, you and I are in the same boat. You have lost your husband, and I have no wife. For my part, I would consider myself amply compensated for saving your life if you would marry me."

This piece of gallantry sent a shock of alarm through Widow Cai. "Sir," she stammered, "your timely rescue deserves to be rewarded, for sure. But I have been widowed for many years, and I am now old. If I remarried at my age I would become the laughing stock of the neighborhood. When I get home, and I promise I will give you all the money you ask for."

Zhang the Dog was at a loss how to reply, when his son butted in. "If it hadn't been for us," he reminded the widow, "you would have already lost your life. Offering us money for that is an insult. Do as my father suggested. And besides that, I'll have your daughter-in-law for my own wife. How about it?"

Zhang the Mule's menacing attitude struck terror into Widow Cai, and she begged the scoundrel not to be angry with her.

Seeing that he had managed to frighten the old woman, Zhang the Mule continued his intimidation. "The cord that was used to try to strangle you is still here," he reminded her. "If you don't consent to what we propose, I'll finish off the job!" And with that, he stooped, as if to pick up the discarded noose.

His father, meanwhile, in feigned agitation, urged Zhang the Mule: "Don't be so hasty, my boy. Give this good woman time to think over our offer." Then, turning to Widow Cai, he said, "Madam, you should know that such an arrangement would be beneficial for both sides. What need is there for hesitation? I must warn you that my son here is a person who means what he says. If you don't go along with his desire, I cannot be answerable for the consequences!"

Widow Cai realized that she had no choice. "All right, all right, all right," she gabbled, "I agree to do what you say. But I cannot answer for my daughter-in-law. You see, she has a mind of her own, and she's very stubborn."

The two Zhangs were delighted that their scheme seemed to be working, and they said in chorus: "That will be no problem!" They then went on to assure the old woman that since they had her consent, her daughter-in-law's objections could soon be overcome. "Today is a day of great rejoicing," they assured her, for it was the very day when they were to move into her home as a pair of bridegrooms!

"Well, if this is my fate," muttered Widow Cai, "I suppose you'd better follow me home. By the way what are your names?"

The two scoundrels were only too pleased to impart this information. Following this formality, they dusted themselves down, straightened their clothing, and followed Widow Cai in high glee.

CHAPTER THREE

Inviting Wolves into the House

AS THEY WALKED, Widow Cai wondered how she was going to explain to Dou E how she had managed to go out alone and come back with two men who intended to marry them and move into their house. "I had no choice," she thought to herself. "If I hadn't agreed, this villainous-looking pair would have strangled me. But if, when we get home, Dou E refuses to go along with their scheme, who knows what calamity that will bring on our heads?" The old woman could think of no way out of this predicament, and was still puzzling over it when they arrived at her door. She turned to the Zhangs, and said, "Please wait in the courtyard while I go in and speak to my daughter-in-law. If I can get her to agree to your proposal, I will call you in."

Zhang the Mule was pleased to see that the house and its courtyard were big and spacious. "Please proceed, madam," he urged the widow, "and tell your daughter-in-law that her future husband and father-in-law are waiting eagerly to pay their respects to her and to fasten the bonds of kinship."

Dou E, who had been anxious about Widow Cai's troublesome errand, rushed to greet her happily when she appeared at last. "Oh, why are you so late, mother-in-law?" she asked. "I've been worried to death about you. I've got supper all ready for you, so sit down and have something to eat."

At the sight of Dou E, the injustice of what she was being forced to do to her overwhelmed Widow Cai, and she burst into sobs: "My child, I have no stomach for food. I have something to tell you, but I don't know how I can bear to begin!"

The old woman's coming back so late and then straightaway bursting into tears informed the girl that something terrible had happened that day. She hastened to support Widow Cai, and said, "I suppose an argument over the unpaid debt has upset you. We are just two helpless women, living alone here. Besides, you are advanced in years, and you must avoid distressing yourself. Tell me what happened. Don't bottle it up inside, and rack yourself with grief."

But when Widow Cai thought of how the rascally Zhangs had bullied her into agreeing to bring them into the house as bridegrooms, she could not bring herself to tell Dou E of the appalling bargain.

"Whatever can it be that you can't even tell your own daughter-in-law?" Dou E pressed her. "Even if I can't solve the problem for you, so long as I know all the details of it, perhaps I can offer some advice. Please tell me, quickly, and relieve me of this burning anxiety." As she said this, she was startled to notice that there was a red weal circling the old woman's neck. Horrified, she asked her how it had come about.

Tearfully, Widow Cai related how Sai Lu Yi had lured her to a lonely spot and tried to strangle her, and how the Zhangs had saved her from death.

Dou E's first reaction was to exclaim that such benefactors should be well rewarded with silver. "But why are you still weeping so broken-heartedly?" she asked her mother-in-law, mystified.

Widow Cai replied, "I too was all for rewarding them with silver, but they don't want money."

"If they don't want money, what do they want?" asked Dou E.

"That's the problem," sighed the old woman, "the older one wants me to marry him. Shameful, isn't it?"

Dou E blushed to the tips of her ears upon hearing this. Recollecting the reputation of the Zhangs for being scoundrels, her first reaction was to explode with anger. But she checked herself when she remembered that they had, after all, saved her mother-in-law's life. So, after pondering the matter for a while, she said, "Of course, I think such a thing would be most inappropriate. We are comfortably off here, and we have a little money to lend out. No one can force us to do anything. Besides, if you were to remarry at your time of life, people would hoot with laughter, wouldn't they?"

Widow Cai knew in her heart that Dou E was right. But she hesitated, fearing to bring future trouble upon them both, especially as the two villains were waiting right outside the door, expecting a favorable answer. "My child," she said, eventually, "I owe my life to them. How was I to know that when I invited them home to give them a reward, and they learned that we two women lived alone, they would demand that I marry the father and that you marry the son? Moreover, they threatened to strangle me themselves if I did not comply. I had no choice but to promise for you too!"

When she learned that she had been promised in marriage to Zhang the Mule, Dou E was outraged. "Good Heavens!" she cried, "how could you bring yourself to seal my fate too so lightly? All they did, it seems to me, was take advantage of your trouble to force you into this. They are cunning villains. Bringing them here was like inviting a pair of ravening wolves into the house! Well you may have invited them, but I certainly did not!"

Widow Cai pleaded with her daughter-in-law: "My dear, it's too late. They're already waiting outside the door. What am I to do?"

Dou E forced herself to be patient with the frail old woman. She explained, "There is an old saying that from middle age on, a woman must put aside all flighty thoughts. Now, you are in your 60s, and have been a widow for many years. How can you throw away your husband's loving care and affection, and get married a second time? Apart from the fact that other people will laugh at you, I too will lose my respect for you."

But the old woman objected, "The fact is that I have to repay them for saving my life whether other people laugh or not."

Dou E had to make a further effort to control the rage rising inside her, and spoke in tones controlled but severe: "Even though they saved your life, you must not abandon the path of womanly virtue. Think of how hard your husband worked, rushing around all over the country, to set up the household and its modest fortune, so that we can now live in a modicum of comfort. How can you throw away your husband's legacy on a couple of spongers? Mother-in-law, I urge you to send them packing at once!"

"How can I do that?" cried the agitated widow. "They're right outside that very door!"

Exasperated at the old woman's dithering, Dou E yelled, "Well, if you won't, I will. Those Zhangs are a couple of villainous layabouts. If they get their greedy hands on our money, our corpses will lie unburied by the roadside. And then it will be too late to repent!"

In the middle of this commotion, the two Zhangs clumped through the doorway. Zhang the Mule had become impatient with waiting, and grumbled, "Keeping us waiting like this is a deliberate slight. We shall have to show the old woman and her daughter-in-law that we mean business!"

Zhang the Dog was accustomed to being browbeaten by his son, and dared not object to what the young man proposed. So when the latter straightened his clothing, put on an air of affronted dignity and strode into the house, the old man meekly followed him.

Their first sight of Dou E's lissome form stopped them dead in their tracks. Their gaze greedily drank in her radiant, moon-like face, her eyes like shining stars, her cloud-like hair, her wispy eyebrows, her ruby lips and her teeth like pure-white jade. Moreover, even though her brow was clouded with sorrow and indignation, it still exuded a natural charm.

Guessing that the rough-looking intruders must be the Zhangs, Dou E replied to their ill-mannered stares with a contemptuous sneer. Widow Cai, however, trembled from head to toe at the Zhangs' sudden appearance, and hastened to introduce her daughter-in-law to them, and vice versa.

Recovering from the trance that befallen them at the sight of Dou E, the two men bowed and mumbled some words of greeting. Widow Cai bowed in turn, and expressed a cordial welcome. Dou E, however, was disgusted at this hypocritical display, and stood by, with her eyebrows raised in scorn and her eyes blazing in accusation. "You two can get right back to where you came from!" she cried. "My mother-in-law has told me all about you. How dare you set foot in our house?"

The girl's wrath made Widow Cai cower, but Zhang the Mule was unperturbed. "Miss, you can see for yourself what ideal mates my father and I are for yourself and your mother-in-law. Don't miss this wonderful opportunity, but let us go through the ceremonies for becoming one family as soon as possible." So saying, he seized Dou E, and pulled her towards him.

The girl turned pale at this sudden outrage. With a reflex reaction, she pushed Zhang the Mule so hard that he tumbled down on the floor. "How dare a ruffian like you barge into respectable people's houses acting shamelessly?" Dou E burst out in indignation. "That's enough of your odious tricks. I may be a woman without a husband, but you can't bully me!" With that, and a contemptuous flick of her sleeves, she stalked out of the room.

Zhang the Mule climbed to his feet just in time to see Dou E disappearing through the door. He ground his teeth and cursed: "You little vixen! I'm not going to let you get away with pushing me down. I swear that I will have you for my bed, if it's the last thing I do!"

With that, he swung round to face Widow Cai. His face contorted with fury, Zhang the Mule snarled at the old woman: "Your daughter-in-law says that she won't have me. Well, that's just too bad, because my father and I are going to stay here anyway. This is going to be our house from now on. Now you just run along and prepare some decent food and wine for us. Any objection out of you, and I'll flay you alive and beat you to a pulp!"

This outburst reduced Widow Cai to a trembling jelly. She cringed and whined, "Oh, my good sir, I beg you not to be angry. Of course I must reward you for saving my life. It's just that my daughter-in-law has a hot temper, and if she is adamant about refusing you, how can I by myself invite you? Meanwhile, I'll go and prepare a nice meal for you. Please be patient while I try to persuade the girl."

"All right, in that case off you go!" was Zhang the Mule's gruff reply.

Without another word, the old woman scuttled off to the kitchen to prepare some food and heat a jug of wine. When the meal was ready, the two Zhangs scoffed it down like a strong wind blowing away the clouds. Before long there was neither a scrap of food nor a drop of wine left. Belching and breaking wind, the pair started to feel sleepy and told Widow Cai to prepare a place to sleep for them.

The old woman said, "The western side of the house is where Dou E has her quarters, so I'll prepare the eastern side for you two gentlemen for the time being."

"All right, but don't keep us waiting too long," was the gracious response of Zhang the Mule.

When the two Zhangs had retired to sleep, Widow Cai forced herself to drink a drop of soup, and then went to bed herself.

The shock of almost being murdered by Sai Lu Yi and the anxiety caused by being entangled with the evil Zhangs proved too much for the widow's aged and feeble frame. The next morning, she was wracked by fever and delirium, and could not rise from her bed. Dou E was alarmed by the seriousness of her condition, and wanted to summon a doctor. But the old woman stopped her. "It's just a result of fright and over-exertion," she claimed. "I'll be all right in a couple of days. You don't have to bother the doctor. But you must be careful, my child. That nasty pair are still hanging around the house. Don't do anything to provoke them."

Dou E was furious at this. "Mother-in-law," she said in reproach, "here you lie, seriously ill, and yet all you worry about is those two scoundrels. I'll throw the pair of them out of the door right now!"

"Oh, don't do anything of the sort, at least for the time being," the old woman pleaded. "You see, for one thing I do owe my life to them. If you throw them out, other people will consider us ungrateful wretches. For another, they are wicked and unscrupulous. If you drive them out, they are sure to try to get their revenge. Please, for my sake, look after them properly."

Although it went against her inclination, Dou E was forced to acquiesce to her mother-in-law's wish. "Well, I suppose they did save your life, after all. All right then, I will not send them away just yet. But you must consider the gossip that could be caused by two men who are not relatives staying here with us two women. How will we be able to hold our heads up in the future?"

Widow Cai replied, "There's no help for it — at least not for the next few days. Wait until I have recovered my health; then I'll think of a way out of our predicament. Perhaps they'll simply get tired of hanging around, and leave?"

But Dou E was skeptical. "I doubt whether those two loafers will be in any hurry to leave a fine house where they can eat and drink their fill," she muttered.

At this moment, Widow Cai suddenly felt an attack of dizziness coming on, and she said, "My child, please don't say any more for the moment. I want to sleep. Help to make me comfortable, and then go and make me some gruel. And while you're at it, prepare breakfast for our two guests. Make sure they're well looked after."

Seeing that the old lady really was in a poor state, Dou E could not but comply. As soon as she had made the widow comfortable she went off to the kitchen.

In the meantime, the Zhangs, having eaten and drunk to their hearts' content the previous evening, snored away the whole night between fluffy blankets. The sun was already high in the sky when Zhang the Dog awoke and called to his son to get up. Zhang the Mule, without taking the trouble to wash his face or comb his hair, made a beeline for the kitchen in search of something to eat. There he stumbled on Dou E, who was busy cooking. The girl's first reaction was to try to slip away, but it was too late. He prevented her leaving the kitchen, saying, with a hideous leer: "My dear, why are you trying to avoid me?"

Zhang the Mule's sickening attempt at dalliance caused an expression of disgust to spread all over Dou E's face. "Who are you calling your dear?" she snapped. "Have you no sense of decency, you and that old dotard? Taking over the house of two poor widows without so much as a by-your-leave?"

Zhang the Mule pretended to be unperturbed. "We saved your mother-in-law's life," he explained, mildly. "It was she who invited us to stay here out of sheer gratitude. In fact, she wants us to be your ever-loving husbands!"

"You shameless vagabonds!" Dou E cried. "Taking advantage of other people's misfortune, barging into other people's houses, snatching innocent women, and grabbing their property! My kind-hearted mother-in-law has fallen ill as a result of your bullying. Don't talk such nonsense as that about being invited here to marry us!"

Zhang the Mule was an ill-mannered boor, and so, thwarted by Dou E's spirited defiance, he resorted to his old tricks. As she glared at him, he sprang forward, and pulled her to him. With one arm clasping her waist, he started tearing at her clothing. Taken by surprise, Dou E had no time to stop him tearing open the front part of her gown, but just as Zhang the Mule was pressing towards her lily-white breasts, she protected herself with one hand while giving the rogue a box on the ear with the other and leaving five livid red scratches on his cheek.

Zhang the Mule, like all bullies, was a coward at heart. He seemed to shrink to half his size upon receipt of this rebuff. Covering his torn cheek, he hastily stepped back. As he did so, Dou E snatched up a vegetable cleaver. "Get out of here!" she blazed. "If you ever try that again, I'll chop your head off!"

Zhang the Mule shuffled out, looking back at Dou E with sullen but frightened eyes. "All right, I'm going. I'm going," he muttered. He then added, ludicrously: "I'll let you off this time, but you'll catch it from me next time." And with that, he scuttled off back to the eastern side of the house.

The sight of Zhang the Dog contentedly sipping tea and humming to himself didn't do anything to soothe Zhang the Mule's injured feelings. He thereupon greeted his astonished father with a torrent of abuse, and sent him off to the kitchen to prepare breakfast. Zhang the Mule threw himself on his bed. Stroking his burning cheek, his mind in a turmoil, he cursed to himself: "That little slut dared to raise a hand to her husband-to-be, eh?

It's outrageous! I'll have to teach her a lesson." It was then that a diabolical scheme entered his head: He would take advantage of Widow Cai's illness to poison her. Then Dou E would be alone and completely at his mercy!

Having seen Zhang the Mule off, Dou E returned to the western side of the house to change her clothes. As she thought how she had been widowed at an early age, and left to endure such abusive treatment, she could not help tears springing to her eyes, and she burst into a fit of wailing. After a while, she thought of her mother-in-law ill in bed. If she found out about Zhang the Mule's odious behavior, she would be so distressed that her condition would be sure to get worse. So Dou E dried her eyes, adjusted her clothing, and returned to the kitchen to make the gruel the widow had asked for. She spent the rest of the day attending to the patient.

CHAPTER FOUR

Zhang the Dog Dies at the Hands of His Son

ZHANG THE MULE was unable to sleep all that night for vexation, and first thing the following morning he woke his father up, saying, "I heard yesterday that Widow Cai has fallen ill. Let's go and pay a call on her to see how she is faring."

Zhang the Dog, who had been sleeping soundly, was at a loss to understand why his son was so eager to see the old woman at the crack of dawn. Nevertheless, he struggled out of bed. Smiling, he said, "I didn't know you were so soft-hearted, my boy! Well, let's go then." As he did so, he suddenly remembered how reluctant Widow Cai was that they should move into her house as prospective bridegrooms, and how Dou E particularly was dead set against it. Sourly, he observed, "I don't think there's any point in us remaining here, actually. The old woman is reluctant to keep her promise, and anyway she hasn't been able to persuade her daughter-in-law to accept us at all. Now she's gone and fallen ill. What's the point of hanging around?"

Hearing this, the young man realized that his father was afraid of what might happen if they kept forcing themselves on the two widows. "You old blockhead!" he roared. "It was a chance in a lifetime finding a nice big house like this. Who could have expected that we could have got the old woman to invite us to move in and marry her and her daughter-in-law? If we're going to do it, let's do it. If not, then let's forget the whole thing."

Zhang the Dog was reluctant to get into a confrontation with his son, so without another word he shuffled after the latter to Widow Cai's quarters, to ask after her health.

The old woman's condition had worsened compared to the previous day. Dou E found her pale-faced and gasping for breath. She was about to go to ask the neighbor to fetch a doctor, but Widow Cai, old skinflint that she was, begrudged the expense and forbade her to do so. All Dou E could do was make sure her mother-in-law was comfortable, and go off to the kitchen to prepare some gruel for her.

After she left, Widow Cai lay back for a while, half asleep and half awake. Suddenly, she saw through the fog of her delirium the two Zhangs enter the room. In a fright, she struggled to sit up in bed, and was about to call out when Zhang the Dog hurriedly stopped her. "Madam, you are unwell," he said in an unctuous voice. "You should beware of draughts. Please lie back and rest for a while. We have just popped in to see how you are."

"It is very kind of you," answered Widow Cai. "Forgive me for not rising to greet you, but it is difficult for me to move."

"It is no trouble at all, I assure you, Madam," gushed Zhang the Mule. "I trust you are feeling somewhat better today?"

"I'm afraid not. When I woke up this morning, I distinctly felt that my condition had worsened."

Zhang the Dog butted in with, "Perhaps, Madam, you require the attention of a physician? I can send my son here to fetch one for you if you like."

"Oh no, I wouldn't think of putting the young man to so much trouble," said the old woman. "I've caught a chill, that's all. A couple of days in bed will see me right."

Zhang the Dog, who had not given up hope of marrying Widow Cai and was therefore eager to worm his way into her favor, then asked, "Is there anything you would like to eat?"

"Well, now you come to mention it," said the patient, "I was just thinking that I have eaten nothing but some watery gruel for the past few days. I really fancy a bowl of mutton tripe broth. It's a good tonic for the body, too. It's just that my daughter-in-law is very young, and is shy about showing her face outside the house. I'm the one who normally goes into the town to do the shopping. Besides, now that I'm laid up in bed, she is needed here to look after me and do the cooking, and all the rest of it. How can I send her out to buy mutton tripe? No, I'll just have to do without, I suppose."

Zhang the Dog thereupon interrupted her. "My dear madam, why didn't you tell us before that you are partial to mutton tripe soup?" he cried. "I'll send my son to buy some mutton right now!"

Zhang the Mule, taking his cue, nodded his assent, and turned as if to dash off into the town. He made a great show of this, although his pockets were empty, and it was a hint that didn't escape the old lady. Fooled by this feigned kindness, she called to him to wait. "You will need some money," she said, as she fumbled under her pillow, and produced a purse of silver. Taking a few pieces out, she handed them to Zhang the Dog, who made pretence of refusing them. "Oh, no, no, no, Madam," he protested hollowly, "we wouldn't dream of allowing you to pay for such a trifling thing." As he said this, the silver passed from the widow's hand into Zhang the Dog's and thence into Zhang the Mule's with astonishing swiftness. The latter then swaggered out of the door, leaving his father to chat with Widow Cai.

Zhang the Mule hurried away, clutching the silver. The first thing he did was pop into a nearby restaurant and order a slap-up meal. Only then did he buy some mutton tripe and look around cautiously for a pharmacy when he could purchase some poison. The center of the town was crowded with people, and the two major drugstores there heaved with customers. Zhang the Mule hesitated; he didn't want anybody to observe him buying poison and set tongues wagging. Then he suddenly remembered that he had passed a pharmacy a few days previously in an isolated spot outside the South Gate. "Just the place!" he thought to himself.

Making his way to the place, he saw that it bore a sign reading

"Master Sai Lu Yi's Pharmacy". Full of confidence, he strode straight in.

Ever since his attempt to murder Widow Cai had been thwarted by the sudden appearance of the Zhangs, and had fled from the scene, Sai Lu Yi had been trembling with fear of discovery and being hauled off to face the magistrate. He had even toyed with the idea of handing his business over to someone else and slipping away quietly from the area, to start afresh somewhere else. But as he couldn't think of anyone who would take it off his hands at such short notice, and as the days passed no one came to arrest him, he opened up his shop again.

Sai Lu Yi was sitting behind his counter making up a prescription, when he was startled by the abrupt entry of a long-faced disreputable-looking fellow. There was something disturbingly familiar about the stranger, which caused a shiver to run down the pharmacist's spine. Where had he bumped into this lout before, he wondered.

For his part, Zhang the Mule was delighted to discover that there was only one occupant of the shop, and, moreover, that he was the very rascal he had come across in the act of committing murder a few days previously! "Heaven has smiled on me today, all right," he thought. "It's true that, as they say, 'Adversaries will find each other sooner or later.' It couldn't be better: He won't dare to refuse to sell me the poison, nor will he dare to open his mouth about it!" Being careful not to betray any sign of recognition, he said, in a casual tone: "Good morning, I wish to purchase some medicine."

Sai Lu Yi still couldn't think where he had met this customer before. So he put the matter out of his mind, and asked, "What kind of medicine, sir?"

"Actually, it's not medicine as such that I want," replied Zhang the Mule, "but poison."

Sai Lu Yi nearly jumped out of his skin when he heard the man say the word poison. He was still quivering with fear after his fright the other day, when he had been caught red-handed trying to strangle Widow Cai. The last thing he wanted was to get mixed up in some other dark deed. So he hastily protested that he only sold regular drugs. "I don't stock poisons, sir," he gabbled. "I'm sorry, but it's too risky. If I did, and someone died, I'd be in big trouble."

"So you don't want big trouble, eh?" sneered Zhang the Mule.

"Oh, we pharmacists can't just go supplying poisons to just anybody, you know," Sai Lu Yi continued, emboldened. "You're not planning to kill somebody, are you?" he asked facetiously.

Zhang the Mule's response was to lunge across the counter, and grab Sai Lu Yi by the collar. In a low, menacing voice, he said, "Do you think I don't know who you are? Well, what was a respectable pharmacist like you doing trying to strangle Widow Cai the other day? I'd know you anywhere. How about coming along with me to see the magistrate?"

At this point, it dawned on Sai Lu Yi at last where he had seen the stranger before. Frightened out of his wits, he begged, his voice barely a whisper: "Oh please, sir, don't say a word of any of this. My life is in your hands. Spare me!"

Zhang the Mule became all business: "I can do that. Just provide me with what I came here for, that's all."

"I have some rat poison already made up, sir," said the relieved Sai Yi Lu. "I'll get it for you right away."

"That's more like it!" beamed Zhang the Mule. "All right, I'll let you off the hook this time. Go and get it."

Sai Yi Lu took some rat poison from beneath the counter, wrapped it in paper, and handed it obsequiously with both hands to Zhang the Mule. The latter shoved it inside his gown. "I'll pay you later, if you don't mind," he said, as if he were the pharmacy's best customer. "It's just that I came out in such a hurry this morning that I forgot my purse."

"Don't bother about such a trifling matter, sir," said Sai Lu Yi, with an ingratiating grimace. "Please accept it with my compliments."

Sai Lu Yi wiped the cold sweat from his brow as he watched Zhang the Mule stride away in high spirits. "He wants that poison for some evil purpose, I'll be bound," he thought to himself. "And whatever it is, it's going to involve me in deeper trouble than I'm in now. I'd better shut up shop here right now, and set up in business somewhere else." Having made this decision, Sai Lu Yi gathered up his few belongings and left the district.

When he got back to Widow Cai's house, Zhang the Mule straightaway presented the mutton tripe he had bought to the old woman. Pleased, she asked him to give it to Dou E so that she could make soup out of it.

Zhang the Mule found Dou E in the kitchen. As soon as he entered, she tried to escape from his loathsome company, but Zhang the Mule stopped her, saying, "DouE, I have just been out to buy some mutton tripe at your poor, ailing mother-in-law's request. She wants you to make soup for her with it."

The girl had no choice but to leave off what she was doing before, and start rinsing and boiling the mutton tripe. In the meantime, Zhang the Mule hovered around, fiddling with things and pretending to be helping. In fact, he was waiting for an opportunity when Dou E was distracted to slip the poison in the soup. But the girl was so intensely irritated by his presence that she was aware all the time of every move he made. Finally she turned and ordered him out of the kitchen.

Zhang the Mule protested, with a smirk on his face: "But your mother-in-law has been kind enough to give shelter to my father and me. Now that she is not well, and desires this mutton tripe soup, I thought it only right to assist you to make it for her. Just tell me if you need me to do something."

Dou E perceived the furtiveness behind Zhang the Mule's false smile, but she suspected that his purpose was to press his unwelcome attentions on her while she was alone in the kitchen. With mounting fury, she snapped, "I can manage perfectly well here by myself. You have no business hanging around!"

Zhang the Mule was reluctant to leave, but he was afraid that if he didn't he might arouse Dou E's suspicions as to his real intention. So, with a face beaming with hollow radiance, he retreated, saying, "Of course, if I'm in the way…"

He went back to Widow Cai's room. While he joined his father in chatting in a desultory way with the old woman, his eyes were riveted on the window, waiting for the first sign of Dou E coming with the mutton tripe soup.

After a while, Zhang the Dog said, with feigned solicitude, to his son: "My boy, perhaps you should go and see what's delaying Dou E and that soup. Madam Cai has been waiting eagerly for it."

Zhang the Mule sprang to his feet and hurried off to the kitchen once more. When he got there he said, "Dou E, hurry up with the soup. Your mother-in-law's anxious to taste it."

Dou E tasted the soup, found it was ready, and poured some into a bowl. Then she took it, with a spoon, on a tray to Widow Cai's room. But, before she got there, she was accosted by Zhang the Mule. He had decided that the time had come to put his plan into action. "Let me have the honor of offering the soup to your mother-in-law," he wheedled.

But Dou E rebuffed him coldly. "You are not one of the family," she pointed out, "so what right do you have to such an honor?"

Without replying, Zhang the Mule snatched the tray, picked up the spoon and dipped it in the soup. Tasting it, he shook his head. "There isn't enough salt or vinegar in it, I'm afraid. You'd better go back and fetch some."

"I know my mother-in-law's taste perfectly well," she said. "How do you know there isn't enough salt or vinegar in it?"

Zhang the Mule was desperate to get rid of Dou E for a moment, and so he invented an excuse on the spur of the moment. "Old people's taste buds aren't what they used to be. So you have to make their dishes extra salty and vinegary. If you won't do it, I will go to the kitchen myself and add some more condiments." And with that he turned as if to go marching off to the kitchen with the soup.

Dou E, fooled into thinking that Zhang the Mule really was concerned that the old woman would find the soup tasteless and afraid that he would slop it all over the place if he flounced off to the kitchen in his usual clumsy manner, said, "All right, I'll go and get them. You take the soup in to my mother-in-law."

"That's better," said Zhang the Mule. "Don't take too long."

As soon as Dou E was out of sight, Zhang the Mule looked around carefully to make sure that he was alone, placed the bowl of soup on a windowsill, and took out the packet of poison from inside his robe. Emptying the contents into the soup, he stirred it briskly with the spoon. He sighed with relief when this task was accomplished before Dou E had time to return from the kitchen with the condiments. Then he solemnly bore the fatal soup into Widow Cai's room.

His father hurried to meet him, took the tray from him and presented it to the old woman. Zhang the Mule was explaining that Dou E had gone to the kitchen for something to spice the soup up with, when the girl appeared with the salt and vinegar. Taking them from her, Zhang the Mule tipped a little of each into the soup, saying, "There now, it should be a bit tastier."

"What a thoughtful boy you are," purred his father, and turning to Widow Cai, said, "Shall I help you to sit up, madam, so that you can take your soup more comfortable?"

Observing this display, Dou E came to the conclusion that the old man and his son were simply trying to get on the good side of her mother-in-law, with marriage in mind. She would have lost her temper with them if the old woman had not been ill. So she just looked on from the side with cold eyes.

Widow Cai tried a spoonful of the soup, but, having taken nothing but thin gruel for the previous few days, her stomach rebelled at the strong taste of the mutton tripe soup, and she spat out the very first few drops. Her stomach heaved, and she retched several times. Her whole body began to tremble. There was nothing for it but to hand the bowl back to Zhang the Dog. Holding her stomach, Widow Cai took several gulps of air, and then said, "It's no good, I can't keep it down."

Zhang the Dog, however, eager to ingratiate himself with the old woman, urged her to try again, reminding her that the soup had been made specially for her.

Dou E too encouraged her to try to take some of it. "Please try to drink some while it's hot," she said. "It'll make you sweat, and then you'll feel refreshed."

"You're right, I'm sure," replied the old woman. "It's just that I'm afraid that if I retch again, it will make my illness worse." She stubbornly resisted their blandishments, finally saying to Zhang the Dog: "Sir, why don't you take it. It will be no good if it goes cold, and it would be a pity to waste such fine soup made specially for me, wouldn't it?"

Years of leading a vagabond life of feast and famine had taught Zhang the Dog not to pass up the chance of a good feed. Besides, the delicious aroma of the mutton tripe soup had been making his mouth water ever since it had arrived. When Widow Cai invited him to take the soup himself, he made a perfunctory show of refusing, and then grabbed the bowl and swallowed the soup like a ravenous wolf.

Dou E was tempted to snatch the bowl from the old reprobate, but he had finished the soup before she had time to move.

In the meantime, while the others were encouraging Widow Cai to drink the soup, Zhang the Mule had slipped back to his quarters on the east side of the house. He wanted to distance himself from the inevitable tragedy to alleviate as far as possible any chance of suspicion being directed at himself. He waited with his ears pricked up for the sound of a commotion. His mistake was to leave his father's greedy nature out of his calculations.

When some time had passed and no unusual sound was heard, he began to grow alarmed. He tiptoed back to Widow Cai's room, and peeped through the window, just in time to see his father setting down the empty soup bowl, wiping his mouth with the back of his hand and saying to Widow Cai: "Delicious soup indeed, madam, and I thank you for so kindly offering it to me."

Zhang the Mule was petrified with horror, realizing that his father had drunk the poisoned soup. Under his very eyes, the old man, in the midst of smacking his lips, clutched his stomach and grimaced. "Oh dear," murmured Zhang the Dog, "perhaps there was something not quite right with it after all. I have a sudden stomach ache. Scarcely were the words out of his mouth than another spasm caused him to double up in agony. He fell to the floor, thrashing around in a paroxysm of pain.

Seeing this, his son came to his senses, and dashed into the room, uttering an ear-splitting wail. At the same time, Widow Cai, forgetting that she was sick, jumped out of bed, screeching, "My dear sir, what's the matter?" Then she turned to Zhang the Mule. "Fetch a doctor at once," she urged him. "Something terrible has happened to your father."

But before Zhang the Mule could budge an inch, his father gave one last scream, blood spurted from all seven orifices, and the stillness of death seized him. Widow Cai too gazed transfixed as the old man's eyes bulged from their sockets, his face turned black and his whole body by degrees stiffened into rigor mortis. She stretched out her hand to his mouth and nose, but not a whiff of breath did she detect. With a shrill cry of "He's dead!" she collapsed in a heap on the floor, sobbing her heart out.

Dou E at first had thought that Zhang the Dog had simply been complaining about stomach ache, and thought that it served him right for guzzling the soup so greedily. But when she saw her mother-in-law leap from her sick bed and throw herself on the floor weeping and blubbering "He's dead!" she was seized with fright. She rushed forward to help the old woman up. "Please don't distress yourself, mother-in-law," she pleaded. "I'm sure it was only the summer heat that overcame the old man. He was not well, you know. The heat in the summer can easily kill a person. Anyway, whether one dies early or late is all determined in a previous existence. There's nothing anyone else can do about it. Besides, he was not one of our family. So why are you upsetting yourself like this? I admit that it was bad luck that he died in our house, but all we have to do is buy the wood for a coffin and the grave clothes and arrange for him to be buried in the cemetery outside the city."

As she thought about this, it sounded like sense to Widow Cai. She stopped crying, fumbled for her purse, and handed 20 pieces of silver to Zhang the Mule, saying, "My dear sir, please restrain your grief. After all, the dead cannot be brought back to life. Since your father died in my house, here is something to help defray the funeral expenses. With these 20 pieces of silver you can buy a coffin and grave clothes. Then all you have to do is choose an auspicious day for the funeral."

Even in his shock and dismay at having taken his father's life with the poison he had intended for Widow Cai, Zhang the Mule's evil mind was already concocting another dastardly scheme. He fell on Zhang the Dog's prostrate body, weeping copious tears. Words of consolation from Dou E fell on deaf ears; only when the silver was produced did he leave off his heartbroken lamentations.

Stuffing the silver inside his gown, he confronted the two women with a fierce stare. "My father was in perfect health," he bellowed. "He had never been sick for even a day in his life. There must have been a conspiracy between you two to murder him. Well, I will not let you get away with it!"

Widow Cai was flabbergasted. She had given this rascal money out of the goodness of her heart, and he had the nerve to turn round and accuse her of murdering his gluttonous old father! But his words terrified her. "But sir," she pleaded, "I was ill in bed. How could I have harmed him?"

Zhang the Mule continued, relentlessly: "Look at the poor old man's face — it's dark-green! And there's blood dripping from every orifice. He's been poisoned, that's clear to see. There's nobody else in the house, and you insisted that my father drink the mutton tripe soup your daughter-in-law made. It was after he had drunk it that he fell down dead — of poison! If it wasn't you and your daughter-in-law who poisoned him, who was it?"

The old woman was too afraid to speak. Drenched in cold sweat and trembling, she turned to Dou E.

Dou E, however, was not at all afraid, knowing perfectly well that she and Widow Cai were innocent. She stepped forward to support her mother-in-law. "There is nothing to fear," she assured her. "Since this pair of ruffians forced their way into our house we have never left it. Besides, you have been ill in bed. How could we have procured any poison? If his father was poisoned, the poison must have been in the mutton tripe soup. And it must have been put in when he complained that there was not enough seasoning in it, and sent me back to the kitchen. Who do you think he intended to kill? Fortunately, Heaven has eyes, and he only succeeded in killing his own father, when that greedy wretch gobbled down the soup! Zhang the Mule, you took advantage of my mother-in-law's misfortune, and forced her to give shelter to you and your father. You poisoned your own flesh and blood, and now you have the effrontery to blame us for the crime!"

Zhang the Mule realized that Dou E had guessed the truth, but that didn't stop him blustering even more wildly: "It is as plain as daylight that you poisoned my father. How dare you talk such nonsense? You were the one who made this mutton tripe soup, nobody else. If you didn't put the poison in it, who did? And you have the audacity to accuse me of poisoning my own father! Who on earth would believe you?"

This bluster failed to shake Dou E. She answered fearlessly: "Zhang the Mule, my mother-in-law took you and your father into our house out of the sheer goodness of her heart. She wined and dined you. And how do you repay her kindness? With this wicked scheme, that's how! You tried to force us to marry you. You tried to take improper liberties with me, and when I resisted your obnoxious advances, you schemed to kill my mother-in-law. But Heaven spoiled your little plan — and you ended up poisoning your own father. This tragedy was your doing; it had nothing to do with me. My mother-in-law was heartbroken at the old man's death, and even gave you 20 pieces of silver for the funeral expenses. But you ... you're worse than an unfeeling brute. With no thought at all for your deceased parent, you immediately accuse us two innocent women of murder! Are you a man or what are you? If you think you can use your father's corpse to intimidate us, you'd better think again!"

This stern rebuff made Zhang the Mule realize that Dou E was not going to bow to threats. He decided on a change of tactics. Noticing that Widow Cai was trembling like a leaf, he seized her roughly. "You were part of the plot to poison my father," he roared. "I'm going to take you to your neighbors and see what they think about your crime!"

The thought of others becoming aware of this shocking occurrence terrified the old woman. "Oh please, sir, I beg you not to be angry. You're frightening me to death!"

Seeing that his new approach was working, Zhang the Mule snarled, "So you've got something to be afraid of, have you?"

"Heaven decides our fates, sir" the widow replied. "When something like this happens, of course I'm afraid."

"Well, if Heaven decides our fates," growled Zhang the Mule, taking a menacing step forward, "how do you expect me to let you off? Do you want me to forget the whole thing?"

The old woman pleaded, "Please let the matter drop, sir. We won't mention it again, and I promise that I will burn incense for your health and happiness every day."

Zhang the Mule glared balefully at her, and hissed, "In that case, you'd better do as I say. Let me marry your daughter-in-law, and I will let both of you off the hook. I will not cause you any more trouble. Otherwise I'll bring ruin on you, and drive you to the brink of destruction."

The old woman was at a loss how to reply. Eventually, she turned to Dou E, and said, resignedly: "My child, we must do as he says. It's best not to tempt fate."

Her mother-in-law's lack of courage infuriated Dou E. But, not wishing to berate her in front of Zhang the Mule, she mastered her anger, and chided her: "How can you say such a thing. We didn't poison his father. He did that himself. What do we have to fear from him? Even if the story of this tragedy becomes the talk of the town, we will still have nothing to fear, for everybody will know the truth about him. There is still some mutton tripe soup in the kitchen. I made it specially for you. Let everybody examine it and see whether there is any poison in it or not. Then they will realize that this Zhang the Mule used the pretext of there not being enough condiments in it to get me out of the way for a while so that he could put the poison in the bowl. We will be found to be perfectly innocent of this crime. Don't listen to his nonsense about demanding to marry me."

Widow Cai was torn between Dou E's reasonable words and fear of another browbeating by Zhang the Mule. With a frenzy of agitation, she paced round and round the room, muttering, "I don't know what to do anymore."

CHAPTER FIVE

Evil Plotters

THWARTED IN HIS attempt to use the death of his father to bully Dou E into becoming his wife, Zhang the Mule rounded on the stubborn girl. "You low slut!" he bellowed, beside himself with rage, "having poisoned my poor father, you not only try to wriggle out of your responsibility with specious excuses, you even go so far as to slander me! Well, I won't bandy words with the likes of you. I will just ask you one thing: Do you want to settle this matter in front of the magistrate, or do you want to settle it privately?"

Dou E coolly replied, "Your father's death has nothing to do with me. You are the one who must decide whether to settle this matter in front of the magistrate or privately."

Further agitated by this exchange, Widow Cai asked fearfully: "What is all this talk about the magistrate? About privately? What do you mean?"

"If I haul you two before the magistrate, you'll be interrogated mercilessly, despite the advanced years of the one and the tender years of the other," Zhang the Mule threatened. "And you'll be tortured to get the truth out of you," he added for good measure.

"You'll confess to the crime all right, once you feel those instruments of torture caressing your weak and tender flesh!" He then changed tack. "However, if you wish to settle out of court, all you have to do is allow me to marry Dou E, and straightaway I'll let both of you off. And from that moment on, there will be no more mention of you having poisoned my father. If you know what's good for you, you'll avoid the magistrate's court like the plague."

But Dou E's reply was, "Since I did not poison your father, I prefer to go with you to see the magistrate."

The old woman was horrified. "My child, what are you saying?" she screeched. "The magistrate's court is no place to enter lightly. Apart from the fact that it would bring disgrace on us, two weak and defenseless women, to be seen there, it is a place as unfathomable as the ocean. I fear that if we once go in, we won't come out again. The fact that his father died in our house is a very ominous sign. It will be better if we settle this privately. Then not only will we keep our family intact, but you will have a husband to look after you all your life. Listen to your mother-in-law, and marry Zhang the Mule!"

Seeing that Widow Cai was so timorous that she was eager to stoop so low as to agree to Zhang the Mule's terms just to keep out of the magistrate's court, Dou E could hardly control her indignation. She addressed the old woman sternly: "Mother-in-law, I have told you many times that my loving union with your son was one for life. This Zhang the Mule here took advantage of your misfortune to force his way into our house. He has taken indecent liberties with me several times. And now he has the gall to accuse us both of poisoning his father. I can't bear to be in the same room with him; how could I consent to marry him? If you had not been so afraid of him in the first place, and taken my advice to drive him and his father from our house, we would not be in the awkward situation we find ourselves in today. You need not say any more. I have made up my mind to go with him to the magistrate to clear this matter up."

Overcome with shame, Widow Cai could find no words to say. She stood silently weeping. Zhang the Mule, too, was at a loss what to do. His threat to drag the two women to the magistrate's court had been nothing but bluster. When Dou E called his bluff without turning a hair, he felt that he had mounted a tiger — it was fatal to dismount! All he could do was to continue with his vindictive hectoring. "So you want to take your chances with the magistrate's court, do you?" he howled. "Ha! Do you think your tender skins and frail carcasses can withstand the tortures they will subject you to there? Dou E, you'd better consent to be my wife and save you and your poor old mother-in-law the agony of interrogation under torture, I think!"

Dou E stepped defiantly forward. "Is the magistrate's court a tiger's den, then?" she inquired.

"What do you mean?" asked Zhang the Mule.

"Is the magistrate a demon?"

"Definitely not! What are you talking about?" answered the puzzled Zhang the Mule.

"Well then, if the magistrate's court is not a tiger's den and the magistrate himself is not a demon, I have nothing to fear, do I? What are we waiting for? Let's go and ask the magistrate to settle this affair."

Zhang the Mule, in his desperation, made as if to seize the two women and drag them off to the magistrate's court. But Dou E flung him off with a contemptuous gesture. "In broad daylight and before the eyes of the general public, we will state our case to the magistrate," she announced calmly. "There is no call for a ruffian's tactics."

Widow Cai butted in with a pathetic plea: "Sir, I beg you to go together with my daughter-in-law to see the magistrate, and leave me here to await your return."

But Zhang the Mule, knowing how easily the old woman could be bullied to his advantage, was determined not to leave her behind. In answer to Dou E's protests, he cried, "I know that you were the one who put the poison in the soup, which killed my poor old father. But I also know that you couldn't have done it without the connivance of this old hag here! How can we get to the bottom of this without her testimony? And if you claim that it wasn't a conspiracy between the two of you, she has to give evidence of that to the magistrate, doesn't she? My aged parent passed away right here in this house. Do you think you're going to get away with that?"

Calm and collected, Dou E turned to Widow Cai. "Don't be afraid, mother-in-law," she said. "When we get to the magistrate's office, leave everything to me. I'll make sure no harm or distress comes to you. Let's go along with him quietly."

The old woman had no choice but to do as she was bid, and, quivering and quaking, went along with the other two to the magistrate's office.

The incumbent magistrate of Shanyang County was a Mongolian named Huxin. He was the son of Ahema, the prime minister of the Yuan court, who had been a favorite of Kublai Khan, the founder of the dynasty. Ahema had performed great exploits for his master in consolidating the Central Plains under Mongol rule and in the overthrow of the Southern Song Dynasty. Unfortunately, he was an arrogant and ruthless man, and his son had inherited these traits. Huxin was muddle-headed and sensuous. He spent his time in the company of idlers, feasting, carousing, gambling and cavorting with strumpets, spending money like water. His overriding passion was lechery. Whenever his eye happened to fall on a pretty wench, he would not hesitate to go to any lengths to possess her, even to the point of kidnap — and then cast her aside. The people of the capital had hated him to the very marrow of their bones. They called him Taowu, after a ravening beast of mythology, but changed the first character to the "tao" which means "peach," to circumvent the wrath of his powerful father. The asinine Huxin thought it was a compliment, and reveled in the appellation.

Ahema had wanted to employ the young man as his assistant in the government. But as Huxin was widely known to be completely brainless, not to mention universally loathed for his dissolute ways, the best Ahema could do for him was to get the emperor to appoint him magistrate of an obscure county, which was a rank of the seventh grade. Indignant at such a lowly posting, Huxin refused to take up the position at first, and his father had no option but to promise that if Huxin handled the job well he would make sure he got promotion.

From the time he took up the post of magistrate of Shanyang,

Taowu showed that he had not the slightest intention of attending to official business, much less inquiring about the problems and hardships of the local people. He spent all day and every day loafing with his dissipated cronies, selling favors and "justice" to the highest bidder, forcing chaste women to become profligate, and encouraging local rakes and rogues to follow suit with abandon. The local people groaned in despair. Apart from his other vices, Taowu had a particular weakness for money-grubbing. Every time someone came to lodge a complaint or lawsuit, Taowu didn't bother to investigate the details of the case or delve into the rights and wrongs of the matter — whichever side offered the biggest bribe got the favorable judgment. So, piles of treasure mounted higher and higher in the magistracy's strong rooms, to the sound of the thwack of the club and the piteous cries for justice and mercy from the innocent. Investigation teams from the higher authorities descended on Shanyang County as rumors of this scandalous situation spread, but as soon as they realized that Taowu was the son of the prime minister, they withdrew immediately, afraid to speak out against these flagrant abuses.

There had been no lawsuits brought before him on that particular day, and Taowu was dozing in his chair in the courtroom of the magistracy, when he was suddenly startled awake by a tremendous commotion.

Somebody was beating the drum outside, which had been set up for complainants to announce their grievances. The courtroom guards rushed about to rouse Taowu, and grinned at each other as they saw his fatuous face, jerked out of sleep, with its bleary eyes and drooling mouth. Taowu hurriedly straightened his cap and gown, wiped his mouth, and bellowed, "Well, hurry up and bring in the complainant!"

The guards cried in unison for the petitioners to enter, making the rafters ring. Following which Dou E, supporting Widow Cai, and Zhang the Mule appeared. The old woman had never been in a magistrate's court before, and the sight of the fierce-looking guards, not to mention the deafening roar of the summons, struck terror into her heart. Dou E was somewhat intimidated too, but, sure that her cause was right, mastered her fears and helped Widow Cai to kneel and kowtow before the magistrate.

Taowu, who had not been expecting to earn a bribe that day, felt that this was a blessing bestowed by Heaven. Leaving his seat, he walked down the hall, and was just about to curtsey to his benefactors, when Zhang Qian, the captain of the guards, stifling a guffaw, stopped him, reminding the fathead that the newcomers were supposed to kowtow to him, not the other way round.

"It's people like these who put food on my table," Taowu reminded him. "Why shouldn't I kowtow to them?"

It was with the utmost difficulty that Zhang Qian managed to choke down his mirth and stop Taowu making a fool of himself. Seeing this pantomime, Zhang the Mule thought that he might as well stand up too, since the usual formalities, it seemed, were not followed in this strange court. But as he did so, he received a prompt slap across the face from Taowu. "How dare you put yourself on an equal footing with your betters?" his assailant spluttered. Then, turning to the guards, he cried, "Give this insolent beggar 30 strokes of the club!"

Zhang Qian barked the same order to his subordinates, who pounced on the unfortunate Zhang the Mule, and pinned him to the ground. They beat him until both buttocks were stained with blood, Zhang the Mule all the while squealing like a pig in a slaughterhouse. Dou E and widow Cai stood watching this, silently quaking with fear.

When the thrashing had been administered, Taowu said calmly: "Right then! Who is the plaintiff and who is the defendant in this case?"

But as Zhang the Mule was moaning and groaning too loudly to hear what Taowu said, and the two women were too scared to speak up, his questions went unanswered. Taowu banged the desk in front of him with his gavel, and yelled, "Well? What's the matter with you? You've come here with some grievance or other, haven't you, you miserable wretches? Speak up, I'll have you beaten for contempt of court!"

At this, Zhang the Mule hastened to explain, while banging his head like a door knocker on the floor: "Your Honor, I am the plaintiff. My name is Zhang the Mule. My wife's name is Dou E. She put some poison in some mutton tripe soup, and murdered my father, who was also her own father-in-law. That old woman is Widow Cai, my mother-in-law. She is involved in this case too. I petition Your Honor for justice."

Taowu thereupon commanded, "Which is Dou E? Which is Widow Cai? Raise your heads!"

Dou E introduced herself, and so did the old woman with a great deal of stammering.

Taowu's eyes glittered as they fell upon Dou E, and his jaw dropped in awe. "What a beauty!" he thought. "A night spent with her would be the crowning pleasure of a lifetime."

When Taowu's leering had gone on for so long that even Zhang Qian was beginning to feel embarrassed, the captain of the guard moved to nudge the magistrate back to the business in hand. "Your Honor, it's not seemly to stare like that," he whispered. "You should start interrogating them."

Taowu hammered the desk with his gavel once more. "Nonsense!" he cried. "What on earth are you talking about? Why shouldn't I look at a beautiful woman if I want to? Get back to your post, and wait for my orders!"

Zhang Qian had no choice but to step back. Taowu then addressed Dou E. "What a pretty girl you are, my dear," he said in an oily voice, and with a repulsive smirk all over his face. "How did you come to poison your father-in-law? Come, tell me the truth, and I will be lenient with you."

Dou E protested, "But I am not Zhang the Mule's wife! I was married to Cai Zongchang when I was very young. Widow Cai is my mother-in-law — she is not the mother-in-law of Zhang the Mule. The Zhangs and the Cais have no connection with each other. Some days ago, my mother-in-law went to the pharmacy of Sai Lu Yi, outside the South Gate to collect a debt from him. Sai Lu Yi, however, had no intention of paying the debt. He tricked my mother-in-law into going with him to a secluded spot, and there he tried to strangle her. As luck would have it, Zhang the Mule and his father happened to come along, and their intervention saved my mother-in-law's life. Out of gratitude, she invited them to stay for a while at our house, as the Zhangs were vagabonds of no fixed abode. But they then had the insolence to insist that they marry us. Well, since I lost my husband three years ago, I have guarded my chastity, determined never to marry again. It has been my steadfast determination to devote my life to looking after my mother-in-law. Now, it happened that my mother-in-law fell ill, and told me to make some mutton tripe soup for her. That black-hearted villain there snatched the bowl of soup from me, saying that there was not enough salt or vinegar in it. While I was away fetching the salt and vinegar, he slipped something in the soup, which he then offered to my mother-in-law. But Heaven must have been watching over her, because it caused her to turn nauseous, and she could not drink the soup. She then offered it to the old man, who slurped it down and dropped down dead on the spot! This had nothing to do with me. I never left the house; how could I have got hold of poison? Besides, I made that mutton tripe soup especially for my mother-in-law. I wanted to help her get better, not poison her! It must have been Zhang the Mule who brought the poison in, hidden on his person. Then, having got me out of the way on a pretext, secretly put it in the soup in order to kill my mother-in-law. But by some strange mischance he killed his own father instead. I am telling you the absolute truth, Your Honor. I trust in your keen perception and expect that you will find me innocent."

Taowu was pleased with Dou E's lucid presentation of her case. Turning to Zhang the Mule, in no friendly fashion, he said, "It seems to me that the matter is as this nice young lady says: You procured the poison, and put it in the soup, with the lamentable result that you dispatched your own father to the next world, eh? And now you are trying to put the blame on her. Isn't that right? Right now, I am inclined to find for Dou E. What do you have to say for yourself?"

Seeing that the case was going against him, Zhang the Mule made haste to kowtow obsequiously. "Most perspicacious arbiter! All-seeing and impartial personification of justice!" he babbled, "As soon as my revered parent had partaken of the mutton tripe soup prepared by that hussy's own hands, blood spurted from all his seven orifices, and he died right there and then! If Dou E did not poison the soup, then who did? Your Honor, how can you take her crafty words at their face value? Another thing, Your Honor: If the old woman had not intended my father and I to marry her and her daughter-in-law, why on earth did she invite us to come and live in her house in the first place? Besides, I have evidence. These 20 ounces of silver are what the old woman gave me to keep my mouth shut about her poisoning my father. Look, Your Honor! As Heaven steers the affairs of men, I would not dare to try to deceive you."

This mention of silver made Taowu prick his ears up. "Well, if you have evidence, bring it here and show me," he ordered.

Zhang the Mule produced the 20 pieces of silver from inside his robe, and handed them to Zhang Qian, who passed them to his master. Gazing at the glittering silver, Taowu thought to himself: "This Zhang the Mule is no fool. But how am I going to handle this matter?" He thought for a while, and then said to Zhang the Mule: "You have acted wisely in bringing this evidence to me. Excellent! However, if you did not poison your father, and Dou E did not poison your father, then who did poison your father? Tell me, who gave you this money?"

"Widow Cai, Your Honor," replied Zhang the Mule promptly.

Taowu rapped the desk with his gavel. "Widow Cai," he cried, "it is clear from the fact that you gave 20 pieces of silver to Zhang the Mule in order to bribe him into silence that you were the poisoner. Are you prepared to confess?"

Already trembling like a leaf, Widow Cai was startled out of her wits when Taowu barked her name. All she could say was, "I didn't do it. I didn't do it" over and over again.

Seeing her in this state, Dou E shuffled forward on her knees. "Your Honor, my mother-in-law gave him the 20 pieces of silver partly to repay him and his father for their kindness, and because it was simply bad luck that the old man happened to die in our house the gift was made partly to defray the funeral expenses. It was certainly not a bribe to prevent the truth from coming out! The old lady had been ill in bed for two days, and so I made the mutton tripe soup especially for her. But she could not face it, her stomach being weak. She thereupon gave it to the old man. Zhang the Mule and I were watching her the whole time. She had no opportunity to put poison or anything else in the bowl without us seeing her do it."

Taowu was taken aback. "But if none of you poisoned him, I suppose you are suggesting it must have been me." He thought for a while, and then, wrinkling his brow, said, "All this wrangling is giving me a headache." Turning to Zhang Qian, he said, "I don't know how to handle this case. Fetch Magistrate Xiao here."

Zhang Qian went into the rear hall, and called for Magistrate Xiao.

Now this Magistrate Xiao was a local ruffian with some pretension to learning. He called himself Sai Xiao He, or "Better than Han Dynasty Prime Minister Xiao He". He invariably brought out the worst in people, and his main role in life was that of a wicked advisor. He had previously been in the entourage of Governor Saputo, who recommended him to Taowu when the latter arrived in Shanyang. Taowu put him in charge of the paperwork of the magistracy, including lawsuits, and trusted him implicitly. Hearing Zhang Qian's summons, Xiao knew that his master had got himself into a muddle in court yet again, and needed Xiao to help him out. Magistrate Xiao hurried into the courtroom, and stationed himself beside Taowu. When the matter had been explained to him, he frowned slightly, and then said to Zhang the Mule: "Were you telling the truth just now?"

"Every word of it, sir," came the reply.

"Well then, since you spoke the truth, sign a statement to that effect," Xiao ordered.

The hapless Zhang the Mule, being illiterate, could do nothing but hold the writing brush in his clumsy fists and pretend to make a few marks on the paper with it. Meanwhile, Xiao whispered something in Taowu's ear. The latter nodded, gave a thunderous rap with his gavel, and announced, "As the day is well advanced, I hereby adjourn this court. The trial will resume in three days' time. In the meantime, the accused, Dou E, will be remanded in custody. The plaintiff, Zhang the Mule, and the witness, Widow Cai, will be released on bail, and the coroner will examine the body of Zhang Gouer to determine the cause of death."

Hearing herself described as "the accused" and destined for prison, Dou E felt as though she had been hit by a thunderbolt. She cried out vehemently: "Your Honor, I am the victim of injustice! It is obvious that Zhang the Mule put the poison in the soup. I am completely innocent, so why should he be let go free while I am to be thrown in jail? Oh Heaven! Can this be justice? Who will be my protector?"

At this moment, Widow Cai uttered a plaintive cry, and clung tightly to her daughter-in-law. Magistrate Xiao thereupon ordered Zhang Qian to expel the old woman from the court, remove the drum used by plaintiffs to announce a request for justice, and escort Dou E to the prison.

The order was duly carried out by the officers of the court.

As he left the courtroom, Taowu gestured to Magistrate Xiao to follow him into the magistrate's office. Once there, Taowu dismissed his servants, and lost no time admitting to Xiao that he did not understand why he had sent Zhang the Mule and Widow Cai home, but had insisted on Dou E being held in jail. "You Honor," the wily Xiao replied, "In the first place, where could either of the women have obtained the poison? And in the second place, why on earth would Dou E have wanted to murder her mother-in-law? For, after all, it was for the old woman that she had prepared the mutton tripe soup, wasn't it? It is obvious that it was Zhang the Mule who..."

At this point, he was interrupted by Taowu. "Oh yes, I see that now," he said, "But why did you arrange to separate them in such a fashion, pending the second hearing?"

"Just think, Your Honor," replied Magistrate Xiao, "When Zhang the Mule came here today, crying about an injustice, claiming that the two women had conspired to poison his father, it was obvious that he was lying. He must know that it would be very difficult for Your Honor to find in his favor. And so, what do you think he has in mind...?"

This was the one area in which the muddle-headed Taowu was as sharp as a whip. He slapped his thigh, and chortled, "Of course! I see what you're getting at now. He knows that I cannot find in his favor unless he makes it clear that he will be suitably grateful!"

"Exactly, Your Honor!" fawned Magistrate Xiao. "That was

why I released Zhang the Mule and the old woman on bail. You see that villain Zhang the Mule knows that he is in the wrong. He also knows that in order to get the blame shifted onto Dou E he is going to have to part with a tidy sum of silver to you, Your Honor. Besides that, although the two women have been unjustly accused, if I had simply let them go, Your Honor would be going to all the trouble of trying this case for nothing. Now, as soon as I heard that Widow Cai had been chasing Sai Lu Yi for money he owed her, it occurred to me that she probably had a store of silver at home. So I had Dou E imprisoned as a hint to the old woman that crossing Your Honor's palm with a little bit of that silver might be wise if she wanted to ensure lenient treatment for her daughter-in-law. So, you see, Your Honor, two birds are killed with one stone this way! If both sides pay up, you can dismiss the case, reminding them that they don't want others to find out that bachelors and widows had been living together for some days, and so they should keep their mouths shut about this matter. Besides, the old man is dead, and nothing can be done about that. Just tell the old woman to give Zhang the Mule some money for the funeral expenses, and that will be the end of it. If, however, one side refuses to pay you, you can pass a sentence of death with a mere flick of your wrist. What could be simpler? What do you think of my suggestion, Your Honor?"

Taowu was delighted. "My dear magistrate," he burbled, "you really do deserve the nickname Sai Xiao He! I certainly did the right thing when I chose you for my right-hand-man! Yes, I will do as you suggest. The only thing is, that Widow Cai seems to be one of those prim and proper women who don't understand how things are done here in the magistrate's court. Do you think she'll have the common sense to cough up the cash? If she doesn't, how can I avoid making it look as though that brazen little chit of a daughter-in-law of hers is the aggrieved party?"

Magistrate Xiao was a past master at gauging other people's moods and whims, and knew exactly how to apply flattery to the greatest effect. Smirking obsequiously, he said, "Your Honor's prowess as a lady's man will do the trick, I'm sure. All you have to do is invite Dou E to join you for a few cups of wine. And then, her services in your bed for a few nights will perhaps make it possible to waive the money payment?"

"What a good idea!" cried Taowu. "Go and fetch her from the prison immediately. But make sure nobody finds out. Tell her that I need to question her further. Get a couple of your trusty men to arrange a feast in the Court room. I'll be along shortly."

While Magistrate Xiao was taking care of this, Taowu took his ease before going to tell his wife that he had business to attend to in his office, and returning.

Taowu's wife was the daughter of a court minister, a man named Wanyan Jin of the Nüzhen tribe, which had capitulated to the Mongols many years previously. Wanyan Jin had performed many stalwart services for the Mongols, and was a close confidante of Prime Minister Ahema. His daughter was a stout woman, with a figure like a barrel. Fierce of mien, she had from her earliest days cultivated a vindictive nature. It had not taken her long, after marrying Taowu, to discover that her husband had a roving eye, and she dominated him with an obsessively fierce possessiveness. The slightest hint that Taowu had been involved in extra-curricular dalliance brought down a torrent of invective on the cringing lecher's head from this tigress. Indeed, there had been times when Taowu had not dared to show his face in court until the livid fingernail scratches that marred it had healed. It was ludicrous that this tyrant, who would stoop to any villainy without a moment's hesitation, was reduced to a quivering jelly as soon as his wife appeared.

The court proceedings of that day had been reported to Taowu's wife by one of her spies. She was particularly incensed when she heard of Taowu's sickly leering when questioning a pretty young widow. So, upon hearing his specious excuse about having more work to do at the court, her suspicions — never far from the surface where her husband was concerned — were instantly aroused, and she dispatched one of her trusted maid-servants to follow him.

Taowu strode briskly to the court building, where he found Magistrate Xiao waiting for him together with Dou E, whom he had fetched from the prison. There was a sumptuous banquet laid out, too. Taowu gushed apologies for having had Dou E locked up, assured her that it had been a mere formality and that she could rest assured that this little matter of a charge of murder would soon be cleared up, and invited her to sit down and have a glass of wine with him. Taowu's honeyed words had the initial effect of convincing Dou E that he was sincere in his protestations that he had her and Widow Cai's best interests at heart, and she thanked him over and over again. But soon, as Taowu's flirtatious manner and suggestive actions became more and more outrageous, she began to perceive his real intentions; flushed with indignation and anger, she refused to take so much as a sip of wine, and demanded to be returned to the prison forthwith.

No detail of this farce was missed by the maid-servant sent by Taowu's wife. She darted back to report to her mistress, who bustled over to the Court room in a towering rage. There, she unceremoniously took her husband by the ear and hauled him back home, like a pig's carcass. After giving Taowu a good clattering about the face, she forced him to kneel at the foot of the bed the whole night. Taowu dared not disobey, but cowered and begged forgiveness until at dawn he was released from his penance, by which time everyone in the magistracy knew about the latest scandal. Taowu himself couldn't wait for the day's court session to open so that he could vent his spleen at his abject humiliation on the helpless Dou E. He determined to sentence her to death.

In the meantime, Zhang the Mule and Widow Cai had returned home. The old woman wept and wailed continuously, and could not touch a morsel of food or a drop of drink. Zhang the Mule, however, was in high spirits, and ordered the widow to prepare a hearty dinner for him.

Having eaten his fill, Zhang the Mule found his gaze wandering to the corpse of his father, which lay where it had fallen. The thought of how Dou E had so stubbornly thwarted his plan, to the extent that he had been involved in a lawsuit, maddened him, and he swore aloud: "Only when you suffer the death by ten thousand cuts will my wrath be assuaged, you hateful vixen!"

There is an ancient adage that goes something like this: "The magistrate's gate is open to all, but, penniless, through it doesn't bother to crawl." Zhang the Mule was well acquainted with this piece of wisdom; his dilemma was that not only did he have no money with which to bribe Taowu to execute Dou E, he did not even have enough money to bury his deceased parent. What was he to do? Then the thought suddenly came into his head that Widow Cai, apart from being the stingiest person he had ever met, was a money lender! Not only that: She charged 100 percent interest, and so somewhere in the house must be a hoard of silver! "Aha!" he thought, "She's a frail and timorous old crone, and her daughter-in-law is stuck in the local prison. This way, I have two sticks to beat her with, and extort some money out of her."

Zhang the Mule pranced with delight upon coming to this conclusion. He then went to the kitchen, selected a cleaver and hid it beneath his pillow. When night fell, he would be ready to pursue his dastardly scheme.

Widow Cai, in the meantime, was loath to enter her bedroom while the corpse of Zhang the Dog was lying there. Besides, the imprisonment of Dou E had filled her full of anguish. At this time of the evening, she was reminded how Dou E would come to tuck her up in bed. Now — Oh horror! — the young girl was languishing in a prison cell alongside the scum of the streets, with no money to bribe the guards to bring her food. How would she survive?

Widow Cai cried herself into a stupor, and fell in a swoon on Dou E's bed. She slept for she didn't know how long when a stealthy noise in the room woke her. Opening her eyes, she saw that the lamp had been lit, and that Zhang the Mule was standing before her, a murderous glint in his eyes. In a voice that quavered with terror, she asked him what he wanted at that time of night.

Zhang the Mule knew that the old woman was so timorous that all he had to do was raise his voice, and she would give him all the silver she had. So he shouted, "You ungrateful old hag! My father and I saved your worthless life, and you made an empty promise of marriage, for both yourself and your daughter-in-law. But you went back on your word — not only that, but you and that slut of a daughter-in-law of yours colluded to murder my father. It's an outrage crying to Heaven for vengeance!" As he uttered these words, he produced the cleaver and stepped ominously forward, his murderous eyes as round as saucers.

Widow Cai tumbled out of bed, and knelt on the floor, kowtowing frantically and begging for forgiveness.

"Forgive you? Hah!" spat Zhang the Mule. "With my poor father still lying stiff and cold in your house, poisoned by you and that hussy? You dare to ask for mercy? Well, first of all, you owe me money to pay for my deceased only parent's funeral expenses. Then, what about compensation for the beating I got, having been compelled to complain to the magistrate? I know you have silver hidden in this house somewhere. Turn it all over to me, and then perhaps we can see how we are going to settle this. Otherwise, I will slay you on the spot to avenge my father's murder!" So saying, he raised the cleaver, ready to bring it down on the old woman's neck.

"It's in a hole in the wall behind the head of the bed ..." screeched Widow Cai. "Take it all... Please!"

"That's better," murmured Zhang the Mule. "I'll just go and take a look. And you'd better be telling the truth. If not, you'll not live to see the dawn, I can assure you."

Mesmerized by the evilly glittering cleaver, as Zhang the Mule brandished it before her, Widow Cai jabbered, "Oh no, I wouldn't dare. It's all in there ... where I said... Take it ... take it..."

Her unwelcome visitor lit another lamp, approached the wall behind the head of the bed, and began to feel for a cavity. Sure enough, he found one, a secret compartment. Inside, it was chock full of gleaming silver. Zhang the Mule had never seen so much silver in one place before and he stared at the hoard until his eyes were dazzled. Wild with joy, he looked as though he wished he could swallow the lot at one gulp.

Eventually, he rummaged around the room until he found a wooden box, into which he scooped every last piece of Widow Cai's savings. He took the box to his room in the eastern part of the house, where, perceiving that there was no suitable place to hide it, he went to sleep with it clasped tightly in his arms.

The following morning, Zhang the Mule went back to Widow

Cai's room. He found the old woman already awake, but still wiping away tears. Zhang the Mule roughly ordered her to prepare breakfast, and he had scarcely finished eating it when the coroner from the magistrate's court arrived to examine the corpse of Zhang the Dog. Having returned a verdict of death by poisoning, the coroner took his leave. Zhang the Mule then went out to buy a coffin and funeral clothes. He hired a few layabouts as mourners on his way back, and then forced Widow Cai to accompany him in giving his father a hasty funeral. The next item of business was to tuck several large ingots of silver inside his robe and stride off to make an appointment with Commander Saputo.

When he was finally ushered into the commander's presence, Zhang the Mule lost no time pressing ingots worth a total of 50 pieces of silver on his host. He then made a clean breast of his efforts to possess Dou E, which had involved an attempt to poison Widow Cai and which had resulted in the accidental death of his father. He begged his host to intervene with Magistrate Xiao so that the case would be settled in his favor. Saputo chuckled as he pocketed the silver, and ordered writing materials to be brought. He scribbled a note, and handed it to Zhang the Mule, who stuffed it inside his robe, thanked his benefactor, and scuttled off to find Magistrate Xiao.

CHAPTER SIX

A Confession Extracted Under Torture

MAGISTRATE XIAO WAS not in his office, however, and Zhang the Mule searched high and low before he tracked him down in a house of ill-repute known as the Tower of Emerald Fragrance. The wily Xiao knew exactly what Zhang the Mule had come for, and furthermore he was sure that the visitor had not turned up empty-handed. He told the madam of the establishment to make a secluded room available, and retired there with Zhang the Mule. The latter looked in every nook and cranny to make sure there were no eavesdroppers, even making sure no one was snooping outside the door. Then he explained his business, at the same time placing four large ingots of silver before Magistrate Xiao, together with the note from Saputo. He wanted Xiao to intercede for him with Taowu, so that Dou E would be found guilty of poisoning his father and beheaded.

The silver and the letter did the trick. Xiao agreed immediately. But he added, "It is getting late, and the court will soon be closed. Just run along home now, and wait for what I assure you will be good news."

The two parted. Zhang the Mule went home, and Magistrate Xiao went back to the Court house. There, he gave half the silver he had received to Taowu, told him of Zhang the Mule's request, and advised him how best to handle the case. The unexpected present made Taowu forget his humiliation of the previous night, and he readily assented to Xiao's suggestion. "At the next court session, I will sentence Dou E to death by beheading," he announced.

Three days later, Taowu came to the courtroom and ordered the two parties to the poisoning case to be brought before him. Widow Cai, worried about how Dou E must be suffering as she languished in jail, hurried to the court as soon as she heard the summons, anxious to see her daughter-in-law again. Zhang the Mule, on the contrary, knowing that the verdict was a foregone conclusion, took his time getting there.

When the courtroom doors opened, and the guards bellowed for the litigants to enter, Widow Cai was the first to dash in. She immediately fell to her knees, as did Zhang the Mule, behind her.

Taowu, his robes rumpled, strolled in, yawning. Seating himself with difficulty, Taowu gazed at Widow Cai and Zhang the Mule. Then he cried, "Bring the accused, Dou E!"

Zhang Qian passed on the order to the nearest guard, who passed it on to the next one, and so on, until eventually Dou E, loaded with chains, was led shuffling into the courtroom. Her few days of captivity had seemed like years, and when she caught sight of Widow Cai once more she could not help bursting into tears and throwing herself into her mother-in-law's arms with a heart-breaking wail. The old woman too wept copious tears and sobbed loudly.

Taowu rapped loudly with his gavel. "Silence in court!" he yelped.

The two women hurriedly dried their eyes, and knelt in the middle of the hall, as Taowu cried, "Announce your names!"

This came as a surprise to the three people involved. If Taowu had been studying the case for the past three days, why on earth did he need to ask them their names again, they wondered.

a confession extracted under torture

Zhang the Mule said, "I am Zhang the Mule, Your Honor."

Dou E said, "I am Dou E, Your Honor, and this is my mother-in-law Widow Cai."

"Who is the plaintiff, and who is the defendant? And what is this case about?" were the next astounding questions.

Zhang the Mule thereupon repeated his accusation of the previous day. When he had finished, Taowu turned to Dou E. "What do you have to say for yourself?" he demanded.

"Your Honor," she began, "I was betrothed to Widow Cai's son when I was very young. That was 13 years ago. Three years ago, my husband died unexpectedly, and since then I have preserved my virtue. I have never remarried, nor have I any intention of doing so. Zhang the Mule here is well known in the neighborhood as a wicked scoundrel. Some days ago, my mother-in-law demanded the repayment of a debt from a pharmacist called Sai Lu Yi. The latter lured her to a deserted spot, where he attempted to strangle her. The two Zhangs, father and son, happening to pass by, saved my mother-in-law's life. In gratitude and because she felt sorry for the two homeless vagabonds, she invited them to stay for a while at our house. She certainly never invited them to marry us! But they turned out to have evil intentions; they schemed to get possession both of us and of the family property. Zhang the Mule tried to force my mother-in-law to marry his father, and me to marry him. I firmly refuse to allow any such thing. But now he claims that Widow Cai is his mother-in-law and that I am his wife. Furthermore, he accuses me of poisoning his father. Your Honor, please do not be deceived by his wild statements! If, as he says, my mother-in-law and I had married them, where are the wedding presents? When was the day of the nuptials? Who was the go-between and which neighbors were the witnesses? It is clear that he has told a pack of lies. My guess is that he was so resentful when I spurned his advances that when he offered to go and buy mutton tripe so that I could make a nourishing broth for my mother-in-law, who had fallen ill, he bought some poison. Then he snatched the soup I had made, and on the excuse that it was not seasoned properly sent me back to the kitchen. When I was gone, he put the poison in the soup in order to murder Widow Cai. But, fortunately, she couldn't stomach it, and offered it to Zhang the Dog.

The old man drank it, and died there and then. So, you see, Your Honor, the death of Zhang the Mule's father had nothing to do with me. Zhang the Mule was responsible for that death. I beg you to find in my favor, Your Honor."

This upright and fearless defense speech took Taowu aback. Puzzled, he turned to Zhang the Mule: "How can the accused — your new mother-in-law and wife — claim that you are the murderer? Dou E is your wife, is she not? Speak up! And I want to hear not one word of a lie!"

"Your Honor! Fount of wisdom!" cried Zhang the Mule, "if they did not want us to marry them, why did they take we two homeless strangers into their home? This Dou E may be young, but she is sly and mischievous. She also has a devious and clever tongue. May I venture to suggest that a few strokes of the rod would soon get the truth out of her?"

This seemed to make sense to Taowu, and he gave the order to the court attendants to beat Dou E. But no sooner had he done so that Magistrate Xiao stepped forward and had a word in his ear: "Please allow me to interrogate her first, sir." Given permission, Xiao addressed Dou E, "You say that your mother-in-law did not invite the old man to marry her, and that you did not marry Zhang the Mule. But the four of you lived together in the same house for several days. How can you expect people to believe that you were not married? You had better come clean!"

"I have already told the truth, sir," replied Dou E. "As I said, my mother-in-law took them in out of gratitude for their having saved her life. She certainly did not offer them marriage. That Zhang the Mule annoyed me on several occasions; every time I drove him off with curses. How could I marry such a creature?"

Magistrate Xiao then took another tack. "Since each side sticks to an opposite story," he said, "I think the only thing to do is to question the old woman. Then we might get to the truth of the matter." He turned to Widow Cai. "Is it not true that you are Zhang the Mule's mother-in-law, having given Dou E to him in marriage?" he asked.

Widow Cai stammered, "When the two Zhang's saved me from being strangled by Sai Lu Yi, I offered to give them money as a reward. But to my surprise, they didn't want money; instead, they said that if I didn't accept them as husbands they would strangle me themselves. I was so afraid of them that I had to take them home, and make them a good supper. But I never agreed to this marriage demand. He is lying, Your Honor, when he says that I am his mother-in-law. In fact, he bullied me so much that I was even afraid for my life!"

At this point, Zhang the Mule interrupted, fearing that the widow would reveal that he had stolen her silver from the secret compartment in the bedroom wall. But he was silenced by Magistrate Xiao, who said, "It is clear that Widow Cai did, in fact, invite the Zhangs to stay at her house because she had agreed to their marriage proposal. When a single man and a widow are under the same roof for several days, what else are people going to think? Nothing more needs to be said."

He then leant to whisper in Taowu's ear. The latter nodded, rapped the desk with his gavel. "Dou E," he cried, "the coroner has examined the body, and found that the death was caused by poison. Did you or did you not administer that poison. Tell the truth!"

"I am not guilty of poisoning Zhang the Mule's father, Your Honor," Dou E said, calmly. "I and my mother-in-law live in the same house as single women. How could we dare to venture out to buy such a thing as poison? Besides, soon after the Zhangs imposed themselves upon us my mother-in-law fell ill, and took to her bed. Since I had to attend to her, I never left the house. How could I have been carrying poison on me? It is my suspicion that when Zhang the Dog sent his son into town to buy mutton tripe, the poison was bought then. If you question Zhang the Mule, Your Honor, I think you will find that this was the fact of the matter."

Dou E's steadfastness and refusal to be browbeaten infuriated Taowu. His first instinct was to order the girl to be given a beating. But again he was restrained by Magistrate Xiao. "Please calm yourself, Your Honor," he hissed. "Question Zhang the Mule first. You can have her beaten later."

Taowu acquiesced: "Zhang the Mule, what do you have to say about Dou E's evidence?"

Zhang the Mule was quick to answer. "Your Honor, on the day I went into town to buy some mutton tripe I was so consumed with worry about my poor mother-in-law's condition, that I bought the tripe and returned home without delay. How could I have had time to go looking around for a shop that sold poison? The reason that I took the bowl of soup from Dou E was that I wished to serve it to my new mother-in-law myself, as a gesture of filial affection. It was then that I noticed that the soup was not tasty enough, and so I sent Dou E back to the kitchen for salt and vinegar. It is preposterous to say that I put poison in the soup. Then, when I saw that the old lady had someone to attend to her, I returned to my own room. When I finally returned, I found my poor father lying dead on the floor of Widow Cai's bedroom."

Hearing Zhang the Mule's testimony that he was not in the room when his father died, Magistrate Xiao was delighted. "If you were not at the scene of the crime, then you could not possibly have administered the poison," he interjected. "But what makes you think that Dou E did so?"

This caught Zhang the Mule off guard. He was silent for a time, and then an idea came to him. He said, "Sir, my father was old, and unfit for work. Dou E resented him, considering that he was sponging off the household. Several times she was extremely rude to him. She called him a useless parasite. Moreover, she herself made that mutton tripe soup; nobody else touched it. If she did not put the poison in it, then who did?" Then he pleaded with Taowu: "Your Honor, I hope you will put right the terrible injustice done to my aged parent."

Taowu bellowed, "Dou E, you cunning and deceitful wench! Your wickedness is unfathomable. In addition, you had the opportunity to slip the poison into the soup. Who else could have done it? And now you have the effrontery to slander this gentleman. This is absolutely preposterous!" Turning to the court attendants, he ordered them to bring a big club. "If you don't confess, you'll be given a hundred strokes," he warned Dou E.

Zhang the Mule was pleased with this turn of events, but even so he urged Taowu: "Your Honor, this sly slut is the sort who will never confess to her evil crimes unless she tastes the cudgel. May I respectfully urge you to beat her first?"

"All right," said the thick-headed Taowu, "Give her a hundred strokes."

Dou E was seized with fright. She did not yet realize why Taowu was so set on finding her guilty, and she appealed to him: "Your Honor, I am the victim of injustice!"

Before she could continue, Magistrate Xiao ordered the court attendants to proceed with the punishment. The attendants pounced on Dou E like hungry hawks on a chicken, pinned her to the floor and gave her one hundred strokes of the cudgel. As strips of skin and spurts of blood flew with every blow, Dou E fainted before even half the flogging was completed. But the attendants dare not stop before the order had been carried out, and they finally left the girl a bloody pulp of mashed flesh.

Already, Widow Cai had thrown herself to her knees before the attendants and begged them to have mercy on her daughter-in-law. "She is so young and frail," she cried, "how can she endure such cruelty?"

"Stop interfering with the work of the court!" barked Zhang Qian. "This is no place for your babbling." So saying, he kicked the old woman so that she fell sprawling on her back. After that, Widow Cai did not dare to make another appeal, but crouched on the ground, shivering and whimpering.

Having carried out their grim instructions, the court attendants stood back. Taowu banged his gavel, and cried, "Confess to the crime of poisoning your father-in-law, you depraved vixen. Or I will make you suffer even worse things."

"She's still unconscious, Your Honor," Zhang Qian reminded him. "She can't answer right now."

"Well, if she couldn't endure a beating, why didn't she confess in the first place?" asked Taowu, genuinely puzzled at what he considered Dou E's odd behavior. "Zhang Qian, throw some cold water on her. Then when she's conscious again, tell her to confess."

Zhang Qian did so, and when Dou E came round, he said, "Dou E, you know that you cannot stand another beating. All you have to do is confess, to avoid suffering all over again."

The girl, with tear-filled eyes, said in a barely audible voice: "I am not the poisoner. How can I confess to something I did not do? I am the victim of injustice!"

Widow Cai managed to stagger to her feet. Weeping rivers of tears, she embraced Dou E, while Zhang the Mule looked on with a smug grimace on his ugly features.

Taowu was filled with rage when he heard that Dou E still would not confess. "Well, it seems to me that you haven't had a sufficient taste of the rod," he yelled. "Beat her with a thicker cudgel!" he ordered the attendants.

The latter dragged Widow Cai away, and again forced Dou E to the floor. Again, she swooned as the savage blows rained down.

Taowu ordered Zhang Qian to throw more cold water on the hapless girl. When she came to, he asked her again: "Are you ready to confess yet?"

Dou E realized now that her interrogator was adamant on getting a confession out of her. She was sure that he must have been bribed by Zhang the Mule. Even though I'm a helpless woman, she thought, I will never confess to something I did not do, even if they beat me to death. Gritting her teeth as she made this determination, she finally blurted out: "I did not poison him. I have nothing to confess to. Even if you beat me to death, I will never say otherwise!"

This drove Taowu into a paroxysm of fury. "Very well," he roared. "If that's your attitude, so be it!" Then he ordered Zhang Qian: "Beat her with the heaviest clubs. And if that doesn't unlock her iron jaws, beat her to death!"

This time, however, the men who did the flogging, being not altogether without human feelings, were careful to land the blows in such a way that they did not prove fatal. Nevertheless, they lacerated flesh and broke bones, and Dou E swooned once again. Her torturers then stopped swinging their clubs. Wiping the sweat from their brows, they could not help thinking that in all their years in their grim profession they had never come across even a hardened criminal as unyielding as Dou E.

Revived by the cold water treatment one more time, Dou E said, in a feeble but steady voice: "I did not poison him. Even if you beat me to death, I will never say otherwise! Oh Heaven, they

a confession extracted under torture

say you are impartial, and the net of your law is cast wide. But if that is so, why is the real poisoner standing there gloating, while I, an innocent victim of injustice, have to suffer savage beatings? It seems that magistrates' courts have always been placed where the light of truth and justice never penetrates, and people are subjected to cruel wrongs!"

By this time, Taowu was yelping like a mad dog: "Keep beating her! Keep beating her! Beat her to death!"

The court attendants looked at each other, and then down at Dou E's body, which was little more than a mass of bloody pulp by this time. None of them moved, even when their captain Zhang Qian cursed them with the foulest oaths and uttered the direst threats. Zhang Qian himself snatched up one of the massive clubs, but could not bring himself to wield it against the pitiful girl.

Seeing the situation, Magistrate Xiao knew that no beating, no matter how severe, could drag a confession from Dou E's lips. He ordered Zhang Qian to put the club down, and whispered in his master's ear. Soon, a broad smirk spread across Taowu's face. He nodded: "It shall be as you say." He then turned to address Dou E. "Well, since you deny it so vehemently," he said mildly, "I suppose you must be innocent of this heinous act of poisoning your own father-in-law. But if you did not do it, who did?"

Dou E replied, "The truth is, Your Honor, that both I and my mother-in-law are innocent. I venture to suggest that if you were to question Zhang the Mule you would find the real culprit."

Taowu said, "But the poison must have been put in the soup after Zhang the Mule tasted it. Clearly, the poison must have been added after he left the room. So suspicion falls upon either you or your mother-in-law. And if you didn't do it, then the old woman must have. No third person comes into it."

"But my mother-in-law had been ill in bed for several days before the tragedy," Dou E protested. "How could she have got hold of poison? And what motive would she have for poisoning the old man? Surely, Zhang the Mule is the murderer; it is outrageous to accuse my mother-in-law!"

Taowu exploded in rage: "How dare you make a mockery of

this court?" he roared. Then, turning to the attendants ordered, "Enough of this nonsense! Bring the thumbscrews and squeeze the truth out of Widow Cai!"

Widow Cai was startled out of her wits when she heard this. All she could say was, "I didn't do it. I didn't do it."

To put a stop to the terrified old woman's pleas and protestations of innocence, Taowu brought down his gavel hard on the desk in front of him. "If you didn't do it, and your daughter-in-law didn't do it, I suppose you mean that I committed this crime! ... You there, this old woman has a sharp tongue — put the screws on all ten fingers, and don't be gentle about it!"

The attendants fitted the thumbscrews onto all ten of Widow Cai's fingers, and clamped them to the point at which they squeaked.

The old woman's moans of pain were more excruciating to Dou E than the pain of her own battered body. Unable to endure the old woman's heart-rending cries any longer, the girl dragged herself towards Widow Cai, and urged her to try to bear up under this brutal torture. "Your very life is at stake, mother-in-law," she said. "If you confess to this crime, which you did not commit, they will chop your head off. You didn't poison the old man, so why should you confess?"

Widow Cai wailed, "The ten fingers are linked to the heart. Any more of this kind of torture will kill me anyway."

Magistrate Xiao was gratified to see that his plan was beginning to work, and he took this opportunity to put pressure on Dou E. "If your mother-in-law did not poison Zhang the Dog, then it must have been you who did the deed. By confessing, you will save your mother-in-law any more of the agony she is now suffering. I have heard it said that you are a devoted daughter-in-law. If that is so, how can your conscience allow this poor widow to endure such awful pain on account of a crime you yourself have committed?"

Hearing Magistrate Xiao's words, Dou E immediately understood his sinister intention to force a false confession out of her by torturing Widow Cai. She roundly denounced Xiao as a spiteful villain, adding, "You have been bribed by Zhang the Mule to bring about my death. Well, you may do what you like with me, only please spare my blameless mother-in-law!"

Xiao sneered, "Since you won't confess, but keep shouting about injustice, I have no alternative but to keep interrogating Widow Cai." Then, turning to Zhang Qian, said, "Tighten the screws!"

Taowu rapped the desk with his gavel, as a sign of approval. "That's right," he rasped. "All ten fingers!"

Dou E's tears fell like rain as she witnessed the merciless cruelty of her tormentors and heard Widow Cai's ear-splitting shrieks.

Meanwhile, Magistrate Xiao, who was keeping a close watch on the girl, decided to step up the pressure. "Don't stop tightening the screws until the old woman either confesses her guilt or dies from the pain!" he instructed the torturers.

Zhang Qian gave the necessary directions, until two of Widow Cai's finger bones snapped, and she fainted. Dou E flung her arms round her mother-in-law, only to hear Taowu call out, "Throw some cold water on the old woman, and continue the interrogation!"

An excruciating decision now loomed before Dou E. But she did not hesitate. "Stop!" she cried. "Do not torture my mother-in-law any further. I confess. I was the one who poisoned Zhang the Mule's father."

Widow Cai revived from her swoon just in time to hear these dreadful words. Horrified, she protested, "My child, you must not confess to a crime you did not commit just to spare me. How could I live with the knowledge that I was the cause of your death?"

"Heaven and Earth always follow the path of righteousness," Dou E said, resignedly. "Even though I suffer injustice, Heaven and Earth will never forgive these evil officials, and in the end they will get their just deserts."

As the two women clung to each other, weeping, in the middle of the courtroom, Taowu and Magistrate Xiao glanced at each other with repulsive smiles on their faces. They had finally got Dou E to confess! Taowu ordered Xiao to record the confession. Dou E had no choice but to sign the damning statement, and Taowu lost no time writing the sentence of the court below it. The sentence consisted of the one word "Beheading." He then ordered Dou E to be kept in custody, while Magistrate Xiao submitted the documents concerning the case to the prefectural magistrate for ratification. "As soon as we receive the ratification," he said, smugly, "Dou E will be taken to the place of public execution, and there beheaded."

As Dou E, loaded with chains once more, was being led away, Widow Cai howled, "My child, you are to lose your life all because of me!"

But the girl's quiet reply was "I regret that I will no longer be able to take care of you, mother-in-law. Be sure to look after yourself."

The old woman tried to hold on to Dou E to prevent the guards taking her away, but she was thrust roughly to the floor. By the time she had recovered sufficiently to rise to her feet, Dou E had already been locked in a death cell.

When the court was dismissed, Magistrate Xiao buttonholed Zhang the Mule, who was bubbling over with expressions of gratitude, and warned him: "Don't thank me yet; wait until Dou E's head rolls. The prefectural magistrate has to examine the documents first, and I'm afraid this case is full of holes. If the prefectural magistrate does not affirm the sentence, all our efforts will have been wasted."

Startled out of his complacency, Zhang the Mule stammered, "But, sir, what is to be done?"

The other replied, "Go to the prefectural magistracy, and take some silver with you. I have a good friend there named Li. He is well trusted by his superior, and is in charge of all the documentation. I will give you a letter of introduction, which should smooth your way. But you must leave first thing tomorrow morning; there is no time for delay."

"I fully understand," Zhang the Mule assured him.

The two men then parted.

The following morning, armed with the letter and a pocket full of silver, Zhang the Mule went directly to the prefectural seat. He soon found Li, who did not hesitate to sign the ratification himself, once he saw the gleam of silver. Thus was formal approval obtained for the public execution of Dou E for the crime of poisoning her father-in-law. In fact, so smoothly had the matter been arranged that Zhang the Mule noticed that the announcement of the forthcoming execution had already been posted on the gate of the magistracy in Shanyang when he got back that evening.

CHAPTER SEVEN

Appeal to Heaven on the Execution Ground

UPON BEING CAST into a prison cell, Dou E's first thought was that the powerful county magistrate Taowu had been temporarily confused by Zhang the Mule's sly and flattering sophistry, and that before long he would see the justice of her case and judge in her favor. But after his odious behavior at the private little dinner party he had arranged for her she had begun to fear that the old lecher, having failed to have his wicked way with her, would now take Zhang the Mule's side. When, in fact, this turned out to be so, and not only was cruel torture applied to herself but even her frail mother-in-law was threatened with torture in order to force Dou E to confess to a crime she had not committed, all the girl's illusions about getting justice from the magistrate's court were shattered. But even after she had heard the sentence of beheading pronounced upon her, and she had been shut up in a death cell, a shred of hope still remained when she heard from one of the guards that the sentence could only be carried out after the prefectural commander had authorized it. She firmly believed that right would be repaid with right, and evil would be repaid with evil. Surely, Heaven would not allow Zhang the Mule to get away with his wickedness? Having been pure-hearted since she was small, and having sacrificed her own happiness in order to serve her mother-in-law, Dou E firmly believed that the day would come when this injustice that had been inflicted upon her would be righted. She had faith that not all officials were as fatuous, rapacious and venal as Taowu, that once the prefectural court had examined the case, this false accusation would be seen for the travesty of justice that it was, and that she would be exonerated. This was her only comfort as she languished in jail, praying to Heaven to let her soon walk in the light of day once more.

But, to Dou E's horror and dismay, it was no more than a few days before the guard came to inform her that the prefectural magistrate had confirmed the sentence of death, which was to be carried out the following day. She found it difficult to comprehend this dreadful news, and raising her head, she cried out in a trembling voice: "Oh heaven! This is a terrible injustice. Why have I been compelled to suffer so cruelly, and then, completely innocent of any wrongdoing, to forfeit my life upon the execution block? Oh Heaven, you have the sun in the sky during the day and the moon at night, shining down and revealing to you the right and wrong that men do. You also have spirits and Bodhisattvas who control the lives and deaths of all people, and who unfailingly reward the good and wreak retribution upon the bad. But now you fail to distinguish between the clear and the dark, the right and the wrong. Why do you allow an innocent person, who has been fettered by poverty and misfortune to suffer the cutting short of her life in this way, while evildoers are allowed to enjoy long lives wallowing in riches and rank? I have always been devout and respectful: For what reason have I been overtaken by such a dire fate? The sky is forlorn and the earth is desolate; the strong bully the weak. Those in power are false-hearted officials! Oh Heaven, your vastness is in confusion, unable to distinguish truth from lies! Oh Earth, you are topsy-turvy, with the rascally exalted and the noble cast down! Where now can virtue and benevolence be found? Dou E is the victim of a monstrous injustice!"

Dou E's lamentation was a cry from the heart against the villainy of grasping and black-hearted officials. She would have gladly suffered death, going like a lamb to the slaughter, had only her appeal been heeded by Heaven, and the plague of corrupt officialdom swept from the land.

As she pondered how she could have herself vindicated following her death, even though she would become a wandering ghost down the ages, her ringing cries and appeals to Heaven were unaccompanied by tears. Her fellow inmates of the death cells were moved by her sincerity, and joined in her bitter condemnation of monstrous and muddle-headed officials who did not have the slightest understanding of justice. Even the guards wept silently as Dou E continued with her tirade all night, until her voice was hoarse and drops of blood started from her eyes.

The following morning, while the chief executioner went to prepare the execution ground, Zhang Qian led a posse of guards to escort the prisoner to her doom. As the door of her cell was flung open, Dou E cried once more: "This is a monstrous injustice!"

Startled, Zhang Qian ordered her to be silent, but Dou E glare at him, and declared, "I am innocent of this charge of murder. I have fallen foul of a rascally magistrate, and a terrible injustice is being done!"

"The prefectural magistrate has endorsed the sentence," replied Zhang Qian. "My orders are to escort you for immediate execution. It will do you no good to wail and protest." He then gave a sign to the guards accompanying him to load Dou E with chains and hang a board with the details of her crime and her sentence around her neck. They then escorted their prisoner to the market place, where the execution was to be carried out.

The news that the infamous poisoner of her father-in-law was to be beheaded had spread all around Shanyang County the previous day, when the prefectural magistrate's notice endorsing the sentence had been pasted up. The streets had been packed with people eager to glimpse the morbid spectacle since the early hours of the morning. Lamentably, not one of them was aware that an innocent young girl was about to suffer the supreme penalty.

As she was pushed by her guards through the thronged streets, she was the object of contemptuous stares and accusing fingers from all sides. Many of the onlookers remarked on Dou E's beauty, and knowingly remarked that the heart of a scorpion must lie beneath that bewitching form if she could commit one of the ten crimes for which there could be no pardon; others wondered how a girl who looked so virtuous and kind could conceal such a vicious nature; again there were others, of a more callous nature, who made threatening gestures and uttered imprecations, and were of the opinion that beheading was too good for a girl who poisoned her father-in-law, and that the death by ten thousand cuts would be more appropriate. All this of course caused Dou E agonizing injustice! There were not a few among the onlookers who were touched by her piteous wails, even to the point of shedding tears, and even some of the jeering boors in the crowd were left stunned, with mouths agape.

Dou E herself noticed none of this, as her guards hustled her through the crowds. She shouted over and over again, "This is a monstrous injustice." It was not only mortals who were moved by her piercing cry of injustice — a certain deity too found his attention caught by it. This deity was none other than the Local God of Shanyang County. The Local God resided in the Imperial Shrine in Shanyang City, and that is where he was sitting on that day, when he suddenly noticed a black column of what looked like smoke shoot into the sky from the center of the city. The black vapor almost blotted out the sun as it spread across the firmament. The Local God of Shanyang shivered, left behind his image on the temple's altar, and sprang onto a passing cloud. Shielding his eyes, he looked around, and soon caught sight of a huge mass of people lining both sides of the main street of the city. A group of soldiers was escorting a young woman to the execution ground. The deity noticed that although the prisoner looked wan and haggard, and her body bore all the hallmarks of savage torture, she nevertheless kept uttering a cry of "Injustice!" in firm and fearless tones. Now this Local God of Shanyang was a spirit who put great store by righteousness. The heart-rending sight below him moved him to tears, and he descended on his cloud until he could mingle with the bystanders and thus got a closer look at what was going on.

As the sorry procession reached the eastern end of the city, it suddenly occurred to Dou E that her mother-in-law's house was quite near, and if the old lady should see her being dragged to the place of execution it would be a terrible shock for her. She halted, and when the guards roughly prodded her to continue, she turned to them and, shedding tears, said, "Kind sirs, I have a favor to ask of you."

"What is it?" asked the senior guard.

Dou E said, "I wish to proceed no further on this street leading east. I pray you to take me by a detour from here to the execution ground, which, although it would prolong my suffering before death releases me from sorrow, I would rest all the happier in the after life."

The senior guard was a shrewd man, and he suspected that Dou E must have some special reason for this odd request. "But the place of execution is already within sight," he exclaimed. "One chop, and it will all be over. Why do you wish to add more moments of anguish to your doomed life? Perhaps there is a family member you with to deliver parting words to?"

"Have pity on me, sir," Dou E pleaded tearfully. "I lost my mother when I was only three years old, and since my father left for the capital to take the imperial examinations 13 years ago, I have had no news of his whereabouts; indeed, I do not even know whether he is alive or dead. Three years ago, my husband passed away, and left me alone in the world."

"Then, why do you wish to suddenly go by a roundabout way?" asked the senior guard.

"I am afraid that I might come face to face with my mother-in-law," replied Dou E.

The senior guard was taken aback. "You are on the point of departing this life for ever," he said, "so why should be afraid of meeting anyone?"

Dou E explained, "If my mother-in-law were to see me loaded with chains like this, being led to my execution, the shock might kill her on the spot. Sir, if you make a condemned person's last moments easier, you will gain merit in the next life, you know."

The senior guard was overcome with pity. "Well, just a

moment," he said, "I'll have to ask the officer."

But before he could do so, from the eastern end of the street emerged Widow Cai, supported by two neighbors and wailing loudly. The sight of Dou E standing in the middle of the crowd surrounded by guards seemed to charge her slight frame with an uncanny strength. Thrusting aside her helpers, the old woman rushed screeching towards Dou E, screeching, "My own beloved daughter-in-law!"

The guards barred her way. "Stand back! Don't interfere!" they shouted. Dou E begged them to allow Widow Cai to approach her. "She is my mother-in-law," she told the guards, "please let me say a few last words to her." Thereupon, the senior guard made way for Widow Cai. "All right," he said, "but make it brief."

Trembling and weeping, the old woman staggered forward, and embraced Dou E. "My child, the thought that it is my fault that you are to be executed, causes me more pain than I can bear," she sobbed.

Dou E knelt on the ground, and kowtowed to Widow Cai. "I was forced to confess to poisoning the old man," she said, "and now I am on my way to the execution ground. I very much regret that you have suffered this shock. How will you live, without me to look after you?"

"It is for my sake that you are being led to your death," sobbed the old woman. "But your thoughts are still for my welfare. Oh, I can't stand the torment!"

Dou E tried to comfort her, saying, "Mother-in-law, it is not your fault. The blame for my sufferings lies with those evil officials who bend the law to their own nefarious ends. Meanwhile, I have something I wish to say to you, but I am not sure if it is appropriate to do so."

"Please say whatever is on your mind," the old woman urged her.

Dou E continued, "As you know, I lost my mother when I was three years old, and my father when I was seven. I moved into your household, where I served you for several years. In fact, we were just like mother and daughter. I would like to request that after my death you place half a bowl of left-over rice porridge before my grave every New Year's Day and on the day of the Pure Brightness Festival, and burn paper money for use in the afterlife — just as you would do for your own child."

Widow Cai, touched to the heart, assured her that she would do so. Then she wept so bitterly that Dou E was afraid that she would faint and do herself an injury. "Please, mother-in-law, don't cry so," she urged her. "It has been my fate to meet with injustice at the hands of wicked men. Don't grieve for me when I'm gone; the most important thing is that you take care of your health."

But this did not stem the old woman's tears. She continued to lament: "But you have been a filial and blameless girl, and you are going to your death all because of me! How will I be able to face your father again?"

At the mention of her father, the scene 13 years before, when she had parted forever from him, flashed before Dou E's eyes. A fresh wave of sorrow swept over her, and she said, "Mother-in-law, when my father left to take the imperial examination in the capital city, he said to me: 'If I become an official, I will come back for you.' But ever since that time, there has been no news whatsoever of him. If you meet him again, please be sure to explain to him how I was executed unjustly. Also, tell him that I appreciate his kind upbringing, and I will not be able to close my eyes in death, knowing that I did not repay him by serving him for even half a day. Ask him, too, to avenge the injustice done to his daughter." So saying, she lifted her face to Heaven, and cried, "Father, where are you now? Do you see the terrible fate that has overtaken your abandoned daughter? I am doomed to become a wronged spirit, roaming to the farthermost corners of Heaven and Earth looking for my father to ask him to right the injustice done to me!"

The two women then clung to each other, weeping their hearts out.

Meanwhile, unseen by mortal eyes, the Local God of Shanyang County had been observing all this, and could not help being moved by the tragic scene. He mounted his cloud, and soared into the sky. He arrived at the Southern Gate of Heaven, where the fairy guards of the Heavenly Palace stopped him, asking him

appeal to heaven on the execution ground

which particular deity he was and his reason for wishing to enter the Heavenly Palace.

"I am the Local God of Shanyang County, below on Earth," the Local God replied, "and I have something to report to the Jade Emperor. Please be so good as to announce my arrival."

He was told to wait, while a guard went inside for further instructions.

Now it just so happened that the Jade Emperor was presiding over his court at that time, and immortals from all over were reporting on the good and bad deeds taking place in the world of men. The Jade Emperor was paying careful attention to these reports, one by one, when he was informed that the Local God of Shanyang County had a report to present. The Jade Emperor ordered that he be shown into his presence immediately.

After the Local God had greeted the Jade Emperor, he was invited to give his report. He did so, as follows: "Your Majesty, I was seated at my ease as usual this morning, in the local shrine, when I suddenly became aware of a thick black cloud of resentment shooting up into the sky. I investigated, and found that its origin was a woman of Shanyang County who was about to be beheaded. The woman's name is Dou E. She lost her mother at the age of three, and her father left her when she was only seven. She was placed in the home of a certain Widow Cai, to be brought up as a future bride for her son Cai Zongchang. At the age of 17, she wed the boy. But, alas, Cai Zongchang died of illness less than three months later. Despite these hardships, Dou E never wavered in her staunch commitment to virtue — unsurpassed among womankind — and her duty to her mother-in-law, whom she devoted herself to serving wholeheartedly. Then one day, a rascally pharmacist named Sai Lu Yi, to whom Widow Cai had gone to demand payment of a debt, lured her to an isolated spot, and there tried to strangle her. Fortunately, a pair of vagabonds, father and son, happened to stumble on this atrocious scene, and the old woman's life was saved. In gratitude, Widow Cai invited these homeless wanderers into her home. Who would have thought that the rascals would then have had the temerity to demand that Widow Cai and Dou E marry them! When Dou E showed that she would not hear of anything so outrageous, Zhang the Mule — the son — decided to get his revenge by poisoning Widow Cai. However, through some muddle, he ended up poisoning his own father. To get out of this predicament, Zhang the Mule complained to the local magistrate that Dou E was the one who had poisoned the old man. Now this local magistrate, Taowu by name, is corrupt and lecherous. Having been bribed by Zhang the Mule, and, moreover, already having his amorous advances spurned by Dou E, Taowu had the girl tortured. Dou E refused to confess to a crime she had not committed, but when the fiendish Taowu tortured her mother-in-law, Dou E was forced by her sense of devotion to the old woman to take the blame on herself to save her from further suffering. The result was that Dou E was forced to sign a confession, and was held in custody to await confirmation — or otherwise — of the death sentence by the prefectural magistrate. But the crafty Zhang the Mule, having managed to get his hands on all Widow Cai's silver, bribed a clerk at the prefectural magistracy to authorize the sentence, and Dou E is at this very moment being led to the execution ground. It is noteworthy that, since time immemorial, executions have always been carried out on earth after the start of the autumn season. But right now, the mortal world is still in the grip of the blazing-hot days of the sixth month. To carry out an execution now would be going against all natural principles. I venture to suggest, Your Heavenly Majesty, that it is clear that the magistrate in charge of this case has manipulated the law for his own private ends. Dou E, as she faces the headsman's axe, feels that virtue has been repaid with evil, and she has openly accused both Heaven and Earth of conniving at injustice, and the spirits and deities of self-serving chicanery. Her indignation is such that it has spouted up in a huge black cloud, right up to Heaven itself! When I chanced to see it, I realized that if this virtuous and innocent woman is allowed to suffer this terrible injustice, then not only will the principles of Heavenly rectitude, under which all wrongs are put right, be besmirched, but the people down there in the mortal world will be led to abandon the way of goodness and espouse that of wickedness, and social ethics will be undermined. I myself mingled with the crowd, and observed how Dou E conducted herself and how forthrightly she spoke. There can be no doubt that she is a person of the utmost probity and filial piety. Now there is nobody in Shanyang County who does not know that Dou E is the victim of an earth-shattering injustice. They all curse Heaven and Earth for being unfair, and the spirits and deities for being self-seeking fiends. I am very much afraid, Your Heavenly Majesty, that unless you vindicate this paragon of virtue and reassert the impartiality of Heaven's justice, mortal men will become perverse and difficult to govern. This in turn, I fear, may shake the very foundations of the Heavenly Palace itself! I beg Your Heavenly Majesty to save this girl who today stands upon the execution ground, not only as a way to commend her virtue before the whole world and reaffirm the commitment of Heaven to justice, but also to avoid the disaster of mortal men's anger and outrage building up to a point at which it could boil over and bring about some unconscionable disaster! If my report has offended Your Heavenly Majesty, I tremble in terror, but I felt that it was my duty to report what I had seen with my own eyes."

The Jade Emperor listened to this with growing indignation. When the Local God of Shanyang had finished his report, he said, "A thousand years ago, there was a filial maiden in Donghai County who was unjustly put to death. Apprised of this, I personally commanded that not a drop of rain should fall in that County for the next three years, to show Heaven's displeasure and redress the wrong. Who would have thought that one thousand years later, there would still be blockheaded, arrogant and corrupt officials in the world of mortals, who perpetrate injustices! By the way, what family does this Dou E have? Who are her parents?"

The Local God of Shanyang answered, "She has no mother, Your Heavenly Majesty. Her mother passed away when the girl was only three years old. As for her father, Dou Tianzhang, he placed her with Widow Cai to be brought up as the bride for her son. He did this in return for traveling expenses he needed to journey to the capital to take the imperial examination. That was 13 years ago, and there has been no news of him since. In fact, nobody even knows whether he is alive or dead. Dou E's husband having died not long after the marriage, the girl's only known relative is her mother-in-law, Widow Cai."

The Jade Emperor turned to his aides. "Bring me the Book of Life and Death," he commanded. "I wish to find out if Dou Tianzhang is still in the land of the living or not."

The aides scurried off to fetch the tome, and the Jade Emperor perused it. Putting it down, he said, with a frown: "This Dou E is fated to suffer the injustice you spoke of. Her father has joined the ranks of officialdom. He abandoned the girl to seek fame and fortune, and so he is the one who is destined to right the wrong. Three years from now, it is decreed, he will be dispatched to Chuzhou to inspect the record of criminal cases there, and he himself will redress the injustice done to his daughter. Now, you, Local God of Shanyang, go back to the place of execution, and whatever last wish Dou E has make sure you fulfill it. I will send the host of immortals to assist you. That way, retribution will be seen to assert the Way of Heaven!"

The Local God bade a hurried farewell to the Jade Emperor, and sped off back down to Earth on his cloud. Peeping over the edge of the cloud, he observed all that was taking place at the execution ground. The host of the immortals rallied behind him, ready to carry out whatever last appeal Dou E made.

Meanwhile, as Dou E and Widow Cai clung to each other, weeping and lamenting, the guards were becoming impatient. "It's nearly noon," they reminded the two women. "You mustn't delay any longer, or the chief executioner will be angry!"

Zhang Qian ordered the guards to drag Widow Cai away and force Dou E to make her final steps. The old woman had no choice but to follow along with the crowd.

The chief executioner himself could not help but feel sorry for the bedraggled girl who tottered towards him. Her tear-streaked face was haggard and wan, her clothes were in tatters and her blood-caked body bore all the hallmarks of torture. But he said, gruffly: "Are you the female criminal Dou E? What do you mean by standing, defiantly facing your executioner, instead of kneeling?"

"Yes, I am Dou E," was the reply. "I am the victim of a monstrous injustice. I was forced to confess to a crime I did not commit, by corrupt officials. I will not be able to close my eyes in death. So why should I kneel to you, who is about to deprive an innocent person of life?"

The executioner saw that Dou E had an unyielding spirit and was filled with righteous indignation. Without more ado, he turned to his assistants, and said, "This woman has been identified as the criminal Dou E. Remove her bonds, and prepare to carry out the sentence!"

The two assistants, fiendish-looking ruffians carrying huge scimitars, stepped forward, and removed the chains and shackles that weighed so heavily on Dou E's wasted frame. Then, one on each side, they took her arms preparatory to tying her to the execution stake.

But Dou E shook them off, knelt down in front of the chief executioner, and said, "Sir, I am the victim of injustice!"

The chief executioner motioned his two assistants to stand back, and said, "Just now, you refused to kneel to me. Why are you kneeling now?"

Dou E replied, "I was overcome with fury at the unjustness of my treatment, and so refused to kneel. But now I wish to make an appeal to Heaven. If you will allow me to do so, I will resign myself to my fate, and you may carry out your duty."

The other said, "I heard that you protested vociferously all the way here that you are the victim of injustice. I presume that this case is a complicated one. However, I have my orders, and must carry them out. Nevertheless, to ease your ordeal, you may say what you wish to say."

"If I were to go mute to my death, wronged as I am," explained Dou E, "the Way of Heaven would be obscured, and there would be no distinguishing between good and evil. I have heard that during the Zhou Dynasty, there was a loyal minister named Chang Hong, whose downfall was brought about by the slander of sycophants. After his death, his blood turned into jade, preserving his body from decay. Then there was Du Yu, King of Shu, who was driven from the throne by rascally ministers. He died of a broken heart, and his soul turned into a cuckoo. Every time spring came around, it cried tears of blood. These are two examples of how Heaven and Earth, reminded later generations of the bitter injustices that had been committed. But the injustice done to me, Dou E, far surpasses in atrociousness those done to Chang Hong and Du Yu. I want a clean mat to stand on, and a ten-foot-long piece of white silk hung from the flagpole. I make a solemn declaration to everybody, right here, that if I am innocent, the moment my head falls from my body not a single drop of my blood will stain the ground. Instead, it will all fly up and soak into the silk. Then everybody will be able to see that I have been the victim of injustice and have wrongly become a headless ghost. This will be known for all time to come. If you, sir, will agree to this, I hereby render my deepest gratitude in advance."

The chief executioner hesitated. "I can see no objection to your request," he said, "but where can I find such things as a clean mat and a long piece of white silk on such a pressing occasion?"

Dou E said, "You are most kind, sir, and I am sure that someone in this huge throng will be able to produce these items in no time at all, without delaying your busy schedule."

The chief executioner gazed upon Dou E with profound pity. Then he spun round to face the crowd of onlookers. "Pay attention!" he cried. "This condemned person has one last request to make. She desires a clean mat and a ten-foot length of white silk. If you have any charity in your hearts, please look around and find such common objects, so that she may go to the netherworld content!"

The response was instantaneous. Dozens of people scurried around, and soon came back with a clean mat and the required length of white silk. The chief executioner ordered his assistants to hang the silk from the flagpole and place the mat for Dou E to stand on. All was set for the execution to go ahead.

Dou E drew herself up to her full height. Exuding righteous indignation, she raised her face to Heaven. Not a word did she speak. The noonday sun blazed down upon her. In fact, it was the time for the sentence to be carried out.

The two assistant executioners, despite being hardened takers of life, were somewhat disconcerted by the sight. "Dou E," they urged, "if you have something else to say to our master, please say it. Why this delay?"

Dou E thereupon said to the chief executioner: "Sir, I stand here, under the scorching sky of the hottest part of the year. If I am the victim of a heinous injustice, may this be proved by a fall of three feet of snow which will cover my corpse as soon as death takes me!"

Astonished, the chief executioner could not help but lift his eyes to the sky, where he saw a merciless sun beaming its fiery rays down on the baking earth. He sighed, and said, "Dou E, perhaps it is true that you have been grievously wronged. But to expect Heaven to send snow during the Dog Days of the year, when the sun is roasting the earth and parching the crops, is preposterous!"

Dou E calmly replied, "Sir, have you not heard the story of the loyal minister Zou Yan of the State of Yan during the Warring States Period? He was cast into prison on account of base slander. Unable to express his anguish, he simply gazed up to Heaven and wept — and, sure enough, there was a snow flurry in the sixth month! You say that a scorching sun is blazing in the sky, and this is not the season for snow. But I assure you that the injustice I am suffering and the overwhelming resentment I feel will so move Heaven that it will send snow as a white mourning garment to cover my wronged spirit and martyred bones."

The chief executioner was doubtful, and all he could do was shake his head and sigh over Dou E's pathetic condition. Just then, there came a chill gust of wind, the moaning of which grew steadily louder. Black clouds rolled across the sky, until the sun was hidden by them. In an instant, the air and the ground became icy cold. The two assistants, naked from the waist up, were already shivering violently. The bystanders were astonished, and began to mutter among themselves.

This strange phenomenon caused a thrill of emotion to run through Dou E. She was sure that this was a sign that Heaven and Earth had been moved by her sad plight. She immediately fell to her knees, and addressed Heaven once more: "Oh vast firmament, if you really have a soul which recognizes that an injustice is being done to me, I pray that you will afflict Chuzhou with three years of drought."

This last appeal angered the chief executioner. "What are you saying?" he demanded indignantly. "How can you pray for three years of drought for the whole of Chuzhou just on account of a supposed injustice caused to you alone?"

"Sir," came the reply, "It is the duty of the Emperor of Heaven on high to discern the good and bad deeds of mortals here on Earth. How can the Emperor of Heaven allow corrupt officials to run rampant, misusing the law for their own ends, and beheading innocent people? Surely this is not a matter that concerns one person only? During the Han Dynasty, there was a filial girl who lived in Donghai. When she was unjustly executed there followed a severe famine that lasted for three years in the Donghai area. Later, when the head of the prefecture exonerated her, Heaven released the rain. The reason for my appealing to Heaven just now for it to send snow in the hottest part of the summer followed by three years of drought was to prove to later generations that I am the victim of injustice." With that, Dou E stood on the clean mat, and said no more.

Seeing that the time had come to carry out the sentence, the chief executioner ordered his two assistants to bind Dou E to the execution stake. Throwing down his warrant, he called out, "The time is at noon. Carry out the sentence!"

A scimitar flashed, and Dou E's head rolled upon the ground, as fresh blood spurted from her neck cavity. At this very moment, the Local God of Shanyang, who had been watching the seen, together with the posse of immortals, from behind his cloud, blew a strong puff of breath. The blood shot straight up into the air and spattered the strip of white silk, not a single drop staining the ground. At almost the same time, large shining-white snowflakes began to fall, filling the sky and blanketing the earth. Dou E's corpse was soon completely hidden in snow.

The two executioners had never seen anything like this in their whole careers of dispatching people to the next world. Shaken, they cast aside their scimitars, and howled, "We have killed a dutiful woman! We have slaughtered an innocent person! The Emperor of Heaven will never forgive us!" Wailing and crying, they fled from the uncanny scene as fast as their legs would carry them.

Watching them as they disappeared, the chief executioner

sighed, and said to himself: "This execution of an innocent person is bound to bring down the wrath of Heaven!" He then ordered the guards to march back to the magistracy, while he went to the same place to report on the happenings of that day.

When the officials left the place of execution, Widow Cai and her neighbors fetched a coffin, placed Dou E's corpse in it, and buried it outside the city. A gravestone was set up, and the grieving old woman performed a sacrifice before it.

CHAPTER EIGHT

The Emperor's Inspector

AS THE CROWDS dispersed from the execution ground, the Local God of Shanyang and his escort of immortals returned to the Heavenly Palace to report to the Jade Emperor. They found him already waiting for them in his Golden Bell Hall. The Local God kowtowed, and said, "Your Heavenly Majesty, just before her death, Dou E made three appeals. One was for her blood to be spattered on a piece of hanging white silk, another was for snow to fall right now in this hottest part of the summer, and the third was for a three-year drought to afflict the Chuzhou area. Well, Your Heavenly Majesty, I took it upon myself to carry out the first two tasks. As for the third, I thought it wise to consult you first."

"I will take care of that," said the Jade Emperor. "You don't have to worry about it. In the meantime, Dou E now being dead, her aggrieved spirit will soon start wandering all over the place, and we might even lose her whereabouts altogether. Then how could we redress her injustice? I want you to go straight back down to Earth and take Dou E's spirit into your shrine with you. Then, after three years her father Dou Tianzhang will arrive in Chuzhou to inspect the magistrate's records. At that time she will meet her father again and be able to pour out her grief to him."

The Local God kowtowed, and hurried off to carry out his mission.

He came across the spirit of Dou E hovering around not far from the scene of the tragedy. He explained how he and the host of immortals had been delegated by the Jade Emperor to carry out her final behests. "The Jade Emperor, moreover, has instructed me to look after you for the next three years." he added, "When your father arrives in Chuzhou to inspect the magistrate's records, he will be able to right the injustice which has been done to you."

When she heard that her father was still alive, and, moreover, would come to avenge her, Dou E's spirit was transported with joy and thanked the Local God over and over again. The latter then escorted her to the imperial shrine, where he made arrangements for her to stay, enjoining her to have patience.

From the very day on which Dou E had been executed, not a drop of rain fell on the Chuzhou region for three years. The reason for this, stemming as it did from one of Dou E's last requests, was soon universally known to the local people. They uttered rancorous curses against the venal officials who had caused them so much hardship. Taowu, however, relying on his father's influence at court, made sure that no news of the drought reached his superiors and was even promoted to the position of prefectural magistrate of Chuzhou. Despite the severity of the drought, with the farmland parched for miles around, he continued to report to the court that the weather was favorable, the rains timely, harvests abundant, the people living long lives in contentment, and the law-and-order situation excellent. At the same time, he continued with his tyrannical and extortive ways, while living, as usual, a life of idleness and dissipation.

During these three years of drought, throughout the Chuzhou region wells dried up, the tips of the trees were scorched, and the crops withered. Grain became as expensive as gold. The farmers left their villages in droves, a pathetic sight as they supported the old people hobbling along, carried infants on their backs, and half-dragged their children and womenfolk. To add to their distress, the local avaricious officials and hired ruffians plundered them of what little they had, and cases of murder and arson were too numerous to count. The whole of Chuzhou resounded to laments.

In the midst of this calamity, Widow Cai, now well advanced in years and robbed of her silver by Zhang the Mule (who had also by this time sold her house), was reduced to begging by the roadside. She never knew from day to day where her next meal was coming from. Whenever she reminisced about the old days, when she had been looked after by Dou E, she shed bitter tears of anguish. It was fortunate for her — although she was not aware of it — that the spirit of her daughter-in-law and the Local God of Shanyang were watching over her; otherwise she would have starved to death long ago.

After he had left his daughter with Widow Cai, Dou Tianzhang traveled alone to the capital. There, he sat for the imperial examination, passing with flying colors. At this time, the country had been pacified, and the emperor's policy direction had turned from military campaigning to enhancing civil administration. Dou Tianzhang was appointed magistrate of Gaoliang County in Jiang Prefecture. Eager to be reunited with his daughter, one of the first things he did was to send one of his trusted aides on a swift horse and with plenty of money to Chuzhou to fetch her. But, to his dismay, the man reported that Dou's old neighbors had told him that Widow Cai had moved away, unable to endure the bullying of some of the people she lent money to. Nobody seemed to know where she and his little Duanyun had gone.

The grief-stricken Dou Tianzhang wanted desperately to go and look for her himself. But he had an imperial mission to undertake, and dared not delay his departure for Gaoliang County.

Dou Tianzhang came from humble origins, and knew well the sufferings of the common people. In his new office, he did much to lighten the burden of the people he governed. As if to show its approval, Heaven blessed Gaoliang County with favorable weather and bumper harvests, and prosperity and joy were the order of the day under the benevolent stewardship of Dou Tianzhang. At the end of his three-year term of office, the local gentry sent a memorial to the throne, thanking the emperor for sending them such a diligent and kindly magistrate. Pleased, the emperor promoted Dou to prefect of Jiangzhou.

In his new post, Dou Tianzhang acquitted himself with equal credit, whether in administration, supervising the officials under his command, visiting the peasants in their fields or sitting in judgment on court cases. His sympathy for the people, coupled with his mastery of the law, which he had acquired at an early age, ensured that Jiang Prefecture was well governed, and its people lived in harmony and in the midst of plenty. The local officials were honest; justice was dispensed impartially; the common people were full of appreciation for the work of Dou Tianzhang.

When the emperor heard reports of this, he was highly pleased. "This official is a credit to my rule," he mused. "Wherever he is sent, he gladdens the hearts of the people. Theft becomes unknown, and people don't even bother to lock their doors at night. There have been many faithful officials in the past — indeed, bulwarks of the state — but none that I have heard of can measure up to this man Dou Tianzhang!" The emperor thereupon ordered that a decree be issued appointing Dou Tianzhang a court minister, with the portfolio of special assistant to the emperor himself.

Upon receiving this news, Dou Tianzhang left straightaway for the capital. He was received in audience without delay, where the emperor congratulated him on his sterling efforts. Dou Tianzhang kowtowed, and replied, "I did nothing but my duty, Your Majesty. But it was because Your Majesty follows the will of Heaven and complies with the people's wishes that the land is content and thrives under the administration of such humble servants as myself." At this, his first face-to-face meeting with Dou Tianzhang, the emperor was impressed by the man's modesty and sincerity. As a result, he promoted him to a post in the secretariat, with special responsibility for reviewing court cases and impeaching corrupt officials.

Thenceforth, Dou Tianzhang enjoyed immense power and prestige, being especially trusted by the emperor. Nevertheless, he was as upright, hardworking and immune to flattery as before. In his rare moments of leisure, he read, cultivated flowers and seemed outwardly carefree. But there was a cloud hanging over him that he could not dispel, and that was the anguish of not knowing what had happened to his daughter Duanyun. This was especially so when, in the dead of night, his dying wife's last injunction to him to look after the girl would steal upon him unawares. For ten years, he had been dispatching men all over the country to search for the girl, but not a single scrap of news had they managed to obtain. Every time he recalled that moment of parting, Dou Tianzhang would be so overcome with grief that he would break down in tears. As the years went by, this weight of mental suffering made his eyes grow dim and his hair and beard turn a sickly white.

Then one day, quite unexpectedly, the emperor fell ill. The court physicians tried every remedy they could think of, but all to no avail. Before long, it seemed that the emperor was hovering on the brink of death. At this point, Minister Ahema took advantage of the power vacuum to seize control of the government. He then formed a faction, and farmed out magisterial posts all over the country to his cronies.

When the emperor finally did die, which was only a few days later, a mere three days of mourning was observed. Ahema then emerged as the most powerful figure at court. He placed his own favorite on the vacant throne, as Emperor Chengzong, with the reign period title Yuanzhen. The usual general amnesty for criminals was proclaimed. With the new emperor under his thumb and his picked men in all the positions of power in the country, Ahema instituted a reign of ruthless extortion and oppression. Dou Tianzhang and the handful of upright officials still remaining at court viewed the situation with growing alarm. They were adamant that Ahema should be impeached before the emperor, but the former was so powerful at this time, that they dared make no rash move, and were forced to bide their time. However, before a year was out the new emperor became fully aware of the misdeeds of his chief minister and of how he had placed his own trusted subordinates in key positions in both the court and the provinces. He became aware too of how most of his officials were mere toadies, whereas in reality he himself was held in contempt as a mere puppet throughout the empire. Emperor Chengzong was careful to hide his anger, while quietly gathering evidence of Ahema's treachery. When all was ready, he secretly summoned

Chief of Military Affairs Jin Gui, Minister of Personnel Affairs Cui Gun and Chief of Administration Dou Tianzhang to the palace for consultation as to how to deal with Ahema. The plan they finally came up with was to send loyal officials to the provinces, where they would deal severely with Ahema's henchmen who had committed crimes, thereby tightening the noose about Ahema himself.

The next morning, after the court officials had greeted the emperor, he addressed them thus: "Since I ascended the throne, I have been gratified to see that you all have made every effort to assist my administration wholeheartedly. As a result, the empire is at peace; the seasons are timely and the people joyous. This is a great comfort to me. Now, those of you with memorials to present to me, may do so. Those without any may withdraw."

Cui Gun immediately stepped forward. "Your Majesty, I, Minister of Personnel Affairs Cui Gun, have a memorial to submit to the throne," he said.

"You may do so," said the emperor.

Cui Gun continued, "Your Majesty, recently I have received a flurry of complaints from all over the empire that officials in charge of prefectures and counties are acting in cruel ways, bending the law to their own advantage and oppressing the people most heinously. Yet the court does not heed the people's calls for justice. If this situation continues, I fear it may lead to an uprising and great chaos under Heaven." He continued, "I venture to propose that Your Majesty send honest and upright officials to the provinces to check on the conduct of the local magistrates, especially by re-examining court cases. In that way, evil magistrates will be punished and the grievances of the people will be redressed. The empire and the people will then thrive once more."

Emperor Chengzong expressed anger at hearing that local magistrates were not behaving themselves. "The local officials should act as the parents of the people, as well as acting as my brothers," he exclaimed. "How dare they neglect their duties and oppress my subjects? Very well, it shall be as you suggest. Pick honest and upright officials from the court to make inspection tours of the provinces. Give them instructions to strictly punish corrupt magistrates and put things to rights in the name of the emperor!"

The assembled court officials then jostled with each other to offer their opinions, and eventually a dozen trustworthy men were chosen to go on circuits throughout the country. Dou Tianzhang was sent to the area of what is now Anhui Province. Upon receiving his commission, Dou Tianzhang said, "Your Majesty's decision to root out evil wherever it may be found throughout the country, and promote good, to rectify government administration and solidify the foundations of the state will bring great rejoicing among the people. For my own part, although I lack talent, I can assure Your Majesty that I will do my utmost to help Your Majesty sweep the bane of misrule from the land."

Pleased, Emperor Chengzong replied, "Dou Tianzhang, you are a loyal and upright minister. Moreover, you are a master of the law. Your responsibility for inspecting Anhui is a great one, and sly villains may attempt to hinder your investigations. So, I hereby invest in you the highest authority an emperor may delegate, as symbolized by this precious sword and gold tablet. If you uncover instances in which local officials have committed atrocious crimes that have aroused great indignation among the people, you have the right to execute the perpetrators first and report afterwards. I am relying on your good faith not to fall short of my expectations."

Dou Tianzhang kowtowed, and thanked the emperor for this special mark of favor, adding the ritual vow: "Even though it would mean my liver and brains being splattered on the ground, I would never dare go against Your Majesty's will! I will dedicate every fiber of my being to sharing the country's burden."

Meanwhile, Ahema watched this unexpected development unfold with growing alarm. His first impulse was to object to this forthcoming inspection, but was afraid of rousing the emperor's suspicions if he did so. Therefore, for the time being, he had to pretend to acquiesce in the plan. But as soon as court was dismissed, he dashed off messages to his cohorts all round the country, warning them to take care to hide all traces of their past wrongdoings, at least until the "storm" had passed.

Back in his office, Dou Tianzhang ordered his manservant to pack for the journey, as they would be leaving for Anhui on the morrow. The orderly was delighted to hear that his master's errand was to inspect the system of justice and examine court cases in Anhui. "You will be returning to your native place resplendent in the trappings of success, sir. Congratulations! What's more, you will surely be able to mount a thorough search for your long-lost daughter when you get there."

"This mission involves a heavy responsibility; I fear that I may not be up to the task. You have served me for many years, to my great satisfaction I may add. And so I will entrust the search for my daughter entirely to you."

Early the next morning, Dou Tianzhang and his retinue boarded a boat, which was to take them south to Anhui along the Grand Canal. When they arrived, a few days later, Dou Tianzhang insisted on disembarking in civilian clothes, and making an investigation of local conditions incognito, accompanied only by his trusted manservant. Having ascertained the feelings of the local people and whether the officials of the place were honest or not, he returned to the boat, gathered his belongings, and proceeded with his full escort to Chuzhou.

In the few days it took to reach Chuzhou, Dou Tianzhang found himself appalled at the desolation he saw all around him. The land was parched, and littered with the bodies of those who had died of hunger. What few crops there were had withered. Whole families were fleeing the drought-stricken land in countless numbers. Puzzled, he thought to himself: "This drought is obviously one of long duration. But over the past few years there have been no reports to the court of such difficulties in Chuzhou! This is most odd!" He found the local people reluctant to talk to this high court official, learning from them only that not a drop of rain had fallen in the district for three years, resulting in a total crop failure.

As they neared the seat of Chuzhou Prefecture itself, Dou Tianzhang said to his orderly: "I intend to go straight to the magistracy, where I will rest and hold discussions with the magistrate. I want you to spend the next three days making inquiries about my daughter. Then, whether you find her or not, report to me."

Prefectural Magistrate Taowu, having been forewarned by his

father, was already awaiting his illustrious visitor at the gate of the magistracy, together with all his subordinates both civil and military long before Dou Tianzhang hove into view. Taowu hastened to usher Dou Tianzhang into the reception room, where tea was served and polite pleasantries exchanged. Then the magistrate ordered refreshments. Dou Tianzhang was taken aback when he saw the sumptuousness of the feast that was produced — no delicacy of farm, river or vineyard was absent. As the scenes of desolation in the countryside he had only recently witnessed crowded back into his mind, Dou Tianzhang lost his appetite completely for the banquet laid before him. Glancing at the florid face of Taowu, munching and quaffing, apparently quite oblivious to the sufferings of the common people in his care, Dou Tianzhang could not help thinking bitterly: "Unless this tyrannical parasite and his ilk are eliminated, the ordinary people will never be at ease, and their hearts will be difficult to win!"

After a while, Taowu, by this time well into his cups, asked Dou Tianzhang where he was lodging and how long he intended to remain in Chuzhou.

The other replied, "I intend to lodge here, at the magistracy. I have been sent by the emperor to inspect the Anhui region. I am only able to spend three to five days in each place, and Chuzhou is no exception. I am quite content to find that this prefecture is in your safe hands, sir, as your noble father was most kind to me before I left the capital. I have called on you merely as a matter of routine. If you would be so kind as to send for the prefectural court records, I will peruse them at my leisure."

Greatly relieved to hear this, Taowu sent a man to fetch the documents. At the same time, he sent another man to bring a large wooden box from the rear hall. Turning to Dou Tianzhang, he said, in a wheedling tone: "Sir, our humble prefecture is nothing more than an impoverished backwater. I hope you will not find these shabby welcoming gifts too ludicrous."

Dou Tianzhang knew perfectly well that he was about to be offered a bribe. He recoiled at the thought, but at the same time was afraid that he might put Taowu on his guard. So he lifted the lid of the box. The inside was crammed with pearls and jewels, equivalent to the wealth of several cities. He feigned delight. "You are so thoughtful, sir!" he gushed. "It would, of course, be impolite of me to refuse to accept. However, I feel I am unworthy such a gift. I must leave it to one side for the moment." Thereupon, he ordered the man who had brought it, to take the box back to the rear hall.

Deceived into thinking that Dou Tianzhang had accepted the bribe, Taowu found himself in the mood for carousing contentedly. His guest, however, was in no mood to accompany him, and used the excuse of a fatiguing journey to retire early to bed. The magistrate and his cronies escorted Dou Tianzhang to his quarters, and spent the rest of the night making merry.

CHAPTER NINE

A Ghost Appeals for Justice

THE NEXT DAY, Dou Tianzhang started the task of examining the court records of Chuzhou Prefecture. These records going back several years had all been carefully doctored by Taowu, and after three days of minute examination Dou Tianzhang could find nothing more incriminating than a few minor flaws. He was convinced that Taowu was involved in corrupt practices up to his ears, and it grieved him to be unable to unearth concrete evidence. He was thus in low spirits when his orderly, whom he had sent to try to find news of his daughter's whereabouts, returned. Putting aside the document he was examining, he asked the man eagerly what he had learned. But the report was disappointing. "Sir, the outskirts of Chuzhou these days are a wasteland, and few people remain there," said the manservant. "I first went to Your Honor's old home, only to find it in ruins and the neighborhood deserted. I next went to the shrine where you once took shelter. It too is derelict. Then I traced the old home of Widow Cai. This also is in ruins. The only person still living in the vicinity was a white-haired old man, and he didn't even remember Widow Cai. So I decided the search was fruitless, and returned to report, sir."

Dou Tianzhang was lost in thought for a long while. Finally, he said, "I have instructed inquiries to be made in those places you visited several times in the past-all to no avail. Clearly, Widow Cai has moved to another district to avoid the famine. In the meantime, I have examined the Chuzhou court records going back several years, but I can find nothing really wrong with them. They've been tampered with by Taowu; I've no doubt about that. If I want to find solid evidence of his venality and misgovernment, it will be necessary to make discreet inquiries. Tomorrow I want you to visit the poor people in the town — without revealing your identity, of course — and ask them about Taowu's conduct. That way, perhaps we can get enough facts to indict him on criminal charges. The search for my daughter will have to be postponed."

The orderly was about to retire, when Dou Tianzhang called him back. "First, bring me the records of penal sentences for the past few years. I will make a search through them for cases of miscarriage of justice."

The man did so, placing them on Dou Tianzhang's desk and lighting the lamp, as dusk was closing in. After he had left, Dou Tianzhang sighed for a while, and then started to read the new batch of documents. But he found it difficult to concentrate. Ever since he had returned to Chuzhou, a place he had left as a poor scholar 16 years previously, as an envoy of the emperor his heart had been in turmoil. The area had been ravaged by drought for three years; the land was cracked and arid for a thousand *li* in every direction; famine stalked the land. Yet not a word of this had been reported to the imperial court. And during all this terrible time, the local magistrate never ceased to wallow in luxury and debauchery. This monster must be made to answer for his crimes as soon as possible, Dou Tianzhang was convinced. But, he recalled with anguish, the documents he had seen so far were all in order; there was no legal hook to hang Taowu on. What disturbed him in addition was his orderly's report that there was still no news of his beloved daughter. He still did not know even whether she was alive or dead. He reflected bitterly that for all his sword of state and other credentials as the emperor's envoy, which made him one of the most powerful men in the country, he could not gaze on his own daughter's face.

He was afflicted by a terrible sense of having let the girl down. From the time that she had been born, she had suffered privation and hunger with him. She had only been three years-old when her mother passed away, and at the age of seven she had been placed in another's house to be brought up as the bride of the son. For 16 years he had had no news of her. It was possible that she had not survived this terrible three-year drought, when the price of rice had soared until it was more expensive than pearls and firewood was more expensive than the rarest teak. The people had fled from the land in droves. It was more than likely that she had joined the exodus. If some catastrophe had overtaken his beloved child, how could he face her mother in the next world?

Locked in these gloomy reveries, Dou Tianzhang was suddenly startled by the drumbeat announcing the second watch of the night. He mumbled to himself: "Well, that's enough of such idle speculation. There's never an end to regret and resentment. Perhaps my man will bring back some news of the girl when he has finished his inquiries this time. Meanwhile, I'd better get on with examining these records of penal sentences."

He looked at the case document on top of the pile. It bore the title, "Criminal Dou E. Beheaded for Poisoning her Father-in-Law."

"That's a coincidence," he thought. "Same surname as mine! Poisoning one's father-in-law: That falls into the category of the ten felonies for which there can be no forgiveness. Death by beheading: Standard procedure. No, I can't find anything wrong with this case."

He muttered aloud to himself: "There are plenty of people with the same surname in this world, I suppose. This Dou was probably not even remotely related to me. Horrendous crime, poisoning one's father-in-law. Anyway, that's enough of that. Let's move on to the next case." He put the document on the bottom of the pile. As he was reading the next document, he felt a wave of fatigue sweep over him. He yawned, leaned his forehead on the desk, and fell into a deep slumber.

All this time, the spirit of Dou E had been living in the shrine of the Local God of Shanyang, feeding off the sacrificial offerings. Every time she thought of the injustice she had suffered, her heart was pierced with anguish, and she shed secret tears. The kind-hearted Local God did his best to make her comfortable, and in this way three years passed.

One day, the Local God was sitting on his altar as usual, making supernatural calculations, when he suddenly realized that something unusual was about to happen that very day. That evening, he summoned the spirit of Dou E, and said to her: "My dear, your father has been appointed an imperial inspector, with the special duty of inspecting the Anhui area. In fact, he has been in Chuzhou for three days already. He's staying at the magistracy. Now is your chance to get the injustice you have suffered for three years righted. Tonight you can appear to your father in a dream, tell him about the wrong done to you, and appeal to him to redress your grievance."

Hearing this, Dou E's spirit burst into a flood of tears. "I was only seven years old when I parted from my father," she sobbed. "Sixteen years have passed, and I thought we would never meet again, now that I am in the land of the dead while he is still in the land of the living. But, dear Local God, may my father and I only meet in a dream?"

The Local God replied tenderly: "My dear young lady, you dwell in the netherworld, and your father is a court official of the second rank on earth. You inhabit different spheres; how can you meet in daylight? Do as I say: Go to the magistracy tonight, and appear to your father in a dream. But don't tarry too long; you must be back here before dawn breaks. Once you have explained to him the injustice that has been your fate, he will come straight to Shanyang County, I'm sure, to redress this case. And in due time, you will be able to help him to do so."

Dou E thanked him, and sped through the wind and dew to Chuzhou, where she alighted in the rear hall of the magistracy. She perceived that a lamp was burning in the study. Moistening the paper of the study window with her tongue, she poked a peephole in it. She saw a man with grizzled beard and hair slumped over a desk, as if sleeping. Tears scalded her eyes as she uttered a strangled cry: "Father!" Without more ado, she pushed open the door, and entered the study.

In his sleep, Dou Tianzhang seemed to hear someone call out

"Father!" And, in a dream-like trance, he seemed to reply, "Duanyun, my child! Where are you?"

Dou E's spirit flitted into the shaded part of the room, where she stood still without making a sound.

Dou Tianzhang woke up, rubbed his eyes, and mumbled, "How strange! I had only just closed my eyes when I heard what sounded like Duanyun calling me. It was as though she were standing right in front of me. But I can see that she isn't. My old ears and eyes must be playing tricks on me. Well, now that I'm wide awake again, I suppose I should continue examining these documents." With that, he took a dossier from the pile, and began to read it.

As he bent his head to the page before him, Dou E's spirit stole out of its hiding place, and covered the lamp flame with its hands. The sudden dimming of the light caused Dou Tianzhang to look up in annoyance. "What a nuisance!" he grumbled. "Just when I was getting down to work again, there's something wrong with the lamp. I'd better go and trim the wick." As he left the desk to go and attend to the lamp, Dou E took the opportunity to take her own file from the bottom of the pile and put it on the top.

Having trimmed the lamp wick, Dou Tianzhang returned to his work. He was startled to find that the document on the top of the pile clearly read "Criminal Dou E. Beheaded for Poisoning her Father-in-Law." He thought to himself: "Surely, this was the first file I examined. And I know that I put it on the bottom of the pile. How did it get back on the top of the pile? Perhaps I only dreamt that I read it."

He then put the document back on the bottom of the pile, and picked up the second dossier. Seeing this, the spirit of Dou E wanted to alert her father of his negligence. But, not wishing to frighten him, she simply blew a stream of cold air, which made the lamp flame flicker. Dou Tianzhang rubbed his eyes, and then, deciding that there was something wrong with the lamp, got up to trim the wick again. As he did so, the nimble Dou E put her case file back on the top of the pile.

When Dou Tianzhang resumed his reading, he was flabbergasted to see once more before his eyes the words "Criminal Dou E. Beheaded for Poisoning her Father-in-Law." He exclaimed,

"Good Heavens! I definitely put this document on the bottom of the pile. I'm absolutely certain. And then, when I went to see to the lamp, it somehow jumped back on top! Surely, there can't be a ghost in here, can there? There must be something fishy about this particular case if it keeps shoving itself under my nose like this. I'll put it back on the bottom of the pile, and see what happens."

Sure enough, when Dou Tianzhang put DouE's document on the bottom of the pile for the third time, the girl's spirit again made the lamp flicker. This time, Dou Tianzhang only pretended to be going to fix the lamp, all the time keeping his eye on the pile of documents. As Dou E anxiously darted out from the shadows, and replaced her dossier on the top of the pile again, Dou Tianzhang saw her quite clearly. What he saw in fact was a young girl with disheveled hair and a tear-streaked face interfering with his documents. She was also uncannily vague and vapor-like in outline. Astonished and affrighted, Dou Tianzhang snatched up his sword of office, and bellowed, "Who or what are you, to invade this magistracy at the dead of night in the shape of a young girl? How dare you keep meddling with the business of the emperor's special envoy? I am Dou Tianzhang, dispatched to Anhui to check that justice is being done and examine the conduct of officials. What I grasp in my hand right now is my sword of office, a symbol of my power to expel evil. If you dare to indulge in any more of this sinister trickery I will slice you in two!"

Dou E saw that there was no point trying to hide any longer. Instead, she threw herself on her knees, and cried out, "Father, don't be afraid! I am your daughter, Dou E, whom you have not seen for 16 years!"

Dou Tianzhang was perplexed. "But my daughter's name is Duanyun," he said. "At the age of seven she was delivered to the Cai household to be brought up as a bride for Widow Cai's son. I have not set eyes on her since then. You may have the same surname as myself, but there is no Dou E in our family. How then can you be my daughter? Stop talking such nonsense!"

"Father!" wailed Dou E, shedding tears, "For the past 16 years there has not been one day when I did not pine for you. And now that I finally meet you again, you refuse to recognize your own daughter! Father, I really am the unfortunate Duanyun. Widow Cai gave me the name Dou E after I went to live with her."

At this, Dou Tianzhang looked closely at the girl. When he perceived that her arched brows bore a distinct resemblance to those of his deceased wife, he was convinced that the mysterious apparition was indeed his long-lost daughter. Unable to control his emotions, he burst into tears. He raised Dou E to her feet, and said, "Yes, I am convinced now that you really are Duanyun, whom I have missed for 16 years. When I left you with Widow Cai, I went to the capital to take the imperial examination. To my great surprise, I passed first time, and entered the ranks of officialdom. The first thing I did was to send men to bring you to me. But they returned, only to report that Widow Cai had moved away, and nobody knew where she had gone. Then for the next ten years or so, I had men scour the whole region of Chuzhou, but to no avail. All this time, I wept until my eyes grew dim, and mourned until my hair and beard turned white. Finally, I have found you here, of all places!"

The spirit of Dou E hugged itself to Dou Tianzhang's breast, and wept silently. Her father also shed bitter tears. After a long while, Dou Tianzhang suddenly asked, "Duanyun, my child, where are you living now? And why have you come here, to the magistracy in Chuzhou, so late at night?"

Still weeping, Dou E prostrated herself on the floor. "Are you still unaware, father," she groaned, "that Duanyun was unjustly put to death? What you see before you is no more than a grieving ghost crying for vengeance."

Dou Tianzhang tottered backwards, in a state of shock. His voice wavered and he demanded, "My child, what is the meaning of this? Who caused you to be put to death unjustly? When we finally meet again after 16 years, we are still divided because we live in two different worlds — one of light, and the other of shadows! Oh, I can't bear the pain of this too cruel fate!"

At that moment, the remembrance of the document he had read hit him like a thunderbolt. His hair stood on end with horror. "Are you the person who poisoned her father-in-law?" he demanded.

"I am the person mentioned in that case file," came the reply.

Dou Tianzhang was incensed. "You accursed vixen!" he roared.

"While I was weeping till my eyes dimmed, and sorrowed till my beard and hair turned gray, you committed one of the ten most horrid crimes imaginable; a crime for which there can be no pardon. For this, you paid the extreme price, and quite rightly so. How will you be able to face your mother in the nether world. When I entrusted you to the Cai household, I impressed upon you the importance of adhering strictly to the Three Obediences and Four Virtues by which a woman is required to be obedient to her father before marriage, to her husband during marriage and to her son in widowhood; and to exercise the virtues of fidelity, charm, propriety in speech and efficiency in needlework. Is this how you repay me for educating you in the classics and rites until you were seven years old? By committing a dastardly crime? For three generations there has been not one man of the Dou family who has committed a crime, and not one woman for five generations who has disgraced the clan by remarrying. Not only have you besmirched the honor of our ancestors, you have tarnished my own good name! I am amazed that you have the audacity to approach me!"

Her father's tongue-lashing cut the spirit of Dou E to the quick. Weeping even more uncontrollably, she pleaded, "Father, you must know that I am the victim of a most dreadful injustice. Let me ask you this: When you handed me over to Widow Cai to be brought up as her daughter-in-law, was her husband still alive?"

Dou Tianzhang was puzzled. "At that time, she had already been widowed for some years, as I recall," he said. "She had a son, but no husband. Unless, of course, she married again later."

"I can assure you, father," replied the spirit of Dou E, "that she did not."

"Well, that is indeed strange!" mused Dou Tianzhang. "If Widow Cai did not remarry, how did you come to have a father-in-law? It really does seem that there has been a miscarriage of justice in this case. Sit down, my dear, and tell me what happened. I will then be able to right the wrong done to you."

So the spirit of Dou E, which for three years had not been able to open her heart to anyone, now poured out the full story of her sufferings to her father. She told him how Widow Cai, having been saved quite by accident by the two Zhangs from being strangled by Sai Lu Yi, had been bullied by them into promising to accept them as husbands for herself and Dou E. She related how Zhang the Mule, rebuffed by Dou E, had plotted to poison the old woman, but ended up poisoning his own father instead. "Zhang the Mule, to save his own skin, charged me with the crime," she said. "At that time, Taowu, who is now the head of Chuzhou Prefecture, was magistrate of Shanyang County. He invited me to a feast, and told me that if I let him have his way with me he would find a way to get the charge against me overturned. When I refused his advances, he determined to punish me. While I was being held in the prison, Zhang the Mule forced Widow Cai to reveal where she kept her money. He then robbed her of all her wealth, and used some of it to bribe Taowu. The villainous Taowu then subjected me to ferocious torture. I told him that my conscience was clear, and that even if he tortured me to death I would never confess to a crime I had not committed. But, upon the advice of his henchman Magistrate Xiao, he left off tormenting me, and started to torture Widow Cai. I could not bear to see the old lady's sufferings, and so I confessed to the false charge of murdering my father-in-law. Then I was sentenced to death. While I was imprisoned in the death cell, Zhang the Mule, with the connivance of Magistrate Xiao, came to Chuzhou, where my sentence was under review. He bribed a clerk in the magistracy to approve the sentence, and I was beheaded at the height of the summer."

She then explained how, just before her execution, she had made three appeals to Heaven: One, that as her head tumbled to the ground, her blood should all fly up and stain a length of silk; two, that three feet of snow should fall, and cover her body; and three, that from the moment of her death the Chuzhou area should be afflicted by a severe drought for three years.

"The injustice done to me was so enormous that a great column of outrage shot up into the sky. This was brought to the notice of the Jade Emperor, and he dispatched a band of immortals to fulfill my three appeals. Father, these three wonders — the blood-spattered silk, snow in midsummer and this three-year drought — are all manifestations of Heaven's indignation at the injustice done to me!"

She added that the Jade Emperor had ordered the Local God of Shanyang County to accommodate her spirit in his shrine for three years until her father arrived in Chuzhou as the emperor's special envoy, at which time the injustice would be redressed. This is the day for which I have been waiting with such longing — the day when my dear father would come to avenge the injustice I have suffered, and wipe away my disgrace."

Dou Tianzhang stood staring in amazement as what he had just heard slowly sank in. At length, he exclaimed, "I had no idea that such scandalous miscarriages of justice were occurring anywhere in the country. Or that Chuzhou, my own hometown, was such a sink of iniquity! Corrupt officials manipulate the law for their own benefit, perpetrating all kinds of excesses, while the common people are too afraid to voice their complaints. Oh, my poor child, how could I have been so neglectful of my parental duties as to allow this calamity to descend on you?"

So saying, Dou Tianzhang hugged the spirit of his daughter tightly, and wept silent tears. The latter murmured, "Father, although I have been reduced to the status of a grieving, wandering ghost, now that I have found you again at last, and have been able to pour out my sorrow to you, I will be able to close my eyes in death at last, in the knowledge that you will blot out the injustice done to me."

Dou Tianzhang said, "My child, for 16 years I sent men looking for you time after time. Not a day passed but I was anxious for you. My purpose in coming to Anhui was not just to perform my mission, but also to search for you in person. Now that I find that we have already been parted by death, my heart is racked with agony. This pain can only be assuaged once I have brought all those vipers that infest the positions of authority to justice. This I am determined to do, so, grieve no more, my child."

As he said this, the drum tower sounded the fifth watch. Dou E's spirit suddenly remembered the admonition of the Local God, that she must return before daybreak. She hastily explained this to her father, and said that she must leave immediately. "Take care, Father," she added, "and I will assist you from the world of the shades in you efforts to rectify this terrible case." She then kowtowed to him, weeping.

Stifling his sorrow, Dou Tianzhang said, "Just now, you told me that one of the requests you made just before your death was for three years of drought to descend upon Chuzhou. It is recorded that during the Han Dynasty there was a filial daughter who endured all sorts of hardships to support her mother-in-law. The old woman, to lighten the girl's burden of toil and suffering, hanged herself. The magistrate of Donghai Prefecture made a mistaken judgment on the case, concluding that the girl had driven her mother-in-law to take her own life, and condemning her to death by beheading. Following this, rain ceased to fall in the prefecture for three years. Then Duke Yu visited Donghai to inspect the records of court cases and put right miscarriages of justice. He held a memorial ceremony at the filial girl's tomb, and immediately thereafter rain began to fall in torrents. Now, a thousand years later, Chuzhou too has been suffering from three years of drought. Can this be on account of you, I wonder?"

Dou E replied, "Father, the three appeals I made on the point of death have all been fulfilled. The three years are up. You have arrived to reverse the malicious verdict, and as soon as you have done so, Heaven will send sweet showers, and all the people will be saved."

"If that is so, you may return to the Local God's shrine with a light heart," said Dou Tianzhang. "I will put this wrong right, and will hold a memorial sacrifice at your tomb. This way I will not only comfort your anguished soul, but also get Heaven to send divine rain to succor the people of Chuzhou."

These words gladdened Dou E's heart. She kowtowed several times in gratitude, and then reluctantly took her leave.

Dou Tianzhang felt a sense of anguish as he watched the form of his beloved daughter whom he had not seen for 16 years fade away before his eyes. He stretched out his hands to clutch her and hold her back, but they clutched at empty air. He awoke with a start, and looked wildly around him. There was no one else in the room. The lamp had almost burned itself out. He was sitting at his desk, but somehow the front of his robe was soaked in tears. He pulled himself together and thought of the strange apparition — or had it been real? Had he been asleep or awake? He didn't know. Then his eyes fell on the document that lay on the desk before him. It was the one titled, "Criminal Dou E. Beheaded for Poisoning her Father-in-Law." He snatched it up, and read it carefully several times. There was no doubt about it: It corresponded in every detail with what Dou E's spirit had related to him. He thought hard, trying to find some flaw in the case as presented in the official statement. And then it came to him. There had been no investigation into the source of the poison! This was a serious omission, he knew.

Dou Tianzhang was wide awake by this time. He crashed his fist onto the desk. "This Taowu has been deceiving the imperial court all this time!" he growled between clenched teeth. "While the Chuzhou area has been suffering from disaster, he has been carousing and stuffing his greedy face, but reporting to the court that all is well. I should have known that there was something wrong when he offered me that lavish bribe as soon as I arrived. He is a wicked scoundrel who puts innocent people to death. Even when his wrongdoing brings about three years of cruel drought to Chuzhou, he shows absolutely no remorse. If I fail to rid the world of this parasitical vermin, I will not be doing my duty to the emperor, nor will I be able to relieve the people of their sufferings. On top of that, I will not be able to right the injustice done to my daughter. Then what kind of a petty wretch would I be? And what use would be my sword of office and golden tablet, and all the pomp and power I am invested with?"

Dou Tianzhang thereupon made up his mind that as soon as it was light he would go to Shanyang County, and make an on-the-spot investigation of the case, clearing up its doubtful aspects and revealing the terrible wrong done to his daughter before the whole world.

CHAPTER TEN

An Injustice Avenged

AT DAWN, DOU Tianzhang summoned his faithful manservant into his study. He told him: "Today, I want you to come with me to Shanyang County. I'm going to reopen the case of Dou E. But you must not reveal this to anyone else. If anybody asks, just say that I have to visit every county in Anhui."

The man assented, and then went to make preparations for the journey.

Dou Tianzhang then donned formal attire, and took his place in the main hall of the magistracy. When Taowu and all his officials, both military and civil, were assembled before him, Dou Tianzhang addressed Taowu thus: "Prefectural Magistrate, on my way to Chuzhou, I could not help noticing that the area is suffering from a serious drought. The people of the city tell me that rain has not fallen in this region for three years. Why is it that you did not report this situation to the imperial court and request relief assistance?"

Taowu had long before this realized that he would not be able to disguise the fact of the drought from Dou Tianzhang, and he had an answer ready: "Your Honor's observation is correct; there is indeed a drought in the Chuzhou area. But it is not true that rain has not fallen for three years. It is just that this summer has been an unusually torrid one. I have been consumed with worry night and day, but I dared not trouble His Majesty. However, I took prompt action to procure relief grain from neighboring prefectures and counties to help the poor suffering peasants. I myself have gone down to the villages to condole with and encourage the common people. The planting has been completed for this year, and if rain falls within the next couple of months there will be no question of a disaster."

Dou Tianzhang pretended to be taken in by this claptrap. He nodded. "If that is the case, then all is well," he said. "Today, I intend to continue my tour of inspection of the counties, to check the extent of the problem. If I find that the ordinary people are able to support themselves, then I will agree that you do not need to petition the court for assistance."

Taowu knew that were the imperial inspector to go down into the counties he would be besieged by people clamoring for help. So he said, "Perhaps I should accompany Your Honor, and be your guide, so to speak?"

Dou Tianzhang guffawed. "There is something you do not know, Prefectural Magistrate," he said. "And that is that I lived right here in Chuzhou for many years. Now that I have returned, I intend to take advantage of my inspection duties to see the old places once more. I would not dream of dragging you away from your busy schedule on a needless errand." Then, lowering his voice, he added, "You and I have spent much time inhabiting the official sphere, Prefectural Magistrate. We both know that it does not do to overstep the mark. So I urge you to set your mind at rest."

Taowu, thought that his bribe of a box of jewels had bought the imperial inspector's discretion, and, in an equally low tone, replied, "Your Honor, it was not that I had any worries whatsoever; it was just that I was concerned that Your Honor might find traveling unescorted inconvenient. But now that I know that Your Honor is well familiar with this area, I will not presume to delay you, but will stay here and eagerly await Your Honor's return."

To lull the rascally Taowu deeper into a sense of false security,

Dou Tianzhang said, "If I find that the situation is not serious, and that the people are content, there will be no cause for concern. I will return within a few days. By the way, I read through the court cases last night, and found nothing inappropriate. But I still need to sign them. After that, I shall send them back to you."

Secretly gleeful, Taowu said a few token words of appreciation.

At this point, Dou Tianzhang's man announced that the carriage was ready.

Shanyang County was less than a day's journey away. Dou Tianzhang lost no time inquiring of the county magistrate, who came out to meet him with all his officials: "Three years ago, there was a case here of a woman poisoning her father-in-law. The criminal, Dou E, went to the headsman's axe protesting her innocence. Moreover, she appealed to Heaven to afflict Chuzhou with drought for three years following her death. Is this true?"

The county magistrate was taken aback at this abrupt request, and wondered whether it boded ill or good. He quickly replied, "I have heard of the case, Your Honor, but it was handled by my predecessor, who is now the magistrate of Chuzhou Prefecture. The death sentence was authorized by the then magistrate of Chuzhou. The dossier on the case is kept there. It has nothing to do with me."

At this, Dou Tianzhang was incensed. "You worthless imbecile!" he roared. "If Dou E was not the victim of injustice, how could she move Heaven to blight the Chuzhou area with three rainless years? How can you claim that the case has nothing to do with you? In the three years since you've been magistrate here, have you never once examined the file on this case, or questioned the witnesses?"

The Shanyang County magistrate's knees began to knock. He prostrated himself in front of Dou Tianzhang, and babbled, "Your Honor, this case was taken care of specially by Taiwu. I didn't dare presume to review it. Besides, it was one of the ten crimes for which there can be no forgiveness. It was all cut and dried — evidence and everything — there was no call for a person such as myself to question the verdict!"

Dou Tianzhang saw that it was a waste of time questioning this muddle-headed coward any longer. He barked, "I have a particular interest in this case. Issue an order without more ado for the arrest of the people involved in it — Zhang the Mule, Sai Lu Yi and Widow Cai. Bring them here right now, and don't breathe a word of this to anyone else. Do you hear?"

The Shanyang County magistrate realized that Dou Tianzhang was well acquainted with the case, and was well prepared to handle the review of it. So, without prevarication, he did as he had been ordered.

Before long, the constables announced that they had brought Zhang the Mule and Widow Cai, but that Sai Lu Yi had disappeared three years previously, no one knew where.

"Sai Lu Yi was a leading criminal suspect in this case," Dou Tianzhang commented. "How could he have been allowed to simply go free? He should have been arrested straightaway. Hold Zhang the Mule in custody for the time being. As for Widow Cai, taking her advanced age into account, hold her in a room here in the magistracy. Try not to alarm the old woman. I will hold a hearing into this case tomorrow." He then rose, and left the Court room.

The Shanyang County magistrate and his entourage uttered cries of assent, and also left.

Withdrawing to the rear hall, Dou Tianzhang remained lost in thought for some time. He then summoned his faithful manservant, and said, "Take a couple of trusty fellows, and pick up Sai Lu Yi, wherever he is. He obviously fled to save his own skin."

The following morning, Zhang the Mule was led into the court. Dou Tianzhang cast his eyes over the cringing and despicable form presented before him. He noted that Zhang was clad in gorgeous apparel, like a dressed-up monkey. With ill-disguised wrath, Dou Tianzhang asked him: "Zhang the Mule, do you know what crime you are guilty of?"

Zhang the Mule fell to his knees. "No, Your Honor," he squeaked. "Will Your Honor please tell me what crime I'm guilty of?"

Dou Tianzhang rapped the table in front of him with his gavel. In a voice quivering with rage, he asked, "Do you remember the case of Dou E, who was beheaded three years ago?"

Zhang the Mule had never dreamed that a case that had been closed for three years would be brought up for revision. He broke out in a cold sweat, desperately struggled to calm himself, squinted up at the stern figure seated above him, and realized in a sudden fit of panic that this man had been sent by the emperor himself to right a terrible injustice. He stammered, "Er, well, yes, Your Honor... I do seem to recollect that case. In fact, Dou E was my wife. We lived together with my father and Dou E's mother-in-law — who was then my second mother-in-law, you understand, as she, that is, Widow Cai, had been the mother of Dou E's first husband, who was of course by that time deceased — er, anyway, on account of Dou E and my old man not getting along very well ... er ... well ... to cut a long story short, she ... er ... poisoned him. That was three years ago. And so ... er ... I took her to the magistrate. The magistrate said that the case was quite clear ... er ... and then he ... er ... had her head chopped off in the market place."

Dou Tianzhang was livid with rage. "You say that Dou E was your wife, and that Widow Cai was your mother-in-law?" he thundered.

"Er ... yes. That is correct, Your Honor."

Dou Tianzhang turned to the court ushers: "Call Widow Cai."

For the previous three years the destitute Widow Cai had had to beg for a living. By this time, her hair was as white as snow, and her face was a mass of wrinkles. Daily grieving over the fate of Dou E had dimmed her eyes. The shock of being picked up in the street, held overnight and dragged into the magistrate's court had left her petrified with fear.

Dou Tianzhang hardly recognized the grimy aged creature who knelt speechless before him as the same person whom he had known 16 years before. He addressed her gently: "Are you Widow Cai?"

The old woman acknowledged that she was, in a barely audible whisper.

"I am the emperor's envoy sent to investigate the carrying out of justice in the Anhui region," Dou Tianzhang explained. "I have found some discrepancy in the dossier pertaining to the Dou E case, and that is why I have summoned you here. Now, there's no need to be afraid. Just answer my questions truthfully, and everything will be all right."

Although Widow Cai didn't quite understand what this grand official who had come all the way from the emperor's court was talking about, nevertheless his kindly manner comforted her somewhat. Then she remembered that he had mentioned Dou E, and she burst into tears, wailing, "Oh my poor child, you died because of a terrible injustice. I hope the emperor's envoy will right the wrong you suffered!"

Dou Tianzhang then started his inquiries. "Widow Cai," he said, "I want you to cast your mind back three years. When Zhang the Mule accused Dou E of poisoning his father, Dou E was your daughter-in-law. Therefore, her father-in-law must have been your husband. Just now, Zhang the Mule said that you were his mother-in-law. Is that true?"

Widow Cai raised her head, and glared at Zhang the Mule. "Your mother-in-law?" She spat the words out in disgust. "You took advantage of us having no man in the house to bully me and steal my money. You then bribed the magistrate to sentence my innocent daughter-in-law to death. After that, you commandeered my house, and for the past three years I have been a homeless beggar. If I were really your mother-in-law, would you have treated me so abominably?"

"Madam, please calm yourself," Dou Tianzhang urged, "just tell me the details of this case from the beginning."

Widow Cai thereupon related, accompanied by a flood of tears, how she had been inveigled by Sai Lu Yi to a deserted spot in the suburbs, where he had tried to strangle her; how she had been saved by the unexpected arrival of the Zhangs; how the Zhangs had bullied their way into her house; and how Zhang the Mule had contrived the death of Dou E, robbed her of her money and bribed the magistrate.

When she had finished the sorry tale, Dou Tianzhang said, "Widow Cai, from what you have told me, your daughter-in-law cannot be considered to have poisoned her father-in-law, as Zhang the Dog did not stand in that relationship to her. How did the indictment come to be written that way?"

Widow Cai explained how Dou E had raised the ire of Taowu when she had rejected his unwanted advances, and how he had accepted a bribe from Zhang the Mule, who harbored a similar grievance. She described how Dou E had been interrogated under torture, and had only confessed to the false charge after torture was applied to the old woman herself.

"What do you have to say to this?" Dou Tianzhang asked Zhang the Mule, sternly.

The latter had been growing more and more appalled and alarmed as the truth came out into the open, item by damning item. But there was nothing for it but to try to brazen it out. "Your Honor," he pleaded, "it is quite clear that it was Dou E who poisoned my father. The case is cut and dried. I humbly ask Your Honor: What is the point of reopening it?"

Dou Tianzhang replied, "I would have you know that I have been sent by the emperor himself to investigate the dispensing of justice in the Anhui region. My remit includes examination of criminal records and official wrongdoing, and I am especially concerned with cases of miscarriage of justice. This particular case is seriously flawed; how can I overlook it?" He went on, "Now I will ask you one question. And that is, where did the poison that deprived your father of his life come from? There is nothing in the dossier about the person who prepared the poison. Did it just drop down from the sky?"

"It was Dou E who obtained it, Your Honor," came the hasty reply.

Dou Tianzhang objected, "But Dou E was a young girl. Whence would she have got poison? Do people normally keep poison in their homes? The poison must have been made up at an apothecary's shop. Zhang the Mule, did you have it prepared?"

"I have no idea where she got the poison which she put in the soup, Your Honor," Zhang the Mule protested. "And anyway, if I had procured it, would I have used it to kill my own father?"

This argument took Dou Tianzhang aback. With anguish, he realized that there was no evidence with which to refute it, and that his effort to vindicate his unfortunate daughter might well be futile. Inwardly, he cried, "My dear, wronged daughter, without you here to reveal the truth, I fear that the injustice done to you will never be avenged. Where is your spirit now?"

Something made him look up suddenly. He saw the ghost of Dou E enter the Court room and bow to him. It then addressed him: "Imperial Envoy, I am the spirit of Dou E. I heard that Your Honor had been sent here to investigate cases of miscarriage of justice, and so I have come here to unmask Zhang the Mule." So saying, she turned to point an accusing finger at the worthy in question. "Zhang the Mule," she cried, "You know very well that you got the poison from a pharmacy in the city, and here you are trying to blame me!"

Zhang the Mule, who a moment ago had been smugly congratulating himself on having stumped Dou Tianzhang, was frightened out of his wits at this sudden turn of events. All he could do was stand there, jabbering: "A ghost! A ghost!"

Dou E approached him with eyes glaring: "Zhang the Mule, I accuse you of intending to kill my mother-in-law when you put the poison in the soup. That way, you calculated that it would be easier for you to pressure me into marrying you. You never thought that she might be too delicate to take the soup, but would give it to your father. Do you still deny your guilt?"

Zhang the Mule was trapped. He fell back before Dou E's relentless advance, gibbering, "A ghost! A ghost!"

The Shanyang County magistrate and his retinue witnessed this extraordinary spectacle in amazement. They thought that Dou Tianzhang must have divine power to summon witnesses from the other world to rectify cases of miscarriages of justice. Widow Cai was so overcome with joy at the sight of Dou E's spirit that she prostrated herself on the floor before the apparition, weeping copious tears.

Dou Tianzhang rapped with his gavel for silence, as he prepared to pass sentence. "Zhang the Mule, you slandered Dou E, accusing her of the crime of poisoning her father-in-law. Not only that, but you brought about her unjust execution. Her restless spirit still haunts this place, and has appeared before me to appeal her case. Do you still dare to claim that she was guilty? I advise you to confess without delay, and save yourself a great deal of physical pain!" With this, he turned to the court attendants, and ordered them to prepare clubs for flogging Zhang the Mule.

The attendants responded so enthusiastically to this command that the very rafters of the Court room rang.

Zhang the Mule, knowing that his crime deserved the "death of ten thousand cuts" trembled from head to toe. But he staked his life on one last gamble. "Your Honor," he pleaded in a terrified squeak, "if the person who sold the poison can be brought here to accuse me to my face, I will gladly confess and face the supreme penalty."

Dou Tianzhang was enraged by this piece of insolence, and was about to order a flogging for Zhang the Mule, when a posse of court officers appeared in the doorway, dragging some wretch with them. The officers fell to their feet before Dou Tianzhang, and reported, "Your Honor, we have found the apothecary Sai Lu Yi, a material witness in this case."

Seeing that Sai Lu Yi had been tracked down, the spirit of Dou E knew that Zhang the Mule's fate was sealed, and that the injustice done to her would now inevitably be redressed. Thereupon, she quietly faded away.

Dou Tianzhang again banged his gavel. "Is Sai Lu Yi present in court?" he called out.

The physician kowtowed. "I am Sai Lu Yi, Your Honor," he acknowledged. "I have been engaged in business far from here. I have had nothing to do with bad people, I assure you, Your Honor. And so, I have no idea why I have been summoned here."

After giving the poison to Zhang the Mule, and dreading the thought of getting mixed up in more villainy, Sai Lu Yi had fled to Zhuozhou, where he had continued his pharmacy business. In the three years he had been away, he had often been homesick for Shanyang. Eventually, he thought to himself: "Surely, people must have forgotten that affair concerning Widow Cai by this time. And that fellow who extorted the poison from me, well, he may not have harmed anybody after all. Even if he has, I've been away from there for so long that I can't possibly be implicated. There is an old saying, 'The fallen leaf returns to its roots.' I've saved up enough money to live comfortably; why not return to my hometown?"

But as soon as he crossed the threshold of his old pharmacy in Shanyang, he was arrested by the court officers dispatched by Dou Tianzhang, and straightaway hauled into the county court.

Dou Tianzhang read out the charge: "You, Sai Lu Yi, are accused of attempting to strangle Widow Cai three years ago, to avoid repaying a debt you owed her. How do you plead?"

Sai Lu Yi was flabbergasted at having his attempt on Widow Cai's life hung round his neck the minute he set foot in his hometown after all this time. He kowtowed furiously. "Your Honor," he wheedled, "it is true that I borrowed money from the old woman. Pressed by force of circumstances, I was not able to repay it, and did hatch such a plot. But two men came by, and foiled my plan ... and so you see, Your Honor, everything is all right. The widow is alive and well. No harm done, as I am sure you will agree! Besides, in these past three years I have not done anything bad. I swear it, Your Honor. I hope that in your wisdom you will see fit to let me off this time."

Dou Tianzhang said, "Did you recognize the two men who disturbed you in the act of strangling Widow Cai? If so, what were their names?"

"Your Honor, I was in such a panic at that time that I scarcely glanced at them. I ran for my life. I don't know who they were. However, three days later, the younger one came to my shop looking for me. I would recognize him for sure."

"Why was he looking for you?"

"He wanted me to make up some medicine for him."

"What ailment was he suffering from? What kind of medicine did you prepare? Be sure to tell me the truth. One single word of a lie, and I will punish you most severely!"

Sai Lu Yi thought, "Oh, my God! I should have known that ruffian was going to do some mischief with that poison. The best thing for me to do is to tell the truth, and maybe I'll get off lightly." He kowtowed several more times. Then he said, "I would not dare prevaricate in Your Honor's all-seeing presence. The fact is that the young man wanted me to prepare poison for him. I tried to fob him off by saying that I only stocked officially approved drugs. But he produced the cord I had used to try to strangle

Widow Cai, and threatened to drag me before the magistrate. Well, I've always been terrified of magistrates. So I made the poison for him, but as soon as he was gone I packed my things and hurried away from Shanyang, in case I was implicated in whatever skullduggery that roughneck was planning. In fact, I didn't stop until I had got as far as Zhuozhou, where I set up in business again. But I didn't prepare any more poison after that. And that is the truth, the whole truth and nothing but the truth, Your Honor. I humbly beg forgiveness for the misdeeds I committed long ago."

Dou Tianzhang gave an inward sigh of resignation, and said, "You claim that you would recognize that man again. Take a look at the person next to you, and tell me whom you see."

Sai Lu Yi, eager to ingratiate himself with the emperor's envoy, scrambled to his feet, and looked to his left. His heart skipped a beat when he saw Widow Cai kneeling there. "This is Widow Cai, Your Honor," he said. "I haven't set eyes on her for three years. Good Heavens, how she has aged in that time!" He then looked to his right, where a man was kneeling. The man's mean and shifty eyes belied the splendor of his garments. Sai Lu Yi looked at him closely. There was no doubt about it but that the man was the same one for whom he had prepared the poison three years previously. He fell to his knees once more, and kowtowed to Dou Tianzhang: "Your Honor, this is the man who forced me to make up the poison."

Dou Tianzhang ordered Sai Lu Yi to be taken away to sign a statement. Then he turned to Zhang the Mule. "You have been identified by the pharmacist Sai Lu Yi as the person who collected a preparation of poison from him," he said. "Whom did you intend to harm with that poison?"

Zhang the Mule knew that the noose was tightening. He decided to stake all on one last desperate throw. He shuffled forward on his knees a few paces, and said, in a low voice: "Your Honor, I still have some silver left at home. You can have all of it, if you will refrain from pursuing this case any further."

Dou Tianzhang, boiling with wrath, roared, "How dare you have the barefaced effrontery to attempt to bribe a judicial officer? It is clear that you are completely ignorant of the imperial code of law. Three years ago, the innocent Dou E was put to death all because a corrupt official accepted a handful of silver. This was an injustice that outraged Heaven and Earth. As a result, Chuzhou was punished with three years of drought. Hundreds of ordinary people fled. Families were ruined and lives were lost. And here you are, trying to play the same old game! What do you take the imperial envoy for? It seems that a crafty villain like you needs a sharp taste of the rod before he will confess the truth!" He turned to the court attendants. "Give him one hundred strokes of the cudgel," he ordered. "And lay them on with gusto!"

The attendants sprang to their task. At the 20th blow, Zhang the Mule could stand no more, and begged for mercy, moaning that he was ready to confess.

He admitted everything in his statement — from the time he and his father stumbled on Sai Lu Yi attempting to murder Widow Cai, to their forcing themselves on the family home, to Zhang the Mule's rebuff by Dou E, to the poison plot that went wrong, to the bribery of Taowu to put Dou E to death, and to the robbing of Widow Cai. He did not omit Magistrate Xiao's unsavory role, either. Following this, Dou Tianzhang ordered that Zhang the Mule be held in chains in the death cell, to await the company of his fellow conspirators.

Retiring to the rear hall, Dou Tianzhang fell deep in thought. He felt that even though he had found out the truth about the injustice done to his daughter, he still needed to remove the much bigger problem of official corruption — which had allowed the injustice to take place — from the shoulders of the people. This was not going to be easy, he knew. Taowu, for instance, one of the major villains in the whole affair, was under the protection of his father, Ahema, who was powerful at the imperial court. But if he did not bring Taowu to justice, he would not in the end be able to clear Dou E's name. At the same time, if he arrested Taowu, that would be like beating the grass to give advance warning to the snakes. Ahema had made it quite clear that he was ambitious to seize the throne for himself; any precipitous move would spur him to stage a rebellion, with dire consequences for the country. After racking his brains for some time, Dou Tianzhang decided that the best thing to do was gather concrete evidence of the wrongdoings of Ahema and his son, and submit a petition to the emperor. At the same time, he would write to Jin Gui and Cui Gun, appealing to them to be ready to act in concert with him when the time came to expose Ahema. And once Ahema was out of the way, he could set about devising a strategy for rounding up Taowu and his many lackeys who infested all levels of the Chuzhou administration.

Having made this decision, Dou Tianzhang lit incense, washed his hands, and sat down to write a memorial to the throne. He described how Ahema and his son Taowu abused their authority, extorted bribes, took the lives of the common people at will, and sold official posts. In short, he warned the emperor, "These men are scourges of the country and the people." He listed ten major crimes of deceiving their superiors, which he laid at their door, and urged that they be executed to soothe the anger of the people. He also gave a detailed account of the appalling conditions in the Chuzhou area. His righteous anger and his outraged feelings of loyalty to the throne, he said, could not be expressed in words. When he finished the memorial, he proceeded to write letters to Jin Gui and Cui Gun. He attached seals indicating Top Secret to the three missives, and entrusted them to his faithful manservant, with orders to deliver them to the capital as soon as possible.

Dou Tianzhang then summoned the Shanyang County magistrate, and told him to arrest Saputo and Magistrate Xiao that very night, and at the same time to confiscate their property. Following this, he wrote a letter to Taowu in Chuzhou, in which he said that he had found conditions in Shanyang worse than he thought, and Taowu was to come to him in order to discuss relief measures.

When he read the letter, the wily Taowu's instinct told him that something was wrong. The fact that Dou Tianzhang had suddenly made a trip to Shanyang County for no apparent reason was suspicious enough, but his summons to join him there definitely smelled fishy. However, Taowu consoled himself with the thought that Dou Tianzhang would not dare move against him while his father was one of the most powerful men at court, and so set off for Shanyang, taking with him only a few trusted henchmen. But no sooner had he presented himself at the magistracy in Shanyang than court officers pounced on him from all sides, stripped him of his official robe and bound him with convict's ropes. By the time the astonished Taowu started to struggle, it was too late. He was well and truly trussed up. He called out to Dou Tianzhang: "What is the meaning of this? I am an imperial court-appointed official. How dare you have me bound like this for no reason and in broad daylight too? Just you wait till my father learns of this; you will smart for it!"

Dou Tianzhang smiled mirthlessly, and said, "Oh, so you're an imperial court-appointed official, are you? Well I have a special commission from the emperor himself to inspect the Anhui region and especially to rid it of corrupt officials. I bear the sword of office, which, as I'm sure you are well aware, authorizes me to execute transgressors first and report to his Imperial Majesty afterwards. So what need have I to fear the power of your father?" He then ordered the court attendants to lock Taowu up, to await judgment.

And so Taowu, together with the cohorts he had brought with him from Chuzhou, spent the night in the cells. He passed the night railing against Dou Tianzhang, and speculating on the gory fate that would overtake that upstart when his father heard about this little farce.

The next miscreant to be nabbed was the scribe Li, who had forged the prefectural magistrate's signature, which had finally sealed Dou E's doom.

It had taken about ten days to snare all the culprits in the case of the injustice done to Dou E. But before making his next move, Dou Tianzhang waited until he received news from the capital. When his man finally returned, he learned that Emperor Chengzong had acted immediately he had read Dou Tianzhang's memorial. In a state of great anger at learning of the scandalous state of affairs in Anhui, and of the evil collusion between Ahema and his son Taowu, the emperor had dispatched Jin and Cui to arrest Ahema and all the members of his clique. He had read to Ahema the list of the latter's crimes, as reported to him by Dou Tianzhang, and sentenced him to be beheaded on the spot.

Upon receipt of this news, Dou Tianzhang faced in the direction of the imperial palace and voiced his heartfelt thanks to the emperor. He then ordered the magistrate of Shanyang County to bring Taowu and the other culprits before him to learn their fates.

He started with Zhang the Mule: "For poisoning your father in a plot to take advantage of a helpless widow and her daughter-in-law, bribing a magistrate, slandering an innocent person and bringing about the tragic death of Dou E, I sentence you to be dismembered in the public market place."

Next, it was Taowu's turn: "For colluding with scoundrels, corruption, misuse of the law, excessive use of punishments, disdain for the lives of the common people, putting an innocent person to death, which resulted in three years of drought for Chuzhou and the exodus of large numbers of its inhabitants, deceiving your superiors and scandalizing both Heaven and Man by riotous living in the midst of calamity, I sentence you to death by beheading."

Saputo was then hauled forward: "For indulging in unbridled whoring, depriving people of their property and wives, and selling official posts, I sentence you to death by beheading."

Sai Lu Yi was sentenced to serve with a border garrison for attempted murder and preparing poison, which led to a death. As for Magistrate Xiao and the scribe Li, they were given one hundred strokes of the rod each for misuse of authority, corruption and perverting the course of justice. In addition, they were never to be employed in government posts again.

Dou Tianzhang concluded by announcing, "The injustice done to the filial heroine Dou E has now been put right. The girl's chaste and true nature was proved by the fact that the three appeals she made just before her lamentable death moved Heaven and Earth. Later, I will hold a memorial service before her tomb, and erect a stele and a banner. In the meantime, Widow Cai's house and all her possessions shall be restored to her, to enable her to support herself for the rest of her days."

Taowu was the only one of the miscreants to protest his sentence. "You can't behead me in the public market place without the emperor's order!" he cried. "Does my father know about this? Well, when he finds out, you won't be long for this world either, Dou Tianzhang! If you want to live, you'd better set me free so that I can intervene for you with my father."

Dou Tianzhang received this diatribe with a sardonic smile. "My commission is to inspect the Anhui area," he explained mildly. "Moreover, I have received from the emperor himself the sword and gold tablet which authorize me to execute first and report afterward. There is another thing I must tell you, which you do not know, and that is that your father has already been put to death by order of the emperor for his arrogant ways, his sale of offices, deceiving the emperor, bringing disaster on the country and incurring the wrath of the people. In addition, all his property has been confiscated. His case was similar to yours. Do you still expect him to save you?"

Taowu forthwith collapsed in a heap, wailing in despair. Dou Tianzhang, ignoring him, ordered that he and Zhang the Mule be taken to the place of execution. Their deaths were watched with glee and relief by just about everyone in Shanyang County.

Dou Tianzhang commanded the county magistrate to construct an elaborate shrine where people could pray for blessings from the soul of Dou E. He himself held a sacrificial rite before the girl's grave, and prostrated himself there, weeping.

Strange to relate, as soon as the sacrificial rite was over, the clear blue sky clouded over, there was a roll of thunder, and the whole Chuzhou area was plentifully sprinkled with divine rain, which did not let up until three feet of water had accumulated on the ground, to the great delight of the drought-racked people.

Dou Tianzhang retired early that night, worn out by the exertions of the previous few days. In a dream, Dou E appeared to him, to say farewell. Shedding tears, she said, "Father, for three years I suffered a grievous injustice, and my spirit was unable to rest as I waited for you to come and wipe out my shame. Now, my only wish has come true. The Jade Emperor has vindicated me as a faithful and filial woman. He has decreed that I will escape the torments of Hell, and will be in the care of the Local God of Shanyang until I am reincarnated as a good woman. Your daughter now bids you farewell."

His heart breaking, and tears rolling down his cheeks, Dou Tianzhang reached out to hold her back. "My child," he cried, "I failed to keep my last promise to your mother, and caused you nothing but hardship. Now that I have cleared up the injustice done to you, we must never part again. Oh, don't go! How can I go on living without you?"

Dou E kowtowed. "Father, it is the command of the Jade Emperor. How dare I disobey? Take care of yourself. I am going now." With that, she glided through the door.

Dou Tianzhang leapt from the bed, and dashed from the room, just in time to see Dou E turn her head, and say, "Father, I forgot one thing: Please take care of Widow Cai for me, now that she is too old to take care of herself. And make sure that she has a decent burial when the time comes. Promise me that, and I will be content."

Dou Tianzhang nodded, and said, "I promise that I will do so." Whereupon the spirit of Dou E vanished. Her father, flustered, looked around, but she was nowhere to be seen. He woke with a start, to find himself covered in a cold sweat. When he gathered his wits together, Dou Tianzhang realized that his daughter had gone to her new reincarnation, and that he would never see her again. He wept bitter tears.

The following day, he sent for Widow Cai. The old woman was in high spirits as she entered his presence. She kowtowed, and thanked him profusely for redressing the grievance done to Dou E and for getting her house and belongings back for her.

Dou Tianzhang raised her to her feet, saying, "Madam, do you recognize me?"

She peered at him for a long while, but finally shook her head. "No, I'm afraid not," she said. "Anyway, my eyesight is dim these days, so how could I?"

"I am the Dou Tianzhang who left his daughter with you in return for traveling expenses to go to the capital to take the imperial examination. I passed first time, and became an official. I am here now with an imperial commission to inspect the Anhui area. For 16 years I sent men looking for you, but you had moved away from Chuzhou, no one knew where. I have finally found you here in Shanyang. Please forgive me for being so late in coming."

Widow Cai trembled with emotion upon hearing this. She wailed, "So it is you! You are a member of my family, but I let you down by allowing Dou E to suffer a terrible injustice. Oh, I cannot bear the pain of this sorrow!"

Suppressing with difficulty his own grief, Dou Tianzhang said, "Please put aside your distress. The cruel fate visited on my daughter was no fault of yours. Now that I have redressed that injustice, Dou E can rest easily in the other world. Last night, she appeared to me in a dream, and urged me to make sure that you are looked after in the evening of your life, as she is unable to do so. Therefore, I would like to ask you to accompany me to the capital and live in my mansion there, where I can take care of you. You can begin disposing of your house and property here this very day."

Widow Cai was overcome with emotion. "Even after death, Dou E is still concerned about my welfare," she sighed. "Where was there ever such a loving and filial daughter-in-law? If that was Dou E's last request, then I will gladly go with you to live in the capital."

Having settled the matter of Widow Cai's future, Dou Tianzhang led a group of prefectural and county officials to inspect the results of the drought. He found that the recent timely rain had solved the problem completely. The countryside was springing back to life. The scattered peasants were returning home, and busily engaged in tilling the fields, just as before. The whole of Chuzhou Prefecture was a hive of activity.

When a new magistrate for the prefecture arrived, it was time for Dou Tianzhang to start on his way back to the capital. The local elders flocked to express their gratitude for all he had done for them, and along both sides of the road he took out of Chuzhou there were offerings of food, wine and incense.

Meanwhile, Emperor Chengzong was greatly relieved at having got rid of that thorn in his flesh Ahema. He quickly proclaimed a general amnesty, held more examinations for recruiting civil servants, and gathered around him a host of talented men.

As soon as Dou Tianzhang reached the capital, he was summoned by the emperor, who loaded him with commendations and rewards, and appointed him to the post of Prime Minister. From then on, Dou Tianzhang, as one of the most senior court officials, devoted all his energies and loyalty to the service of his ruler, winning the complete trust of the emperor, the reverence of the other officials and the love and affection of the people. Both he, and Widow Cai, lived to a ripe old age and passed away peacefully.

Meanwhile, the story of how the injustice done to Dou E moved Heaven and Earth spread all over the country. It came to the ears of Guan Hanqing, a genius of his generation, during a period of feckless wandering. He was impressed by the tale, and lost no time using it as the theme for a *zaju*, a kind of poetic drama, set to music, which flourished during the Yuan Dynasty, which he titled *The Injustice Done to Dou E Which Moved Heaven and Earth*. It is still performed today.